STOLEN ANGELS

A JAKE STORM NOVEL

WILLIAM JOHNSTONE
TAYLOR

FOREWORD

by Gail H. Johnson,
Investigative/Security Consultant

WARNING! The reading of this book will open your eyes and have your emotions on edge as you turn each page, wondering, "Did this by chance really happen or is it just another great systemic exploration into the world of international investigation?"

The author, William (Bill) J. Taylor, a world-renowned private investigator with over fifty years of hands-on "boots on the ground" experience, has done an extraordinary job in creating a dramatic thriller novel. It will make people aware of what lies in the shadows and what needs to be dealt with but is seldom handled in the appropriate manner unless the right type of person steps in, no matter the consequences. That person, in this case, is Jake Stone!

I personally have known Bill for over forty years, and in that time, I have seen, lived, and experienced so many nearly inconceivable things with him, as one of his Special Investigation Consultants, that many things ring true in his writings about some of the missions he has experienced. But, of course, nothing in his novel really happened or is true. Right?

This novel offers in-depth insight into the horrible world of "human trafficking," where young people become the prey and tools of corrupt individuals. These are the people where power and greed take over their better judgment. The value of human life is of no concern to them.

Bill's book is by far the best book ever written on understanding the nature of human trafficking so the layperson can experience it firsthand! It is an important and necessary book, and one that should be required reading in every investigation agency so every rookie and up-and-coming agent can get a comprehensive look into this international trade—the merchandising of people.

From the reader's standpoint, this book is nothing short of riveting. It will take you places you never knew existed. Jake takes you there, and the turning of each page will allow you a look into the horrendous world of *Stolen Angels*.

1

"**T**his is going to be a tough one, Jake. A hell of a challenge," my old friend, Doug "Major" Partin said in his gruff, all-business voice over the phone.

A hell of a challenge for a hell of a hellraiser, he was probably thinking. But, I had undoubtedly earned that name over the years.

I just knew, from Doug's tone of voice, that this was another big one. (A "black op" or something similar).

As usual, I replied to his challenge with: "What else is new?" He spoke very quietly into his phone and nearly whispered that a friend of his' young daughter was missing near where I lived in Florida.

All of my life, my fights were not for my own benefit, but to protect those who were young, passive, handicapped, or who could not otherwise defend themselves. In school, I protected kids who didn't have the talent I possessed with my fists. Hell, I'd had a permanent seat outside the principal's office at my grammar school. My adult years weren't much different from that.

I joined the Marine Corps at the age of seventeen because I was "guaranteed to be a fighter pilot." What I didn't know then was that the recruiter would've promised me the moon if I would just sign the papers. But, I didn't do that until the next morning, when I woke to find the Marine Recruiting Sergeant sitting at my family's dining room table, drinking his morning coffee with my mother. He already had her signature, and he was holding the pen out to me in his outstretched hand, which hovered just above the enlistment contract. The amazing part was that it was about seven o'clock in the morning and we were nearly sixty miles east of the Marine Corps Recruiting Office located in Orlando, Florida. He would have had to leave his home before five o'clock in the morning. That should have told me how hungry he was for recruits. (I should have asked for a Cadillac.)

Truthfully, I was not very happy about my home life at the time. When I was younger, my father had beaten the hell out of me with a belt almost every night up through my pre-teen years. My stepfather wasn't too fond of me, either. As a result, I had been working for a group of multi-agency Federal Agents in the Cocoa Beach area by going undercover and letting bartenders serve me alcohol as a minor in nightclubs. A close friend had brought me into the gig to get me out of the house at night. (That's a story for another time!)

Within a few days, I was on my way to Parris Island, South Carolina, and the Marine Corps Recruit Training Depot. There I was introduced to the three guerrillas who would teach me how to survive the rest of my life.

I did well in boot camp, and, upon graduation, I was promoted to Private First Class. Eventually, I was sent off to Camp Lejeune, North Carolina, for infantry training and then ordered to Pensacola, Florida, and flight school—which I never made.

On the day of my graduation from ITR (Infantry Training Regiment), a big, black staff car pulled up in front of the headquarters building at Camp Geiger. A very large man in a black civilian suit, white shirt, and black tie waved me over, and, after I did a couple of double takes over my shoulder to make sure he was motioning to me, I walked over to the passenger side window.

This very large gentleman introduced himself as Master Sgt. John Kemper, USMC, the Chief Investigator of Marine Corps Base, Camp Lejeune, Criminal Investigation Department. Chief Investigator Kemper invited me to climb into the front seat of his car for a little meeting. He told me he had been waiting for me for a couple of months and was getting impatient.

Sitting there nervously in the front seat of that large staff car, I learned I had come highly recommended by certain government agents (never to be named) for a position with the United States Marine Corps Criminal

Investigation Department. I told Kemper that there must be some mistake. I was on my way to flight school in Florida and, in fact, was currently waiting for my bus.

As it turned out, over the next few years, I came to perform, among other responsibilities, the duties of a Criminal Investigator and Intelligence Operative for the Marine Corps. I was given the opportunity to play in Southeast Asia a few times, which I gracefully accepted. There, I was utilized in numerous undercover positions, but you won't read about those war moves until later, and not the complete stories, as I'm sure some of my former Marine colleagues are still out there and still feeling victimized by my shenanigans.

It was 0630— (6:30 AM for you Army guys)—on a Monday the day the Major called about the missing girl. A bright, fall morning outside my beautiful island home on Isle Del Sol off Merritt Island, Florida. The Banana River surrounding my island, which I could see through the window, was as smooth as glass with an occasional mullet jump causing a few circles over the surface. My boats were perfectly still against the long dock, and I could see the water move near the transom of my thirty-eight-foot Morgan sloop, *The Deep Secret*. A closer look told me it was a small Manatee grazing on the bottom grasses under the boat.

I have a panoramic view of the east from my home office. I looked out over the Banana River and across to the western shore of Patrick Air Force Base on the long Canaveral barrier island that stretches from Ponce Inlet to the north to the Sabastian Inlet to the south. The island is broken up by man-made canals and lochs at Port Canaveral, about ten miles north of my island. Numerous barrier islands from Key West to the north of Maine protect the mainland from storm surges and tidal shifts. I call my barrier island "Canaveral," as I am not sure it has a proper name.

I had just gone out to my west dock, which serves as a maintenance area for my two-small speedboats and the pontoon boat I use to transport machinery and other large items. As usual, I could see Dave Bright, my Island Keeper and good friend, skimming down through Newfound Harbor in his Boston Whaler boat. Dave has been my friend for about twenty years and helped me build my island home from a tent an into the four thousand-square-foot paradise it is now. He would rival Angus MacGyver for ingenuity. He can do anything!

Dave lives in a small cabin on the shore of Newfound Harbor right next to the Merritt Island Airport. He can sit on his front porch dock and look southeast to see my island and northwest to see my small hangar where I keep my single-engine Cessna 182. Dave is one of my most trusted friends.

Earlier, he slid the nose of his boat onto the beach in the same spot he always uses and tossed me my morning newspaper and a hardy, "Good morning, sir."

I caught the paper before it sailed by me and into the water and gave him a snappy Marine Corps salute. He had some groceries and a couple of packages in the back of his boat, so I threw the paper up onto the back lawn, grabbed a couple of bags from him, and carried them to the end of the dock.

As I was walking back to retrieve more bags, I heard my office phone ring. I decided to let the answering service catch it and continued back to Dave's boat. Just as I was bending over for more bags, the phone rang again. Apparently, someone was anxious to speak to me at this early hour, so I ran back up to the phone box on the back patio.

The caller ID indicated that it was my old friend Doug Partin. (His nickname is "The Major" from an old movie we had seen many years before.) The Major is a well-known Civil Rights and Criminal Defense Attorney who lives in California. That meant it was about 0400 where he was. It was totally unlike him to call me at this hour from his home phone. That spelled "Important."

I grabbed the phone before it went over to the answering machine again and immediately asked him if he had wet the bed.

He chuckled a bit but told me to start taking notes. I had to put him on hold for a few moments until I could run into the house and to my office. I signaled to Dave with a twirling of my index finger to stand by for instructions. He nodded and started hauling his goods up toward the house. Dave knew enough of my business to understand my body language. He knew that when the phone rings before ten in the morning, I'm probably on my way off somewhere. All he was waiting for was the signal: *Plane or boat.* He could have either of them ready in one hour, fueled up, packed with provisions, and loaded with my ever-ready packed suitcase.

I grabbed the office phone and my notepad and slammed myself down on my couch in front of my desk.

As soon as I picked up, the Major said, "Signal Dave the plane."

(Did he know my routine or what?)

Dave was looking in from the kitchen as I pointed my finger up. He nodded his understanding and walked back toward my bedroom for my travel bag. As he walked down the hall, I could hear him speaking to his friend at the airport FBO (the "Fixed-Base Operator"—an organization granted the right by an airport to operate at it), to get my plane out of the hangar and preflight ready.

The Major asked me if I was ready to take notes.

I said, "Shoot"

I'm not the fastest note-taker in the world, but I knew if I wrote down every fourth or fifth word, I'd be able to read my notes well enough later.

He said he had received a call about an hour ago from Thom Cohen of Ocala, Florida—a man I had met several times in the past. A good friend and funder of the Major's many crusades, Cohen told the Major that his eighteen-year-old daughter, Angela, had not come home from her day trip to Daytona Beach the day before. The friends she was with at the beach said she had left about 1900 that evening, but by 2200, she still had not made it home.

Thom told the Major that he and his wife, Blanche, had tracked her route down Highway US 40 toward the beach and found her car on the side of the road at the intersection of US 40 and State Road 11, near Barberville, Florida. They found the keys in the ignition of the car and her pocketbook on the seat. Thom notified the local Volusia County Sheriff's Office and they were currently investigating. Thom and his wife felt they needed far more help than the Sheriff's office could provide. So, they'd called the Major.

The Major instructed me to drop everything I was doing and fly over to Ocala, interview the Cohens more thoroughly, and find this girl.

I hung up the phone and walked swiftly to the rear of the house. Dave was standing by the bow of his boat. I pushed the remote control next to the back door that locked and alarmed the entire property. As I climbed down into Dave's boat, he passed me my Smith & Wesson 9MM pistol in a plastic Ziploc bag. He asked me if I needed to file a flight plan or if I was flying visual (VFR). I told him I was headed to Ocala and that I would fly visual.

I stepped to the back of the boat next to Dave as we sped up through Newfound Harbor toward the Merritt Island Airport. I filled him in on what I knew of the case so far. He offered to contact some of his sources from the North Volusia County area to see if there were any rumors skimming around the area. I thanked him and requested that he do just that.

We pulled into Dave's dock behind his house. He grabbed my bag and both of us took off running for my plane parked at the end of the runway. Even though Dave's friend had already completed a preflight on my plane, I repeated the effort, as I always did. I climbed into the left seat and asked Dave to stand by his phone for any instructions. I also asked him to contact my friend Gage Copeland, my intelligence source over at Patrick Air Force Base, and tell him to expect my call as soon as I had more information.

I took off west from the island airport and followed the Indian River until I passed Titusville off my left wing. There, I turned toward the St. Johns River basin. This way I avoided all the commercial air traffic going in and out of the Sanford Orlando International Airport. Forty minutes later, I announced on my radio, to any other plane in the area that I was landing at a private airfield just north of Ocala. I'd gotten permission to use the airfield many years ago by a former client who'd owned it at one time.

I placed a call to Thom while I was on route, advising him to meet me as soon as my wheels touched the tarmac. As I rolled out across the short taxiway, I could see him driving toward me in his black Chevy Suburban. Blanche was sitting in the passenger seat, and I could see, even at this distance, that she looked terrible.

Thom jumped out of his SUV and ran over to my hatch before I even wound down my engine. After I shut down my engine and electronics, I unlocked and pushed my hatch open and greeted Thom under my wing.

After tying my aircraft down, I grabbed Thom by the arm and walked him to his SUV. Blanche, who was standing outside her open passenger door, gave me a quick hug.

She cupped my face between her two hands as she looked up at me. "Please bring my baby home."

The sound of her voice and the look in her eyes choked me up, and I felt like I had never been as motivated to perform a miracle as I was at that moment.

As we rode in Thom's car to his house, he briefed me on everything he knew. When we arrived, he showed me a picture of Angela that, frankly, surprised me. She was of light complexion and very, very blonde, unlike her mother and father, who had dark complexions and dark hair. Blanche noticed my curiosity and told me Angela had been conceived through artificial insemination.

As I stared at this extremely beautiful, blonde young girl in the picture, I began to get a very bad feeling.

After hearing the Cohens' story, I telephoned a couple of Angela's friends who were with her yesterday at the beach. But, other than confirming the time she'd left alone, they were of little help. Paula Davis, the fourth member of the quartet, did not answer her phone, nor did her parents return my call on their answering device. The girl lived close to Silver Springs, so I asked Thom if he would give me a ride to her house.

After assuring Blanche that we would keep her posted, Thom and I drove to Silver Springs.

As we reached the road where the Davis' lived, Thom pointed to the driveway and said, "Those are their two cars."

I asked him to pass the house and stop at the next block. As we went by, I could see Paula through the window, standing in the front room.

Thom pulled over to the side of the road and stopped. I asked him to call Paula's phone again and then her parents'. When no one answered, I nodded to Thom that something was up. He wanted to go up and knock on the door. I advised him to wait. Paula was nineteen years old and no longer a minor. We didn't need her parents' permission to speak with her.

About that time, I received a call from Dave back on Merritt Island. He told me he had spoken with a few of his friends from the North Volusia County area, but no one knew anything about the missing girl. Dave said if it were a kidnapping, these characters would have some knowledge of it. (Dave knows some interesting folks.)

I told Dave about the problem and he suggested it might only be because her parents didn't want her involved for her own safety. I told him he was probably right, but I needed Gage to check the family out as soon as possible.

Gage Copeland is my link to the universe. I have known and worked with him for about forty years. A computer genius with contacts all over the world. Gage is a government employee with more power than anyone I have ever come across. His headquarters and master computers were in the Technology Laboratory on Patrick Air Force Base near Cocoa Beach, Florida. The Tech Lab is across the runway from the Banana River. I can look out any east-facing window of my island home and see the Lab to the east, and he can look west and see my house clearly, but we never planned any of that.

Gage claims my intervention in a problem he was experiencing many years ago saved his life. Frankly, I was just doing what was right for a fellow human being. What does matter is that he's my best friend in the universe and the most important asset I have. Truth be told, he has saved my bacon more times than I can list.

After I talked to Gage, I asked Thom to drive me to an Enterprise Rent-A-Car office, where I rented a small four-wheel drive SUV. He offered to lend me one of his cars, but I was worried about winding up in harm's way.

The next thing I needed to do was view the ground where Angela's car had been found. Not only was it possible for me to pick up on some visual clues, but I might also pick up on some spiritual ones, as well. (Don't ask.)

I drove an hour east to where they had found Angela's car, parked about fifty yards up the road, and walked the rest of the way. Thom pointed out the spot where Angela's car had been found parked partially in the bushes on the south side of the road. She would have been traveling west, so her car should have been on the north side if she pulled over. The location was about one hundred yards west of the crossroad of State Road 11, which had a traffic light at the intersection. I walked back and stood on the westbound side at the light. There was a faded rubber line from the stop line to where Angela's car was found. In fact, it was exactly in line with her car tires and curved, as if her car had been pushed from behind and forced to the left. I asked Thom if there was any damage to her car, and he said he didn't see any, but that she already had some dents on her car. Again, I was getting that same bad feeling.

I asked Thom to call the sheriff's detective who was handling the case and request that he give Thom access to her car. I told him not to mention that he had hired a PI to work the case. Police tend to frown on outside interference. They might start screaming obstruction of an official investigation and try to eat my license.

The detective told Thom where it was and said he would call ahead to give him permission. The car had been towed to a private lot near Barberville on US Route 17. I kicked around a bit more at the scene and then we left. I knew I wanted to come back later to get a little closer to the ground, but without Thom looking over my shoulder. I also wanted to see who was cutting through the woods so frequently that they'd left a fresh trail near where her car was found. I didn't want to drag Thom into any hassle I might encounter, so we took off to the wrecker yard to check out her car.

When we approached the car lot, I saw a man standing near a rear gate. He put his hand up to stop us as we approached. Thom got out and told him he owned the car and had permission from the Sheriff's office to look it over. The man, we later learned, was named Buddy—or maybe that's just what I'd called him when I approached him. I don't recall now, but he answered to it well enough. Ole' Buddy was used to getting his palm scratched from all the DUI folks eager to retrieve the empty booze bottles and hidden drug stashes from under the seat before the Sheriff's Office had an opportunity to inspect.

I walked up to Buddy —perhaps that was when I named him—and said, "Hey, Buddy, is this your twenty I've just found lying on the ground?"

He grabbed it and pushed open the gate for us. He mentioned that the cop who called said there would be a uniformed deputy along shortly to make sure no one tampered with anything before the crime guys finished up with the car. I told him he could count on us to steer clear of any tampering. Buddy took a hike.

As we turned the corner beyond the gate, Thom pointed to a fairly beat up Honda Civic and announced, "Here it is."

Thom had given hundreds of thousands of dollars to Civil Rights groups and more to just Doug's legal campaigns, and his only child was driving a wreck? Thom looked at me, then at the car, and then back to me. "This car is only two years old."

Could have fooled me.

I looked through the car and saw nothing notable until I looked at the rear bumper and the scuffed dirt marks on the trunk lid. The scuffed area was clean of dirt and road dust. The bumper was scraped from recent pressure from behind.

I walked over to the fence and yelled at Buddy if he was the tow operator on the car and he said, "Yes."

I asked him if he towed it frontward or backward. He said from the front. I went back to the car and looked closer. I could see small deposits of rubber or rubber flakes on the scuff marks. I told Thom I had seen enough and said we needed to get gone before the deputy arrived and warned me off of the investigation.

We drove back down to Route 40 and headed west. About a half hour later, Gage called my cell and said he had something interesting for me regarding Mr. and Mrs. Davis. I told him I would call him back in a few minutes and hung up. I didn't want Thom to overhear what Gage had to report, so I looked for a good place to pull over.

We came upon a small store and gas station a couple of miles down the road and I pulled in. I told Thom I needed to call a friend of mine and he should call Blanche and fill her in. I asked him to refrain from mentioning that the Davis' were avoiding us until I had an opportunity to be there with her. I didn't want Blanche rushing over there and accusing them of anything when we had nothing to back it up.

I got out of the car and stood around the back to call Gage back. He answered on the first ring and I could tell he was excited and proud of himself. "Just spit it out," I told him.

Gage said the Davis' had filed bankruptcy some months ago. Poppa Davis was out of work and Mommy Davis was clerking at a convenience store down in Lake County for minimum wage. They were in debt up to their chins and their house had been on the foreclosure list for a year and was waiting on a court date. I was getting impatient, but I knew I had to endure Gage throwing in one of his famous aphorisms.

"Well, you know money can't buy happiness...but somehow it's more comfortable to cry in a Cadillac than a Yugo." (Ya gotta love 'em.)

He then said that in the last two weeks, the Davis' had paid off many of their debts. They had dropped the bankruptcy case and made up the arrearage on their mortgage payments enough to satisfy the bank. Poppa was still unemployed, but Mommy hadn't shown up for work in a week and a half. But, here comes the best part: Poppa Davis made a flight from Orlando to Brazil and then was back two days later with new luggage and a nice smile for the Customs and Immigration camera. A smile he was looking at right now in the picture lying on his desk.

"But...that's not all. Poppa had a brand new...wait for it...*Cadillac*."

I thanked Gauge and hung up. Time to see the Davis' again, but this time alone and individually.

I drove Thom back to his car near Silver Springs and told him I would call him later. I then called Dave and told him where I was and that I needed two of the largest, ugliest men he knew in Marion County and that I would pay them a hundred dollars each to just stand still and look as menacing as they could. He put me on hold and was back in twenty seconds saying he had two gorillas on their way right now and not to pay them a cent. They owed him money.

Ten minutes after I briefed Dave and hung up, an old Ford pick-up truck pulled up behind me and revved its engine. The windows were tinted so I couldn't tell who was in it, but I decided to take the chance and walked over to it. The doors popped open on both sides and two very large human beings stepped out and grinned at my obvious apprehension.

The truck suspension groaned as they exited, and it gave one last shudder as they slammed the doors.

They both spat tobacco juice out on the ground at the same time and the driver said, "We're Dave's friends."

2

I was sure glad to hear those words. I relaxed the trigger on the pistol in my pocket that I'd been pointing directly at the space between one of Dave's friend's eyes. I pulled my hand out to shake the catcher's mitt of a hand he offered. I introduced myself and he and his look-alike partner stayed quiet. I decided to name them Tweedledee and his brother, Tweedledumb—not to their faces, however. We walked around the front of my rental car and I prayed they wouldn't decide to sit on its fenders. They must have had the same idea, as Dumb thumped the hood with his finger and mumbled something about defecation. I was sure he didn't need the men's room.

We stood there in the dirt lot and I gave them a brief of what I wanted them to do for me as soon as I lured Poppa Davis away from his house. Dee pushed the issue and asked what kind of information I needed from the guy, and I explained about Angela's disappearance. He shrugged and walked back to his truck. Dumb continued to stand there, looking at me from the passenger's side of the car. I thought he was going to ask me to unlock the doors, but he turned with a grin and walked back to the truck.

I told Dee that I was going to drive to the end of the Davis' street and wait a while to see if he was unlucky enough to decide he wanted to take a ride. As I pulled up to the Davis' street, I saw the brand-new Cadillac in the driveway. One of the cars from earlier was now gone. I could see Poppa looking down the street from his front door and right into my eyes. I had no choice but to continue to the front of his yard and up to his door.

He had shut it by the time I arrived, but just as I was about to ring the doorbell, I saw a foot and leg fly past me and the entire door and frame turned into splinters and a very large hand reached in and yanked Poppa Davis out and threw him halfway across the yard. I wasn't sure any human being could withstand that kind of abuse, but I was encouraged to see his chest rise and fall a couple of times before Dumb picked him up and held him about seven feet in the air.

Dee walked over, looked up at him for a moment, and said very quietly, "Where's the chick?"

Mr. Davis, through the tears and spittle running off his face, did not hesitate to say he would tell us all he knew.

After Dumb dropped him onto the ground, I stood over Mr. Davis as he told us a very bizarre story.

His daughter, Paula, had been doing some modeling for an agency out of Miami about six months ago. This agency would send her to model for advertisements and magazine covers all over North and South America. While she was in Brazil some months ago, a man approached her, asking if she would like to make some serious legitimate money. Paula, knowing the family's financial situation, sat down and listened to the man's offer.

He told her that she and any of her friends, models or not, could make a great deal of money acting as escorts to wealthy South American businessmen when they were in the States on business. As he was explaining this, he passed her an envelope, thick with hundred-dollar bills spilling out of the top. He told her there was $25,000 in the pile, and that was hers only to just consider the offer. Paula was shocked to the point of being dizzy and could not find the words fast enough to accept.

For the past three months, she and some of her friends had been going back and forth between Miami and Tampa, telling their families they were modeling for this agency and making large amounts of money for little to no sex play. Mostly, these men just wanted to see them take their clothes off and act as if they were modeling on stage in front of them.

I asked if Angela was one of the friends who made the runs to Miami, and he said, "Yes." I had been afraid of that answer from the start of his story.

Davis said he had discovered his daughter's business affairs while he was driving her car in for repairs about a month ago, and instead of scolding her, decided to join her as a sort of business partner. His first order of business was to contact the Escort Service in Miami. The service then invited him to Rio for a face-to-face meeting.

During this meeting, Davis told the two gentlemen he was meeting with that he had contacts all over the country with folks who were out of work, and/or in desperate need of financial help. Prior to flying to South America, he had called several his former co-workers and filled them in on the deal. Many of them had attractive wives and young daughters who were game—so long as there was no real sex involved.

It was decided very quickly that they had a deal, and Davis was given a hundred thousand American greenbacks as a sign of good faith.

Since that meeting and his return home, he had set up over fifty matches around the country and had made nearly a half a million dollars for his efforts. Davis said he had no idea how or why these rich South American men were so willing to part with their money for the brief time they spent with the young ladies.

Davis went on to say that about two weeks ago, he received a call from one of his associates in St. Louis that one of the young ladies in the ring had failed to return home after being out on an escort service. Two days later, he received another call informing him that another young girl had disappeared. Later, that same day, he received still another call telling him that a third young lady had gone missing. It didn't take Davis long to realize this entire affair had been a ruse for a kidnapping ring from South America and perhaps parts unknown.

Davis called his contact man in Miami to get some answers but was unable to reach anyone he had talked to previously. He then called the man in Rio and left a message on his answering device. The following afternoon, he found a note tucked under his windshield-wiper blade on his car warning him that he was to continue doing business as usual or his daughter would be next. Davis became terrified that he would lose his only child to his greed.

The next day, he received a call from his Miami contact ordering him to make Angela available for service. Davis knew they were planning to kidnap her, as he had never received a direct request for a particular girl before that.

He didn't give Paula the message to call Angela and give her the escort message. He knew Paula and some friends, including Angela, were going to the beach. He knew he should have warned Angela and her parents but was afraid for his own family.

17

Late yesterday afternoon, Paula called him as she was leaving Daytona Beach to tell him there were two Latin-looking men talking to Angela next to her car in the parking garage. Angela looked irritated. Davis told her daughter to drive straight home and only answer her phone if she recognized her father's number.

Later that night, he received a call from Angela's father and did not answer it. He instructed Paula to do the same and made plans to get to the bank's safety deposit box today and leave town.

This morning, the Marion County Sheriff called to question him about Angela and to say they wanted to interview Paula as soon as possible. Davis said he had all his ready cash in his car and was just picking up some odds and ends when I'd pulled up. He said his wife and Paula were already on their way up Interstate 75 and were to meet them in Atlanta tomorrow. He said he had no further plans beyond that but needed to hide out before they caught him and made good on their threat.

Davis gave me the phone numbers of his contacts in Tampa and Miami. He also gave me his contact's home address in Petropolis, Brazil.

He said the man called himself Frank Schultz, but Davis did not know the names of his contacts in Miami or Tampa. They would just answer the phone with a "Hello."

Gage should be able to get me some info on this hombre with little problem, I thought. His business address was on the shoreline road south of Mage, Brazil, in a large, south-facing building facing over the bay. He said it was the only structure that looked grand enough to house offices, and it was close to a large dock where he'd spotted a big yacht. He said he had been driven up there by a couple of thugs and was told to keep his eyes facing forward, but he could see from his peripheral vision the name of the town and other details he felt he needed to remember for his own safety— should he need to escape from these people.

I looked at the man-mountains providing shade for us and told them to get scarce. I pointed to Davis' new Caddy and told him we were going for a ride. He did not hesitate.

I had Davis drive back to Silver Springs and park on the side of Highway 40. I took the keys from his ignition and stepped around the back to call the Major. After I had thoroughly briefed him, he asked me only one question. "Do you think she is still alive?"

I thought about it far longer than I needed to, but finally answered, "Yes."

Angela might very well be dead in the woods somewhere, but that would be a waste of good, profitable flesh.

His next question was what I was expecting. "Can you get her back?"

Again, I took a little longer to answer than I really needed to. I had been thinking and planning my moves well before I called Doug. I believed we had a chance if we could keep the Cohens from informing the police or the FBI until I was ready. A very good chance. If it became an international incident and a news item on TV, Angela was surely dead. I also called Gage and fed him the info on Rio and assorted folks. He said he would send me his research by email as soon as he pulled it up.

Doug and I decided that I should take Davis over to the Cohens and have him tell them what he knew. I signed off with Doug after promising to keep him briefed.

I needed to make one more stop before we went to the Cohens' home. I climbed back into the Cadillac with Davis and told him to drive out to US highway 40 to the intersection of State Road 11.

When we arrived at SR 11, I had him park on the side. I again grabbed his keys and told him to stay in his car.

I headed for the worn path I had noticed earlier where Angela's car had been parked. There, I walked it down through the brush. When I came to the first clearing, I found a pile of beer cans and about a hundred cigarette butts. I continued and found a couple of campfire remnants and a badly maintained bicycle lying in the bushes. Then, before I saw or heard it, I sensed a baseball bat swinging alarmingly close to my head. I twisted around and blocked it before pulling the skinny arm attached to the other end of the bat to the ground. I was about to deliver a killing blow to the back of the neck of the Evil Doer when I noticed the bulge of a small breast under the now nearly broken arm. Not a dude.

I checked my kick and snatched her up from the ground. While holding her tightly by the neck, I asked very unpleasantly, "What the hell are you thinking?"

She began to sob and shake all over, unable to speak.

I gave her a few moments to stop crying and again asked her why she'd attacked me. Finally, able to speak through sobs and coughs, she said she had run away from home and had been living here for two weeks, hiding from her abusive father. She thought he had sent me to bring her home to Bunnell, about twenty miles north. I assured her I had no knowledge of her father. I was a PI looking for a missing young girl last seen the night before out near the road. She started to cry again and, after quieting down, told me that she had seen what happened early in the evening.

She said her name was Emily Ruskin and that she was about to turn eighteen in two days. She told me she had been hiding in these woods for the last two weeks, only riding her old bike to a distant convenience store down Rte. 40. She said she had a tent about fifty yards in the bushes and had managed to avoid the few people who frequented the woods every few days.

She said that at about six o'clock the night before, a big SUV pulled off the road and backed into the bushes on the other side of Route 11. There was one man in the car, and he looked to be Spanish. A few minutes later, a small car stopped at the light and the big SUV pulled out and pushed the car up the road and into the bushes near her camp. She said another car pulled off the road. There was one man in that car who also appeared to be Hispanic. She said both ran to the small car and pulled a blonde girl out and forced her into the second car. The car and the SUV then sped off west on Highway 40 toward Ocala.

Emily went on to say that later that same evening, a man and woman stopped at the abandoned car, and, shortly thereafter, some sheriff's cars arrived. She said that a wrecker towed the car to the west. She said she had been hiding in the bushes ever since as she believed if she was discovered, the cops would send her home.

After Emily filled me in with a few more details about her home situation, I called Mr. Cohen and asked him if he and his wife would mind housing a material witness for a few days until I had time to catch up to Angela's captors. They immediately agreed and never questioned me. I told them I would explain everything when I arrived back at their home.

I asked Emily if she had anything important, she wanted to bring with her, and she said, "Absolutely not."

There was no doubt she was ready to be out of these bear-infested woods. (Her story brought back some memories of my Uncle Joe and the culvert hidey-home I used during one of my Uncles drunken rages. Another story for another time)

While Mr. Davis, Emily, and I drove back to Ocala, I called Dave and asked him to use up a bit more of his Tweedledee and Tweedledumb credit to pay Emily's stepdad a visit and convince him to play nice from here on out.

Dave never questioned me, just said, "Got it." After I gave Davis directions to the Cohen ranch, he said he was afraid Mr. Cohen would try to kill him after he heard his story. I told Davis I would kill him if he didn't. Emily asked if she could move to the backseat and away from him.

I called Mr. Cohen again at his home and told him Davis, Emily, and I would be there in ten minutes. I asked him to keep an open mind and an even temper when he heard Davis' story. He tried to get me to explain but I told him it would have to wait until we arrived.

Davis asked me if he could call his wife, as she would be worried that he hadn't informed her that he was on his way. I told him to go ahead but to leave the phone on speaker so I could hear what she had to say. I told him that it was not in his best interest to warn her off, as we may need her help—and Paula's—in the next couple of days. I told him to instruct her to continue to Atlanta and to call him later with her location. He spoke with her briefly and, although she sounded apprehensive, she agreed to do what he'd instructed.

We pulled up into the Cohen's driveway. Mr. Cohen was waiting for us in front of his house. Again, I took the keys out of the ignition and stuck them in my pocket. Mr. Cohen stood there with his hands on his hips, glaring at Davis through the windshield. I waved him over.

I asked Emily to stay in the car until I signaled her to get out. I pointed at Davis and said, "Get out."

I told Mr. Cohen that I had a pretty good idea of what had happened to his daughter and that I needed him to stay calm while I had Mr. Davis tell his story. I told him I wanted Mrs. Cohen to hear his story, as well. I could tell that Mr. Cohen was anxious, and I certainly couldn't blame him. However, I needed him to be cool and go along with my plan.

While Davis repeated his story, I only had to intercept Mr. Cohen from punching him out three times, but, to their credit, in the end, he and his wife looked to me for my plan.

I'm not known for having long-range plans, or, if I do, not following them very well.

Mrs. Cohen took Emily upstairs to get cleaned up and changed into some of Angela's clothes. I placed Mr. Davis in the small bathroom in the hallway off the living room while I briefed the Cohens on the first part of my plan. I told them I was going to have Davis call his contacts in Miami and tell them he had seen the light and would cooperate fully. I had already tasked Gage with tracking the phone numbers Davis had given me earlier. I knew Gauge would have the rest of the information available on the owners of those phone numbers. With any luck at all, I would be conducting a seance with one of those contacts by first light the following day.

I also talked the Cohens into allowing Mr. Davis to bunk with them for a while until he had worn out his usefulness. They didn't like it any more than he did, but I knew I would need him soon to buy me time with these bad guys, and I also wasn't sure if he wouldn't double-cross me in order to curry favor with them.

Before I left to retrieve my car and get back to my plane, I took Mr. Davis for a walk out back. I warned him that Mr. Tweedledee and Mr. Tweedledumb would be close by, watching his every move while he was still useful to me, and that they had my permission to make him disappear as soon as he fell out of line. I told him to do everything the Cohens told him to do and to answer my calls on the first ring. He quickly agreed and asked that I afford his wife and daughter some protection if they needed it. I told him I was the biggest threat to him now but assured him if he continued to cooperate, I would protect them, as well.

I had Thom drive me to my plane and asked him to get my rental car back to the lot in the morning. He agreed and complained a bit more about having to entertain Davis at his home. I explained that it was the only way we could keep an eye on him while we still needed him.

3

Before I did my preflight and took off from the little airport, I called Dave and briefed him. I would be landing in about forty-five minutes at Merritt Island to refuel and load up some necessary hardware that I would need before flying on to Tampa. He knew from my briefing what hardware I needed, and I knew it would be waiting for me as soon as I landed. He asked if he could ride along to watch my back, and I agreed it would be a good idea. I also asked him to call Gage and tell him to email me the background info he had on the folks I was about to visit.

The landing and turnaround at Merritt Island went smoothly and Dave and I were in the air in less than fifteen minutes. He contacted the night FBO manager and had a fuel truck parked on the taxiway as soon as I touched down. David made a run to my island and picked up the necessary articles I had requested, as well as some extras I hadn't. I did not file a flight plan; I only contacted the tower at Patrick Air Force Base to tell them I would be flying on the edge of their airspace for a few moments while I headed for the greater Tampa area. As I flew, David tracked us on the chart and guided us around all the restricted airspace along the way. Dave was also a pilot—far better than I was—but he hadn't kept his certificate up to date for a few years. (I believe there were some other reasons, too).

Dave had also downloaded Gage's email containing the names, addresses, and background info on these bad hombres I was about to confront. The main character in Tampa was a man named Juan Compos. I'm sure that was not his birth name, but it was what he answered to now. He lived a little southeast of Tampa in a community called Brandon. His office was in Ybor City, a Latin community located near downtown Tampa.

It was now just after midnight on Tuesday morning, nearly thirty hours since Angela's abduction. I had decided to go to Tampa first, thinking that it was right down Interstate 75 on a straight line from Ocala. I figured I'd be able to get some information from Mr. Campos that would help point me in the right direction.

Dave and I decided to land at the Tampa Executive Airport just north of Tampa, near Interstate 75. That put us at nearly the same distance north of Tampa as Brandon was south. I enjoyed having some maneuvering room during my operations. It was late, however, and a night attendant at the FBO rented cars for an outfit like Rent-a-Wreck, just not nearly as nice.

I have oftentimes joked to rent-a-car employees that I would take any car they had except a red Yugo convertible. This guy had a red Yugo with a slide back canvas roof for rent. I couldn't believe it—and I did not rent it. Instead, we rented a Kia SUV. Far better than the Yugo. It even had four-wheel-drive.

After tying down the Cessna and loading up our gear, we drove through the winding roads and onto southbound Interstate 75. David remembered to take along his faithful GPS, which said we had to cover about forty miles to Old Juan's adobe-style hacienda. As usual, I offered to drop Dave off at a truck stop along the way, so he didn't have to involve himself in my shenanigans. As usual, he gave me the same old disgusted look out of the corner of his eye and instructed me to take exit 256, near the Brandon Mall, about ten miles on.

I enjoy working with Dave. He seldom says anything and leaves me to my thoughts and plans. When trouble strikes, he is right there beside me online—and, often enough, a bit ahead of me for good measure.

When we got off at the exit, I stopped to top off the fuel tank and to make a head (latrine) call. You never know when you will be afforded the use of a urinal, and one of the greatest lessons I'd learned in the Marine Corps was to relieve yourself as often as you could. Because when the crap hits the fan, you don't need it lining the inside of your trousers.

We cruised the area around the Compos home and found it to be a sleepy neighborhood of two-acre lots guarded by an imposing gate that had not one but two very large uniformed security guards. There was a

Hillsboro County Sheriff's patrol car parked alongside a small pickup truck across from the guard shack. That told me that at least one of them was an off-duty cop. I continued to drive while Dave suggested we cut over a few roads and look for a service entrance. Sure enough, there was one at the opposite end of the neighborhood. Even better, the gate was all bent and leaning over from lawn mowers and delivery trucks striking it.

We drove on and parked the Kia next to some brush. I had been looking for security cameras around the perimeter but had not seen any. Folks were getting more guarded about their privacy and becoming less concerned about safety. They were more concerned about being able to skinny dip in the pool or make love on the patio lawn chairs without a security guard joining in with a night vision camera.

I told Dave to get behind the wheel of the Kia and let me do a recon of the house before we made any plans. He reluctantly agreed. I plugged in an earpiece, slid a black stocking watch cap over my head and face to reduce the light that was bound to reflect off my neon-white hair and beard, and slipped out into the night.

I stayed on the opposite side of the road from the gate and squatted down a few moments to get the lay of the land. I could make out the overhead lights from the main gate about four hundred yards east of where I was and see the street signs marking off the roads to the short, residential cul-de-sacs. According to Dave's GPS, the Compos' home was at the end of the second cul-de-sac from the rear gate and four houses in. Domestic GPS devices are not always dead accurate, so I wanted to make sure by verifying the number on his house before jumping the wrong guys.

I didn't see any cameras or movement from the direction of the guard shack, so I darted across the road and squeezed through the side of the gate. I ran two houses in and stopped again to see if I had set off any alarms. Nothing so far.

I continued, staying close to any existing bushes for cover, and turned down the second road until I could see the house where I believed Compos lived. I verified the number and slid into the bushes of the house next door. I radioed Dave and gave him my position. He clicked acknowledgment and remained quiet.

After a few moments, I crept along the side of the house to the backyard. The place was completely dark. Not even a night light or a security motion detector outside. No curtains or blinds on the windows. No patio furniture. No BBQ grill out back. Nothing. This house was empty.

I went around the front and saw a realtor's box attached to the front doorknob, but there was no For Sale sign in the yard. I went over to the side where there was a pad for the trash cans and found an envelope in the bushes that had Compos' name on it, so I had the right house. Back to the drawing board

When I got back to the Kia, I briefed Dave and we drove back out to the northbound on-ramp to I-75. Dave pulled over and we both read more of Compos' background papers. We found he also listed an address near his office in Tampa as a residence. It was only one month old, so it fit the picture of moving from the big house to an apartment in town. Back to Tampa.

The Ybor City area of Tampa is unique for its history and colorful, scenic portrayals of twentieth-century Cuba. Although a bit more modern, and far cleaner, it looks like it has been cut from a block of old Havana and transported here from a hundred years ago. This is where good Latin food lives and never varies. Truly one of my favorite getaways. Up until twenty-some-odd years ago, it was also the dinnertime headquarters of the Santos Trafficante Mob bosses, out-of-town visitors from New York cartels, and various Miami mob celebrities. Sitting at your table at the Columbia Restaurant, waiting for your meal, you could visualize the smoke from the famous Cuban cigars leaking out of the numerous side rooms. There, bodyguards would stand their watch, protecting their bosses, as ill-natured business was carried out night after night. I wonder where it is conducted now. Probably at some dark Capitol Hill back room where lobbyists walk in, take a number, and then wait their turn to pour greenbacks on the table next to the Long John Silver's empty take-out boxes.

Dave and I sat in the Kia in the parking lot of a BankAmerica, looking up at the second-floor apartment not far from the center of Ybor City, wishing for an order of fish and chips—or even a box of crackers. I hadn't eaten anything since yesterday morning, but if I asked Dave about his last meal, I'd probably have gotten a shrug at best.

There was a light on in the front of the apartment in what I thought might be the living room. The rear was dark with a window open, curtains flowing in and out with the brisk breeze. The interesting thing about that open window was that it was right above the old, steel fire escape decorated with some small flowerpots scattered around the landing. Looked like an invitation to me! The only problem was that there were no stairs leading down to the ground from the platform.

I looked at Dave and he pointed to the roof of the Kia. A little short, but with a good up-and at-'em from Dave and a spring off his hands, I might make it. Of course, my ability to pull myself up at my age left much to be desired. If I fell back down, the roof of the Kia was going to sound like a bass drum to whoever was snoozing in that room up there. Never know till one tries!

Dave pulled the Kia out of the bank parking lot, did a U-turn up the side road, headed back at a good clip, and then shut off the engine, coasting just below the fire escape balcony and window and finally stopping exactly where I needed him. Standing beside the Kia, there was a six-foot gap between my height and the bottom of the balcony. Up close, the fire escape looked extremely rusted, and the corrosion was flaking off the bottom of the wrought-iron rails. Dave looked up for a moment, opened the car door, and stepped out with a pair of light-colored leather gloves. I wondered if he could find a few years in there to shave off for the Jake of my youth who could have nearly jumped from the ground to the rails with a good run. He didn't offer me any of those years, so up onto the roof, we went.

I asked him to stand by with his silenced .22 pistol in case I was met by a shotgun on the opposite side of those pretty curtains. He twisted a bit to show me he was, as usual, one step ahead of me. I had my modified Buck fighting knife tucked into my waistband, as well as a small .22 pistol in my pocket. Any more weight and I would need a crane to get up to the window!

The wind was making enough noise blowing the leaves and limbs together that it covered the clunking and groaning of the Kia roof. (There went a couple of hundred dollars to the rental company to pop the roof up after this. I don't know why I think of things like that at a time like this. I guess it keeps me sane to know I have a normal life somewhere.)

Dave stood close beside me as we balanced each other on the roof.

I looked him square in the face and he immediately whispered, "No way," as I considered that perhaps being younger than I was, he should be the one to climb up. Nope on that one. I slid on the offered leather gloves.

The plan was to get me up on the balcony so I could climb in the window, sneak through the room to the front hallway door, and let Dave in to assist me in my endeavors. Dave bent down and clasped his fingers together. I stepped into them and he lifted me like a shot put so all I had to do was flat-palm my hands on the edge of the fire escape and sit down between two very dead aloe plants in their dry, soil-filled, red ceramic pots.

Great job, except for the one pot that tumbled over the opposite edge and fell—praise the Lord—into Dave's waiting hands! I thumbed-up him a good job.

I could now hear a rather loud fan blowing the air around in the room behind the curtain. That helped keep the noise of our infiltration at a moderate level. I inched forward, dared a peek into the room, and then quickly pulled my head back. I can take a picture with my eyes that I can reflect upon for a few moments afterward to get the general layout of an area. In this case, I had a dark shadow accompanied by a couple of more dark shadows that meant absolutely nothing to me. I wasn't even sure I had penetrated the room far enough to have seen anything.

I looked down at Dave again and gave him a salute. He gave me a shrug and I went for the window. As I parted the curtains, I saw a bed, a chest of drawers, and two doors on the opposite wall. I figured that behind one of those doors was a hallway and behind the other was a closet.

I placed my feet inside, pulled out my Buck knife, and took a step toward the doors. Just then, I heard a faint whimper and saw something move on the bed. I moved closer to the bed and saw only one lump under the covers. A small one, at that. As I drew closer, I saw it was a young girl with her mouth covered with a cloth gag and her hands and feet tied to the headboard and footboard of the old-fashioned bed. She was wide awake and looking right at me.

At first, I thought I had found Angela, but then quickly realized this girl was only about ten to twelve years old. Blonde hair like Angela, but the wrong age. How could these people place someone's daughter in such a compromising position?

I bent down to her and whispered that I was one of the good guys and here to get her out. I told her I would remove her gag and bonds, but that she had to be very quiet and not say a peep. She nodded. I had just cut her bonds off with the Buck knife when she sprang up from the bed like a jack-in-a-box. I put my arms around her, both to comfort her and to prevent her from jumping out of the bed and clunking to the floor as I pulled the gag away from her face.

I waited for an outcry, but she just continued to hold onto me. I lifted her from the bed and looked out the window to see if Dave was still down there, but he must have gone around the front to wait for me. I needed to get her out of the building before any action began, and it looked as if she was going to have to go with me to the front door.

I asked her how many people were in the house and she said she had only seen two men. She said they were speaking Spanish and she had no idea what they were saying. They spoke English to her and said she would only be there until morning, when she would be taking a long plane ride into a new life.

I had many more questions for her but only asked two more. What was her name and where was she from? Her name was Emily Little, and she was from St. Louis, MO. I realized she was one of the abductees that Davis had spoken about yesterday.

I told her we were going to go out the door into the hallway and then down the steps to the outside. I told her I had a friend waiting at the door down below and he would take her away as soon as we got out. She again nodded and I, very quietly, opened the door and looked right into the closet. Emily was standing at the other door, pointing at it as if I was as dumb as a stone. I can't be sure in the dark, but I think I saw her shake her head in disgust as I quickly moved to the proper exit. (She and Dave were going to get along famously!)

I opened the door and saw the door leading outside. It had a deadbolt on it. There was an open door to a small living room where a table light was on, and, farther down the hall on the same side as Emily's cell, another door that was open. I could see that the hall turned toward the rear of the building and wondered if another bedroom or bathroom was down there.

I held Emily close and exchanged my knife for my small pistol. We then made for the door leading out. Just as we arrived at the door, I heard a slight clicking of the knob and the door slowly opened. I pointed the pistol at the crack of the door as it opened, and there was Dave's face staring back at me. He looked at the pistol, pushed it away with his finger, and gave me a Dave shrug when he noticed Emily wrapped up in my arm. I whispered to him to take her down the stairs and get out. I would contact him later when I finished here. I asked him to find out all she knew about what was going on here and if she'd seen any other girls here or anywhere else after being abducted. I pushed her into Dave's arms and pinched her cheek with a smile. Then they were gone.

I waited until I could hear the Kia driving off and moved to the second bedroom. The room was even smaller than the other room and held one bed with one very large, broad man in it. He didn't stir when I entered the room, so I stepped back out and rounded the corner of the hall to see if there were any other guests slumbering away. That turn led to a small bathroom, but no other occupants.

I walked back to the occupied bedroom and stepped close to the bed. There was a flat looking, 1911-style, semi-auto pistol on the nightstand, which I quickly picked up. Judging by its weight, it was loaded. There was also a long-handled, Maglite on the table, which I also picked up. The bedroom window was closed and the curtains drawn tight.

I decided it was chat time in Ybor City and I struck Sleeping Beauty in the crotch with a grand swing of the Maglite. He woke up very quickly and only made the briefest of moans as he grabbed his manhood with both hands. As he sat up and played locate the tootle-o, I hit him across the throat with only slightly less force than the crotch. He went right back down on the pillow. Before he passed out from lack of oxygen, I squeezed his larynx from side to side so he could get a little air.

I introduced myself as El Diablo and told him I was going to ask him a few questions. I said that I would beat him with the flashlight every time I thought he was lying to me. I asked him if he understood and he hesitated a moment too long, so I whacked him on his right shoulder hard enough to shatter the bone and cause him to start passing out again. In that moment, it also dawned on me that I had rendered him unable to speak with the throat strike. I could picture Dave shaking his head at me and shrugging his shoulders.

I had to get this handled quickly as the sun was rising and Emily said she was going for a ride early in the morning. I figured we'd have company real soon.

I asked fatso if he was Mr. Compos and he nodded. I asked him if he knew where Angela Cohen was, and he nodded. I waited a beat. He was trying his best to please me with her location, but he couldn't get the words out. So, I decided to give him only yes or no questions.

Was she in Tampa? No. Was she in Florida? No. Was she in Brazil? Yes. Rio? No. Near Rio? Yes. Marge? Yes. Were the other girls with her there? Yes and no. This was tricky, but I thought I knew the answer already. Are they being sold? Yes.

I heard the front door open and someone climbing up the stairs. I quietly asked him if this was Emily's ride to the airplane and he nodded yes. I asked him if it was only one man and he said. Yes. I then swung the flashlight down on his head and told him, "Wrong answer."

I could hear two sets of feet climbing the stairs.

I quickly moved out of the room, leaving the hamburger-headed guy on the bed, and into the spare bedroom with the fire escape balcony. Just as I climbed through the window onto the platform, I heard the door open and someone called for Juan. I didn't wait for an introduction, hung down from the rail, and dropped to the ground.

Fortunately, it was a soft sand landing and I walked briskly around the front of the building and noted the white Ford van parked out front. As I passed it, I bent down, slashed both tires on the passenger side with the Buck, and then kept walking.

Two blocks down and two to the right, I stopped to call Dave. He was at a McDonald's a few streets over, waiting for my call. I told him to pick me up as soon as they were finished. The next call I made was to Thom Cohen. When he answered, I gave him a brief rundown on our night's work. I told him I needed him to transfer fifty thousand dollars into my Bank of America account immediately and then I needed to speak with Davis right away.

I gave Thom my account number and he put Davis on the phone. He confirmed that Emily was his friend's daughter from St. Louis. I told him we had her and that she was safe. I told him again that I needed to keep this quiet from the authorities for a little while longer. I also needed him to contact Mr. Little in St. Louis and explain that I needed him to keep a lid on this. I told him I was going to have Dave fly Emily up to Thom's house from Tampa. Mr. Little could retrieve his daughter from there. He said he would handle that as soon as we hung up.

Just then, Dave pulled up with Emily in the front seat of the Kia. I jumped into the back seat and told Dave to drive me to the Tampa International Airport. I then told him what Compos told me and that that I wanted him to fly Emily to Ocala. He agreed and took the on-ramp west to the airport. Before I climbed out of the car, I gave Dave my Derringer, my Buck knife, and my newly acquired 1911 Kimber .45 caliber pistol.

I retrieved my actual passport from my Maxpedition backpack and made sure it was in order. I also checked the little secret compartment where I kept two extra alternative passports with various names that I used in certain matters when I didn't care to be identified. Everything was in order and I returned them to their little compartments. I took all the weapons out of their hidden compartments and checked to make certain I still had my emergency comfort items and the change of socks and skivvies that Dave had packed for me.

4

I was not very familiar with the Tampa Airport, so I had Dave drop me off in front of the Delta Departure area. I gave Emily a hug, told her she was a great date, and then jumped out. I could see Emily looking at me the whole way until they made the turn out of view.

I whispered into the wind, "Have a good life, little one."

As it turned out, Delta had a flight to Rio leaving in three hours. It had a seat available in First Class and the airline could leave an open return, so I booked it. I told the attendant that I would return in an hour to drop off my luggage and fill out the customs forms.

Next, I shopped in the International duty-free shop for a small suitcase to compliment my backpack, some casual clothes, and a few more toiletries for the trip. I needed to look the role of a traveler as much as possible and not raise any suspicion from the TSA folks at security or the Brazilian Customs in Rio. The flight was about ten hours long with a tailwind, and I needed every moment to try to get to Angela before she was sold off to some rich Brazilian or Arab businessman. Any number of dark possibilities for her future ran through my mind, should I not be successful.

If Mr. Compos was telling me the truth, and I had every reason to believe he was, Angela was at the Brazilian businessman's home or office. This was the information that Davis gave me when he briefed me.

Next, I called the Major and informed him of *most* of the night's activities. (Some things he really did not need to know!) He was very concerned that we may be too late already, but I assured him that my gut told me I was only a few hours behind her. From what I was told from folks in the know, these human sales were far too complicated to be handled overnight, and it would take the people involved a few days to hash out the details. The seller also did not want the buyers to think it was too easy or the price might be drastically reduced.

I signed off with the Major and walked to the front of the airport to stretch my legs before the flight. As I approached the big glass doors, I saw what I believed to be the white van I had disabled this morning in Ybor City. Two men wearing light green hospital scrubs were exiting the front doors, and the passenger-side guy was sliding open the side door. I stood there and watched as they lowered a small ramp and rolled a wheelchair onto the sidewalk.

The occupant of the chair was a slender, young girl with a bandage wrapped around the top of her head, leaving only her face exposed. She appeared to be in a trance or drugged. Behind her, coming out of the van, was an older woman in a flowered dress and flat, slip-on shoes. She was carrying a small carry-on bag and a purse. The driver reached past the slider, took out a bigger suitcase and nodded to his partner to head into the building.

I could now see that at least one of the tires on the van was new as it still had the paper sticker on the tread. The older lady placed a blue, disabled sign on the inside passenger door window and closed it and the slider. She then caught up with the group as they entered the terminal.

I walked over, stood beside them at the Delta ticket counter with my new bag in tow and looked at the young girl in the wheelchair. I could see from her eyes that she was out of it, but not entirely unconscious. She had dark, exaggerated eyebrows, which, at a closer inspection, were colored in with a makeup pencil. I also noticed a large dark mole on her cheek that they had tried to cover with makeup. This wasn't Angela, but was it someone else's angel being missed right now?

As they approached the counter, the attendant asked me if I was next and I told the attendant to wait on the folks with the girl first. The taller of the two men, the passenger from the van, said they had three reservations to Rio on the next flight. My flight! The lady produced two passports and the man put his own on the counter with them. The ticket attendant took the three passports and looked at one of them but kept staring back at the girl in the wheelchair. The shorter man in scrubs was looking uncomfortable and started to move away from the counter area.

I knew I had to do something to stop this girl from being placed on that plane, but it had to be something that, at the same time, would not leave me held back here in Tampa, answering a thousand questions for the Tampa Police, the FBI, and everyone else who wanted the credit for stopping a kidnapping.

Just then, a Delta Red Coat Supervisor walked up to me as I stood away from the counter and asked if I needed any assistance. I told him no, that I was fine, and then I noticed he was wearing a Marine Corps pin on his lapel. I gave him the Marine-to-Marine greeting of *"Semper Fi,"* and he returned it with a handshake.

I decided to take a chance on my brother Marine and quickly told him I was a former Marine Corp CID and was now a private investigator. I showed him my credentials and told him I was working a big undercover case. I nodded toward the counter and said the girl in the wheelchair looked exactly like a photo I had seen of a missing young girl from up north somewhere. I also described the makeup she was wearing and explained that I felt she was drugged and not the brain surgery patient they were attempting to pass her off as. I explained that it would blow my case if I went to the cops or the TSA and asked if he would investigate it more closely before she could board the plane.

He did not hesitate at all—especially now that I could see a little commotion going on at the ticket counter. It seemed our Delta Ticket Attendant was not only pretty but wise, too. She wasn't buying the makeup job. My Red Coat buddy was moving in that direction, talking into his radio microphone as he approached the counter. I could see several Delta officials moving toward the counter from every direction. A uniformed deputy had his back to the excitement, so I caught his attention and pointed to the crowd gathering at the counter. He grabbed his shoulder microphone, shouted a ten code, and headed that way.

Meanwhile, the short driver in scrubs was slipping out the front door toward the van. I sure wished I had a little time to speak with him, but it was now a half hour before boarding time and I needed to get through the security checkpoint before I got caught up in some police dragnet. I pulled my roller bag out of the exit door next to Dr. Shorty and followed him to the van. As he went around to the driver's side, I opened the passenger door and asked if he was a taxi.

He looked up, surprised, and said, "No, shut the door."

At that point, I grabbed him from across the seats and smashed my fist right into the tip of his nose, a blow that should have driven his cartilage into his small brain and killed him instantly. Unfortunately, he went out but continued to breathe. I took the keys from his fingers and closed the door. As I walked away, I threw the keys in a trashcan and told one of the Red Cap bag handlers there was a man who appeared to be unconscious in the van by the unloading ramp. He looked back, and, as he walked over, I could see that he too was on his radio. (I put Mr. Motorola to work today.)

As I passed my Red Coat Marine on my way to the security checkpoint, I pointed out the van commotion outside the front doors and told him the guy in the front was part of the kidnapping gang trying to get away. He winked and got back on his radio as he approached another deputy sheriff nearby.

I sailed through the security checkpoint and made my way to the International flight gates. I called Thom Cohen again and filled him in on the information about the girl here at the airport. He was upset it wasn't Angela but told me he had transferred the money into my account and then passed the phone to Davis.

I described the girl to Davis, including the mole on her cheek. He said she was another missing girl from up north that he had been told about. I told him to contact her family but, again, to keep it quiet and to keep my name out of it. The folks in Rio were likely getting a bit nervous by now, and they would be even more so when no one they recognized got off the flight.

I again called the Major to keep him in the know.

I was the last to board so I could get a good look at my flight mates. I saw no other wheel-chaired young people or any scrub-wearing doctors or nurses.

The equipment we were flying in was a Boeing 767, and I had seat 5B on the port aisle. A good place to observe my fellow passengers—and a great place to snooze, if I could for a few hours. As soon as I boarded, I requested a screwdriver and a couple of bags of peanuts for breakfast. While I was trying to remember the last time I had eaten, my seatmate, an attractive Latina who looked about forty, excused herself to get by me and walked into the passageway. She had her cell phone in her hand and dialed it as soon as she stopped. She spoke in Portuguese, so I only understood the names she was whispering. One of them was Compos. No snooze for me.

35

I used this opportunity to check my email on my phone and saw I had one from Gage. I read a couple of lines regarding Frank Schultz in Rio but shut it down quickly when I saw my seatmate walking back toward our seats.

When she climbed back by me and into her seat, I offered her a pack of my peanuts. She graciously declined and went silent. She looked at her watch a dozen times a minute and kept looking out the window toward the boarding ramp. (Anxious to get away from Tampa and back to *Rio*?)

When we lifted off and banked left toward the south, I thought I heard her release a great sigh of relief. I turned and looked at her and asked if she was alright. She smiled and said she was and went silent again.

The little I had read of Gage's report was that Schultz was a second- or third-generation German brought up in Brazil, and he was considered a shady character at best. He was on Homeland Security's watchlist, both in the States and in Brazil. I would read more of it later when I had some privacy.

About an hour into the flight, I did fall asleep and woke up to find everyone, including my seat companion, doing the same. I slipped off my seatbelt, made a quick head call, and then returned to my seat. I sat there, trying not to stare at her. She was a real beauty. The rich kind of beauty that has never appealed to me very much. Skin so clear it was translucent and hair that was black and shiny. This lady was just shouting for someone to do something to her hair as she slept. I had to chuckle at that old joke but really considered it a possibility.

As she continued to sleep, I slowly examined the outside of her carry-on bag, which was stuffed under the seat in front of her. It was an embroidered carpetbag with a psychedelic design. Through the long slit in the top, I could see a thin laptop or tablet. I was sitting there, trying to figure out how I could slip that little grey bit of information out of her carry-on when I noticed her beginning to stir.

I slowly put my head back on the headrest of my seat, turned slightly in her direction, and pretended to sleep. A few moments later, she woke up, stretched, and looked out the window for a while. After a few minutes of window gazing at the top of the clouds, she turned back, bent down, and pulled her laptop out of the bag. She pulled her tray table up from out of the armrest, laid her computer on it, and split it open. Through my barely open left eye, I watched her boot it up. Occasionally, she gazed in my direction to see if I was still sleeping. I must've been convincing as she turned it on and, through the aircraft's Wi-Fi system, brought up the Internet.

She angled the laptop toward her window and away from my view only to turn it back again because of the glare coming in the window. I could see she had numerous unread emails. Unfortunately, they were all in Portuguese. She trashed most of her messages and read two or three. I tilted my head up slightly to focus one of the lenses of my trifocals in order to see if I could read any of the words in her message. My center lens setting was best, as it was set so I could read the instruments on the dash of my aircraft. The name Compos jumped out of the page about ten times. I could tell this message upset her because she kept making and releasing a fist. The next message she read was from someone different, or from a different email address. What jumped off that page was a capital "A" about four times in different paragraphs. There were five or six other letters capitalized on the page that may or may not have been reports on other captives.

About that time, a flight attendant walked down the aisle and asked her in English if she wanted some lunch. I could no longer pretend I was asleep, so I sat up stretched and blinked my eyes a few times, smiled at the flight attendant, and looked at my seat companion to wait for her answer. She quickly turned her computer screen away from me and declined any food. Asking me if I were hungry, I nearly shouted "Yes!" Those peanuts had done little to satisfy the hunger pains in my gut.

As I began to raise the tray out of my armrest, my Brazilian cutie put her hand on my arm and asked me to excuse her for a moment so she could use the facilities. She folded up her laptop without turning it off, tucked it into the seat pocket in front of her, and pushed the tray up against the window. I stood up, let her pass, and sat back down in my seat. From where I was sitting, I could see her go to the latrine on the opposite side of the plane behind me. I judged I had about one to three minutes before she came back. I figured I'd better go for it and grabbed her laptop out of the pocket, quickly opened it up, and pressed Enter.

It lit back up immediately, and I copied down the email addresses from the last three emails she'd received.

As I was getting ready to close and put it back in the pocket, another email popped up—this time in English—marked urgent. The heading read "American authorities waiting for you at the airport in RIO." I didn't open the message to read it, but I figured I knew what it said. Someone had ratted her out back in Tampa, and the U.S. Feds were going to nail her before she got off the plane. I wasn't sure about the law, but I had heard that until she'd deplaned, she was still technically in American territory.

I quickly folded up the laptop and placed it back in the pocket just as I saw the latrine door open out of the corner of my eye. She slipped back into her seat and immediately lifted her laptop out of the pocket and lowered her tray back down in front of her. When she opened the lid and brought up her email again, I saw her visibly shudder as she read the message. I tried not to make it look too obvious as I attempted to read more of the message, but she immediately turned away and started gazing out the window again.

The pretty flight attendant delivered my meal and asked my seat companion if she had changed her mind and wanted to eat. She continued looking out the window and shaking her head no. I dug into the food as if it was the end of the world and even ate the strawberry pie for dessert. I signaled the flight attendant to bring me a Coke, and my seat companion ordered a double rum and Coke.

I said, "That's the spirit," and she looked like she was about to cry. I had nothing to lose at this point, so as soon as her drink arrived and she had polished half of it off in one gulp, I told her I knew there was something wrong and asked if there was anything I could do to help. She said no, but I could tell she was thinking it over. After she finished the rest of her drink, she signaled to the flight attendant to bring her another and, halfway through that drink, she asked me what I did for a living.

I had been prepared for this question and immediately answered that I was a lawyer. Now, I knew back in the States, I could be prosecuted for claiming to be an attorney, and I had just made a case for it, still being on U.S. sovereign property, but if I could get her talking, thinking I was an attorney, it might save me a lot of time on the ground.

She asked me what kind of law I practiced, and I told her Criminal and Constitutional Law. I could see lights flashing out of her brain as she tried to figure out how she could use me to her advantage. I acted like a love-struck idiot and pretended to be completely caught up in the aura of her beauty. She wasn't far from wrong, had the circumstances been different, and it seemed like my demeanor, along with the rum, gave her the encouragement she needed.

She loosened her seatbelt a bit, turned her ample bosom toward me, and told me I was going to find it hard to believe her story. I asked her if she had a one-dollar bill to retain me, explaining attorney-client privilege to her. She really liked that one and quickly grabbed her purse and gave me a hundred-dollar bill. I could see at a quick glance in her wallet that there were plenty more where that came from!

I folded up the hundred-dollar bill and held it in my hand, encouraging her to start her story by giving me her full name and date of birth. She said she called herself Linda, but that her real name was Melinda Famino, and she had been born in Quincy, Massachusetts in 1978. Two years ago, in Miami, she met a man from Brazil who had swept her off her feet, but she discovered that he was involved in some illegal activity between Rio and the United States. She said she had no idea what was going on until it was too late.

I encouraged her to continue even though she had already contradicted herself once or twice. She kept beating around the bush until I asked her about the nature of her boyfriend's criminal activities. She then came right out and told me it involved kidnapping and selling young children all over the world.

I know it seems far-fetched that her story was about the very people I was after, and that one of them—someone who appeared to be a very important part of this criminal organization—was sitting right beside me. I also know it's hard to believe, but she was admitting to almost everything that I was interested in learning about.

Well, therefore I'm in this business. It happens to me often. I can watch a breaking story on TV and know that I would be involved in the case. I don't know why, but I just do. Call it serendipity or synchronicity.

As she continued to tell her tale of woe, I kept encouraging her to give me more and more details so I could help her get out of this terrible situation.

She told me that she just received an email from one of her associates telling her that the United States authorities in Rio were coming to meet the plane and arrest her before she deplaned. I told her that I had worked many of these cases in the past and might be able to cut a deal for her if she could give me more information about her associates. I first asked her if she had a list of the names of the young girls who'd been abducted. She told me she had absolutely no knowledge of who the girls were and that she hadn't taken any part in their abductions.

I advised her that lying to her attorney was the worst thing she could do in this case. I'd have to dangle some information in front of the federal agents that would encourage them to deal right off the bat. She said she might be able to remember some of the names she overheard between her boyfriend and his potential customers. I asked her if she had a notepad in her carry-on so she could write down some of the names she remembered, including when they might have been abducted.

She rummaged through her carry-on bag, came up with a fancy leather portfolio and opened it to a blank page. I noticed that tucked into the fold of the portfolio cover were what appeared to be email printouts.

I encouraged her to start writing the names as she remembered them, as well as any other information she could recall. She thought for a moment and wrote *First name: Angela*, a line, and then *Florida*. As she wrote, I asked her how long-ago Angela had been taken. She said within the last three days. I asked her where Angela was now, and, without hesitating, she said at the lockup facility just outside Rio. I asked her to write down the address of that facility and she said she didn't know. Again, I reminded her that I was there to help her, and she needed to be completely honest with me. She said she understood that but that she really didn't know where it was except that her boyfriend would go there from his office two or three times a week, and it would only take him about five minutes to get there. I asked her to write down his name and his home and office address. She wrote down the same info I had received from Davis yesterday. She wrote the name *Francis Schultz*—the same name I had received from Davis.

I then asked her how long these girls were kept at this holding area before they were sold. She said it depended on whether the girls had been special-ordered or were just picked up as available stock. (Wow. This lady was heartless. I could feel that from the bottom of my soul.)

She wrote down about ten names and stopped. She said there were more, but that was all she could remember right now.

I asked her how much these girls sold for and she started to say she didn't know, but then stopped and said, "Anywhere from half a million to five million American dollars."

I was floored. But, on hearing how much Davis and his partners had been paid in the last couple of months, I was not completely surprised.

We were about half an hour from landing in Rio and she said she needed to erase a bunch of stuff she had on her laptop. I told her that would not be necessary if she gave it to me since it would be covered under the same attorney-client privilege. I also told her to give me her portfolio for safekeeping. I told her that if they were in her attorney's possession, the feds couldn't touch them. I told her that some of the information on her computer could be used in her deal with them. (I was talking right out of my ass.) She told me she was trusting me with an awful lot. She hoped I would do everything I had promised her I would.

I turned in my seat, gave her my most honest look, and asked her, "Do I look like I would do anything to hurt you?" (I could just hear Saint Peter repeating that one to me from his list.) She stared at me for a moment, stuck out her bosom again, placed her left hand on my right cheek, and kissed me right on the lips. They were nice lips, and it was a nice kiss, but I felt like I was kissing a zombie.

I took her laptop, her portfolio, and her notes. I stood up and placed them in my backpack in the overhead compartment. Just then, it was announced that we were preparing to land. I told her that when we landed, we would likely be boarded by some federal officers before we arrived at the gate. I told her that I was going to move to a vacant seat across the way so that I would be able to confront them when they boarded. I also told her that she would be brought to the American Embassy to be interviewed and that I would take a cab directly there. As an American citizen, she could demand her attorney be present during her interview. I told her that I would be right out front in the lobby, waiting for them to call me in.

As I rose to change seats, she remembered something very important to ask me—my name. I told her it was "Nat Frank." (I thought "Ball Park" would not work even with this bad character.)

She reached up again, set the palm of her hand on my cheek. She told me that once she was released, she would reward me back at my hotel room. Just before I changed my seat, I told her to give me her cell phone as well, as they could use the numbers and text messages against her during her interview, but she said she needed to make some phone calls as soon as we had landed. I told her not to contact anyone but me after she was released.

I grabbed my backpack, cut around the back of the First-Class bulkhead, and sat down in a vacant seat on the opposite aisle. As we landed, I looked over at her a couple of times and winked and she smiled back at me.

Just as I'd predicted, as we taxied toward the terminal, the pilot announced that we would be making a quick stop before we arrived at the gate and that everyone should remain in their seats unless otherwise instructed. I glanced over at Linda. She was looking out the window and wringing her hands.

5

The plane stopped short of the concourse. A stair-truck drove up to the plane and, after someone knocked on the forward port hatch, a male flight attendant opened the door slightly. Three men suddenly pushed the door wider and rushed into the plane and down the aisle to where Linda was sitting. Because of the jet engine noise coming through the open front hatch, I could only imagine that they were warning her of her rights and placing her under arrest. One of the agents took her handbag and carry-on without handcuffing her, walked her up the aisle, and then out the front door. She never even looked in my direction as she walked forward.

As soon as Linda and her three new boyfriends left the plane and closed the door, we drove to the gate without further incident.

As I walked toward the baggage claim area, I saw two young Brazilian men standing across the way at an empty gate, studying the passengers disembarking our flight. I could only guess that they were hoping Linda and all the incriminating information she had in her brain would get off that flight and slip into their car for a long ride off a high cliff.

After I grabbed my bag from the luggage turnstile and cleared Brazilian customs, I rented a car from the Hertz folks, walked to a phone kiosk, and made arrangements for a hotel room on the north side of Rio.

I found my hotel, drove past it to the next hotel about three blocks up the road, and parked my car. If I was being tailed, I didn't want to make it easy for them to ambush me. I was quite sure that only my own team knew where I was at this point, but it never hurts to be careful. I grabbed my bag and walked back the way I came to my hotel and checked in. Fortunately, I carry several different identifications and matching credit cards and, so, I used one of those to check in. (The only downside to this is that I must remember who I am each time!) I also noticed a FedEx Drop Box and some shipping supplies in the business lounge just off the lobby. After retrieving my keycard to my room, I used it to access the lounge. I took a medium box and placed Linda's laptop, phone, and portfolio in it. Sealed it and addressed the label to the major's secure Mailboxes Etc. address outside of Washington. I paid for the shipping with one of the Visa gift cards I carry and used one of my mail-drop locations as the return address. I then quickly sent a text to the Major to watch for it.

I went up to my room and took a shower, and then, remembering that it was an hour ahead of Eastern Standard Time, I called Dave and Gage on a conference call to inform them as to where I was and what I had done to get to this point. I asked Gage to call Thom Cohen and his wife and brief them, and then I put Dave on notice to possibly FedEx me more cash and supplies, should it prove necessary. Gage stayed quiet during most of the call. I could hear him typing notes into his computer as I spoke. I knew he would be coming up with some assistance very soon, as he always had in the past. It also helps that he has three daughters of his own and can relate to the grief the Cohens were going through. We hung up with my promise to keep in touch and to text my locations often as I moved about.

I was in desperate need of some sleep, so I set my phone to wake me at six in the morning and crashed. I was asleep for what seemed like ten minutes when my cell phone rang, playing the Marines' Hymn. That always gets my attention, especially in the middle of the night in a foreign city while I'm about to face a group of kidnappers without any close support. But, then again, the Marines' Hymn grabs my attention under any circumstance!

As it turned out, it was my friend Gage informing me that he had located my old friend Ron Sorensen, my all-too-often partner in crime—or, should I say, my right arm during most of my crusades. I had not asked Gage to locate him yet, but knowing me as he did, he took the initiative to run him down and put him on notice that, once again, I had stepped into a sticky mess and would need all the help I could get. I needed to do a little recon work around Rio and Mage before I called Sorensen for any assistance, but from the feeling in my gut, I knew I'd need him soon.

I grabbed my camera and phone-charger cord and left the hotel to walk to my car. I walked in the opposite direction of my car and made a few right turns until I was sure I had no active tails.

My car was still in the other hotel parking lot and it didn't seem that anyone had fiddled with it. I scoped out this hotel lobby to see if there were any observers lurking around but found none, so I climbed into the rental and headed on a joyride around the city to familiarize myself with some of the main roads before I drove up to Mage for a bit of surveillance. I had a nagging feeling that I did not have a great deal of time left to get Angela back.

The first thing I noticed was that the streets had more potholes than Connecticut in the early spring. I didn't think anywhere could top those holes. I once considered collecting lost hubcaps and opening a used hubcap shop in the middle of the state. Seems it would have been extremely profitable. Instead, I have continued to putter around the world, fighting windmills.

The second thing I found was that the beaches on the shore of Guanabara Bay, the coastal area east of the downtown business district, were...

(You know, rather than describe the conditions of the beach at this time, I think I'll let that be a surprise for all the Olympic watchers present or past, depending on when this story is read. I knew I didn't want to take a dip.)

I had checked Google Maps before I left the hotel and viewed a Google Earth map of the Mage area. It appeared to be about forty hard miles northeast of the city at the top of the bay.

After driving around for a bit and being more confused than when I started, I followed my GPS north and then east toward Mage. I can't remember how I ever navigated without a GPS. Even my phone has GPS. I had to change the GPS in the rental from Portuguese to English, a language I'd had a short handle on when I was a kid. I'd spent some school vacations on my Portuguese uncle's boats out of Plymouth, MA, and I knew many of the cuss words, but now I'd be lucky to understand a warning!

I drove north for a few miles until I reached Route 116, and then turned east toward Mage. Fortunately, many of the road signs were in English as Brazil was preparing for the upcoming Olympics.

I decided to look at Mr. Schultz's office first since it was the middle of the day and he was most likely there. I also figured he was preparing to flee considering his friend Melinda getting arrested and being held at the American Consulate's office.

As I drove through the western outskirts of Mage, I watched for the main road leading south toward the bay as I had seen on Google Maps. There was only one long dock stretching out into the bay on any of the roads south of Mage, and the dock would be quite visible from any point on the beach. After that, all I had to do was look for the office building Mr. Davis had described before I left Ocala.

I got lucky and drove right to the beach on Estr. da Ponta da Piedade, the only road I could find heading south, and finally saw the dock with the yacht tied up and pointing away from shore as if it was preparing to cruise any minute now. I also noticed that there were more than two men holding AR 15 rifles standing right alongside the yacht on the dock. I couldn't make out if there were more guards on board but figured there must be and that there had to be some precious cargo to call for this kind of security.

I drove on by and parked in a lot next to a fish market and saw, to my surprise, the only office-type building about two blocks farther east on the same waterfront road. There were two more armed guards at its entrance, and they looked well disciplined in their trade. I decided to walk back toward the dock and carried my camera, which was hanging from its strap on my shoulder. I decided to look like a tourist and walked briskly out to the dock. Fortunately, many small fishing boats appeared to be outfitted for charters all along the dock. I walked past the yacht and barely received a quick glance from the guards. (My advanced age has been handy for me lately as I look harmless with my white hair and beard).

I walked about twenty-five yards out and stood looking at a sport fishing boat tied up on the same west side of the dock. There was no one on board, so I climbed aboard and pretended I was talking to someone while I glanced back at the large yacht. The name of the boat was the *Lady Katherine* and it appeared to be about a hundred or more feet long. It had a bar over the flybridge like the Chris-Craft Roamer, but much longer than I had ever seen one before.

I studied the boat out of my peripheral vision and noticed that all the port-light windows were covered on the inside and that the generator was running. The generator meant the air-conditioner was running, which in turn meant there must be someone on board being kept comfortable. The temperature was pleasant enough on the outside, but I knew it would be too warm inside the boat if it weren't being regulated. I found this very curious. I was even more curious when I saw what appeared to be a small hand pressed up against one of the portside windows. Too small to be a man's hand and too light complexioned to be a sunbathing female. My gut feeling told me I had just had a bit more good luck.

I climbed off the fishing boat, saluted the imagined captain I hadn't really been talking with, and pressed my camera button a few times as I passed the yacht on my way off the dock.

I made my way back to my car and drove past the office building and then about a half-mile down the road before pulling into another parking lot. By now, it was about 15:00 and I had about four hours of sunlight left to wait out. I had a plan taking shape in my head when my phone vibrated in my pocket.

I quickly answered my phone. I was happily greeted by the thunderous bellow of my good friend Ron Sorensen singing a very off-key version of "The Girl from Ipanema." My mind started formulating an even better plan after he told me he had just left the airport, and would I care for some company? He went on to explain that he was taking some time off from his normal duties at his day job with the Central Intelligence Agency, a job he has occupied far longer than the forty years I have known him.

Sorensen and I had been Marine Corps Criminal Investigator partners in Vietnam in the late Sixties. I'd had no idea he was undercover CIA long before that. He didn't tell me until a few years later when I happened to see him standing in front of a Sears store in Beaufort South Carolina in the early Seventies. He gave me a little wave and a "let's meet" signal by rubbing his nose with his right pointer finger, a well-known gesture in the spook business.

Ron and I met, and he told me he was a card-carrying CIA agent and had been since the early Sixties. I wasn't really surprised and told him so. He apologized for snowing me and went on to tell me why he was in South Carolina. (Another story for another time). There has been a lot of water under the bridge since then and we've had many, many adventures together since.

I explained where I was and briefed him on my latest endeavor. Gage had briefed him the day before, and he knew that I was heading into trouble. So, he'd decided to take a South American vacation and tag along. He told me he would meet me in about an hour and added that he would bring me a Big Mac if he passed a Mickey D's. He was joking. But, wait until he saw how many McDonald's there were on his way from the airport. Dinner was guaranteed.

I don't know how he's managed to keep his job with the government after working with me on so many projects over the years—including many anti-government endeavors. On the other hand, what better way of keeping an eye on me? But I've never suspected that he's tried to influence me to change direction on any of the projects we've worked together on. In fact, he took point on many occasions and charged right down the middle of our crusade and in the opposite direction of the US Intelligence community's best interests.

Sorensen stands six foot seven inches in his stocking feet and weighs about three hundred pounds—all of it solid muscle. I am not sure about his age, but I suspect he is a bit older than I am. Still, he looks twenty years my junior. He's the finest friend one could hope for in this business, and the worst nightmare the bad guys could have ever imagined.

As I waited for Sorensen to arrive, I walked back toward the large office building, staying in the shadows of the small shops along the way. I acted like a typical tourist as I moved along, just in case I had missed a surveillance spotter when I cased my surroundings.

The office building was quite large and had only a few cars parked in the lot on the side. I did take note of the long black Mercedes with the blacked-out windows parked in the entranceway with a fully costumed chauffeur dusting the hood and a sentry holding an M16 military-grade rifle over his breast on a sling. Well, hello, Mr. Schultz!

I walked by the building on the opposite side of the road and back toward the pier, clicking a few pictures of the building's front and sides for further study. The lack of cars in the lot was puzzling. Of course, there probably wasn't much call for an office in these parts. The entire village could fit on my island in the Banana River.

I stopped before I got as far as the pier and bought a Coke so I could look down the bottle at different points to study my surroundings a bit further. I did note that there were a few other tourists walking around, which made my presence less noticeable to the sentries.

About an hour and a half had passed, so I walked slowly back toward my car. As I turned a slight bend in the road, I caught a glimpse of a person standing at the rear of my rental car, talking on a cell phone. It was easy to tell he was reading the tag number into his phone and describing the car. I could abandon the car, but I needed my stuff out of the trunk or I would have to spend more of Mr. Cohen's money for supplies. The parking lot was secluded and the shops on the street were set back so no one could see the parking lot. Good for me; bad for him!

I cut behind the shops on the south side of the road and continued past the lot. I then crossed the street, and, by cutting behind the shops on the opposite side, entered the parking lot from the back. I stopped and sent a text to Sorensen telling him I was going have a dance with a shadow and that he should be prepared to swoop me up if it all went south. I made sure my phone was on silent and ducked down behind the parked cars on the way to my dance.

Mr. Shadow was still standing near my car as I slipped in behind him. I did a quick look around to make sure we were alone and grabbed him by the throat, pulling him to the ground. He didn't put up much of a fight, as he knew I could have yanked the tissue off his throat with little effort. I asked him quietly to nod or shake his head in response to my questions. He nodded yes, which answered my first question—if he understood English. I asked him if he knew who I was. He nodded. I asked if he had been tasked to look for me and he nodded. I then saw he was pointing at his lower leg and saw he had an ankle holster with a small caliber automatic pistol in it. I also noticed he had a gold badge attached to the holster. Great!

I asked him if he would remain on the ground if I released his throat and he nodded earnestly. I loosened my grip and he remained still except to cough and rub his neck tenderly. He introduced himself as Captain Tom Lee of the Brazilian Intelligence Agency—the ABIN—and a good friend of Ron Sorensen. He was to meet Sorensen and me here, and Sorensen was supposed to have already told me to expect him. (Oops!) I glanced at my phone and saw there were three text messages from Ron that I had failed to read. One of them mentioned Lee's name right on the face of my phone.

I helped Mr. Lee back to his feet, advised him to squeeze his throat on a front to rear angle, and tried to look sorry. I put a call into Sorensen just as I saw him drive down the street. I canceled the call and waved him down. He looked at me, then at Lee, and shook his head slowly when he realized what had just happened.

He parked his rental car at the rear of the lot and climbed out.

Instead of looking at me, he looked directly at Lee and said, "Asshole. I told you not to get too close, cuz I knew this would happen. You're lucky to be alive."

I said nothing except to look as serious as a heart attack.

Sorensen walked up to me and whispered, "Read your text messages! You don't have enough friends who want to send you good wishes, so when it vibrates, it must be something important."

There was a secluded shade tree in the back of the lot where we gathered to debrief. Sorensen explained that he had known Lee for several years and had recently met with him in Miami to discuss the upcoming Olympics and the problems that would certainly arise during that event. I knew Lee would be a good ally. Sorensen never makes those kinds of misjudgments.

I described what I had seen earlier regarding the yacht and the small hand at the window. Lee asked if I thought it was a signal of some sort or just a motion from someone sitting there. I thought about it for a moment and decided that it had to be a signal. Even though there were covers on the port lights, someone could have easily pulled them aside to look out. If it was an intentional act, then they were surely trying to get my attention, and that meant they wanted help.

Lee said he was familiar with the boat, but his superiors had warned away from it when he had inquired about it. He knew it belonged to Francis Schultz's company, but it seldom left its mooring at the dock. Schultz deeply and politically connected, was said to reach all the way to the president's office in San Paulo. The word in intelligence circles was to stand clear of Schultz or risk your job—or worse.

I asked Lee how he was able to take the time off to be there with us while his country was busting its chops to prepare for the upcoming Olympics. He said that when Sorensen called him last night, he called in that he had a family matter to handle and would be absent a few days. He said he would give up his job for a shot at bringing Schultz down. I looked across at Sorensen and asked him how long he had been aware of this bad guy. He said that his Miami office had been watching him loosely for several years.

Sorensen then related that Schultz was involved in numerous criminal activities but was closely protected by high-ranking politicians in Brazil and the U.S. He described Schultz as a big-time political donor. About a year ago, Schultz was implicated in a prostitution ring operating out of Florida and involving every form of debauchery known to man. A group of civilians and off-duty law enforcement officers discovered it and reported it to the federal authorities, but the feds referred it back to the state level, where it was dismissed as nonsense. Further insight into this ring showed several high-ranking law enforcement officials and politicians were frequent users of this party plan. He said these goings-on involved children and young teenagers of both sexes. I further explained the info I had learned in the past couple of days and he said it fit snugly into Schultz's business plan.

I looked at Sorensen and Lee and asked, "Want to have some fun slamming him down?" They both smiled as I motioned for them to get a little closer to hear the plan I was slowly forming in my head.

The first thing I wanted to do was to get a look at the inside of the office building Schultz used as his headquarters. The second thing was to get inside the yacht to see what that little hand was attached to.

Lee said that just because Schultz's limo was at the office, it did not mean he was there. He said that his senior staff also used it. Lee had been inside the building several times in the past to deliver or pick up documents but had never ventured beyond the lobby.

He believed Schultz's office was on the third floor, facing south and toward the bay. From there he could look over and see the *Lady Catherine* moored, the yacht pointed toward the bay and open water. Lee also related that Schultz had a G5 passenger jet at a private airfield about five miles north on a large tract of land he owned. He said the runway ran north and south and had no landing lights for night landings. He took off from there at night using several vehicles that would shine their headlights on the end of the field as guides for the pilot to judge his distance. I said that was dangerous because a crosswind could alter his lift in a large plane like that and, if I didn't miss my guess, a crosswind could cause the plane to plunge into the city of Mage dead south of the field. His method went against every flight rule on the books internationally. Lee smiled and said that was the nature of political influence.

I also realized the enormous scope of Schultz's reach. The man owned a G5, a plane that has a fuel range to reach most any major city in the world.

While we talked, the sun was setting and cooling the day down, as well as affording some nice shadow cover for our first scout of the office building. We headed north, then west a few blocks, heading away from the building. From every north and south road we crossed, we could see the building with its mirrored windows looming above us about three blocks away. We only watched it from our peripheral vision in case there were watchers on the inside or on the roof. I did see a windsock flying on the roof edge, indicating a helicopter landing zone on the roof. Lee said he had never seen a copter land there, but it was possible.

Once we were a bit west of the building, we walked down a small dirt road and stopped next to a tree to wait for a bit more darkness. As we stood there, leaning on the tree, I heard voices behind one of the small houses next to us. Alerted, we moved to the north side of the tree. Sorensen slipped me a small .380 automatic pistol, and I saw he had a silenced, long-barreled .22 caliber silenced pistol pointed toward the sounds. Lee stood to our rear and I knew even without even looking that he had his little automatic from his ankle holster in his hand. I turned my head slightly to the side and could see another group of people walking toward us from the north, putting them in the line of fire behind us, and if they were bad guys, we were going to be pinched in the middle. Lee told us to hold fast and walked up to the folks to our south. To my relief, I saw him direct them to walk back the way they had come.

Just as Lee arrived back at our tree, I saw the people attached to the voices to the south emerge from a side road and turn the corner toward us. Two men, both carrying M16 rifles, raised their weapons toward us. I could clearly hear them click the safeties off as they prepared to shoot. I was a bit surprised that they were preparing to shoot without challenging us first, but I didn't have time to dwell on proper procedure. Just as I raised my gun to fire, I saw one of the men fall forward and the other twist around while his head stayed front and center. It looked like his head had been severed from his body, but without any of the nasty bloodletting that normally occurs when that happens.

Both Lee and I held our fire, and that was when I first noticed that Sorensen was not next to us under the tree. The next thing I noticed was Sorensen bending over from around the corner and quickly dragging the two men into some bushes next to the road. Somehow, during the past few minutes, while he was dealing with the folks to our north, Sorensen had slipped away and was waiting for the sentries about fifty feet ahead of us. Lee and I hurried over to Sorensen and helped kick some dead leaves over the deadies. It was clear that they were both quite dead. One had a wound in his chest just opposite his heart, and the other had a very broken neck from a violent blow to his spine. That would be a "Sorensen Special."

Lee said these men were part of a security force set up to protect Schultz and his property. He described them as former military or police who were known to shoot first and ask questions later. It still didn't explain why they were prepared to shoot at first glance. I was sure I hadn't been made by the sentries on the dock or the guards at the front of the office building. Lee suggested that we had just blindly walked into something else going on.

Whatever. We needed to find young Angela. We were only two days behind her, at most.

6

We stood behind a small house about a block north of the office building, doing quick peeks at the building and trying to determine how many guards there were on the outside or around the front. We could see two on the side. The two we'd taken out may have been a roving patrol for the area, or they may have been walking home after their shift. We'd never know now.

Just as the sun set enough to allow us to get closer, we heard a helicopter approach from the south over the bay. I looked at Lee and shook my head. He shrugged as we pressed ourselves closer to the building in case the copter was looking for us. It appeared directly over us and did a quick turn to the south, flared, and landed on the roof of the building. It kept running. I tried to see if it was visible by moving away from our hide, but it was completely out of sight where it rested in the middle of the roof. Moments later, it took off, swung toward the north, and disappeared. Lee said either it was heading for Schultz's home or his airstrip. Both were in the same direction. I thought it unlikely that it was heading to the airstrip, as that was only a couple of miles away. But the cargo might be determining the mode of transport.

I looked at Sorensen and Lee, nodded my head toward the building, and took off running toward the east side and the two guards standing there casually and looking the other way. Lee, being the younger and faster of us, arrived first and landed a jump-kick to the closest guard. I struck the second behind the left ear with my small pistol. That left them both still alive and lying on the ground. A quick roll put them both in the tall grass next to the wall. They both had M16s, and one had a Sig 40 with four magazines of ammo, including the one in the pistol. I took the Sig and three clips. I also took the small Motorola hand-held radio that he had on his belt and passed it to Lee. I wouldn't understand the chatter anyhow. I passed the little .380 back to Sorensen, who quickly made it disappear in his side pocket. He and Lee grabbed the rifles and extra magazines the guards were carrying, and then we ran to the corner near the front of the building.

Just then, we heard the exhaust from a very large jet plane winding up, and from the sound of it, it was taking off away from us toward the north. I hoped that that wasn't our angel flying away.

A quick look around the corner to the front of the building revealed the big limo still parked in front of the main entrance doors, and only one guard standing there. Lee passed his rifle to Sorensen and started to walk around the corner to confront the guard. At the same time, Sorensen popped around the corner with his silenced .22 pistol and shot the guard three times before Lee could take his second step.

Amazed, Lee looked at the big man, and all Sorensen said was, "He would have shot you as soon as he saw you walking toward him."

I agreed, based on the actions of his partners before him. We ran up to the front door and, while Sorensen pulled his latest dead body to the bushes next to the entranceway, I took a quick peek into the lobby. I pressed myself against the wall to process what my eyes had just scanned and told my companions that I saw no one in the lobby, only a set of elevator doors straight across from the entrance.

Again, Lee walked around us and into the lobby. Sorensen and I followed with our weapons at the ready. There was an unoccupied reception desk to the right of the elevators and doors on both sides of the wide lobby with red illuminated signs above them that I assumed were exit signs indicating stairwells leading to the upper floors and emergency exits outside. I didn't see any cameras mounted on the walls or anywhere else in or on the building, so we were safe there.

We wasted no time heading for the stairs. Sorensen and Lee toward the staircase on the right and me toward the left. I signaled with two fingers to meet on the second floor and they disappeared behind the door. I pushed my door open and found, to my surprise, a uniformed guard coming down the stairs with his pistol in his hand pointed down and a surprised look on his face that reflected mine. I took a half step, cold-cocked him with my right fist, and followed it up with a crunching blow to the back of his head with my new Sig .40 automatic. He never made a sound except for a *crunch* when he hit the deck.

I listened for a moment for more sounds of footfalls from above but heard none. I ran up to the second floor two steps at a time and slowly opened the fire door. I saw Lee standing in the hall, and then Sorensen came out of a door to the right. He shook his head no, signaling to me that there was no one there. I quickly pushed open a couple of doors, and not only were there no folks lurking around, but there was no furniture, either. I walked up to Sorensen and suggested we go to the top floor where we knew Schultz's office was and work our way down. I warned them that I had encountered a fellow on the stairs coming up and that he'd had his pistol out and was prepared for action, so it might no longer be a secret that we were crashing the party.

We again headed for the stairs in the same order we had come up from the lobby, but we were a bit more cautious when opening the fire doors. I again skipped every other stair or more with my aged legs and was surprised when I was not more winded than I was. Adrenaline is my friend.

I reached the fifth floor—the top—and saw that the stairs continued to what I believed was the door leading to the roof and the landing zone that the copter had taken off from a few minutes earlier. I opened the fifth-floor hatch and saw a hall like the one on the second floor. But this floor had a short hall and an ornate door about three-quarters of the way down. That meant Sorensen and Lee would already be in the main office. I didn't hear any gunfire or fighting going on, so I quickly moved to the big, fancy door. It was locked. A keypad to the right wasn't helpful at all.

I also noticed that the door had a fancy antique doorknob and latch system that completely came apart when I used my size eleven and a half boots as an entry key. The door swung open to an incredibly fancy lobby with ornate furniture and chandeliers hanging from the ceiling.

There was a young woman lying face down on the floor in front of the reception desk with Mr. Lee standing beside her, speaking Portuguese to her. She was motioning "up" with her hand and shaking her head "no" to some question Lee was asking. I quickly scanned the area and went through the door to the inner offices, where I found Sorensen standing over four more ladies and a young man on the floor and one very dead male guard against the wall.

The guard's rifle was lying next to one of the ladies, and I could see her looking at it with that "what if" look in her eye. I kicked it away and shook my pistol "no" at her. She looked disappointed.

I looked around a bit more and decided we must have gathered up all the folks working late on this floor and walked into the big office where Schultz conducted his evil ways. I noticed four large filing cabinets that I would have loved to get to a safe place for later scrutinizing. I thought perhaps Lee could arrange that through his local contacts.

Right now, it was important to get as much information on Angela as we could before the local authorities came storming in. I grabbed Lee by the arm and handed him the picture of Angela her parents had given me. I asked him to show it to the people lying around us on the floor and see what they had to say.

He showed it to one young man who looked prosperous enough to be in the know, but he looked away without answering Lee's question. Sorensen walked over, placed his right foot on the guy's crotch, and pressed down a bit. The guy quickly sat upright but Sorensen backhanded him back down.

The guy began to sing, in flawless English, that the girl was on the boat at the dock. I asked him when he last saw her, and he said the day before yesterday in the back of a car that Mr. Schultz used for client transport. Sorensen asked him what the kids were used for and the man shut up again. As Sorensen used his interrogation technique again, I said we had no time, as I was sure one or more of our sleeping beauties would be coming to and would be making a lot of noise that we didn't need or have the luxury to deal with right now. So, we had all the nice folks on the floor climb into a small, snug closet. I broke the doorknob off the inside and Lee closed the door. Sorensen slid a huge credenza in front of the door and then a desk for good measure.

I yanked on one of the filing cabinet drawers and that popped the lock. It slid open and I saw it was filled with file folders labeled with numbers and some names. There were all sorts of names, including those in English, Asian, and Arabic. I grabbed a stack and urged my partners to do the same. I glanced into Schultz's office and noticed a large briefcase of the type lawyers bring to court and I grabbed that. As I was heading out, I saw a piece of paper that appeared to be a flight plan in English lying on the side of the desk. It had today's date on it. I grabbed it and folded it into my pocket.

We ran for the eastside staircase and raced down. On the second floor, which I knew to be empty, I found a closet and kicked a hole in the Sheetrock wall inside it big enough to hide the few records we had and shut the door. If Schultz were able to beat a search warrant to his files, Lee would know where to send the authorities for the samples we'd hidden. That, hopefully, would lead to a search warrant for Schultz's house, but you never know with politics. I lugged the briefcase with me as we left the building.

We tried to act as normal as we could as we walked back to the parking lot where our cars were hanging out. It was difficult not to run when I felt Angela might be just moments away down the narrow street.

We arrived at the lot and decided to take just two cars, Sorensen and Lee's official government cars. Lee had all the bells and whistles of a cop car mounted discreetly in the car's grille, as well as flip-down light inside, above the windshield. I decided to leave my rental there and pick it up later as Sorensen had a full-sized Ford sedan that would carry far more. I retrieved my small suitcase from my rental and walked toward Sorensen's car.

I stopped Lee as he was getting into his car and asked him if it would be wiser for him to start an official investigation and get the search warrants requested before the "great shredder" went into action. What I was really saying was that he might not want to participate in the next phase of this project as there were going to be a couple more body bags to fill and, once I found Angela, she and I will be leasing a fast jet to Florida. But I believed that would be delayed if we waited for the Brazilian court system to sort it all out.

He agreed on the search part of my suggestion but wanted desperately to be part of the boat raid. Sorensen agreed with him and my vote dwindled to nothing

Lee drove his cruiser and Sorensen and I followed in his car. I checked our weapons over to make sure they were loaded and the safeties on. We had quite a collection now and decided that we would just take sidearms, as rifles would be too visible, even in the dark. Lee parked outside the pier's parking lot and Sorensen pulled in behind him. I quickly advised Lee on our decision to carry only pistols and he agreed.

We could see two guards standing at the boat ramp, just as they were earlier. A rack next to the parking lot contained a stand with a few fishing rods and small tackle boxes, all unlocked and out in the open. I motioned for everyone to take one of each and proceeded to walk down the dock. As we approached the *Lady Catherine*, one of the guards became alert and lowered his M16 a bit. Lee said something to him that appeared to relax him.

I was in the lead and, as Sorensen watched the guards, I scanned the well-lit salon as we approached. I could see the movement of at least two more folks through the curtain liners. This was the tricky part of our anti-plan. I looked at Sorensen and could tell from our many years of playing these same games that he had the same thought. I just nodded and he dropped both guards with two shots from his silenced automatic. Fortunately, the sound of the boat's generator exhaust muffled the two pistol cracks, and nothing seemed to change behind the curtains.

Lee took the initiative to roll the two bodies into the water and Sorensen, still carrying his fishing rod, moved up the gangway onto the boat. I pointed to his fishing rod and he tossed it over the dock and into the drink. Lee and I had dropped our fishing equipment as soon as Sorensen's pistol had finished its latest job. We couldn't see anyone who needed to be fooled with our props any longer.

A sliding door opposite the gangway led to the salon. It was closed tightly but moved when Sorensen pressed it a bit. A large, aft deck behind the salon had two wide doors that opened out. This was where I'd seen the movement moments ago. I climbed aboard, past Sorensen, and made my way to the rear doors of the salon. Lee passed Sorensen and walked toward the salon where the inside helm-stand was located. He leaned forward and sideways to look in the large windshield. He quickly pulled back and held up four fingers. Then he positioned his hand like a pistol and held up three fingers to signal that three were armed. I motioned for him to come aft toward me, and when he arrived, I told him to walk around to the other door and position himself on the port side like Sorensen was on the starboard.

Just as Lee passed me, I heard the little radio that I had confiscated earlier come to life. Someone was speaking Portuguese rapidly and, I could tell, shouting orders. Lee looked at me and shouted, "Go, go, go!"

Neither Sorensen nor I needed a translation of the foreign language. We had been outed.

I stooped down low on the deck and pulled open the right-side hatch to the salon. As I did, I saw a large man swing his pistol in my direction and fire two rounds into the door above my head. Just as I was about to send him to hell, his whole face blew out toward me, followed by a pink mist.

Sorensen. I wasted no time shooting quickly into a man to my right who was bringing his pistol around toward Sorensen. He went down like a bowling pin. Lee managed to grab the third man with his pistol around his neck and slammed him to the floor. The last one was a female dressed in hospital scrubs just sitting on a long couch, holding a cigarette midway to her mouth. I grabbed her and pulled her to the deck by her hair as Lee said something to her in their language. She said something back. He told us that there was one more guard down below, as well as one more nurse.

At that moment, I heard the radio come to life again as someone whispered through it. Lee said it was the guard calling for help from the shore and said that the whispered voice said there were two down below, him and another guard. I looked at the prone nurse on the deck beneath me and entertained the notion of placing a round in her lying head. Instead, I whacked her good on the back of the head and she went to slumberland.

I went to the ladderway leading to the below area and heard children crying and someone responding to them in a sharp, threatening way.

I looked over at Sorensen as he picked up the dead guard lying at his feet. He placed the guard in front of him as one would a shield and moved toward the ladderway. Lee ran quietly out the starboard hatch and turned left toward the front of the boat. I knew he was heading for the forward vent hatch that would be positioned aft of the windlass and above the forward cabins. I lay down on my belly and tried to see the area below the ladderway. Sorensen began to walk down the stairs and I heard two shots ring out and watched as the corpse shook a bit from the impacts. Sorensen's pistol sounded off three times and then he jumped the rest of the way to the lower deck. I followed, still on my belly, and saw movement to my left at the hatchway. It was the second guard. I dispatched him nicely with two shots from my brand-new best friend, the Sig Sauer .40 caliber automatic.

Sorensen threw the dead guard he was using as a shield on the deck and popped the lock on the forward hatch. Immediately, Lee's hand and the pistol went down through the opening and he fired two shots behind Sorensen into the starboard side cabin. I figured Sorensen would probably need to change his trousers from that startle. Lee jumped down onto the deck and said that the nurse, who was now quite visibly lying there, had had a knife to the throat of the young blonde girl that we now saw was lying on the bed, not uttering a word.

I went over to the young girl and was disappointed to find it was clearly not Angela. She had a small cut on her neck that was bleeding slowly. I motioned for Sorensen and Lee to search the rest of the boat as I placed my handkerchief on her wound. She still had not uttered a peep. She just lay there, looking up at me.

Just then, I saw three more young girls come from the aft cabins with Lee following. He said that these were all of them and I realized with disappointment that we were still a few steps behind Angela.

Sorensen came back but said nothing. I now had to start all over again in my search.

From the singsong voice on the other end of the radio, the speaker had started spitting out questions and orders. Lee said it was a dispatcher of sorts and he was trying to reach any of the guards who were listening to converge on the little seaport and remove the cargo. It was clear to us that that meant to get rid of any evidence that could be used against them—not excluding the young ladies now standing around us, some weeping and some silent.

I told Lee to get going in his official capacity and begin his investigation. I suggested that he contact people he knew who were not in Schultz's pocket and exclude any law enforcement local to this area. He tapped me on the arm and said he would try to make it through the crazy hornets' nest that we all knew had been kicked and was headed our way. He ran up the ladderway and was gone.

I gathered the girls around me, introduced myself as Jake, and told them to find and put on some life jackets that Sorensen would locate for them.

I then ran to the helm stand and recognized the engine controls that were very similar to my own yacht sitting at my dock up in Florida. I turned on the engine compartment's exhaust fans and cranked both engines as soon as I felt it was safe enough to do so. Although this ship was diesel-powered, there could be some combustible gas lingering in the engine rooms and bilge. Both engines sounded sweet and were ready to go.

I ran out the starboard hatch and started throwing off the electrical lines and everything else I could find that was attached to the boat. I kept the one starboard spring-line attached and ran back to the helm. I engaged the starboard transmission. At idle, this action snugged the boat up against the dock and held it there.

All the girls were sitting or standing in the salon with life jackets securely fastened around them. I motioned for Sorensen to help me carry the dead—and maybe dead—to the dock. It was going to be too time consuming to determine who was still alive and who was being fitted for red suits and pitchforks, so we laid them all out on the dock to let them sort it out themselves.

I then asked Sorensen to take the briefcase I had left in his car and drive back to Rio. I told him I would meet him on the beach—or, rather, the hotel near the beach—before dawn. I told him that I would call him once I figured out where on the beach. I had a plan, but there wasn't enough time to explain it now. I kept one M16 rifle with me and the .40 sidearm. The rest we threw out onto the rear deck as evidence for Lee, if he made it.

Sorensen cast me off and jumped to the dock. He saluted me and mouthed *Semper Fi.* I returned the salute and the Marine Corps motto. I walked over to the helm and placed the starboard engine in forward and the port engine in reverse, which walked me away from the dock and toward the other boats tied up forward of me, and then threw the port engine in forward at the same time as I advanced the throttles.

It was pitch black as I slowly cruised out of the Marina area. I knew from memory that it was a straight shot south into the large bay area east and north of Rio. I could see distant lights to the west and southwest, as well as a plane landing at the airport. There were a few more planes circling overhead as they lined themselves up for their landings.

It was too difficult to see out of the windshield of the boat from the inside helm, so I pulled both throttles down and neutralized the shifting levers. I told the young ladies to remain in the salon and to listen to my commands if I shouted them. I told them I was going up above the salon to drive the boat from there, where I could see the water better. One of the girls asked if she could come up with me and I nodded. We went aft and through the rear hatch and climbed the ladderway up to the flybridge. I had the running lights turned off and noticed that the anchor light on the equipment mast was on, glowing our presence to the entire area. I saw the red-light indicator on the dash and switched it to the off position. I then sent the shifting levers to forward and again advanced the throttles. The huge yacht jumped forward and we were underway again.

I had been carrying the M16 rifle with me and had four full magazines of ammunition in my pockets. I leaned the rifle against the helm stand and took all but one magazine out of my pockets. I kept the Sig .40 tucked into my waistband.

I decided to turn a bit to the southwest and follow the north shore of the bay. I watched the beach for any sign that I was being followed by land. As I cruised along, I watched the depth gauge and turned on the radar to see what the shoreline looked like. I could just make out some of the landmarks I remembered from my Google Earth study earlier. The boat seemed content for the moment.

About ten minutes later, I heard about a dozen gunshots but couldn't see if they were aimed at us. I couldn't see any muzzle flashes but decided it was time to turn to starboard and run south. Just then, my cell phone rang. It was Sorensen. I answered with a smart-ass greeting about not liking phone solicitors to wake me up. He, getting right down to business, told me he and Lee had encountered a large truck with a .50 caliber machine gun mounted on its roof heading down the shore road just after they saw me turn west on the bay. He said the large boat was quite visible from land as it blacked out the distant shoreline lights as it moved along. I told him that I'd heard gunshots a few moments ago, so I'd turned south.

He said the fifty was no longer a problem, but Lee had received some reports that there had been a terrorist attack south of us and the government was about to get involved. He said Lee was unsure of whom to trust at this time and they were heading into Rio to see what kind of trouble I was going to cause. I hadn't told him my plan, but he knew it was going to be interesting if I wanted him to meet me at a beach. (Sorensen knows how I think.)

I pressed the throttles a little more forward and watched the water around me. I hadn't looked at any navigational charts of the Bay of Guanabara, but I did know from looking at the bay earlier that a lot of small watercraft were anchored offshore. I also could see the outline of some small islands in my path. I was still running without lights and did not want to turn on the big spotlight above the bridge until I was clear of the hostile area we'd just left. I watched for any buoys to show me the channel, but so far, I hadn't seen any.

I remembered that I was not alone on the bridge and turned to look at the young, life-jacketed girl, who must have been older than she appeared sitting behind me. I hadn't even asked her name yet. When I did, and she said she was Mary Tabor, and she was from Danbury, Connecticut. I told her I was familiar with the Danbury area and, at one time, I had lived in Newtown. She smiled briefly and then continued to look to the side in a way that told me she was terrified. I asked her to help me not run into anything out here and again got a quick smile. I asked her how long she had been on the boat and she said she thought about a week. She said that one of the attendant ladies told them that they would be leaving soon on a plane ride. She said to be ready as soon as word came from the office. She said she had been on an interview for a job in Miami when she was forced into a car and then drugged. She then woke up in a fancy plane that landed not far from the boat. She said they were not allowed to look out the windows on the boat or they were struck with a rubber strap. She knew the attendants were not allowed to put any marks or bruises on them, as, following a strike, the attendants would examine the areas they hit and put ice on any welts or swellings. She also said they had no idea where we were geographically but thought somewhere in Florida as she did get quick looks outside from time to time and saw palm trees on the shore.

I told her I had a cell phone and I wanted her to call her family and then go below and have the other three call home. I explained that we were not completely safe yet and did not know if we could trust the local police to do the right thing and get them in touch with their families. I told her I wasn't going to tell them where they were just yet, as their families would start calling the authorities and I wasn't sure that was a good idea yet. I gave her the country code and she dialed her parents' number. After a few moments of sobbing and a description of what happened to her, she passed me the phone. I took it and, after a mild threat from her father, I explained that I was a private investigator and was desperately attempting to get his daughter home to them. I again refused to give him our location and that he would know by early morning if my plan went right. I told him that I had to let three other young ladies contact their families and only had one battery for my phone. I promised I would guard his girl's life with my own and hung up.

I called Doug Partin, the Major. He answered on the first ring and told me that he had gotten a message from Sorensen. Sorensen had called Thom Cohen. I told him that I thought Angela had been flown out earlier, but I had no idea where at this time. I suddenly remembered the printed flight plan I had in my pocket. I quickly pulled the paper from my pocket and ran my finger down the list until I reached the last destination. Hong Kong. I didn't tell the Major that, as I had no idea if someone was listening. I also did not want Mary to overhear me and carry that info with her to the authorities once she was on shore. I told the Major that I needed a bit more money placed into my account as I was about to travel to a distant land. He said he would get it handled and signed off.

I passed the phone to Mary and told her to have the girls call home, but first explained that no matter what they thought they knew about their whereabouts, to please not tell their families now. She knew why and promised to relay that to them.

I cruised south until I came abreast of the airport to the west, then turned south. I knew there was a large bridge I would have to negotiate to get to the place where I planned to stop. Just then, I saw some flashing red and green lights that signaled a channel. The question was whether I was leaving port or returning to it. If returning, I would need to keep the red markers to my right. "Red right return." If leaving port, then the green would need to be on my right. "Green side up." As I studied the channel, I saw clearly that I was returning, as the lights were staggered—green left, red right. Now that I knew I was in the channel; I pressed the throttles forward even more and the large boat surged ahead.

Far ahead, I could see the bridge that I needed to go under and the runway lights from still another airport. I did not remember seeing this airfield on Google Earth but assumed it was either a municipal airport or a government military field. From the brightness of the lights to the west of the field, I knew we were coming up on Rio.

I heard a muffled sound like a weak voice and realized it was coming from the small radio in my pocket that I had lifted from the guard back at the village. I pulled it out but could not understand what the speaker was saying, except that the return call was far louder and that made me look behind, beyond my wake. Sure enough, there was a small boat racing up behind me. It, too, was running without lights, which was a bad thing. This certainly was not a friend. I couldn't make out how many souls were aboard, but I was sure there was a high-powered rifle aimed at my spine.

7

I stomped on the deck rapidly and shouted for everyone to lie on the floor. A moment later, Mary climbed up the ladderway and passed my phone to me. I could see that the line was open and said hello. It was Sorensen and he was telling me what I already knew. Lee had called him after monitoring the guard's channel and had heard that a patrol boat belonging to the Brazilian government had spotted us cruising down the channel. Lee heard the agent on the boat say that he was going to prevent us from getting ashore. The radio dispatcher had instructed the agent to silence everyone on board.

I was not really surprised. Schultz had many politicians and government employees in his pocket, and all these folks' involvements in his schemes were at risk of being revealed during an investigation. I asked Sorensen to call Lee and have him get a hold of some news reporters he may know and have them stand by to film and report on an event about to present itself in the next few minutes in the harbor area south of downtown Rio.

I told Mary to get below with the other ladies and lie on the floor. She started to protest when a bullet passed by my head and splintered the windshield over my shoulder. I pushed Mary to the deck and grabbed the M16 leaning on the wall next to me.

I made sure we were still in the channel and stepped back to the rear of the bridge. I lined up my sights as best I could on the small boat and fired a three-round burst. That got their attention, as the small boat swerved to the right, hit my large wake, and nearly flipped over. I lined up my sights again and this time emptied my magazine into the side of the boat. Again, it changed course and sped off to the west. The next thing I saw was a large flash and a tremendous explosion on the water that lit up the bay for a mile in every direction. The small boat had struck another boat that must have been anchored outside the channel, and the impact had exploded the gas tanks on both boats. I hoped there was no one aboard the anchored boat—and that the flash and sound woke up the city.

I jumped back to the helm and noticed a few more holes in the cabinets under the instrument panel. I hadn't heard the rounds hit in all the excitement and quickly scanned Mary for any wounds. She was clean, so I asked her to go below and check on the three girls. She quickly ran down the ladderway and was back in about thirty seconds, saying everyone was okay. She said there were a couple of bullet holes in the rear windows of the salon, but they were all high up and had missed the girls by a few feet. I asked her to sit on the deck and watch our rear for any other boats.

I called Sorensen and told him about the latest event, and he said Lee had been monitoring the radio and relaying the info to him. He said that the government was telling the media that a terrorist was on the big boat and that they were launching their patrol boats to prevent the large yacht from fleeing out to sea. I told Sorensen to head down to the beach hotel district and park. He asked what I had in mind, and I told him that very soon Rio was going to have another monument to celebrate the coming Olympics. I told him to contact the American Consulate and tell them to be ready at the beach area to receive at least one American citizen, if not four victims of an international kidnapping ring. That would ring the bell on some very important people in the world.

I hung up and put the phone into a plastic baggy I always carried in my pocket. I put my wallet and real passport in beside it. After sealing the Ziploc top, I stuffed everything in my pocket—when I suddenly felt and remembered the flight plan. I took it out and stuffed it into the bag. I had a feeling that that flight plan was the only hope Angela had.

Just as I looked up, I saw the large bridge dead ahead. My bow was heading right through the middle. I glanced up to make sure there were no sharpshooters or snipers looking down from above. I didn't see any and pushed the throttles all the way forward. I did not know what kind of engines were pushing this boat, but they were powerful. We must have been plowing ahead at over thirty knots. This was very fast for a boat of over a hundred tons. This boat could cross the Atlantic, and I had a feeling it had made that trip several times, with very precious and very profitable cargo.

I followed the channel past a point of land with very few lights and, as I rounded the point, I headed south about a half-mile. I could now see the large hotels I had seen as we circled to land last night in Rio. I turned to the west, where I could see more cars running beside the beach, and after about five minutes, I saw the looming sign that read "Flamingo Palace." Next to it, on both sides, I could see other large hotels.

The beach area in front of the hotels appeared deserted, so I told Mary to go below and tell the ladies to lie on the floor and hold onto anything that seemed to be anchored down. I told her I was going to run the boat up on the beach as far as I could. I told her to tell the girls to stay aboard until an American or news reporters with cameras were there. I told her that if they fled right away, bad people might stop them and send them back to where they'd been. She said she understood and climbed below.

I pulled the throttle back about halfway and the boat came down off its plane. I threw the M16 and spare magazines over the side but kept the Sig pistol. I aimed the boat for the center of the beach. I turned on all the running lights and the boat lit up like a Christmas float in the Macy's Holiday Parade. I shined the large spotlight right at the windows of the hotel in case what I was about to do missed the attention of some of the folks. I steered the boat into an area that was clear of any folks and just as we were about to run up onto the beach, I blasted the huge air horns and held the button until I felt the land lift the boat and it skidded up the sand.

The impact nearly threw me over the windshield. I managed to shut down the powerful engines and jumped more than climbed down the ladderway to the deck below. I opened the rear hatch and asked if they were all right. One of the girls told me that this was not the way you docked a boat. Everyone laughed a bit and I felt good that there was still a sense of humor left in them.

I heard sirens off in the distance and threw a kiss to the girls, telling them I wished them well and would visit them in my dreams forever. With that, I jumped to the rear swim deck and then to the beach, surprised that the boat had completely run up the beach and out of the water. All the stuff in the Ziploc bag stuffed in my pocket was safe, after all.

I ran west along the beach, and, as I looked back at the boat, I was amazed at how far the boat had ridden up the sand. Going to take a lot of manpower to remove it. Perhaps my joke about a "new monument" was closer to the truth than not. I imagined the headlines of an advertising campaign for the new permanent fixture on the popular beach: "Stay on a luxury yacht that boasts a seasick-free cruise."

I crossed the wide beach and then the boulevard to the Flamingo Hotel. I stopped near the entranceway and saw the first police car arriving, soon to be joined by a fire rescue truck and about a hundred folks, all speaking English, as they came running out of the well-lit hotel. I grabbed one of the ladies on her way to the beach and told her there were kidnapped American girls on the boat and she should pass the word to everyone she saw. I picked the right lady, as I could hear her screaming about the girls from fifty yards away as she ran to the beach.

I called Sorensen and told him that I was near the Flamingo Hotel and was in desperate need of a ride. He said he was close and would be there in ten minutes. He asked me to send him the picture of Angela, as Lee had been in touch with a State Police officer, he trusted who had been at the airport last night when Schultz left on his plane. He said there were two young girls with him, and he got a good look at both. He told Lee that he often saw Schultz take off with young children, and he thought that Schultz was doing humanitarian work for the government. Sorensen went on to say that that was Schultz's cover story even in the States. I took a picture of the Angela photo with my phone and sent it to him while we spoke. He said he would see me in a few moments.

I continued to monitor the excitement around the boat when I saw a large, black Chevy Suburban pull out onto the sand with red and blue lights flashing. As soon as it stopped, the rear door opened and a distinguished-looking gentleman, as well as an equally distinguished-looking lady, ran to the boat. Two broad-shouldered men in black jumped out of the front seat and took off after them. The American Consulate, I presumed. That was a good sign for the girls and a sign that politics were about to prevail. There was no doubt in my mind that since the Olympics were on the horizon, this whole deal would be made as quiet as possible.

My mind was already devising ways to sabotage every effort they made to cover it up. I needed these young ladies returned to their homes and families and a stop placed on international human trafficking. (Wish I wasn't so darn old. "So many windmills; so little time.") Just then, my phone rang, and I saw it was Sorensen. He told me he was there and would see me in a minute. I told him I was standing next to some bushes in the driveway near the front of the hotel. He said he could see me already—as well as a group of uniformed police gathering together on the opposite side of the hotel. He said they looked like they were preparing for riot control duty. I did not like the sound of that and told him to cut across the parking lot and meet me at the American Consulate's side. I ran across the grass and back to the beach and met Sorensen as we hit the sand. I asked him if he had his little badge and picture card to get the consulate's attention, and he showed me his hand, already palming his wallet.

As we got closer, I saw that the girls, with Mary in the lead, were talking to the consulate with news photographers filming every move. Sorensen badged his way past security and grabbed the man from the consulate by his arm. The man appeared to recognize Sorensen—or maybe just the little badge—and turned his full attention away from the news folks and huddled with Sorensen for a few moments. The man from the consulate looked back toward the hotel and then back at Sorensen. I stayed out of view until I saw Mary's bright smile shining at me from the crowd. She nodded her head a bit and brought her attention back to the news people shouting questions at her.

A moment later, the consulate man walked back to the four girls and motioned for them to follow him and his lady friend back to their official car. Sorensen watched them as the crowd and news cameras trailed them to the big Suburban until they disappeared inside. The security men climbed in the front and the car blasted off toward the city, barely missing the feet of some of the spectators gathered around. At least they would be safe on American soil at the consulate building.

Sorensen and I walked back toward his car and saw that the riot squad was breaking up and dispersing. There was an evil-looking, dark-haired man in civilian clothes yelling something at one of the officers, and I was sure it did not carry one word of compliment. There was going to be some very unhappy folks in the government as soon as the morning news came on. Sorensen told me Lee was communicating with some of his sources in the news media. Telling them the story and who was behind it. Of course, the two handsome mystery men would be kept out of it.

I told Sorensen that we needed to get to a municipal airport right away. He said there was one not far away; he had seen signs for this airport on his way to meet me. I then broke out the flight plan from my pocket and showed him the destination—Hong Kong International Airport. There were two refueling stops listed, but the plane was now hours ahead of us.

Sorensen said he liked long plane rides in order to catch up on his sleep.

I told him that it was stretching his employment obligation to take off time whenever he wanted. As usual, he said, "What are they gonna do? Shave my head and send me to Vietnam?"

Over the years, I had heard that remark a thousand times from him. He went on to say that what we were up to right now was in the national interest and all would be forgiven since we had rescued the girls here in Rio. I had to agree, but I knew someday the very people he worked for would lock him up due to political pressure. I have been involved in a great many national and international matters and, by proxy, so had he. Life goes on.

As he drove, I called Captain Lee and inquired if he knew anyone in the charter plane business in Rio that had any Gulf Fours or Fives that we could lease for a very long haul around to the other side of the world. He said he did and would call them right away and put them on notice that we were coming in. He said the name of the outfit was Ipanema Air and that they had most every aircraft made for charter. He said they were an American company gearing up for the Olympics and already had a corner on the market of American folks traveling down for the festivities, including some of the U.S. Olympic teams. He said he'd met these guys when he was charged with backgrounding them for their charter licenses.

I asked him if the next thing he was going to tell me was that their names were Smith or Johnson.

He said, "No. Jones."

I looked at Sorensen, who was listening to my conversation with Lee on the speakerphone, and he just shrugged. (Sometimes, I believe my whole life is one big, pre-written movie script!)

Lee went on to say that the news was entirely dedicated to our girls and the boat on the beach. The media had not yet mentioned Schultz, or the Americans believed to be involved, but they were close, and we needed to get in the wind ASAP before we were detained as "persons of interest."

I told him we were turning in now and I could see the sign for Ipanema Air straight ahead. Lee hung up to call Ipanema before we arrived. It was now just six o'clock in the morning and the sun was bright on the horizon. Sorensen turned toward the front office and parked in the space marked. Jones, President." I wouldn't have been surprised if it turned out Sorensen was Mr. Jones.

I could see two or three people moving around in the office. It sure was early and they looked all bright-eyed and bushy-tailed. I suddenly remembered that I had not had a great deal of sleep in the past couple of days, and none in the last twenty-four hours.

We walked into the office and up to the counter. One of Mr. Jones' people looked up from the phone he had just put down and asked if we were friends of Captain Lee.

I said, "Yes, sir, and we're in a big hurry."

He said he understood, looked closer at Sorensen, and said, "Hey, Ron. *Semper fi.*"

I never batted an eye. This happened all the time. I followed Sorensen with a *Semper fi* of my own and sat on the barstool at the counter. Mr. Jones, or whatever his real name was, made a quick call, and I overheard him saying to get the five ready. He then turned around and shouted at a closed door, "Wake up Sleeping Beauties, time to go to work!"

Moments later, two young ladies came out of the closed-door wearing military-type flight suits. They rubbed their eyes and headed right to the coffee machine. Both gave us quick once-overs, immediately judged us as too old and too grubby to be of any interest and poured themselves a cup.

Sorensen smiled at me and shifted his attention back to Mr. Jones, who asked, "Where to? Miami?"

Sorensen looked at me and I passed Mr. Jones the Schultz flight plan.

He looked it over and said, "Whoa! I know this plane and the creep who owns it."

He also knew it had taken off last evening for another long haul. He said that Schultz had tried to buy him out about six months ago, but he had turned him down. Jones' cell phone rang and, wouldn't you know it, it played "Girl from Ipanema." One of my all-time favorite tunes. He spoke in both English and Portuguese in the same sentences, but I understood what he was saying.

The Gulfstream V, (Commonly referred to as a G5) was the plane we would be flying on, and the person on the other end of the line was getting it ready to go. Mr. Jones was instructing the person to place a fuel bladder—a spare, portable fuel tank—into the cargo hold just in case we needed it. He also instructed the person to take out ten of the seats and some other articles I could not translate to save weight and conserve fuel. At the same time, the man passed the Schultz flight plan to one of the female pilots and whispered for her to wait to file her flight plan to follow Schultz's plane until she was airborne. What Jones was doing was making certain we would get clearance to take off. Jones knew the game.

His TV was on behind the counter and it was blasting out the news about the boat on the beach. It mentioned that an American man was being sought as a person of interest. You didn't have to be a mind reader to figure out that either Sorensen or I was "the American." Thus, getting us in the air as soon as possible was Mr. Jones' goal.

8

The two pilots came around the counter carrying flight bags similar to the briefcase's lawyers carry with them to court, even though most long-distant flights no longer need bulky charts. Larger, expensive planes have computer systems that hold so much information that you would have needed a trailer to carry it all. Most flights are guided by GPS satellite systems that circle the Earth. Just climb in, set the GPS for where you wanted to go, and take off. The plane does the rest.

I walked over to Mr. Jones and passed him my Black American Express card and he passed it back, saying we would settle the costs later. I looked at Sorensen and he looked away quickly. I had a sneaky feeling the CIA had a bigger role in this than I was being told. I walked up to him and asked if there was something I should know, and he replied that Uncle Sam had been after Schultz for a long time, and they had seen a great opportunity with our current project and didn't want to miss out. I told him we would talk a bit more when we were airborne. Mr. Jones excused himself and pointed us to the door.

Just then, we heard the jet engines winding up as a tow truck dragged the incredible looking G5 out of the huge hangar next to the office. I shook Mr. Jones's hand and thanked him sincerely for his help.

He held my hand a bit longer after I had released my pressure and said quietly, "Get that bastard."

I winked at him as he released my hand.

As Sorensen and I walked to the plane, I saw the bright green Brazilian flag with the round globe-shaped symbol inside a yellow diamond on the tail. I was hoping for the stars and stripes. The tow truck stopped, and the side hatch and stairs folded down. From the top of the stairs, one of the lady pilots motioned for us to come aboard. As we stepped into the cabin, she offered to take my small suitcase for stowage. I thanked her and said I would keep it for now.

She introduced herself as Former U.S. Marine Corps First Lieutenant Sally Moore and that the Flight Leader was Former Marine Captain Val Cline, who was clearly busy setting up the plane for takeoff. She turned slightly and mouthed a *Semper fi* in my direction. I had to admit that I was feeling more and more like I was really in a scripted movie.

Sorensen and I strapped ourselves into two comfortable seats and waited for the rollout to the main runway. It didn't take long. I looked out of the portlight and watched the ground slide by beneath us. I saw the reflection of red lights strobing from the direction of the Ipanema Air Service office we had just left. I unhooked my seatbelt, slid closer to the porthole, and saw two unmarked police-type cars pull to the front of the office. I yelled over the sound of the jet engines to the flight deck that we had better get in the air.

The Flight Leader turned with a thumbs-up signal that she was aware of what was going on. Just then, she turned the big bird to port and started winding the engines up for takeoff.

We were in the air like a rocket ship. As we climbed, I figured we were flying in a northerly direction. As we leveled out some, the plane turned west and then south. I knew we needed to be headed northwest in our route to China and figured Captain Cline was playing hide and seek in case the Brazilian Air Force decided to pay us a visit.

The plane then dove like a dive-bomber and leveled out about a hundred feet below the dirt, in my estimation. We then turned right, toward the west, and began to climb again. I could see the flashing lights of a large aircraft just in front of us that was also climbing—apparently an airliner taking off from Rio's main airport. I then understood the Captain's actions. She had dropped below the radar and popped up closely behind the commercial airliner and was hiding in its radar signature to escape detection. Captain Cline turned slightly toward me and Sorensen, and I gave her the thumbs-up signal, letting her know I knew what was happening.

The sun was nearly fully up now, and I could tell we were still in the wake of the larger aircraft. I had lost track of our direction, but from the look of the sun's position out of our starboard portlights, I figured we were traveling due north. I released myself from the seatbelt and walked to the cockpit. Captain Cline was still flying the aircraft and Lt. Moore, in the right seat, was busy typing info into the flight computer.

I interrupted Cline and asked her what she planned on doing after she broke away from the huge aircraft presently filling the upper third of our windshield. She said that when we took off, the Rio Flight Control Center had ordered her to stop and return to the hangar. She replied that they were breaking up and couldn't understand their transmission. She told them that she had planned to do some touch and goes (practice take-offs and landings) at the airfield and just took off. She told me that she had turned off the Flight Center's frequency and set her radio to the common frequency. She knew that the Rio Air Force would follow her flight signature on radar, so she dipped below the western mountain ridge and waited for the next civilian aircraft to present itself and, with all her transponder ID units in the off position, tucked up behind the larger craft and had been riding it ever since. I knew what she was up to but let her explain it anyway.

I asked her again what her plans were, and she said she was going to fly as far as she could in the same position behind the big Delta plane we were tailing. Then, once we were crossing over French Guiana, she would file a flight plan as normal through the computer as if we had just taken off from some remote airfield near the capital city of Cayenne. The rest was a matter of normal flight plans and fuel stops. I told her it sounded like a plan and asked her how it was that she and Moore were already at the flight office when we arrived. She referred me to Sorensen. I looked back and saw him stretched out in his seat; sound asleep. He could sleep through anything. I decided to let him nap for the time being and set about gathering my thoughts so I could report to the Major and Mr. Cohen.

I jotted down some notes in my notebook and started thinking about what we would do once we arrived in Hong Kong. For all I knew, Schultz may have pulled a similar stunt while getting out of Rio. He may not be heading for Hong Kong at all. I made a note for Sorensen to check in with Captain Lee as soon as he woke up. I made a head call and fixed a cup of tea in the full kitchen galley at the rear of the cabin. I hit the switch on the already set-up coffeemaker for those I knew would need it very soon.

I returned to my seat and used the satellite phone next to me to call the Major first. He answered on the first ring, as usual. I explained where we were—approximately—by using a code that we had developed over the years. I started to tell him about the boat on the beach in Rio when he stopped me and said it was worldwide news and on every channel. He said the authorities were investigating what they were calling a "hijacking of an international registered vessel" from a port near Rio. I laughed at that one. He said that many of the news stations were beginning to report the rescuing of four young American girls who were on board the craft. It was implied that the hijackers were now being sought for the kidnappings. Again, I laughed and then asked him if the perpetrators were now being sought for stealing a multi-million-dollar aircraft.

He said, "Not yet."

Using our code talk, I explained about Hong Kong and Schultz's flight plan. He said he knew something about human trafficking in Hong Kong and it would be like finding a needle in a stack of hay. I agreed and told him that my tall friend—codename: "The Tree"—was sleeping right behind me now. He said that put us closer to the winner's circle, having all the resources that came with him. I had to agree. Not only did Sorensen have all the resources of the CIA, but he had an entire world of confidential sources to call upon at a moment's notice.

Just then, I thought of our most important source, Gage. I hadn't spoken to him since yesterday. I requested that the Major call and brief the Cohens for me and tell them that I would keep them in the loop. He told me he had spoken to Thom a few minutes ago. He and his wife were disappointed that none of the four rescued girls was their Angela. Thom asked the Major to tell me that he had faith in me and knew I would bring their daughter home soon. (I was trying to keep up the same spirit.)

After signing off, I called Gage on his personal cell. He answered by saying, "It's about time." He said that he had to get all his updates from the news channels!

I apologized and explained that I had been a bit preoccupied over the past few hours. He said that he had seen my exploits on the news this morning. He had been following the intel on his computer since he'd arrived at the Tech Lab early this morning. I told him not to believe anything he'd heard and half of what he'd seen.

"Yeah. I'm sure it's ten times worse!" he said.

I had no comeback for that.

He said that he had been following our plane on his computer as it crossed the equator and he knew my pilots had just filed their first flight plan with the Guiana Authority and that it was approved for passage. Gage never ceases to surprise me with his knowledge and spot-on information!

After signing off with Gage, I found some instant oatmeal in the galley and popped the tab on an ice-cold Coke. I downed half of its energy-supplying sugar in one gulp. The belch it produced caused Sorensen to stir a bit and open his eyes. He gave me a disgusted look and went right back to sleep.

Next, I called Dave on his cell phone. He told me that he too had been watching the news and knew that I was causing all the trouble down there. I told him to call Gage and get the rest of the scoop from him. He said all was quiet at the island and that all my critters were fine. I thanked him and asked him to be prepared to send me whatever supplies I needed at my destination. He said he would be staying on the island, as usual, while I was gone. I thanked him and signed off.

When Captain Cline shouted back that we were landing in Panama City to refuel, I woke Sorensen up. I had a feeling he had been awake for a while and was pretending to be asleep to avoid the questions he knew darn well were coming.

Before we went into our landing sequence, I went aft and poured Sorensen a cup of coffee and carried it back to him. I strapped myself back into my seat, and after he took a couple of sips, I said, "Let's hear it."

He looked a bit squeamish. "It was all quite a coincidence."

He said that the government had been working a case against Schultz for nearly two years for various crimes. As I had already surmised, Schultz was so deeply embedded into Washington that he couldn't be touched. Sorensen said Schultz even enjoyed diplomatic immunity in many countries and that he'd been given access to many government intelligence reports. He was even a consultant where he was the prime suspect!

Sorensen went on to tell me that Schultz provided whatever contraband one could dream of and even frequently invented new ones. Drugs and counterfeit currency were his main resources, but in the past few years, he has begun to deal in human slavery sales, more popular in the Middle East. He said our current journey to China was connected to Schultz's foray into a more sinister market: human body parts sales.

Sorensen went on to explain that human body parts had been in great demand ever since the early Sixties when heart transplant advances were made, and human organs were of enormous value on the open market. I had read that some folks were selling their extra kidneys for as much as $25,000. I had also heard that Chinese prisons were condemning inmates to death if they had a certain blood group in high demand. The executed prisoner was chopped up and the organs sold to the highest bidder— sometimes prior to his death. He went on to tell some more gruesome stories and then hit a home run with the worst of it: living spare parts. Sorensen told me that over the past couple of years, the incredibly rich were buying living donors with perfect blood and DNA matches who lived on standby in case the recipient needed an organ transplant or two.

He went on to say that there was some evidence coming out of Thailand that whole bodies were being experimented on, including brain and head transplants. Nothing surprised me anymore. However, it struck me that the super-rich could very soon buy their way into everlasting life, giving a whole new meaning to "taking it with you."

As we touched down on a smooth, well-kept runway, I began thinking about Angela. Was she destined to be chopped up for her valuable body parts? Had she been special-ordered by some rich zillionaire? Was she even now being prepped for surgery at some private Hong Kong clinic because she had a certain rare blood type or DNA match?

I quickly wiped the thought from my mind and looked out of the porthole at the passing taxiways and buildings in the distance. I was sure our troubles were just now beginning. There could well be a reception party waiting for us right here in Panama, or anyplace along the way to our destination. I asked Sorensen to hold the rest of his story for a while until after we refueled, and we were back in the air.

Instead of pulling up to one of the FBOs' (Fixed Base Operations) full-service gas stations, we instead rolled right into a hangar. Captain Cline shut the engines down as we cleared the entryway. Sorensen told me to grab my stuff, as we had to change planes quickly in case we were being watched. I wasn't surprised.

We exited the Gulf V through a side door and into a waiting van. Captain Cline and Lt. Moore were right behind us. Climbing in, Captain Cline winked at me and said we were stuck with them for a while. I said I was delighted and looked forward to our next surprise adventure.

I didn't have to wait long. We circled the runway and passed a few large hangars until we had doubled back to where we had landed. It dawned on me that I had not seen one human being since we landed. I couldn't even see who was driving the van. I looked at Sorensen and saw that he was about to fall asleep again, so I kicked his shoe and gave him a questioning look. He just shrugged his massive shoulders, a move he was so good at, and closed his eyes again.

I noticed that Lt. Moore was typing away on her notebook computer and whispering to Captain Cline. I tried to read their lips but, as usual, it all looked like "Boy, that guy Storm is one manly-man. I'd like to jump his bones right here." (Not really. I could tell she was filling out a flight plan to our next mysterious destination and checking it with Cline.)

Sorensen was now sound asleep. I found that aggravating as all get out. I concentrated on thinking about Angela and anyone else she was traveling with. I knew she was terrified and probably felt all was lost. Little did she know that there were as many as a thousand people working around the clock to save her and the rest of the girls. Sorensen and I were spearheading this operation—and, I was making it up as we went along.

The van slowed and I could feel it turn sharply to the left. Moments later, it pulled into some shade—that or we were inside a building of some sort. Seconds later, I heard a *bang, bang* on the side of the van and the rear door opened. Standing there were two fully dressed out combat soldiers. (Army or Air Force. Hard to tell anymore. Certainly not Marines. That I could tell.)

The commandos motioned for us to climb out. They saluted our pilots as if they knew them. Sorensen and I didn't get a salute, although one of them tried to assist me as I was getting out. He'd misinterpreted my lifting the little suitcase as advanced age instead of awkward leverage, which it was. I felt like challenging him to a foot race or arm wrestling, but instead thanked him and let it slide.

I turned and saw another Gulfstream V setting there with open hatches, waiting for us to board. Sorensen pointed to the aircraft and we all climbed swiftly aboard. We would have our same pilots, but different equipment. I was somewhat sure it was a different plane. The inside looked identical, even down to the empty cup in the holder next to the seat Sorensen was sitting in. (Hmmm.) Lots of expense for this operation. I hoped their faith in me worked out!

Lt. Moore buzzed the stairs up and closed the hatch. I looked around at the interior of our plane again, and then at Sorensen, getting that sleepy look on his face. I kicked his shoe, looked him in the eyes, and asked, "This devil is so politically connected that they want me to take him down because they can't?"

I could tell by his famous shrug that I was right. Oh well. It's happened before. I'm still here. They can always blame me if I fail and try to throw me in the can. Bring it on!

We took off to the west and as we climbed into the sky; I could see a Brazilian G5 out of my side porthole as it banked left toward the south. I was sure the pilots on that plane were going to get a thorough interrogation when they arrived back in Rio.

I had no idea where our next stop was going to be, and I was now too fatigued to care. I closed my eyes, imagined myself lying on the comfortable bed in the cabin of my custom sailboat, *The Deep Secret*, and was out like a light.

9

I woke and looked at my watch. I was not sure what time zone we were in and hadn't set my watch since Rio. According to my watch, six hours had passed since we left Panama. I figured we were about halfway through our first fuel leg of twelve hours. I knew a bit about the G5 and its performance. Fully loaded, it had a range of about six thousand miles and was the champion of long-range civilian aircraft. I figured our pilots would make two fuel stops over the 16,000-mile trip to Hong Kong. I had made this trip a couple of times in the past—once by a military aircraft, and once in an airliner. Long, slow ride. Especially sitting on a rope seat in a KC 130.

I wasn't surprised when we passed over the city of Honolulu and circled in for a landing. Following what I guessed was the plan, we taxied over to the Air Force hangars and the pilots shut down the engines. Captain Cline walked from the flight deck and requested we stay on board and keep the portlight shades drawn. She asked us not to look out of the portlights or the hatch when she opened it. I then noticed she had pinned on the duel rails of captain's bars to the front of her flight suit. I didn't have to say anything. She winked and again mouthed, *Semper fi.*

Sorensen and I walked around the cabin, and then I wandered up to the flight deck and asked Lt. Moore if she was filing a flight plan for Guam.

"Made this trip before, huh?" she stated.

I just smiled and recalled how many trips I'd made from the States to

Vietnam along this route. I asked her if she would like a coffee or sandwich and she pointed to a small, well-equipped kitchenette over her right shoulder. I was surprised it was there but then thought about the status of the folks who fly on these airframes and figured the pilots would want to be segregated from rich passengers who were conducting meetings and conference calls. I didn't see a latrine on the flight deck, but there was one just aft of the flight deck hatch.

I stood away from the instrument panel and marveled at the cluster of gauges and switches. My Cessna wasn't much more complicated than a microwave oven and did less. I have taken the stick on a few of these complex airplanes, but I've never done any long-term piloting or navigating. I was tempted to ask for a couple of hours while we flew to Guam. (No chance.)

I heard Sorensen speaking on his cell phone and remembered that I needed to check in with the Major. I dialed his cell and before I said anything, he asked where I was. I told him that I did not want to say on the open line, but I was on my way to a much farther destination.

He said that the stir in Rio was still the top news story and had even been mentioned as a possible reason to stop the Olympics from being held in Rio. He said that two of the young ladies we had rescued were from affluent families that had been being blackmailed by someone in Rio for "influence" during the games. That is, to influence officials or for special seating. Numerous things came to mind that a parent might be compelled to do to save their child.

I wondered if Mary was one of the girls from those families. Then again, I'd thought Mary had the street smarts of a survivor, not a pampered rich girl. I'd check them out upon my return to the States, just for my own curiosity.

As I hung up, so did Sorensen from his call. He said he had been speaking with Captain Lee and briefed me.

Lee had briefed one of his superiors on the Schultz matter and learned that Schultz was no stranger to the Intelligence folks but was elusive because of his political contacts. However, the deaths of a few Security Guards who worked for Schultz had caught everyone's attention. Lee told Sorensen that even though he was reluctant to tell his bosses that he'd been in on the shootings, he did tell them he had reliable source information regarding what had happened at the little port community.

Turns out, there were many documents in the office building that named some very important people involved with Schultz and his criminal enterprise. Sorensen said that telling Lee's boss about this could lead to many of those documents disappearing. Lee had thought of that beforehand and had driven back to the office building and secured the documents from the wall in the closet, as well as many more documents from Schultz's office. Lee had taken these documents to a safe place and would turn them over to a newspaper reporter he knew and trusted in the event the authorities tried a cover-up. Sorensen went on to say that there was a search going on now and early reports were not favorable for Schultz and his friends. (If I knew politics, certain bits of information were being analyzed and sorted out for someone's "influence" gain.)

I heard the refueling truck's pump engine wind down and drive off. Captain Cline re-boarded the aircraft, smiled, and said she was sorry we couldn't get a little fresh air and a leg stretch, but was under orders. I smiled back and told her I understood. I could see out of the corner of my eye that Sorensen was sizing her up for a more fitting apology sometime later.

We taxied out onto the main runway and blasted west toward Guam and the western Pacific. I looked down as we climbed and saw Pearl Harbor and the remnants of the Japanese attack so many years ago. (I oftentimes wish I could investigate what really set that war off. So many secrets; so little truth.)

I turned to Sorensen and said it was talk time and that he had the stage. He squirmed in his seat, asked if I wanted a Coke or something stronger. I just sat there, looking at him, and crossed my legs. What he had to tell me was far more than I had imagined, and I wished I hadn't heard any of it when he was finished.

First, he asked me if I remembered an incident about four years ago that involved a container ship off the coast of Los Angeles. It was a very large ship registered in Shanghai, China. I recalled that there was a story in the papers about some Chinese refugees discovered in a sunken shipping container. Sorensen referred to it as a CONUS ("Continental United States") Box—a shipping container that had brought supplies to and from the U.S. during the Vietnamese Conflict. I answered in the affirmative and he went on.

During the interrogation of the Chinese crew of that ship, the U.S. learned that that same ship had been smuggling young American children, mostly females, to China. Hong Kong, mostly, but other ports in the Far East, as well. These children were the fruit of a large kidnapping consortium that provided young males and females to an in-demand slave market in Hong Kong and other places. This consortium was one of the richest crime syndicates in the world and had been in existence since nearly the beginning of time. I thought back to the African slave markets that flourished in the U.S. two centuries ago. Sorensen looked at me and asked if I was thinking about those past centuries. I said, "Yes." He said to go back before Jesus and Moses. Perhaps before the beginning of time as we know it. I tried to get a grasp on that, and he said as far back as "desire," there was human slavery.

This was all provided at the request of the very rich. Those folks who could afford to satisfy their sexual fantasies with live players, just as common folks bought magazines and videos for the same purpose. I put my hand up for him to pause for a moment.

I had heard and seen proof of these affairs for years. I had investigated groups of people involved with "sex and you ask for it" parties in central Florida. More recently, I had been searching for missing Lakota children from South Dakota and had recovered some who had been used as playthings at these parties. That was disgusting all on its own, but far more disturbing were the rumors circulating about the children being shipped to the Far East for even more sinister purposes. I put that out of my mind for the time being and asked Sorensen to go on.

He told me it was learned during these interrogations that the American children, like the Chinese individuals, were placed inside containers that were suspended on the outside of the cargo decks of the ships so they could be dropped quickly into the ocean in the event an inspection party boarded. These containers were heavily weighted and had shuttlecocks that aided in their sinking quickly. Sorensen told me that many of these ships and human cargo belonged to Schultz and his band of investors.

I reflected on the horror going on inside one of those containers as they slammed into the water from thirty or forty feet in the air, quickly sinking as the water filled them, followed by the tremendous pressure that would build from the outside as they plunged a mile or two to the bottom. I had to quickly erase the image from my thoughts as it put me in a very dangerous place. In this business, you need to stay calm and calculated to survive. My thoughts of making Schultz pay dearly for the misery he'd inflicted needed to be controlled or I would lose the ability to focus on the mission at hand.

I signaled Sorensen to continue. He told me about a cargo ship off the coast of northwest Africa about two years ago, where a group of South

84

Americans who had been kidnapped were thrown overboard in shark-infested waters when the captain saw a ship on his radar closing in on him. The ship's owner had ordered him to dump the cargo. Nearly a hundred young children went to their deaths. He found out later that the ship was another cargo vessel following the same course. The ship's owner was none other than Francis Schultz, and his radio order sending these kids to their deaths was recorded by the CIA, who were monitoring the ships at sea as part of their normal duties.

Sorensen said that upon being reported to the powers that be, it was designated "Top Secret" for national security reasons and never made public. The entire intelligence community knew it was Schultz. They also knew his political power within the U.S. and other countries around the globe. Sorensen said he could go on for an hour with stories of Schultz's exploits, but suffice to say he was truly the living Devil on this Earth.

10

As we were cruising west toward Guam for another drink of jet fuel, the co-pilot, Sally Moore, came aft from the flight deck and handed Sorensen a long piece of fax-type paper. He took it and thanked her with a couple of flattering remarks and feel-good questions I had heard many times before while he was sizing up the next member of his world harem. Here we were in the middle of an operation, with no less than a hundred or so extremely well-armed enemies searching for us, willing to blow up half the world to prevent their secrets from being exposed, and Sorensen was apparently picturing this very pretty, very professional young Marine lieutenant in a very unflattering pose. (Got to love him.)

Sorensen read the paper and then lifted it up and re-read again. I waited for him to finish and, as I was about to ask him what it said, he passed it to me. I didn't understand all the heading initials and code words showing its origins, but I did recognize that the form was official and restricted.

It was a report from some agent or resource in Hong Kong detailing the arrival of Schultz's jet at the Hong Kong International Airport. He had six passengers, including two security men and three young girls. After being carried off the plane, the girls were placed on gurneys, placed in one ambulance, and then driven away from the airport. The ambulance drove toward Hong Kong and was lost in traffic. Upon catching up with the ambulance, the resource team writing this report discovered that another ambulance had been substituted as a decoy and went on to say they were reviewing the highway traffic videos to see where the ambulance left the highway. The young girls appeared to be well and did not show any signs of injuries. It was not known why the subjects were carried off the aircraft and placed on gurneys.

I thought about the city and its maze of roads and highways, as well as its wide areas of urban and suburban buildings and homes. The Major was correct. It would be like looking for a very small needle in a very large pile of hay. I handed the paper back to Sorensen and shook my head.

He looked at me for a moment and said, "These people are very good. They will find the trail. We just have to get to the kids in time to bring them home in one piece—not small coolers."

I quickly removed that picture from my mind, closed my eyes again, tried to build up the energy I would need over the next couple of days, and again fell fast asleep. I wasn't fond of my dreams.

I woke up in what I believed was a few moments but soon realized was an hour or two.

I decided to make myself another cup of tea. When I opened the cabinet where the coffee and tea were stowed, I found the same opened Lipton Tea Bags box that I had opened earlier. We were on the same aircraft we took off on in Rio. I figured there was some reason other than just hiding our progress and knew I would find out soon enough.

We landed on the old, long runway on Guam—the same one I'd landed on so many times years ago. This old Air Force base was the home to many B-52 aircraft and their crews, who flew endless missions back and forth to Vietnam. It was also the refueling stop for hundreds, if not thousands, of military and commercial planes ferrying troops to and from Vietnam—a dreaded last stop before "Nam," and a happy first stop after surviving and leaving "the Nam." I'd flown through here many, many times in the Sixties and Seventies. Pretty island, with very nice people living here.

We followed the same routine as at our other refueling spots and taxied into a large hangar on the Anderson Air Force Base side of the airport. This time Captain Cline told us we could deplane and stretch our legs. Sorensen reluctantly climbed out of his seat and out the hatch. I followed and, as I reached the bottom of the stairway, saw two military men approaching the rear of our plane as two others in civilian clothes hooked up the hoses to the aircraft for refueling.

Neither they nor the guys fueling our plane ever looked in our direction. It was as if we were invisible. I figured it was part of the complete deniability the government would claim, should we stub our toe and cause another international incident. The CIA probably had Sorensen's personnel file permanently attached to a burn bag. Me? I would be referred to as a known terrorist who was being sought for everything from murder to sea turtle abuse. My obituary would be short, announcing that my ashes had been flushed down a toilet in Hoboken, New Jersey. (No offense, Hoboken, but it's what my grandfather asked for before he died.)

Lt. Moore was doing a preflight. She smiled as she approached and said everything was fine and we were on schedule.

I thought, *Yeah, but about seven or eight hours behind our objective in Hong Kong.*

I was about ten feet from the left wing of the aircraft when I saw a motion from one of the same servicemen at the rear of the plane. Just as I was about to continue toward the side of the hangar, I saw Lt. Moore pull a silenced pistol from inside her jumpsuit and point it right at my head. I was always good at determining the target of a bullet from the barrel of a gun, especially when it was pointed at me. I quickly spun to my right, toward the plane, and in one fluid motion, pulled my own little .380 pistol from my hidden holster inside my waistband. As I hit the deck, I heard Moore's pistol pop three times in quick succession. That was a good sign since if she had hit me in the head, I would have heard nothing and been following the great white light to my grandmother's waiting arms.

I continued to sight down at her while she lifted the barrel of her pistol and raised her other hand in the air in a surrendering motion and nodded her head to my left and rear. I held my pistol on her, glanced to where she was nodding, and saw a very dead pile of Air Force uniform lying on the hangar deck. Still clenched in the right hand of this dead pile was a large pistol that also had a long silencer attached to its barrel. (Was I the only guy left in the world who wasn't concerned about noise pollution?)

I lowered my gun, slid it back into my holster, and rose to my feet. Lt. Moore motioned for me to get scarce for a moment as she spoke into her cell phone. I walked the other way—this time more conscious of my surroundings. I did notice that no one I could see through the office windows or open doors of the huge hangar had even noticed our little moment of drama.

Captain Cline had disappeared into the aircraft and never even poked her head out to see what had occurred. I had been the target of a whack, and no one had noticed except Moore, and now she was back checking the aircraft like it never happened. I heard someone grunt behind me and then feet shuffled across the floor as if they were moving a heavy load. I didn't look.

I noticed for the first time that Sorensen was missing, but figured he was up to spook stuff or had found an old friend in a shadowy corner. No sooner had I thought that, but I saw him step out of a hallway with another equally large man in casual civilian clothes. Another spook by the looks of him, but very familiar with Sorensen. He had a hand on Sorensen's shoulder as they walked, and both were smiling and whispering secrets back and forth. Most normal folks would never think to place a hand on Sorensen for fear of having it bitten off. Neither of them looked behind me where my late and not so great assassin was still being dragged off to a burn pit somewhere.

They walked right past me and never gave me a single glance. I was beginning to feel like I wasn't there. I saw a sign that announced the Men's Latrine a short walk away and figured I would take advantage of it. (For you Marines out there, that meant "head.") I pushed the door to go in and heard Sorensen's whistle, which was familiar to me. I looked at him and he pointed to the Gulf-V. I figured he meant we were ready to go, but I still had time to relieve myself.

As I continued to walk through the door, he whistled again and waved me over. I walked back and he said, "No DNA traces."

I looked at him weirdly and he said, "We were never here."

I nodded, looked at Sorensen's large friend, and put out my hand and said, "Hi, I'm Paul Revere."

He never blinked an eye. Didn't look at me or flinch as I continued to hold out my hand. (I wondered if he would have just stood there if I kicked him in the shins. I guessed, from the looks of him, that he would have.) I walked back to and climbed aboard the plane where Lt. Moore was now back in her co-pilot's seat and Captain Cline was doing pilot stuff in a locker over their heads. Moore turned toward me, winked, and went back to work. I went aft and used the plane's head without anyone scolding me.

Sorensen climbed back aboard and sat in his seat. I knew him well enough to know he had used an off-plane latrine, or he would have been making for the fore or aft aircraft's head right now. Perhaps it was just me that no one wanted to be associated with. Of course, I hadn't washed or brushed my teeth in a couple of days. Perhaps I was offending folks with my redolence. (Marines, before you run for a dictionary, that means "stench.")

I asked him who the friendly guy was, and he looked at me as if I had two heads and asked, "What guy?"

I went along with it and asked, "Heard anything interesting lately?"

That rang his bell and he told me that Schultz had been spotted in a skyscraper near downtown Hong Kong and that the building was under complete surveillance right now. I asked what he meant by "right now," and he said that once we were on the ground, the local assets would be pulled for political reasons. I didn't expect anything less, the way this trip was going. Next thing I expected was an international warrant for my detention and a purple suit to wear through Customs. I knew there was more, but I gave him a break while we were being towed out of the hangar and into the sunlight again.

We took off to the northeast and I looked down at the sheer cliffs that marked the end of the runway—the graveyard of the many planes during the Nam years that were too overloaded or had their engines fail on take-off. After we leveled out, we turned to the west and were on our last leg to Hong Kong, I was looking forward to getting on the ground and doing my job. I was starting to believe that I had a spiritual connection with Angela. When I concentrated on my plans of action, I felt she was guiding me to her. It's not unusual for me to get these feelings. It happens often enough whether my principal is alive or has passed. I pay attention and try to get it right. Angela's message to me that she was still alive and very scared. All I needed was for her to tell me where she was, and I would be there soon.

Sorensen moved from his nesting place and sat in the seat across a small table that I had pulled up to write notes on and to look at some maps that I had copied from online. I was trying to do a psychic move on the street map of Hong Kong. See if a sign popped up saying, "Angela is here." Didn't work, but I did have the building Schultz was spotted entering circled and figured that was a good place to start. I pulled my thoughts off the table and looked at Sorensen waving at me with two fingers and calling me back to Earth. He took a clump of papers from his shirt pocket and unfolded them on the table.

He said the guy who wasn't there back in Guam gave him these printouts of intel and that they may be useful to us. The first thing I noticed was a picture of a small airliner with a Middle Eastern flag on its tail—which one, I didn't recall, but it had the Arabic symbols associated with the Middle East. The next photo was of another aircraft. It was large enough to fly trans-continental and was parked beside the first. There were more photos of individual planes, and then the bottom picture was of a Gulf-V with the unmistakable flag of Brazil—clearly Schultz's plane. They were all parked in a row at what appeared to be an FBO at the Hong Kong Airport.

I asked Sorensen about the significance of the other planes, and he said that they had all landed and parked at the FBO within two hours of one another, and that all the occupants had been driven by limo to the same high-rise building in downtown Hong Kong. Including Schultz and company.

I immediately thought, *Auction.* Schultz had three girls with him, and perhaps the others had similar wards who were also for sale. I certainly did not think that our Angela would be of such a high-quality catch that these people would travel from around the world to try to own her. This was getting interesting. I also thought that how, with this breed of Internationals, there also comes a lot of security.

I asked Sorensen who he thought the would-be assassin was working for and he started to ask me, "What assassin?" when I put up my hand and stopped him. I said the time for games was over. In a couple of hours, we would be in full combat mode. I needed to know everything he could tell me about our opposition. He looked at me for a moment or two, realized I was dead serious, and sat back in his seat.

He said there were so many perpetrators involved in this human trade business that it may be easier to name those who weren't. He said it ran the gambit from the very rich and lazy to politicians in the White House, people in every political office, intelligence, law enforcement, and religious leaders.

He went on to say that the plane we were on was disguised to not only fool Schultz's comrades in and around Brazil but our own intelligence folks, as well. He said Ipanema Air was a CIA front and had been set up to help with U.S. matters during the coming Olympics. In fact, Mr. Jones at Ipanema had been paving the way for us since we left Rio. He said Jones set up the number switch on our plane and a phony crash of the look-alike plane off the coast on its alleged trip back to Rio. He said that it had not crashed but had flown low and given out a phony mayday distress call and then flown under the radar to a remote airfield, where it again changed identification numbers and was standing by for its next adventure.

Sorensen had been informed by his contact back at Guam that there had been a great deal of communication interest in our mission, and all the powers that be were pulling out the stops to bring us down before we caused too much more damage. He had ceased to communicate with his employers, as he did not know who he could trust anymore. I asked him how that was any different than his everyday policy, and he just shook his head.

I reflected on what Sorensen had just told me and realized that my wisecrack pertained to me, too. I suspected a spook in every corner and even questioned my own judgment from time to time. I had stayed alive all these years by keeping a sharp eye out at every turn. As a friend of mine once wrote, "Look for the manicured fingernails on the mechanic's hands as a sign that he isn't what he claims." I trusted some folks to death. One was sitting across from me and another was earnestly working for our benefit back in Florida. There were a few others, including Dave, but for the moment, Sorensen and Gage were my lifelines.

I fixed us both a cold cut sandwich and we drank Cokes to wash them down. Sorensen and I took a little catnap before we had to face the wilds of the next couple of days. I wondered if our pilots had had any sleep before we took off yesterday.

I woke when I heard the drone of the engines changing pitch as we lost altitude. We were about to enter the Hong Kong landing pattern and our pilots were switching from auto to hands-on. The "Fastened Seatbelts" sign came on, and a quick glance out the window showed the bright lights of the brightest nocturnal city on Earth. I'm not sure a Manhattan resident could take this much light. We circled around the city and, after a couple of turns, the landing gear silently dropped down and we leveled out toward the runway.

Sorensen turned on a cell phone that he had slipped from his trouser pocket. I had never seen this one before. He looked at me and said, "A gift." As soon as it glowed on, he punched in a text message. He received one back in a moment and made some notes on a pad he was holding.

We touched down and, before we had braked to normal taxi speed, he popped his seat belt and walked to the flight deck. He passed the sheet of paper to Capt. Cline and came back to his seat. He told me that there was a change of plans for our FBO and that he had informed the crew. He said that we were under surveillance and our "Guardian Angels" here in Hong Kong were looking out for us. I hadn't forgotten that we would be on our own once we got there, but Sorensen never left anything to chance.

The pilots taxied toward the darker freight side of the airport. I could tell because of the UPS, FEDEX and other initialed logos on the big transcontinental planes' tails. We slid in between a couple of these huge cargo planes and, as I watched, a hangar door slid back just in time for us to glide in without breaking our speed. The pilots wound down the engines and swung the plane around in the same movement. I could see the big door was already half closed.

Lt. Moore climbed out of her seat and quickly stepped back to our cabin. She pulled on a corner of the carpet and threw it to the side. She then stuck two index fingers into holes recessed in the deck and pressed. The middle section of the floor popped up and she lifted it out of the way. Inside, I saw a vast array of rifles and pistols all shiny and clean. There were a few hand-grenades in little egg carton-like holders and boxes of ammunition for every weapon there.

Sorensen leaned down and told me to grab what I wanted and get a move on. He took what I recognized as a .45 Kimber and three or four grenades, stuffed them all in the pockets of his signature, multi-pocket trousers, and then got up and out of the way. I grabbed a couple of grenades—and then two more, not to be outdone. I also grabbed a Smith and Wesson Shield .9MM auto. I grabbed five magazines for it and placed them into multiple pockets in my jeans. I looked into the hold to see if there was a change of clothes hiding down there, as, while filling my pockets, I'd caught a whiff of my body fragrance, circa nearly three days old. Nope, no clothes.

Captain Cline, who I now saw was no longer wearing her rank insignia, powered the hatch open and lowered the stairs. Before disembarking, I put my arms around the young Lt. Moore and kissed her on the cheek, whispering, "Thank you for my life."

She turned her head and kissed me right on the lips—a long, memorizing kiss—and said I owed her more upon my return. Well, that sure made living more interesting. I hoped I was reading the message right. From the look in her eyes and the rub of her pelvis on my leg, I thought I understood. I thought to myself how incredible the mind of man was that when about to go into battle, he can still fantasize about romance. None of this was lost on Sorensen as he shoved me out of his way toward the hatch. I grabbed my small carry-on and headed out.

The first thing I noticed upon stepping on the cement hangar deck was that no one was there to greet us. Someone had to open the sliding door and close it. Captain Cline was kneeling on the floor with an M-16 military rifle in her shoulder, and Lt. Moore came down the stairs equally armed. I nodded toward them and quick-stepped behind Sorensen as we made our way to the door on the side of the hangar.

Sorensen pulled his Kimber from his pocket and slipped out into the darkness. I could already hear the big sliding door of the hangar opening, and, a moment later, one of the G5's engines began to wind up. I wondered where I would ever find Sally to pay my debt. Time to clear my head and get back to Earth.

Sorensen jogged to the rear of the hangar and then cut across a grassy area near the fence. I followed as closely as I dared without making us both one target for one bullet. I could see the bay beyond the fence and bright lights on the distant shore. Sorensen continued as if he had done this before, which I was sure he probably had. Eventually, we came to a narrow, paved road. We followed the road for about a hundred yards, and there before us was a white van parked on the side with police markings in English and Cantonese, the two most often spoken languages in Hong Kong.

Sorensen double-timed around the van and slid open the side hatch. He pulled out two sets of police uniforms with assorted attached badges and name tags. We quickly changed and threw our civilian clothes in the brush—except for Sorensen's signature trousers, which he kept on. The shirt he put on was two sizes too small and I could hear its seams straining with the fit. I, on the other hand, was delighted with my attire and felt clean and refreshed, except for my skivvies, which were ready for the trashcan. I quickly stuffed my new pockets with my newly acquired belongings.

Sorensen climbed behind the wheel of the van and took the keys from over the visor. The steering wheel was on the right, as we were in a former British Colony and they still practiced the Brit's ways. The little engine started on the first spin. He engaged the transmission and we rolled back toward the taxiways. About fifty yards down the narrow road, Sorensen turned on the headlights and the red lights on the roof and flew down the side of the taxiway. He picked up the microphone from the dash and checked in with some local dispatcher, telling them he was back in service. (Boy, working for a large outfit like he did sure made life easier.)

We drove to a side gate and, just as I thought we were going to be challenged by the gate sentry, he waved us through. We were now on our way to Hong Kong, dressed as cops and driving a cop van. Neat.

Sorensen had turned off the overhead flashers and we cruised along with the traffic to the brightly lit island city. I asked Sorensen what we were going to do for civilian clothes once we finished playing policemen, and he said, "He will provide." I knew he was talking about the Lord, not himself.

After we crossed the bridge and were on Hong Kong proper, we turned off the expressway to a side road in a very shady-looking neighborhood full of small high-rises. I spotted cars and bicycles all over the sidewalks and door entryways. I couldn't figure out how anyone gained access to the buildings.

It was late. I wasn't sure how late, as I hadn't adjusted my watch. We stopped at a crossroad and he turned his lights on and off three times. About a half-mile ahead, I saw a headlight flash once. We drove on and I discovered it was a motor scooter signaling us, and the guy driving it turned in front of us and waved us to follow. I saw Sorensen shift his pistol to his right hand. Close to the window. A couple of blocks down the road, the scooter pulled to the left and waved us to pull over. The young man got off the scooter and walked over to my window. Sorensen shifted his gun to his left hand and pointed it across my chest. I was glad this kid didn't reach for his comb or a ham sandwich, as he would have been flying back toward his bike in an uncontrolled hurry.

The kid was smart enough to keep his hands in sight as he rested them on my windowsill. Sorensen greeted him with a one-word code "Ron."

The kid said "Lu," or "Lou." Maybe it was his name and they were just getting acquainted. Whatever it was, it seemed to satisfy both.

Sorensen asked for a brief of the last few hours that he had been out of communication.

The kid said there was a big party the evening before and his brother was a waiter at the dinner. He said several pictures of light-complexioned young girls had been passed around to the guests.

After dinner, these men went into a different hall and the doors were shut. There were at least ten bodyguards and some off-duty police at the dinner, and some of them went into a second hall, while others stayed outside, guarding the doors. I asked him if his brother had seen any of the girls in the photo in person. He said no. A maid his brother worked with helped the girls get dressed and prepared for whatever was going on.

I asked Lu how many girls were there, to his knowledge, and he said three. He added that the strange thing was that all the photos looked like the same girl. He said his brother thought that there was only one girl being bandied about until this woman friend of his said there were three, and that they all looked alike. I couldn't figure out the significance of that right then. I thought that perhaps Schultz was passing them off as sisters or triplets.

Sorensen asked if we could visit this lady and ask her some questions. Lu said he would call his brother to ask. When he walked away, I asked Sorensen who this kid was and why he trusted him. He said he'd known the kid's father, now deceased, for many years. His father was a former police officer in Hong Kong well before the British turned the former colony over to the Chinese in 1997. He said that Lu's father, also Lu, was an asset to U.S. intelligence and that Lu's entire family still aided us with bits and pieces. The family had more than a hundred members and all of them were sources. Sorensen said that he had worked with them for over thirty years. He said "trust" was a much-overused word, but he liked these folks and they were reliable.

Lu came back a few minutes later and told us to secure our van and follow him on foot. I asked if the maid was close and he pointed up to the building we were parked in front of. I looked at Sorensen and his shrug was what I got back. Lu figured we would want to meet with this lady, so he had made this our first stop. I liked this kid already.

We walked up to the double door entrance of the six- or eight-floor building and Lu pressed one of the many intercom buttons on the wall. The door clicked immediately as if someone were standing at the receiver, anticipating our arrival. We walked into the entrance hall and I looked for the elevator. My knees were not looking forward to a multi-stair climb. I only saw a wide set of stairs going up into a gloomy darkness. We walked toward the stairs and, as I prepared myself for a climb, Lu turned to the first door on the right and lightly knocked. The door opened wide and a very pretty young woman stood aside and invited us in. (Not only was she standing at the door, but she was also more than likely looking at us through the window six feet away.)

Lu introduced her to us as the maid he had mentioned. No name, only who she was. I wondered why he'd brought us to her home if he didn't want to reveal her name. Maybe this wasn't her real home. She was dressed in pajamas like she was going to bed. Then it dawned on me that here in China almost everyone not working was wearing PJs. Or, to be more politically correct, "traditional clothing."

We all stood at the front door of what I thought was probably a one-room apartment as Lu told her our interest in the three young girls, she had assisted that afternoon. She nodded in the affirmative.

I took out the picture of Angela and she, for the first time, spoke. She said Angela was one of the girls, and that she had begged her, our informant, to call the authorities. Angela also said she and the other two girls were Americans and had been kidnapped. The maid said she and the other maids were instructed to never speak to these girls for any reason. She said that if there was any reason to speak to them, it was left to the Boss Lady, who was her direct supervisor. If they violated this rule, they were fired or "worse." I didn't ask.

I did ask how many of these young girls she had seen over time. She said over a hundred, but she had only worked there for about six months. I asked if they had all been Americans and she said mostly. She said that some of the girls and young boys were dark like Latinos. There were also a few African-looking young people. She said they were all very healthy looking and clean. She related that once, two of the young ladies got into a confrontation and one of the girl's faces was scratched. She said that the girl was taken from the living quarters and she never saw her again.

She then told us that the building belonged to one of the richest families in Hong Kong, but she had never seen a family member at any of the functions when she worked. She knew these young people had been kidnapped, but it was a common business in China, and nearly every person of influence in the area was involved in these dealings. She went on to say that many of these young people worked at the numerous strip clubs or were whores, pimped out by large crime families in and around Hong Kong.

She also said that the young people she'd met at her new job were a completely different class of people. She explained that she'd overheard that these young people were bid on and sold for millions of dollars in a room just a few feet away from where she worked and spent her days.

She went on to say that she and her fellow workers had their own entrance and exit to the floor in the building and were searched going in and going out. Sometimes, she was made to strip completely naked and had even had cavity probes conducted on her. She said they were all paid very well and were given gifts of all kinds, including clothes and jewelry taken from the captive kids.

I asked how far the building was from where we were, and Lu said we were about a mile east. I looked at Sorensen and asked him if he had any plans to raid this building and extract the girls.

He looked back and said, "I'm thinking."

I took that as a no and told Lu I wanted to see this building before the sun came up. He quietly said something to his female friend and then walked past us and out to his scooter. Sorensen nodded at the truck and we climbed in.

Sorensen drove, following Lu at a safe distance. We passed police cars and vans like ours several times and he waved to them as they passed. They were all going the other way, which may have indicated a shift change. Shift changes were always a good time to perform your skulduggery.

We drove into a business area of the city with even brighter lights (if that was possible) and turned down a side road to a parking garage. Even at this late hour, there was a gate attendant in the booth. With a quick word from Lu, the attendant waved him through. We were in a police van, wearing police uniforms, complete with badges and sleeve patches, so I was sure we would pass. The attendant stopped us with an outstretched hand and asked us for money. Sorensen looked surprised and, for once, appeared speechless. I, on the other hand, was quick of mind, grabbed a fifty-dollar bill, U.S., from my pocket, and passed it to him. He never batted an eye and waved us through.

Sorensen pulled the van forward and then turned it around, toward the entrance. He turned off the engine, placed the keys over the visor, and got out. He asked me for another fifty. I gave it to him, and we left the van parked right there. He walked up to the gate attendant and upon passing the fifty over, said, "Nobody messes with the van." The young Chinese man nodded a couple of times but didn't seem able to comprehend Sorensen's size—at least twice as tall as he was.

Lu walked over, said something in Cantonese to the guy, and then motioned for us to follow. (I could have sworn I saw the attendant pass one of the fifties to Lu. Oh well, we all need to make our scooter payments!)

We crossed the street and Lu nodded to a building a little farther on that was so tall, I couldn't see the top. In fact, I couldn't see the tops of any of these buildings. Our building had an elaborate entranceway and awning sticking out about fifty feet from the building. I couldn't see anyone on the outside or the inside lobby area. I could see about ten elevator doors on the opposite wall, which appeared to be plated in gold. Not brass, but gold. I knew the difference. I could see the lit floor position numbers above each door, and only one was not in the ground-floor position. The one on the right was about halfway to the top of its journey from top to bottom. The floor number stayed in that position and did not move as we watched it.

Lu said that some of the elevators went to the twenty-fifth floor and stopped. He said one had to exit it and take other elevators to reach the upper floors, and the floors we were interested in were the fifteenth and sixteenth. He said that the building had seventy-five floors and a huge penthouse at the top. He didn't know who lived in the penthouse, but he suspected it was leased out to clients and friends while doing business with them.

He said his uncle was part of the labor crew that built the building ten years ago and he knew the place like the back of his hand. His uncle was called back to the building from time to time to locate and fix the problems that arose.

He waved to us to follow him and we crossed the street and headed toward the building. He took us down a wide alleyway for what seemed like two hundred yards and stopped near some Dempsey Dumpster-style trash containers. There were four or five Chinese milling around several garage doors at the rear of the building, and I could see a few more inside working. Lu walked right into the garage work area as if he owned the place. A couple of the workers greeted him in Cantonese that got him a smile or two. Sorensen and I got a scornful look or five.

Lu looked at Sorensen and said, "I work with my uncle."

We followed Lu to the back wall, which was about half of a football field from the entrance and stood in front of five large freight elevators. There were no lighted numbers above these doors, but arrows pointed up and down. Lu said that these elevators went clear to the top, except for the penthouse.

I noticed that no one was looking at us and realized it must be the uniforms and Sorensen, who had them spooked. I asked Lu if we should change our clothes before we continued on with our reconnoiter, and he said, "No." It was not unusual for police to come to this building to either work off duty or investigate something for the VIP owners. He went on to say that some of the laborers here were illegals from mainland China and had no work permits. That was why some of them were leery of our presence. It made sense, so we continued.

Lu pushed one of the buttons at the elevator bank and we climbed inside a huge elevator that could literally hold a small car. Lu pressed the button for the eighteenth floor and the door closed. We shot up. I wondered if there was a speed selector on the elevator. As it was, I nearly lost my balance, and my bowels, when it took off. Sorensen must have had the same reaction, as he looked at me and rolled his eyes. He held onto the handrail as we climbed.

We stopped at the eighteenth and the doors slid open. Lu did a quick look left and right, and then we walked out to the vinyl tile floor to the rear of some office spaces. I could see a couple of cleaning people towing carts loaded with cleaning supplies at the far ends of the hall in both directions. They glanced up briefly and then went back to whatever they were doing.

Lu walked briskly to the right and opened a fire door that led to wide stairs. He stopped for a moment and said that we were going to go two floors down to the sixteenth. He said there might be sentries at the door on the seventeenth, but they should not bother us." I asked if the girls were being housed on the seventeenth, and he said if they were still here, that was where they would be. If there were no sentries at the door, then the girls may have already been turned over to their new owners. I didn't like the sound of that, and neither did Sorensen.

We moved to the head of the stairs and Lu gave a signal to be quiet. As we started down the stairs, he began talking normally about the building as if we were taking a tour. As we did a turn in the stairs, I saw a very large Chinese man step into sight on the next floor and look up. We continued down and he stepped back out of sight. Sorensen put his hand in one of his pockets and looked alert. I positioned my pistol in my pocket so I could grab it quickly if needed.

As we arrived on the sixteenth landing, we saw the door leading in. There was no one in sight of the staircase, but I could see that the door was partially open about an inch. There was a small black wedge holding the door from closing and latching. I figured the door might be rigged to lock from the inside, which would lock the sentries out if they wandered out and into the stairwell. That was a good thing for us.

Sorensen moved to the door and pushed Lu up against the wall. Lu understood Sorensen wanted him out of the way and offered no resistance. Sorensen turned to me and asked quietly, "Is this a recon or a rescue?"

I looked at Lu, thought about it, and pulled him away from the wall, telling him to get lost, that we could handle it from here.

Lu looked at me and asked, "Do you know which room they are in?" He followed it up with another question. "Do you know how many rooms are on this floor?"

I looked at Sorensen and told him it was a threesome. He nodded in agreement.

Sorensen whispered that he would go first, as he was the widest and we could hide behind him in the worst possible scenario. I didn't say so, but I agreed. Lu was so small he could hide behind Sorensen's arm. Sorensen lifted his hand and I saw the silenced pistol appear like magic. I pulled out my pocketknife and opened it quietly. Lu did the same with a smaller version of my knife. They were the only silent weapons he and I had.

Sorensen pointed at the wedged-open door and looked at Lu. Lu understood and pulled it open without a sound. Sorensen went through it, bent over at the waist. He fired two quick shots, twisted to his left, and was about to fire again when I grabbed the sentry standing there and pulled him around the corner and right into my knife, which cut his throat nearly to his spine. He never made the first sound as his blood pressure dropped and shut down his brain. I kept his torso away from me so my nice white shirt wouldn't be painted with his blood. A couple of spots on my left sleeve blended with the police patch and, as a result, they were hardly visible.

Sorensen pulled his guy into the stairwell and the three of us dragged them both up to the next landing so they wouldn't be discovered right away.

I asked Sorensen what his sight picture was out in the hallway. He said he saw no one in either direction in the hall. He said there would surely be another staircase at the other end of the hall, and it would probably have two sentries stationed there. I agreed but deferred to Lu. Lu said there maybe two more there and at least four more in the front hallway. He said there were more staircases leading up and down around the building, and that there were three hallways leading right to left or left to right that we could use to get to the living quarters. He had not been here since the place was finished, but he remembered the rooms that had bathrooms, which is where the captives would be held.

We stepped into the hallway, holding our weapons low and at our sides, and walked left toward the closest end. As we approached it, I saw a hallway went right, toward the front of the building. Lu took the lead and walked quietly from the tiled floor to the plush carpeting. That hall ended at another hall that went left and right, like the rear hall. We walked about twenty feet and Lu did a very strange thing. He put his nose to the doorframe of the door he was standing in front of. He then went across the hall and smelled it the same way.

I looked at Sorensen and he gave me the Sorensen shrug.

At the third door, Lu did the same thing and then pointed to the door. I sidled up to him and asked him what he was smelling. He said, "Non-Chinese people smell completely different. Americans are different yet, and there were one or two Americans in that room."

I looked at Sorensen and gave him a shrug back.

Lu walked and sniffed four more doors and came back to where Sorensen and I were standing and said he thought our girls were in that room. I asked him if there would be a sentry or two in there and he shook his head and said he had no idea.

I tried the door, but it was locked. Sorensen sized it up for a kick and I said it would wake up the whole city if he did it that way. Lu told us to hide next to the door, and as we did, he knocked gently. There was a peephole in the door like a hotel room has, and he stood in front of it and smiled. I could hear a muffled sound on the other side of the door and then quiet.

I heard a female voice say something in a whisper in Cantonese, and Lu answered. A moment later, the various latches on the door were unlocked and, as the door started to swing open, Sorensen rushed through. After a slight squeak from the lady, everything was silent. Lu stood out of the way, and I went through after Sorensen, who was walking left and right through the rooms, looking for more trouble.

The middle-aged woman was laying on the floor behind the door with what appeared to be a very broken neck. She'd stood too close to the door upon Sorensen's kick. Lu dragged her into a small closet down the hall, and as she was being dragged, a sinister-looking knife fell from her hand. There went my sympathy!

As he investigated each room, he looked at me and gave me the okay sign. I took that to mean there were no maids or sentries in those rooms but learned upon glancing into the first room that there was a small, blonde girl sleeping in the bed.

It wasn't Angela, but it sure resembled her. I went to the next room and there was another young blonde girl in bed there. Not Angela, either. Sorensen stopped at the end and walked back. I said neither of the girls was Angela. He said the other rooms were empty.

In the interest of time, I shook my head and walked into the first room to wake up the first girl. She woke with a start and I put my hand over her mouth to prevent a scream. She just looked at me as if she had no spirit. I could see from her eyes that she'd been drugged and was somewhat ambivalent to my presence. Lu stood by her and I went to the next room and met the same result.

When I got back to the first room, Sorensen had the girl sitting on the side of the bed and was speaking quietly to her, explaining who we were and that we were going to bring her home. She looked up when he said "home" and seemed to gain some strength. I went back to the other girl and said the same things. She was more aware of us than before and tried to stand up. I held her back and told her we were in a hurry, but she still needed to take it slowly. She nodded and settled back down.

I walked back to Sorensen in the adjoining room and said we needed to get them out. He agreed. I felt awful that Angela was not there.

Just then, I heard someone speaking English out in the hallway. Lu rushed to the door and secured the locks to prevent anyone from coming in. There was a quiet knock on the door and Sorensen walked over and looked out the peephole. He pointed at me to look and I saw two large Caucasian men standing there, and, on closer inspection, saw they had two wheelchairs in front of them.

I motioned for Lu to ask what they wanted and he, in a high-pitched, heavily accented voice, asked them their business. They told him they were there to collect the merchandise. I nodded my head at Lu to open the door and he unlocked it loudly and swung it open. Lu motioned for them to come in and they pushed the wheelchairs through the door and never batted an eye at Sorensen and me. I noticed that the first one had the bulge of a pistol under his coat and figured the other did, too. The second one asked where the bitches' rooms were, and Sorensen dropped them both dead with two quick headshots before they even had time to wipe the grins from their faces. I had to admit that that was really extreme, but it was all he could do under the time restraints.

As usual, I reflected briefly upon the souls of these two men and their families who would probably never know what happened to them. I oftentimes wonder if their family members know what all these bad men are into during their short lives. I try not to judge, but I sure have no trouble being the executioner when it comes down to it. (Am I as bad as they are? I tend not to think so, as the Lord sure looks out after me during these times!)

Lu closed the door and we dragged the bodies up the hall and stashed them in a spare room. The wheelchairs would certainly come in handy.

We wheeled the chairs to the rooms and sat the two girls in them. I took two blankets and wrapped them around the girls to disguise the fact that they were both in nightclothes. They were more alert now and asking questions. I asked them to be really quiet and they nodded. I asked them if they knew where Angela was and they both said in unison that she should be here in one of the rooms. I said she wasn't and looked at Lu in question. He shook his head and glanced back down the hall.

I reflected on the fact that the two thugs had only had two wheelchairs, and with the girls saying that she was here when they went to bed, it got me thinking that we were too late. We needed to get these two girls to safety so I couldn't ponder on it any longer. I pointed to the door and we pushed them out and toward the freight elevators. I was amazed at how similar these two girls were, and how similar they were to Angela. I could see why they were a valuable threesome. Something must not have worked out at the bidding meetup.

I had to get my mind back to our task at hand.

12

We approached the elevators and Lu pushed the down button. I looked down the hall and saw some movement to the left. Just then, the elevator door opened right in front of us and we jumped on. Lu pressed the ground floor button. As the door was closing, we heard someone yell something, but the door shut before I could comprehend what he was saying. I was sure it was not good for us, no matter what it was. The elevator dropped like it was in freefall, and, at the last moment, I pressed the button for floor two. The elevator screeched to a halt on the second floor and the door opened quickly. I motioned for them to push the chairs toward the front of the building. Lu picked up the pace and Sorensen, pushing the second chair, followed in Lu's wake. I went wide to the left and watched to see if there was anyone in the halls in front of us. I didn't see anyone, and we turned left at the end in front of the main elevators.

I looked up and saw all the elevators were still on the bottom floor, except the one in the middle that was still on sixteen. I pressed the down button and saw an elevator light indicate a car was on its way up from below. I also noticed that the one in the middle was coming down in a hurry.

Fortunately, our elevator came first, and we wheeled the ladies in. The door closed too slowly, not like the freight elevators out back, and the car gently descended to the lobby. I didn't bother to check left or right but

106

charged out toward the big glass doors in the front. Locked. Lu signaled to follow him, and we went to the right of the lobby and found a single door with an emergency exit sign above it. There was a wide push-bar, painted red, with some Cantonese writing on it that I was sure read, "An alarm will sound upon opening this door." Lu pushed through it and it did sound off as advertised as we ran down the sidewalk as if our clothes were on fire.

It was just starting to get light out as the sun broke the horizon. More folks were walking down the sidewalks toward us. We crossed a short street and I recognized the parking garage where we had stashed our patrol van. Quickly, we pushed the chairs into the entrance and saw at once that our van was gone. I looked at the attendant, who was the same as when we arrived. He was picking up his phone from the wall of the booth. I pointed my pistol at him, and he dropped the phone on the floor. I asked him where our van was as I shoved my pistol into his nose, and he pointed toward the back. Looking outside, I wasn't encouraged. I saw what must have been his car parked near the sidewall. I asked for the keys and he said they were in the ignition. I clomped him over the head with my pistol and then ran toward his car. Both girls climbed out of their chairs on their own and dove into the backseat of the little car. Sorensen climbed into the passenger seat and Lu pointed to his scooter and told us to follow him.

A couple of cars were waiting for the gate to go up as we cut through the other side. As we passed, I yelled that the parking was free today and to use the outgoing side!

Lu rode his scooter past the side of the big building where there were a few people standing at the side entrance where we had exited. Two of them had pistols in their hands. They were looking both ways up and down the street, but not at us. The girls had ducked down in the backseat and Sorensen was tearing off his police shirt and stuffing it under the dash. I tore at my shirt and popped the buttons. Sorensen helped me pull it off and threw it, too, on the floor.

Following Lu, we drove a couple of miles and turned off a side road to another short-rise apartment building. Lu parked his scooter and signaled to us to get out and follow him. I helped the girls out, and both Sorensen and I helped them walk across the gravel sidewalk. They had no shoes on and it was tough on their feet. Lu led us to a door on the side of the building, and after knocking on it three times, it opened. Standing there was the same no-name maid we had met earlier. She quickly shut the door behind us and turned on a light.

I thanked her for all her help and asked about the third girl who wasn't there. She looked puzzled and said something to Lu in Cantonese. He said something back and took out his phone. After speaking for a few moments, he said the girl, Angela, had been taken out a few minutes before all the alarms went off in the building. That meant that she was only a few minutes ahead of us since we were the ones who'd caused the alarms when we opened the emergency door. Lu said she'd been placed in a private car with two men and one woman. He said one of the men was Hispanic looking. I thought of Schultz right away and figured the bids were not high enough, or he was going to use her as a ransom to get out of the mess he was in. I could just hear all the phones ringing in every major city in the world with him looking for amnesty. I wanted Angela back, not used as a bargaining chip.

If she'd left only moments before we left, then she may still be in Hong Kong. I asked Sorensen how long it would take to get these girls secured with the U.S. Consulate in Hong Kong, and he said that he did not trust them.

He corrected himself right away and said, "It's not a matter of trust, but that I don't know the Consulate, so I'm not going to place their lives in his hands." He said he had a better idea and switched on his phone. He wandered off to a corner, and in about ten minutes, signed off and asked the No-Name Maid if she had any clothes the girls could change into. She said she had and quickly went to the next room and returned with what looked like brand-new clothes for both girls. She said she and the rest of her family helped some of the illegals get settled. As a result, they kept spare clothes for those occasions. She also had clean shirts for the Tree and I. Mine fit perfectly. Sorensen's was a stretch, literally!

I thanked her, took out a wad of money, and asked her to use it to fund their projects. She smiled and eagerly took the greenbacks. She turned to me as the girls were dressing and said, "Lisa."

I looked at her for a moment and realized she was telling me her name. I shook her hand and said, "Jake."

As soon as the girls were dressed, with sneakers on their feet, we were out the door. Sorensen jumped into the driver's seat of the little borrowed car as the girls jumped into the back. They lay down on the seat again as we sped off into the night. I realized that I had not even thanked Lu. I figured I could get him some compensation from Thom Cohen if we ever recovered Angela. I should have been feeling pretty good with myself at this point as we sped to a rendezvous with the girls' safety.

We cruised along for a while until we saw a big Chevy Suburban coming the other way. As we approached one another, the big truck slowed down and pulled over. Sorensen pulled in next to the truck and I saw two men—dressed in black, of course.

They opened their doors and stepped out. Sorensen addressed them, saying they were eating too much and looked old. I hoped he knew them well. They called him a fat, old man and they all hugged. He introduced me as his manservant and invited them to kick my ass if they needed entertainment. (Thanks, Ron.) I told the girls to quickly climb out and get in the car with these guys. I told them not to worry and gave them a phone number on a piece of paper I carried in my pocket of a very trusted couple I knew in Santa Cruz, California—Marshal and Michelle Grant. Also known as Marsh and Mike. They ran an organization called Sanctuary, a group that aided displaced immigrants and such who needed comfort. The number was a burner phone to call so they can leave a message once they got home safe and sound just saying were home, so I would know they were safe. If anything went south, they were to call that number and leave a message for "Jake". They would be called back instantly by one of my two great friends. (This worked so many times while I was locating missing Lakota Native American Children.) They said they would and hugged Sorensen and me as they cried. I asked them again to make sure they left me a message. They both smiled and nodded.

I looked at the two men, and before I said a word, one of them said, "Don't worry, sir. We'll take good care of them." Just as we were set to go, the other one reached for the back floor and produced my carry-on suitcase, which had been in the police van. I looked at him, and then at Sorensen, who shrugged. As we climbed into the little car, he said, "It was their van, anyhow."

I asked him what else he wasn't telling me, and he said he had an idea where Angela was. That was encouraging, to say the least. First, we needed to get some decent clean clothes and a shower. I was concerned about being kicked out of Hong Kong for stink pollution. Lu could smell us down the block if he needed to!

Sorensen pulled into a parking lot next to a couple of buildings that had merchandise businesses on the street level. We went into the first one and found some suitable clothes. Sorensen even found a pair of those multi-pocketed trousers he was so fond of. I, in turn, bought a package of three jockey-type skivvies that I was fond of. Sorensen asked the proprietor where we could take a shower and change, and he offered us his private facility in the rear of his store. I told Sorensen to go first while I made a couple of calls.

My first call was to the Major in our code I proceeded to fill him in on what had occurred since we spoke the night before. I again asked him to brief Mr. and Mrs. Cohen. I explained that we were just a few minutes behind Schultz and told him to assure them that we were doing all we could and more. The Major said they would be encouraged by the news, as well as the fact that we had rescued two more young girls. I told him that I would call him as soon as I had more to report. I never tell him about any casualties we cause to the other side. It gives him a bit more deniability with his liberal following.

Next, I called Gage and filled him in. He said he had seen on the Net that a couple of passports had been requested for two teenage females just moments before. That was encouraging, knowing that those guys were not wasting any time. I felt even better that it seemed that the request had gone through CIA headquarters and not the local consulate office. I then called Dave and he reported all was well on the island, with no unusual activity there. My dogs barking was also a positive deterrent, even though the dogs would lick any trespassers to death who put a foot on the beach. I told Dave to call Gage for a more in-depth briefing and signed off.

Sorensen stepped out of the small bathroom and I told him about the passports that had been ordered. He said he already knew from a text he had just received. He also said the girls would be in disguise and escorted back with legitimate "company" couples, so they looked like families returning home from holiday. I thought that a good idea and relaxed a bit more. He said that he would be notified as soon as they were airborne and heading back to the States. I took my turn in the shower.

When I came out of the backroom, I slipped the businessman a fifty and saw that Sorensen was standing outside, talking on his phone. I walked out as he was signing off and told him that I felt time was running out. I was concerned that harm may come to Angela if we waited too long. Schultz certainly would not want to be caught with Angela since she could clearly identify him as her abductor. The odds were not good for us right now.

Sorensen and I walked back to the car and he said that one of his sources just told him they believed Schultz was hiding out at a Brazilian diplomat's residence not far from where we were. He said it was very close to the U.S. Consulate's office and residence. That told me that storming the place was out of the question. Too many security folks protecting everyone. He said that he had a plan and needed to make another call.

I sat in the car while he spoke to one of his many sources and pondered other matters. I knew I needed to be right on top of Angela's rescue and couldn't risk a minor miss-step. The thing that was bugging me on the peripherals of my mind was this business of body-part sales. I knew it went on and had read about it a couple of times in the past. Here I was in one of the body part business capitals of the world, and I knew that, probably within a mile of me, someone was being prepped to die in order to provide a rich guy with a heart, or whatever else he needed. When my thoughts drifted over to Angela being a possible donor to some rich butthole, I shook my head. I was relieved to see Sorensen walking back to the car.

Sorensen climbed in and said he had just spoken with Captain Lee in Rio. Lee was attempting to get us into the Brazilian's house through one of his many trusted friends in the service. I liked the sound of that, for sure. The downside was getting Angela out in one piece.

Sorensen pecked in some digits on his phone screen and made a couple of notes on the small pad he had in his hand. I could see that he was consulting his phone's GPS and trying to decipher the route from where we were to where we needed to go. Many of the streets had English names, but some had been changed after Hong Kong was returned to the Chinese. In many cases, the phone map reflected both names and there wasn't much room on a phone screen to print all those words.

Sorensen was squinting at his phone screen for the fourth or fifth time, so I suggested he let the phone talk us there. He looked at me as if I was insulting him and pushed a couple of more buttons. I waited a moment and he closed his phone, started the car, put it in gear, and I heard a faint female voice instruct him to make the first turn to the left. I didn't say a thing. (If all the satellites went on the blink, the entire world would be lost!)

I took advantage of the time to check my weapons. Checked the rounds in my spare magazines and readjusted the hand grenades stuffed into my pockets. The new type of grenades was smaller and had a smooth container rather than the old, pineapple-type from the old days. They still had the pins through the levers that John Wayne would pull out with his teeth in the movies. I can assure you that if anyone tried that for real, their teeth would break off before the pin came out. I made sure they were secure in my pockets. I looked like I was smuggling tennis balls. I asked Sorensen about his silenced pistol, and he said it was good and his magazines were full. I hadn't seen him mess with it since all the shooting at the office tower but didn't doubt it was full and ready.

We drove about a mile toward a large hill that we could see from time to time in front of us, and then made a couple of turns. Sorensen pulled over to the side and looked at his phone again. He told me our destination was about two blocks away, down a side road, but we had to wait for Lee to call back. As we sat, I called Dave and asked him to be on the lookout for a call from the young ladies after they arrived back in the States.

He told me there was still news on TV involving the boat on the beach in Rio. The news media had received anonymous information that kidnapped children had been held on the boat and that a mysterious American rescued them in the middle of the night. He went on to say that there was a worldwide hunt on for this American, as the Brazilian authorities were claiming some of its citizens had been murdered during this alleged rescue affair. Dave said there were a few Washington bureaucrats speaking out on behalf of these Brazilians, encouraging the apprehension of this American "bad guy." I told him to make note of those folks, as they were probably part of the conspiracy to market these kids.

Just then, Sorensen's phone rang. I signed off from Dave and waited for Sorensen to stop listening. A moment later, he said, "Thanks, pal," and closed his phone.

Sorensen, after a long moment, told me that Schultz was at the residence but had come with only a male counterpart. My heart dropped to my stomach. Sorensen shut his eyes and gripped the steering wheel so tightly; I could feel the vibration on my side of the car.

I waited a minute and said, "Let's go ask Mr. Schultz where we might find our Angela."

Sorensen looked over at me and opened his car door. He climbed out slowly, in a manner I recognized all too well. He was preparing for battle.

I climbed out of my side, pulled out my small suitcase, and walked around to his side of the car to close his door. He was already twenty feet in front of me, moving faster and faster with his long legs, causing me to run to catch up. I asked him if he had a brief layout of the residence and he just nodded. I tagged along like a Kris Kristofferson song.

We turned the next corner and saw the Brazilian flag flying from the front of a large, two-story house. I could not see any security at the front, but I was sure they were there. Sorensen stopped, and as we watched, a gate at the side opened, allowing a black limousine to pull up to the front walk of the building. The driver got out, walked around the car, and opened the left rear door and stood there. The front door of the residence opened and none other than the man of the hour, Francis Schultz, and a little effeminate-looking guy walked out.

I had seen a few photos of Schultz online and some pictures of him in his office in Brazil. I had no doubt it was him. Sorensen, holding his head down to avoid the camera high up on the roofline of the building, took off like a shot and, as the driver closed the rear door to the limo with his passengers inside, grabbed him by the nape of the neck and threw him down on the sidewalk like a bag of dirty laundry. He pointed at the rear of the car.

I, keeping my head down for obvious reasons, pulled the door open and asked Mr. Schultz if he minded holding my bag for a moment. He looked confused but took it. His seatmate started pulling a small, black automatic pistol out of the inside of his jacket and I, already prepared for it, shot him right in the left eye socket. He bounced off the rear door and never moved again. Schultz just sat there wide-eyed and started to wail.

I pointed my gun in his face and screamed in a Marine Corps manner, "Move over!" He scooted over, being careful not to touch Mr. Dead Guy.

Sorensen jumped into the driver's seat and put the large vehicle in gear. We pulled into the traffic flow and did a few turns left and right to lose any tail that we might have attracted. I kept Schultz's head pushed down toward his dead seatmate and told him to "Shut up!" every time he started to protest.

Sorensen drove about a mile to a less frequented area in a residential neighborhood and parked in an alley. He turned in his seat and asked Schultz where the girl was. Schultz hesitated as if he was about to ask, "What girl?" and Sorensen lifted his hand and shot Schultz in the left kneecap. Schultz howled in agony.

Sorensen, very quietly, told Schultz that he was going to ask him questions about things we knew he knew. If at any time Schultz hesitated, he would shoot him again. He asked Schultz if he understood, and Schultz took a deep breath. Sorensen said, "Too long," and shot him in his right kneecap. This really got Schultz screaming, but screaming he understood, and he begged Sorensen not to shoot him again. I moved as close to the door as I could to keep from being painted with his blood.

Sorensen gave Schultz a moment to catch his breath and let his brain adjust to the pain. He then, very softly, asked Schultz to answer his question. I thought Sorensen was going to shoot him again for hesitating, but he held back a moment until Schultz recalled the girl. Schultz then quickly said that the American girl named Cohen was on her way to Thailand with a man who had ordered her.

Feeling puzzled, I took over the interrogation. "What man?"

Schultz told us that this Thai's name was Benz Mubane and that he was taking the girl to Bangkok. I asked him when he left, and he said last evening from a building downtown. I asked him what he meant by "ordered her." Schultz said that Mubane had met the girl in Miami last month and shortly afterward negotiated with Schultz about buying her.

I asked the question I was dreading the answer to. "For companionship or organ use?"

Schultz said he wasn't sure, but he knew that Mubane had somehow gotten a sample of her blood, and after the results came back, started talking about purchasing her. I asked him how he knew those details, and he said that he had recommended a doctor friend of his to Mubane in Miami and the Doctor had reported the details of Mubane's request. I asked him to provide us with everything he knew about Mubane and his family. This really wasn't making any sense. Why would Mubane want a young female organ donor? I thought about how pretty and healthy Angela looked in her photos and considered that perhaps he was going to sell off her organs for a great profit.

Sorensen asked Schultz where his suitcases were, and Schultz hesitated. Sorensen pointed his pistol at Schultz's arm and Schultz screamed they were in the trunk. Sorensen opened the door and somehow hit a switch that popped the trunk lid with a clunk. He walked back to the rear of the limo and, a moment later, opened the door to the backseat. He looked at Schultz and asked how much money was in the cases. He said there were over ten million dollars U.S. and some bearer bonds worth another twenty-five million. I asked him how much had come from Angela's sale and he said the twenty-five million. He said the entire bidding for the three girls was over one hundred million. The rest of the funds had been wired to his various accounts around the world.

Sorensen held up a ledger and asked if the accounts and names were all listed in the book. Schultz nodded. I took the book from Sorensen and opened it in the middle. I immediately recognized the first name I saw. It was the name of a very important real estate investor from New York. It looked as if this investor was also an investor in human beings. The book was an inch thick, and as I shuffled through it, I saw that every page was nearly full, showing a different name. I stopped looking after I started recognizing so many names that I felt ill.

Sorensen asked Schultz where he was going, and he said he was headed to the airport. I asked him what his destination was, and he said Venezuela had granted him asylum, and he had a home there already. Schultz was very talkative now and said he had done business with many country's leaders and had nearly a billion dollars banked around the world. He then made his last mistake. He told us he could make us very, very rich. Sorensen shot him eight times in the face. I counted the rounds. I didn't know what the significance was, but they certainly disfigured the man.

I figured it would take a bit of time to identify him when the ME examined him. I looked one last time at Schultz and noticed his mouth was still shaped like the word "rich." The first round had hit him right between the eyes. I thought it was too easy a death for that monster. At least he couldn't hurt anyone anymore. I looked again at the book I was holding and pictured the rest of these dirtbags coming to this same end.

We stepped away from the limo and Sorensen opened his phone to make a call. I noticed there were still no folks wandering around. I put my back to the car but continued to hold my head down. Sorensen made two more calls and spoke softly during both before he hung up and told me to get in.

Sorensen drove and I sat up front in the passenger seat. He'd driven about a mile when I saw a police van parked on the side of the road. I couldn't see the driver, but I recognized the front seat passenger as our young friend Lu. He nodded to me as we pulled alongside his van. Sorensen got out and popped the trunk again. This time he stepped forward and placed two Brazilian flags in holders next to the limo's headlights. He nodded at Lu and the police van cut out in front of us, turning on its flashers. Sorensen quickly climbed behind the wheel and followed. I cracked the window a bit to let out the strong odors drifting up from our passengers in the back. I wished we had exchanged them for the suitcases in the trunk.

I recognized the route to the airport and asked Sorensen if he spoke any Thai. He said his knowledge was as good as his Greek. Mine, too. Soon, we passed the airline's terminal entrance and then kept going. We drove to what I remembered as the same gate we came out of last night. The police van turned into the side road and the gate went up quickly. A sentry stood there, saluting the van, and held his salute until we had passed. I turned in my seat and watched to see if he was making any calls, but he stood there, looking after us as the gate went down.

The van followed the narrow road around the runways and crossed a couple of taxiways to a group of hangars. As we approached, a door opened on one of the hangars. The police van parked next to the door and Sorensen pulled into the empty hangar. I was hoping to see a fast military mover parked there, ready to swoop us off to Bangkok. It was empty.

Lu ran thru the open door that was now closing. Sorensen asked him if he wanted to buy a limo and start a new business here in China. He told Lu he already had a couple of paying customers in the back. Lu looked through a window, saw the two dead guys, and asked, "How much?"

I said, "We'll pay you to take it off our hands."

He laughed and said we drove a hard bargain.

Sorensen went to the trunk and started to unload the cases. I gave him a hand and Lu brought a lug cart from against the wall for us to load them on.

I looked at Sorensen and said, "What now?"

He told me it was handled and to be patient. I had no doubt he had something in the works. But I was still concerned with time and checked my useless watch. Lu looked at my gesture and said it was 9:30.

We pushed the cart to the wall next to a little office. Sorensen opened one of the suitcases, pulled out a stack of hundred-dollar bills, and passed them to Lu, telling him to get a haircut and some toothpaste. Lu took the cash and made it disappear in his jacket. I, not to be outdone, reached into the case and took out two more bundles, passed them to Lu, and said here was the money I owed him. Lu laughed and stuffed it away. That was about $30,000 and some change. I was sure he would put it to good use. The limo had to be worth fifty thousand, even with a soiled rear seat. I should have gone into International Relations. I was a hit there in the hangar in Hong Kong!

Sorensen looked at Lu and shook his hand. I smiled at him and thanked him again. I knew he and his family were risking a great deal, and they were not doing it for the money. He walked over to the limo and turned it around as the big doors slid back about twenty feet and stopped. I looked at Sorensen and asked him who was operating the doors. As the limo passed through, he took his phone from his pack and pressed and held one of the keys on its touchpad. The big doors closed.

"Magic." Sorensen told me to relax for about an hour and our ride would be here. Good time to make some calls.

I again called the Major and told him about Angela. I told him I was encouraged by the fact that she, in my opinion, would not be immediately dispatched or cut into parts. I had a feeling Mubane would be doing some bidding of his own before she was used. The Major agreed. I told him I was going to spend some time photographing the ledger and text him the pictures. I told him I would send as many pages as I had time to do, and upon reaching my destination, would FedEx the entire book to one of our mail drops. I would then handle the hand delivery to him with one of my people. He knew that the only person I trusted with such an asset was Dave. I asked him again to handle the task of calling the Cohens. He said he would.

I then called Gage and briefed him. He told me our ride was on route to Hong Kong and that we should be ready to go as soon as it arrived. I, too, was anxious to leave this city. We must have violated every law on the books, including murder. Hopefully, I wouldn't see myself looking back at me from a TV very soon. I noticed that Sorensen was completely out of it, sitting in a chair with his feet on a small desk. I couldn't sleep now if my life depended on it. I did need to use the head. I kicked Sorensen's chair and told him I'd be right back. He snored louder.

As I was strolling to the men's room a short distance away, I looked over the suitcases on the cart next to the wall. There was a lot of money in those bags and possibly more ledgers or files that could incriminate a few hundred important people. Here it was, in an empty hangar, protected by a couple of old spooks, including one that couldn't keep his eyes open once he sat down. The other, me, was on his way to the head, carrying a small bladder and a pocket full of lethal weapons. I looked at my small bag. I had only my shaving gear, new clothes, and three or four sets of identification calling me numerous names and putting me at numerous ages, all old. I wondered where our backup was.

Where were the young people willing to follow in our footsteps and take over saving the world? I hadn't had a single intern come along in years asking for training or to offer assistance. The interns from long ago had bailed to work for large investigation firms that they thought would reveal some of the magic they thought we possessed. Little did they know that our magic was long-ingrained experience and luck. You also had to be willing to look foolish from time to time when you ducked for no reason. So that left me, Sorensen, and a couple of equally old friends and associates to try to live far longer and keep the balance of good and evil in check.

I used the head and walked back out to the hangar, inspected our bounty for any tampering by an invisible force, and then walked to the little office. Sorensen was awake and just signing off on his phone. He told me our ride was here and to help him tow the cart toward the hangar door. He did his trick with his phone and the massive doors began sliding open.

As I pulled on the cart handle, I heard the whine of jet engines getting louder and heading in our direction. When the aircraft came into view and spun on its axis, I saw our familiar Gulfstream V looking magnificent in the bright, noonday sun. I also noticed that it still bore our November numbers and Old Glory flag on its tail. Before it had even stopped spinning, the side door opened, and the stairs began sliding down. Standing at the open hatch was Lt. Sally Moore, smiling as if she had just returned from a South Sea cruise. I smiled back like a schoolboy and immediately thought to myself that I was old enough to be her father, if not worse. Sorensen looked at my grin and shook his head.

The aircraft came to a halt, but both engines continued to run. Moore skipped down the steps and began carrying the suitcases up the stairs and throwing them into the cabin. Sorensen and I did the same and, after the last case and my little bag cleared the hatch, Moore raised the stairs and closed the hatch. Capt. Cline turned in her seat and gave the thumbs-up signal. Moore skipped to her seat. The engines wound up and we were rolling out toward the taxiways.

I grabbed a window seat on the port side and Sorensen took the starboard. I looked at the deck where I knew our store of weapons was hidden, and then I remembered the grenades making lumps in my trousers. I needed to relieve myself of them in order to be a bit more comfortable in the seat as we flew. We turned a couple of times, followed the taxiways, and then I heard the sweet sound of the engines winding up for takeoff. With no hesitation, we were in the air. My anxiety drained away as we continued to climb and turned to the north. Captain Moore came on the intercom and told us she had filed a flight plan for the States, but after we cleared Chinese territory, we would turn to the south toward Thailand. It never ceased to amaze me how efficient Sorensen was in planning. It again made me think of the future without guys like us to run interference.

After we had leveled out, still flying north by northeast, Sorensen and I started moving the scattered suitcases to the rear of the plane and stacking them in the vacant seats. After securing them with the seatbelts, I took the ledger from where it was tucked into the back of my trousers and laid it out on the table in front of me. I started taking photos of the pages one by one and storing them in my phone's memory. After every ten pages, I emailed them to several addresses that I had stored on my phone. One of those was the Major's secret address in Washington, and one was a secure private address somewhere, but I didn't have a clue where. Thirty minutes later, I had sent out about a hundred pages through the aircraft's satellite transceiver and decided to take a break.

Sorensen took the ledger from the table and made little whistling noises as he read some of the names. Both of us were amazed that none of the names were in code, and neither were the bank names or account numbers. Mr. Schultz must have felt damn secure with all his money and sins. It made me wonder about the rest of his organization. There had to be a number two—a "Vise Schultz" somewhere. Whoever they were, I was sure they were aware that he was missing, along with their funds. I glanced back at the suitcases and knew we were in for some trouble soon.

The plane lost altitude quickly and turned to the south. I could see

Capt. Cline speaking on her headset. I figured she was changing her flight plan for Thailand or for a refueling spot en route. As Sorensen read the ledger, he made a couple of notes in his little notepad and then pulled his phone and made a call. He said some gibberish code words and then read from his notes into the phone. He talked further and made a couple of statements that he was equally surprised, and then listened a moment. Whomever he was talking to must have made some suggestions, as Sorensen said he agreed and hung up. I waited for him to fill me in, but he just looked at me and said we needed to stash the contents of the bags in the secret hold beneath our feet. I agreed and pulled up the carpet.

I stuck my fingers into the holes, but nothing happened. I couldn't feel anything like a latch or a button, just a smooth, rounded hole. I looked up, saw Moore waving her left index finger in the air, and understood the latches were fingerprint controlled. She popped out of her seat and came aft. A second later, the lid was off, and then a hatch next to it came off. Plenty of room for our stash. I wondered if a dope smuggler had designed this plane. I thanked her and tried not to think about her embrace and whisper the day before. (Business, Jake, business!)

After Moore had returned to the flight deck, Sorensen and I took the suitcases, one by one, and stacked the cash and bonds into the hold. One of the smaller cases held about a hundred file folders with more recognizable names titled at the top. These perps would be shocked to see that Schultz treated this incredibly dark business like a mom-and-pop operation. Little or no security measures to protect their identities at all. One of the names that jumped out at me as I packed the files away was one, I recognized as an Assistant Director in Sorensen's chain of command. Now I knew why he'd made the quiet call a moment ago. I was sure gears were turning in Washington to block any attempt by this director to buy himself some amnesty.

Sorensen saw me looking at the file and shook his head. I could tell by the redness on his face that he was upset. He was quiet for a minute and then said, "This is why I keep my bosses in the dark until the end of my ops." I already knew that. It must have given him some relief to say it as he returned to less dangerous, Sorensen normal.

After everything was secreted away in the hold, we re-stacked the suitcases on the seats and sat back down. I spoke first, saying that we needed to get the ledger and files secured as soon as possible. Neither one of us cared about the cash and bonds—however, in the back of my mind, I did file the idea that it could provide us with the bait we might need to get to Mubane and Angela.

I leaned back in my seat and tried remembering Bangkok from my past visits there. The first time I was there was in the late Sixties on R&R from the Nam. The last time I was there was about ten years ago. That city had grown fifty times larger and brighter and now rivaled Hong Kong or Tokyo. Every electronics company in the world tried to outdo one another with neon signs, some of which stretched between buildings. It was so bright that if you were approaching the airport from over the city, it was hard to determine the runway lights from the night light clutter. I was surprised there weren't more mid-air collisions by confused pilots. I guessed the air traffic controllers were top notch. The city was as much a "sin city" as any party city I had ever been to, if not more. After we had gained altitude on our southern route, Sally walked back from the flight deck. She asked if we needed anything. After we said we were fine, she sat down across from me. She glanced at the deck carpeting and reached down to adjust its edges, so they were more even with the surrounding carpet. She told us that the hold was designed so that it appeared to be a solid deck across the aircraft, with rivets holding it down. When you opened the belly hold from the outside, all you saw was what looked like the bottom of the deck. Experts had searched this aircraft and its predecessors, and yet they had never discovered the secret holds. She added that the hatch was so airtight that search dogs never even hesitated over it.

I thought that comforting for the sake of the records hidden beneath our feet. I was also thinking that the millions of greenbacks under there were worth nothing compared to the ledger and files we carried. I wondered if we should place the ledger into the hold, too. But then I decided that stuffed into the waistband of my trousers was the safest place right now. I contemplated having someone I trusted meet me here and fly it back like guarded mail. I thought of my friend Nick who was living in New Zealand now. Nick was a former British SAS officer with more combat experience than any ten of his comrades. I could trust him to die before he allowed himself to be relieved of anything he'd been entrusted with. I had to decide, as I knew we would be landing soon in Krung Thep, the Thai name for their city of Bangkok.

I asked Sally where she and the captain went off to while we were touring Hong Kong. She said they had flown to a small military airfield near the city of Gaoxiong, in the south of Taiwan. I was familiar with that area. I had been there on Marine Corps business a few times. I remembered the people as being hospitable and generous.

Sally said that they had been camping out overnight on Taiwan, waiting for our call. I thanked her for her prompt arrival and their faith in us that we would have survived for a pickup. She laughed, and I knew as she looked at me that she figured it was obvious. Sorensen and I had lived this long, and odds were that we were far more experienced than our adversaries. (If she only knew how much harder it was at an advanced age!)

14

Sally patted me on the knee and returned to her flight deck duties. Shortly afterward, Captain Cline announced that we were flying over the Vietnam countryside. She did a female version of "Good Morning, Vietnam!" much like Robin Williams in the movie. It was not morning, and I did not know how the Vietnamese government would feel if they knew I was close. That's another story for another time. I have never gone back there, although I have thought about it from time to time. I certainly think about the Nam a lot, and I have dreamed about it, as well. I thought, *Keep flying, Captain.*

I could feel the aircraft slowing down and losing altitude for our approach into Bangkok. I looked at Sorensen, who hadn't slept or uttered a peep this whole ride, as we flew down. I realized he was far more upset with what he'd seen in that ledger than I'd imagined.

I interrupted him and asked what he thought about getting the ledger and files to a safe spot while we played in Party City. He said he had been thinking about it, but anyone he thought he could trust with the files was now suspect in his mind. I agreed. I mentioned Nick, and he brightened up a bit and asked if I knew where he was, at present. I told him that I thought he was at home in New Zealand with his family for a change.

I hit my speed dial for Nick, and he picked up after the second ring. He made the usual jokes about Yanks and such and then asked if I was okay. I said I was fine, and he asked if I had been in China of late. I replied that I had no idea what he was referring to, but his question didn't surprise me. He filled in the void by saying that he had just hung up from Gage and could be in Sin City by daybreak the next day.

Sorensen spoke up and advised Nick to fly incognito and to keep his plans close to his chest. He would explain everything when we all got together. I told Nick that I would signal him when I found out what airport facility we would be using and that we would also be staying with the aircraft until he arrived. He said he already knew where we were heading and would see us there.

I asked Sorensen if we could use this aircraft and its crew to taxi Nick to his destination. He said he would arrange it and asked the pilots if they wanted to fly back to the States with an even more handsome, younger, and debonair fellow than us, and they dramatically yelled, "Oh, yeah!"

I shouted that I was far younger than the big bloke standing near them, throwing off the weight and balance of the aircraft right now. They laughed and Sorensen gave me a look. When he returned to his seat, he said they were game, but we would have to kick in for the fuel. I looked at the deck near our feet and thought, *No problem!* I told Sorensen that Mr. Schultz had just decided to make up for some of the harm he had caused. Lt. Moore was too busy now to bother asking for her magic finger trick on the deck hatch, so I figured we could open it after we landed and grab a handful of cash for expenses.

We made our approach to the International Airport and landed without incident. I half expected an army of police and politicians whose names were listed in the ledger to greet us on the tarmac. But everything appeared normal as far as I could see from out of the porthole. We taxied toward the hangars opposite the passenger terminals. I continued to watch for trouble. I could see Capt. Cline talking normally on her headset to the Ground Control tower. She appeared to be calm and just looked forward out the windshield. It's tough not to be paranoid while sitting on millions of dollars and enough criminal evidence to put away a good percentage of the free world's leadership. Sorensen was still contemplating his little notepad. He had made numerous notes during the flight, and I had no idea what was going on in his head. Whatever it was, it was not good. I would not want to be the focus of his anger right now. (Or ever!)

Captain Cline taxied through a maze of aircraft and between some hangars to an open area near several parked fuel trucks. Lt. Moore came aft and said they were topping off their fuel now instead of calling for a refueling after we were parked and tied down. I asked her if she would mind opening the deck hold as I had left my "mad money" in the hole. She laughed and quickly pulled back the carpet and did her thing. I lifted the corner of the hatch, grabbed two bundles of cash, and pushed the hatch back down until it clicked into place. I moved the carpet back over the deck and passed one of the bundles to the lieutenant. She took the stack of hundreds and said she was going to the mall for a few hours. Even Sorensen laughed.

Lt. Moore stuffed the cash into the leg pocket of her flight suit and proceeded to open the aircraft hatch. After she lowered the stairs, she climbed down and began her aircraft inspection duties. Captain Cline came aft and took a folder from a small locker on the wall. I could see an Official U.S. seal on the front as she took out a sheaf of paper and walked down the stairs. Moments later, a small van approached the port side of the plane. Cline walked up to the right front window of the van and handed the paperwork to the driver. I couldn't see him or her clearly, but I could see the papers the two were examining and shifting back and forth. Cline turned and said something to Lt. Moore, who was now close to the van. I watched as Moore reached into her "money pocket" and pulled out several bills. I knew they were all hundreds, so I figured she passed about three or four hundred to Cline, who in turn passed them to the van driver. Perhaps it was a landing tax, or the driver was going to the mall, too.

The van drove off and one of the fuel tankers started up and pulled to the rear of our craft. I watched as a young man pulled a thick hose from the side of his truck and dragged it to our starboard wing. Cline came back into the aircraft and put the papers back into the folder. She looked at me and said, "Diplomatic declarations."

I had figured as much.

I wondered if Sorensen's phone could open any of the big hangars surrounding us. From the look on his face the past two hours, I doubted it. I was sure he was going to be very careful in the trust department now and was going to rely on his own backup instead of Washington's.

When the truck finished refueling, Moore went to the hatch and paid him cash for the service. She received a receipt and brought it back to me. I told her to turn it in with her taxes. She laughed and put it on the table. I don't read Thai, but the numbers jumped out at me. No wonder we pay so much for plane tickets. It looked like most people's yearly W-2 return. I figured we had better raid Schultz's stash again and grab twice as much this time.

After a short preflight inspection and instrument check, we cranked up and taxied around to the side of a hangar. Cline turned the aircraft around, so we were pointed the way we had come in. From there we could see most of the airport and the roads. It was still not very secure, seeing how we were literally sitting on millions of dollars. As we sat there for a few minutes, I started to wonder how much we should tell Nick regarding the files. I could have cared less about the money. It was dirty no matter how you looked at it, and that included the bonds. I'd leave the money affairs to the Major. He'd know where it would benefit the people the most. That was the least of my concerns.

Angela was still out there somewhere in the vast, crowded city, and I needed to bring her home.

Sorensen had been working his phone for the last few minutes and now looked more normal than the dangerous, red-faced menace he'd been a while ago. He hung up and looked at me long and hard. I asked him if his sources had any insight on Mubane. He said that he had some leads, and as soon as we figured out the logistics of our problem with the money, we would need to head into town. I told him that I didn't care to leave the aircraft until Nick arrived in the morning. It would have been too much responsibility to burden our pilots with right now. They had no idea how important our cargo was or how much money was in the hold. Sally could buy ten or more malls with it. Sorensen agreed with me.

I informed Capt. Cline that we would be staying on board for the rest of the day and night.

The pilots busied themselves running a large power cord to an electrical box on the side of one of the hangars. This gave us power for the air conditioning and lights. We hadn't used the latrine much on this last trip, so we had plenty of water and septic storage to spare. Food was no problem, either. As soon as the lights came on and the air conditioning resumed, we plugged our various cell phones in for recharging. I re-checked my weapons and made sure the grenades were secured in the pocket of the seat next to me. Sorensen was busy again in his little notebook.

The two ladies said they were going to take advantage of the little pilot convenience rooms at the service center and would be less than five minutes away if we needed them. Sorensen had their numbers and told them to get some sleep. After they left, we sorted out the security watch times and I picked the short stick, receiving the first watch. I moved up into the co-pilot's seat, where I had a fairly good view of the area around the plane. I looked back at Sorensen. He was stretched out on his seat, sound asleep already.

That was a good thing. Sorensen in "anger mode" was not a safe environment. I was having trouble staying awake, but thoughts of Angela being so close kept me alert. I went back, retrieved my phone, and sent a text message to the Major and Gage, briefing them on our location and decision to stay put until morning. I received an acknowledgment from the Major and a message from Gage that Nick was on a non-stop to our location and should arrive before dawn, our time. I sent a text to Nick about our location across the field from the passenger terminals. I used three different phones for my texting just in case one was caught in the worldwide search for us.

The sun was going down and I had about four more hours on my watch, so I made some notes about possible plans for tomorrow. Nothing ever really goes as planned, but it was best to be prepared for the "what ifs," should they came along. The most important plan was how to get Angela out of Bangkok once we freed her. I like to think positively and always look toward the successful end of any mission. I did feel good at this point, because everything else had gone well on this case—even with the surprising turn of events. So, thinking positive, I ran a list through my head of possible means at our disposal to get her home.

As I was sitting there, daydreaming with all the lights out in the interior of the plane, I saw some movement in the reflection on the window. It was just a twinkle, but definitely not natural. Something moved and blocked the light for a moment. I slid out of the seat and went aft. I tapped Sorensen on the foot, and he came alert immediately. I pointed to the outside, port wing, and made a walking sign with my fingers. There was just enough light shining in the portholes for him to see my movements. He rolled off the seat and scooted to the rearmost porthole in the cabin.

He looked quickly, pointed down, and then put up one finger, signifying one person in sight, right outside the rear of the aircraft. Our plane was secure from the inside, but if someone was clever, they could spray pepper spray in the air ducts of the air conditioning system, forcing us to make a break for it.

Now, I wasn't so pleased with our decision to stay aboard. We were captives to our own cleverness, and if we opened the hatch and rushed out, someone could ambush us as soon as we showed our noses. Just then, I remembered our two healthy and able-bodied pilots only five minutes away. Two Marines as combat ready as any Marine on duty today, if not more so. I whispered my request to Sorensen, and he hit a speed-dial on his phone. One of them must have answered on the first ring because he briefed them quickly. He said we could only see one, but there may be more that were hidden.

He hung up and moved to the hatch. I stayed in the center of the cabin and watched out both sides for more movement. Five minutes later, we heard two pops. The distinctive sound of a silenced, small-caliber pistol. As soon as we heard the sounds, Sorensen pressed the switch and opened the hatch. He didn't wait for the steps to go down. He jumped out, and I could see him squat out of a roll and point his pistol at different spots all around himself. He then lifted his pistol in the air and motioned to someone with his hand to stay down. He then moved out of my line of sight and toward the rear of the plane.

I set up a position at the open hatch and watched the area that I could see from that angle. Not much to see except the wall of the hangar. After a few moments, Sorensen came back into view and waved me down. I wasn't going to do a parachute jump as he had done, so I pressed the button for the steps to extend down. I walked to the tarmac and saw one of the ladies and Sorensen bent over a body on the ground beneath the plane's tail. I looked around but couldn't spot the other pilot. Still, I knew she was there someplace. I walked over to the prone body and saw that it was a Caucasian male dressed in military-type fatigues similar to Sorensen's usual get-up. He was also armed with a high-powered automatic pistol of the type that can put a hole right through an aircraft. Sorensen relived him of his wallet, and I could see a California driver's license and some U.S. greenbacks in the cash slots. He had on a small backpack and, as Sorensen opened it, I saw a gas mask and a couple of tear gas canisters.

The next things to come out of the backpack were a few pictures. Two of the planes we were sitting under, with the current November numbers, and a couple of long-lens shots of Sorensen and I getting on the aircraft in Hong Kong earlier today or yesterday, whichever it was. More importantly, there was a photo of the four of us loading suitcases into the plane. The photos appeared to be stills of a video camera's film.

We didn't have to say anything. We knew we were moments away from more company. I took the fellow's phone from his pocket and saw it was still active. It had a photo on its text app of our aircraft, showing the tail numbers, ready to send. I canceled the text and punched up its most recent calls list. The last call was made over two hours ago. That was good because maybe he had not notified anyone that he had found us yet. No matter what, we needed to move the plane and get it into a hangar right away.

Just then, Captain Cline stepped out of the shadows and walked to our position. I asked her if they could roust anyone at this time to tow the plane into a hangar for a few hours. Lt. Moore said there were ground crewmen on standby twenty-four hours a day. She took off toward the office area. I called after her and told her to give us a few minutes to dispose of our California friend here. Sorensen picked up the very dead snoop like a light sack of potatoes and quick-walked to a Dumpster next to the hangar. I searched his pockets again to remove any ability to identify him quickly, and Sorensen lifted him into the trash. Lt. Moore found a water hose next to the building and was busy spraying the blood residue off the tarmac when we returned.

A few minutes later, Capt. Cline walked back from the Service Center and said they had found a hangar space for our plane. Shortly thereafter, a tow vehicle came from the front of the hangar and hooked up the aircraft. After following the plane on foot into a spacious hangar, we all boarded to get some much-needed rest. It was Sorensen's watch time now and he stationed himself next to a porthole that faced the hangar doors. The two pilots sat back in their cockpit seats and appeared to be too wired to sleep. I sent a quick text to Nick's phone telling him we had changed our location to the hangar. I asked him to call as soon as he touched down.

I woke just as the sun was beginning to glow through the hangar's windows. At the same time, my cell phone rang. I saw it was Nick's phone and answered right away. He had just landed and said he would ask the airline folks for a ride to the civilian side of the airport. I told him all was ready for his departure as soon as he got to us and we had briefed him. He signed off and I called for Lt. Cline to open the deck hatch again. I grabbed two more bundles of cash for the pilot's expenses and another bundle for Sorensen and me. I then told them all to gather around as I had changed my plans for the destination of the aircraft and its cargo.

I decided that because there were so many folks involved in the pursuit of us banditos, I thought it better for the ladies and Nick to fly the cargo to New Zealand instead of the U.S. for the time being. Nick had a semi-government relationship there and more sources than Sorensen, if that was even possible. Then again, I believed Sorensen was re-thinking his list of friends after reading the ledger. Nick could secure the files, bonds, and cash until this matter was concluded. If we survived, we could go and get it. If we perished, he could handle it. Either way, it was the best I could come up with now.

I told Sorensen and the ladies that because of the photos California Joe was carrying and the interest he'd shown in the luggage we had loaded, I thought we should perform a bit of deception in case California Joe had a counterpart out there still observing.

We opened the large hangar doors with the help of the crew and made a slow, visible effort to unload all the suitcases onto a cart being towed by a tow tug. After all the suitcases were loaded on the cart, I asked the worker to let us borrow the tug for a while. I slipped him a hundred and he smiled broadly. It was such a nice smile, I slipped him another one.

While we waited for Nick to arrive, the pilots did their precheck. I was sure Captain Cline was filing a phony flight plan with the tower and asking for a departure time. She would probably fly to Hong Kong and then, somewhere over the western side of the China Sea, do a mid-flight "change of mind." She was good at that. They would probably change plans a few times on the way into Auckland. Then I thought of Nick and figured they would more than likely get permission to land at one of New Zealand's military bases. No customs inspectors to mess with and no questions from his military contacts.

Just as I was thinking all that, Lt. Moore walked over with five or six large, nylon mailbags and threw them into the cabin. I also had been wondering how they would get those piles of cash out of the plane upon arriving in New Zealand. I really liked these ladies. I thought about how they might be offered a change of employer soon—if there was a future.

J ust as the preflight was finished and I had retrieved my little suitcase, Nick arrived in a small van. It pulled up alongside the plane, but out of view. He thanked the driver and climbed out with just a small carry-on bag. We greeted with hugs and introductions to the pilots. I warned Nick that they were both U.S. Marine Officers and both could kick his butt single-handedly. He looked at them and promised to be a gentleman.

We got the small talk out of the way and heard a couple of short stories about his latest adventures in the Middle East. Then I told him we needed to brief him and send him on his way.

I gave him the rundown on the documents, bonds, and cash in the hold of the aircraft. I explained that it was totally concealed and only the pilots could access it. I then told him that I wanted him to take it all home with him. He acted a bit apprehensive about that and I explained that I didn't mean his *house*, but somewhere safe that he had access to near his home. He asked me how large an area it would need, and I said, "Large."

I told him the two most important parts of the stash were the records and files, and that he should consider two different places to keep them safe. I could see him running several plans through his head and decided he had it figured out when he smiled and asked the ladies if they were ready to shove off. I then mentioned the weapons in the hold, in case he needed one or two persuaders. He winked and said he would see us soon.

Sorensen and I jumped on the tow tug and headed for the passenger side of the airport. We watched the plane from the corner of our eyes taxi to the main runway, and, with a roar, jump into the sky. I had prepared myself for a gun battle out on the taxiway as the plane made its way to the runway, but all was quiet. I guessed that California Dead Guy wasn't being missed yet. Our luck was holding out for the time being. Now, it was back to Angela.

I drove the tug into the bag tunnels under the terminal and we parked it out of sight near some empty carts. The bags had no tags on them. Later, when someone discovered them, it would be another unsolved mystery, I hoped.

All Nick and the ladies needed was about an hour and they would be over the South China Sea, but we wouldn't know that they were clear until we received a text from Nick. I was confident that the aircraft was fast, if not faster, than many fighter jets, and I felt that the ladies were dogfight qualified.

I still had the ledger tucked into the rear of my trousers and had to figure out what I was going to do with it. Having it and the files gave us a great deal of leverage with the perps. It also gave us the upper hand with many government leaders around the globe. I needed to make some more copies of the pages as proof, should we needed it, and send them off to more safe places. I was thinking about all this as we wound our way to the bag exits under the terminal.

No one looked twice at us in the bag tunnels, and no one cared when we popped out of the bag portholes. I saw a couple of uniformed policemen standing around, but they were looking at the crowds who were waiting for their bags and not the discharge holes.

We decided not to rent a car at the airport and just grab a cab into town. I asked the driver to bring us to the Hilton Hotel downtown and he asked, "Which one?"

I quickly answered that we wanted to go to the biggest one near the residential district. I recalled staying there the last time I was in Bangkok. He acted as if he knew what I was talking about and we scooted off.

I watched the planes taking off to see if there was any change to their pattern in case our plane was diverted, or worse, but saw nothing out of the ordinary. Sorensen was sitting sideways because of his long legs in the short vehicle. I also knew he was keeping an eye out the rear for any tails we may have picked up.

As we drove into town, I sent a couple of text messages to a source I had in Bangkok, asking him to standby for a signal to meet later. I wished I had written down the many aliases I have used here, and who knew me as which one! Confusing, but I recalled that he knew me by my real name, Jake.

I didn't reveal the name Benz Mubane to him until I had a few facts down in my head. Mubane must be a heavy hitter to have paid so much money for Angela. With that kind of money came a certain amount of power. Power to override friendship and loyalty, for sure.

My source, a former British Intelligence Agent with MI6, had lived in and around Bangkok for a dozen years or more. He owned an English-speaking private investigation firm that served the many English and American interests here in Thailand. I had worked with him on a case involving two missing American couples who had vanished, along with their huge sailing yacht, on an around-the-world cruise. He was resourceful and professional, and that led to our discovery of a large, multi-country pirate organization, much like the pirates off the coast of northeast Africa. (That's another story for another time.)

His name was Frank Gowdy and he was licensed as a private investigator in more countries than I could remember, including the U.S. I had consulted with him on several matters, both his and mine. I texted him that I was in the country and may need his assistance. He texted right back that he would standby for my call. I briefed Sorensen and, as he had dealt with Gowdy on his own cases, agreed to his involvement.

Our driver appeared to be oblivious to us in the backseat until I saw Sorensen's hand quickly reach over to the passenger seat and yank out what I recognized as a GoPro miniature video camera. It was in the on position and had been pointed at us from between the front seats. Sorensen took out his silenced .22 pistol, jammed it into the man's neck and forced his head into the right window. He yelped and, at Sorensen's command, pulled off the next exit onto a side road. After we had stopped, Sorensen pulled the man right out of his seat and took the car out of gear. Sorensen slammed the camera into the driver's face and said he had one minute to explain.

The man's face was bloodied from the camera strike and fearful tears were flowing from his eyes. He did not hesitate. He said that the night before, many of the taxi drivers were informed that there was a large reward for information regarding a couple of American men who might arrive at the Bangkok airport. He said that if anyone saw them, they should call a number and leave the information of the American's destination on the answering device, along with the driver's name and number.

I asked him if he had secretly sent a message to this number already, and he said "No." He said that he was going to send a photo first to see if he could negotiate more money.

I asked him why he thought we were the men of interest, and he said that one of the men was huge. That answered that question. I asked him how much the reward was, and he said about two hundred dollars American. I looked at Sorensen and he nodded in understanding. I reached into my pocket, pulled out about a thousand dollars and jammed it into his chest. I told him that I wanted to buy a bit of his loyalty and his camera. He stopped sniveling and looked at the cash in surprise.

Sorensen shoved him back into the driver's seat and told him to keep driving. I asked the cabbie what the number was that he was supposed to call if he encountered these Americans. He gave me the number and I figured it was a burner phone for obvious reasons. More than likely, two or three phone numbers had been handed out to avoid detection. In any event, it was good to know.

The driver dropped us off at the Hilton, the one I remembered staying at some years ago. Sorensen asked the driver for his license and cell phone. He took a picture of the license, which showed his home address, and asked me to give him another couple of hundred for the phone. I did and Sorensen stuck the phone in his pocket.

As soon as we entered the lobby, I pointed to the side door. Sorensen and I walked out and hailed another cab. This time, I asked the driver to take us to the Grand Hyatt Hotel. I had seen an advertisement for it on the way from the airport and figured the driver would think we were familiar enough with the area that he wouldn't associate us with the "all call" information alert from the bad guys. Kind of a stretch, but all we had right at that moment.

The hotel turned out to be near the center of town and convenient for our current purposes. I asked him to stop at the side entrance as if we were already registered there and then tipped him big as I grabbed my bag and walked to the door. When we got inside, I told Sorensen we needed to shift again. As we were driving to the Hyatt, I had noticed the West Bangkok Hotel not far back the way we came. I led the way a couple of blocks south, then east, and then north, right to the front of the massive skyscraper hotel. We went in a side door and I could see a huge pool off to the rear of the building. Nice to know if we wanted to relax and bask in the sun. (Right!)

I checked us into two separate rooms across the hall from one another. That way, we could surveil each other's doors through the peepholes. My room overlooked the pool, and, in the distance, the suburbs of the city. There were a lot of slum areas around Bangkok that held thousands of immigrants from neighboring countries looking for a better life. Sorensen's room overlooked the city.

It was early afternoon and the dust and smog were just getting stirred up over the buildings. Looked like grey soup rising a few inches a minute. As thin as it was in the air above the city streets, it became thicker and thicker the closer you were to the ground. These folks would love the clean air of Los Angeles!

That thought reminded me of Angela. I looked across the vast city from Sorensen's window and wondered just how close she was at that moment. I texted my friend and asked him to meet us in the lobby of the Mandarin Oriental Hotel. Another hotel I had seen advertised along the way. I try to limit the number of folks who know where I am sleeping.

I left my bag in my room and grabbed a few essentials: gun, spare magazines, two different passports, and one hand grenade. (I didn't often get the chance to have my own "object of mass destruction" very often, so I brought one along just in case I had a "John Wayne moment." It was hard to tell what Sorensen was carrying as all of his multi-pockets were bulging.

We left the hotel from the side entrance where we had entered and walked a couple of blocks to another, smaller hotel. There we had the doorman hail us a taxi. I told him to take us to the Mandarin Oriental and we were off. Then again, being off in Bangkok in the middle of the day was like standing still in traffic. As it turned out, we were only a few blocks from the Mandarin and could have walked faster.

As soon as I saw the hotel ahead, I asked the driver to stop and let us out, and, moments later, we were in the lobby of this magnificent hotel. I saw my source sitting in an alcove off the lobby and looking toward the front door and the elevators to his side. We had slipped in the side door in his blind spot. Before we approached him, I located the door to the restaurant. I asked Sorensen to get us a table, so it appeared that we were staying at the place. I waited for a few minutes and approached my friend.

His real name was Francis Gowdy and he was a large man, about ten years younger than me. He kept himself in top shape and appeared to have had a couple of plastic surgeries since I had last seen him. There was also the matter of more hair than I remembered. I walked right up to his side before he sensed my presence. You can do that if you only watch a person from your peripheral vision as you approach. If you look at them, they will sense it right away. (Like the beautiful lady on the subway that caught you looking!)

Frank jumped to his feet as soon as I'd cleared my throat and thrust out his large, tanned hand. Good handshake, firm and dry. That was a good sign. Limp and wet was a sign of worry and deceit. (Not to mention gross.) He appeared sincerely happy to see me and kept a hold on my hand. I finally got control and took my hand back. I also got to pat him down a bit in the almost hug. He was carrying two guns and a knife in a side scabbard on his belt. I figured he probably had another small gun in an ankle holster on the outside of his right leg. He knew I was frisking him just as he was me. I could see him trying to figure out what the bulge of the hand grenade was. I winked at him and told him I was just happy to see him.

He looked worried for a moment and then laughed. I asked him if he had bumped into any of his clients while sitting here and he said, "No."

I casually looked around the lobby area and saw very few people. None appeared interested in us. I pointed toward the restaurant and told him I was starved. He said he could stand to eat something, too.

We walked into the lobby of the restaurant, and I spotted Sorensen sitting at a rear table with his back to the wall and a newspaper spread out in front of him. I guided Frank toward the table, and he lit up and smiled when he recognized Sorensen. They embraced, insulted each other a few times, and then sat down. Frank made a comment that he shouldn't feel so happy about seeing Sorensen, as every time he has seen him in the past, he wound up recuperating for two weeks from wounds and beatings. Sorensen told him that was why he'd chose to work with him in Thailand. He told Frank that he was the only one for a thousand miles fat enough to partially hide behind. They both laughed, but, again, I thought about Angela.

I asked Frank if he had any conflicts with Benz Mubane. He looked at me for a moment and cleared his throat. That was a bad sign. He asked if we were here in opposition to Mubane, and I asked him again if he had a conflict. He said, "Yes. He's one of my clients."

Quickly thinking, I asked him if he was at liberty to give us some information about him, and he said he could tell us the basics. I told him that we would pay him rather than take the time to do the research.

He looked worried, and I could see his forehead starting to dampen up. He looked relieved when the waiter came over to take our orders. After ordering, he broke right in by saying that Mubane was a very rich and powerful man in the Far East. He was into shipping and owned a hundred global merchant ships, and possibly a hundred thousand mobile shipping containers. Frank said he had done work for Mubane's companies—and him, personally. He added that it would be hard to find someone in and around Thailand who had not worked for him. He paid well and treated people fairly.

At that remark, I felt like telling him that he had just purchased someone's child for millions of dollars and may be planning to kill her for her body parts. I held my tongue.

Frank went on to say that Mubane had an enormous security force with many off-duty police and government militia members in its ranks. He added that many of them were senior officers and officials. I asked Frank what the nature of his dealings with Mubane was. He said he couldn't tell us that, but they varied and were mostly offshore matters that dealt with missing property and trade with England. I asked him how much of his current work was related to Mubane matters. He said perhaps over fifty percent. That was also troubling.

I took a chance and asked about Mubane's personal life and if he had any children. Frank said four. The youngest was about fifteen. I waited a moment to allow him to continue. He said that the daughter was ill and had seen many doctors around the world for treatment. (Bingo!) I went further and asked him the nature of the ailment and he said he believed, among other problems, she had a bad heart. I pushed him more and he continued by saying the daughter was not his wife's natural child, but an adopted child from Europe. That stopped the conversation for a moment as Sorensen and I looked at each other. That explained a lot.

I asked Frank if he could describe the girl, and he said he could do better and took out his cell phone. He punched in a couple of keys and turned the phone to me with a picture of a whole family at a celebration. They were all Asian looking except for one young girl with a very light complexion. She was very a thin, blonde, and ill-looking girl. Frank went on to say that he and his wife had been guests at the girl's fourteenth birthday party last year. Her name was Mary. She'd been eight to ten years old when she was adopted.

After our breakfast arrived and we had consumed it, Sorensen asked Gowdy if he felt compelled to tell Mubane about our inquiry. He thought for a moment, looked Sorensen right in the eye and asked if we were here to kill him. Without any hesitation, Sorensen said it depended on Mubane. I watched Frank for any reaction and he just shrugged. He then said he would prefer Mubane be annoyed with him rather than the two of us. I quietly agreed, and Sorensen showed his approval by patting Gowdy on the arm and telling him it was a good answer.

I gave Gowdy a few hundred-dollar bills for his time and he took them willingly. He hesitated a moment and said an idea had just come to him. He suggested that since he may be losing over fifty percent of his business before we left town, that he might be able to help us without violating his relationship with Mubane. He said he knew we would not divulge the nature of our case to him at this time, but he could still help us by handling the peripherals. I told him I would talk it over with Sorensen and call him. He knew we would wait to see if we saw some indication that he had informed Mubane about our presence and interest. He walked off without calling a cab, so I figured he had a car parked nearby.

I was a little bummed by these turns of events. I was counting on Gowdy to be our contact there in Bangkok and to run point for our search. His input was helpful, but now we were further ahead than we had been when we left Hong Kong. We knew the motivation for kidnapping Angela. I looked at Sorensen and told him we needed to get an English street map that we could study. He looked at his phone and realized we needed a large-scale vision of this city. Much had changed in the few years since I'd been here, and I had no idea when Sorensen had been here last. Probably not that long ago, but still…

16

We walked about two blocks toward the noisiest traffic and found a small bookstore. I bought a foldout map of Bangkok and one of Thailand. Afterward, we walked back to our hotel, again disguising our route by walking in the opposite direction and then a block or two beyond before arriving back at our home away from home.

As we walked, I called Gage and asked him to send us a rundown on Mubane. He had already put together some information in case we needed it and said he would forward it to my email. I also told him about Gowdy and his working relationship with Mubane. Gage knew Gowdy personally but was not surprised that he worked for one of the most successful businessmen in Thailand. Gage went on to say that Mubane had relationships with a few politicians in Washington and other popular businessmen in the U.S. He had included that info in the email briefing. I thanked him and asked him to brief Dave for me. He agreed and we signed off.

I told Sorensen that I needed to buy a small laptop computer and that we both needed some new clothes. There was an electronics shop in the little shopping mall attached to the hotel. I looked at Sorensen and doubted he would find clothes large enough to fit him in the limited shops, and so was surprised to see a shop called Big and Tall right at the entrance to the shopping area. I slipped him a few hundred and he went into the shop.

I continued to the electronics store and bought a Samsung Ultrabook. It was thin and looked like it could take a small beating in a backpack if needed. I bought a few accessories that I would need: an automobile charging cable, a few jump drives, and a Microsoft Word program. I asked the clerk if he would program it for me while I continued to shop. I would collect it in a few minutes. I slipped him an extra hundred-dollar bill, and he said he would throw in a few extras. I also asked him to set up a Hotmail account, and he said he would throw in all the major accounts, including AOL. I thanked him and then went looking for a normal man's clothing store. I figured we had better change some of our greenbacks into Thai currency as we had been leaving a generous trail of U.S. cash since Hong Kong. The kind of trail that the wrong kind of fans can use like breadcrumbs.

I found a nice men's shop and bought two complete outfits, from skivvies to sport coat. I also purchased a pair of black-on-black, dressy-looking tennis shoes. In the next shop, I purchased two medium-sized backpacks. One for me in dark gray and one for Sorensen in olive drab. The small carry-on I had been dragging around the past few days was inconvenient, and a backpack would be more useful.

After going back to our rooms, we both cleaned up, and, about an hour later, Sorensen knocked on my door. As I let him in, he said he had some leads. I had been looking at the maps we had purchased. What was funny was that even though they were in English, the names of streets and places were in Thai. I knew that Krung Thap was Bangkok, but the average tourist would be a bit confused. We were going to need a guide, and I would have to lean on Sorensen to arrange that. The first thing he said once he had closed the door was, "I have a friend here in Thailand and he is available to give us a hand. (Amazing!)

Sorensen had found his friend through Gage back in the States. Gage had accessed military retirement records in Kansas City and had found the contact info on retired military folks in Thailand. Barney Friend was a retired Marine Master Sergeant. That was an E-8 in the military pay grades. The Marine Corps has two E-8 designated Sergeants. One is a Master Sergeant and the other is a First Sergeant. The Master Sergeants are mainly combat- and logistics-related, and the First Sergeants are administrative positions. Both are referred to as "Top Sergeants" or "Top," with respect. Friend was a retired Master Sergeant and a Criminal Investigator in the Marines. He lived just outside of Bangkok and was on his way here to the hotel. Sorensen had worked with Top Friend in the past and said he was extremely reliable. I had never met him but had heard some stories from Sorensen over the years. In them, Sorensen was always praising him.

I asked Sorensen if it would be better to meet him away from the hotel, and he said that Top was as trustworthy as they come. I didn't doubt that for a moment but was concerned that he, being a former U.S. Spook, would have a permanent tail following him. I trusted Sorensen's judgment and went on to the next order of business while we waited for Top.

Sorensen had made a few inquiries regarding Mubane at the local U.S. Embassy's Intel Section. He did this without telling the embassy he was in town. It appeared the local U.S. Ambassador was a friend of Mubane's and spent much of his time moving between Mubane's homes and the embassy doing more than official business. Sorensen spoke to the man on the QT said it was a strange relationship, as the ambassador often left his security behind and disappeared with Mubane for hours at a time. After the CIA Station Chief had made it known he was not happy with this arrangement, he was transferred back to the States at the ambassador's request. The acting Station Chief was a new arrival and the ambassador had temporally promoted him to the position over all the other agents who were senior to him. Sorensen said there was a great deal of resentment at the embassy right now that we could certainly use to our advantage. He said that the agent he spoke with already had an indication that Sorensen was starting an inquiry into the ambassador's action and the promoting of the new guy over all the others. Sorensen didn't argue anything to the contrary so we could bleed some info from them as we needed it. The agent was putting together a packet of background info on Mubane and would send it shortly.

I had been charging my new laptop and turned it on to set up my email service for my various accounts. I deleted all the advertisements for home loans and Sears power equipment. I junked the ads for Viagra and cures for Erectile Dysfunction. I wondered why they always seemed to be paired in that order.

I came across two emails from Gage and set the computer aside for a moment and asked Sorensen if Top was a CIA undercover agent here. He said he was a contractor for the CIA. I'm not sure what the difference was. One must get retirement and his name on a plaque when he dies, and the other some cash and a denial that he ever lived. I asked Sorensen if he thought Top would feel compelled to check in with the embassy regarding us being here and he said we were safe with Top. I was trying to be as careful as possible to prevent Mubane from discovering our presence here and moving Angela. I didn't want to lose time locating her again.

I called Gage back and asked him Nick and the girls' status over the Pacific. He said they were about an hour out of Auckland and had encountered no obstacles on their journey. Gage sometimes sounds like a news announcer. I answered in my best "radio talk show" baritone, saying, "Well, we certainly thank you for that report." He laughed and said he had just climbed off a four-way conference call with some higher-ups. They like the phony importance he gives them.

He asked if I had read his info on Mubane. I told him I was just about to do that. He put me on hold for a moment and when he came back, he was all business. He asked how much we had told Gowdy. I told him that we only asked questions about his business and a bit about his personal life. I told him that he had volunteered some info about Mubane's family. He jumped in and said that Gowdy had just arrived at the embassy in Bangkok and had requested an audience with the ambassador. Fortunately, the ambassador was out of the country but was expected to return late that night.

Gowdy was offered a meeting with one of the assistants, but he declined it. Gage said Gowdy then requested to be patched into the ambassador's cell phone. He said he was there at the request of Benz Mubane. That got my attention right quick. I signaled Sorensen with a whirl of my finger. That was the signal to prepare to move. He went to the door and peeked out the peephole before opening it quickly.

Moments later, he was back with his new backpack over his shoulder, and I could see he'd readjusted his pistol, so it was at the ready in his pocket. I asked Gage to keep an eye on the embassy information traffic and hung up.

Just then, our room phone rang. I ignored it as I packed up my backpack with my goods from the old roller bag and we zipped out the door to the stairs. We were on the sixth floor but swiftly descended to the door leading out into the lobby. Sorensen looked out the window into the lobby and said his friend Barney was standing at the lobby phone kiosk and looking back toward the check-in desk. Sorensen looked first left and then right before cracking the lobby door open and whistling at Top to get his attention. Top looked over casually and nodded. Sorensen pointed to our right and Top walked toward the front door and then turned to the right.

Sorensen and I walked out the side door toward the pool area and saw

Top walking up to a small van, not looking at us at all. He climbed in and started the engine. He then jerked his head at us in a signal to come on. Both Sorensen and I cut between the parked cars and up to the side of Top's van. We both slid past the side door and into the rear seat, tossing our backpacks into the rear compartment. Even though it was a van, Sorensen's size was again a problem. We both ducked down as Top drove from the parking lot and joined traffic, casually merging into the flow.

Top spoke for the first time, saying there had been two goons questioning the desk clerk regarding two Americans. Top said he tried to call our room to warn us, but we must have been on our way down.

I asked him to drive us somewhere where we could get up off the floor and be a bit more comfortable. He said that we were far enough away from the hotel now but suggested we stay low in the seat for a while anyway. The windows on the van were tinted fairly dark, but shadows could still reveal Sorensen's size, which would really be noticeable as compared to a typical Thai.

I asked Top how much Sorensen had briefed him on our mission there in Bangkok. He said he knew we were after a kidnapped American teenager and that Mubane had purchased her in Hong Kong. Other than that, he was in the dark. I asked him if he knew anything about the human body part business in the Far East, and he replied that he knew a lot about it and had been gathering intelligence on it for a human rights group from England for about a year.

I told him that we believed Mubane had targeted and purchased our Angela for her organs. I told him Mubane had an adopted daughter who needed a heart transplant and it appeared Angela was a match. Top said that he had seen photos of Mubane's family that showed a young, blonde girl who looked sickly. He suspected that, from the look of her, the girl was on her way out. I wondered if the daughter was another of Mubane's purchases.

Top pulled into a side road and pushed a remote on his visor that opened a garage door under a tall building. As we entered, the garage door started coming down. Lights came on in the large room to show four or five cars and trucks parked neatly in a row to the right, and lockers and boxes on the left. There was another, smaller, roll-up type door on the left wall with a security touchpad next to it.

Top swung the van around and backed into a parking spot that faced out toward the entrance. He shut down the engine and said, "Welcome to the bottom of the Top Building."

We laughed a bit and he explained that most of the building was his, except for two of the ten floors, which a U.S. logistics company that dealt in supplies used by the American residents of Bangkok had leased. I asked him if that also meant spook supplies for traveling agents. He smiled because he knew we knew he was a CIA contractor. Part of his job was to supply undercover U.S. agents with whatever they needed to complete their missions. I'd used these types of facilities from time to time when I was an active agent, and Sorensen still used them often. It never ceased to amuse me when Sorensen arrived at a location with a small carry-on bag and, an hour later, had more clothes and armaments than a Swat Team. Contractors like Top, whom our government could deny, kept our intelligence agencies running smoothly around the world. Top told us to grab our packs and follow him.

He entered a code into the pad next to the small garage door and it rose up quietly to expose a hallway not unlike a hotel's, including carpeting and sconce lights on the walls. A moment after we'd walked through the door, it rolled down twice as fast. I noticed it was made of thick, steel panels that looked both bullet- and blast-proof. The first doors to the left and right of the hallway had steel doors of similar material. The rest of the doors, spaced at different locations along the hall, were standard hotel-type doors with keycard-operated latches. There were no room numbers on or around the doors.

Top noticed me staring at the doors and explained that they used the rooms for various guests. Some were small, one-person suites and others were for medium to large family accommodations. He said that there were guest rooms on this floor, with office and medical facilities on the floors above. Most of the floors were accessible from the lobby at the front of the building, and the building was listed as a visiting dignitary hotel and international business facility. He said that the Thai government had sanctioned its use and asked few questions regarding its occupants and guests.

He explained that he was just a front and assumed it belonged to the U.S. Government. I asked who he thought would be named in a lawsuit if the building fell on someone's head. He laughed and told us that only a very few knew his real name and that it would be hard to verify. I had heard about Top through Sorensen's stories over the years and wondered if even he knew the real Top Barney Friend.

He seemed relaxed and comfortable with us, so I only kept half an eye on him as we stopped in front of a door. Top waved his hand over the keypad on the wall and the door opened like the elevator door it was. We climbed inside and again Top waved his hand over the keypad and the door shut. The car shot up, nearly causing me to collapse to the floor. Sorensen grabbed my arm and held me steady. I then guessed this was not his first time here.

We stopped as violently as we took off and the door slid open before we even came to a complete stop. We stepped into the hall and I could hear voices and phones ringing. I couldn't imagine how anyone could stand working in this environment. It reminded me of the New York Stock Exchange. We walked about fifty paces and again Top waved his hand over a keypad and the door opened.

Inside was a large office space with about ten occupied desks and large monitors on the walls all around. There were maps and satellite images. Talking heads who appeared to be from various newsrooms from around the world manned the desks.

Top stood looking at the monitors for a moment and then said, "Welcome to the brain center of the Far East."

I looked at Sorensen and shook my head. Contractor, my ass. The only good thing was the fact that no one even glanced at us as we stood there. They were all Caucasian looking, although some of them appeared to be Hispanic. Then again, some Thais could pass as Spanish or Middle Eastern. They were all just intent on watching their video screens.

I felt like we were wasting a lot of Angela's limited time, and now we had to re-establish a place to stay and use as a base camp. I had a feeling Top was going to offer us a room at his "skyscraper man cave," and after our experience with Frank Gowdy, I was not sure I could trust him or his network.

Top could be compelled by a threat of losing his plush living, funded by Mubane's ambassador friend, and give us up. But, even if that didn't happen, I was also concerned that if Top didn't give us up, he might be totally compromised, or worse.

We needed to get back on track. I was about to grab Sorensen by the arm and tell him we needed to split, but, just then, one of the computer operators turned in his seat and said something quietly to Top. Top looked toward the wall covered with TV monitors and asked us how long ago we'd met with Frank Gowdy. I found the screen he was looking at and saw a car

145

half up on a sidewalk with four or five uniformed police officers standing around it. I could not see the man who was sitting in the car, but he looked dead. As the picture zoomed in, I saw several bullet holes in the driver's side window and the pinkish film of blood on the windshield in front of the driver.

Top quietly said that someone had attacked Gowdy only moments ago, shortly after leaving the American Embassy. Sorensen asked Top if we could go to another area so we could talk privately. He nodded and we followed him through a side door and into a very plush executive office. It had one glass wall that looked out into the monitor room where we had just been.

There were two Marine Corps emblems on the wall behind the desk and several photographs on the wall of Top, various recognizable dignitaries, and a couple of movie stars from back in the Sixties and Seventies. Obviously, Top's office. Two narrow windows behind his desk looked out across the city. Top pressed a button and the windows turned black. He said they were not windows but monitors that showed the outside of the building.

Top started to tell us the history behind his operation when I stopped him and told him we could take a tour later. I told him we were pressed for time and needed to brief him on our mission. He said he already knew some of it from Sorensen and had been watching the intelligence reports from Hong Kong. He said he was good friends with Gage back in Florida and had fished with him in the Banana River near my island several times over the years. I found that interesting and glanced at Sorensen. He did his shrug number and looked away.

Top looked at me with a quizzical smile. "I may not like it, but I was a celebrity in the intelligence community and was well regarded by most."

I said, "Thanks, Mom. But can we get to our briefing?"

We all sat down, and Top listened to the earpiece I had noticed he was wearing earlier. He said thank you and signed off. He looked at Sorensen and said that Gowdy was dead. The assailants were Mubane security troops, and I knew the authorities would cover up the entire affair as a traffic accident within the hour.

I asked Top if he had any ties to Mubane, as everyone else around here seemed to be beholden to him. He looked at me, hesitated as if I had insulted him, smiled, and said that not even the ambassador knew about this building or its function. Part of his mission was to watch people like Mubane in the Far East and report it to a very select group of people, both government and civilian. He said that even I would be surprised at the good people involved in this outfit and that it did far better than the United Nations or any narrow-focused, aid groups across the globe.

I was beginning to like the Top more and more. He added that Mubane was highly regarded by the rest of the world for his business savvy and generosity. Top stopped for a moment and then continued by saying that few in the world knew he was one of the top heroin smugglers of all time. Mubane was also one of the foremost leaders in the world of human trafficking and body parts sales, Top added. I stopped him there.

I covered what we knew regarding Rio, Hong Kong, and Bangkok. He shook his head and told me that that was only the tip of the iceberg. He mentioned the Chinese trade in prisoner executions. He and his team have been monitoring that business for several years now. But the many politicians involved in the business had hamstrung them.

Top went on to say that he had a great deal of information on Mubane to share with us to try to get Angela back. That perked my interests. I asked if he had any idea as to where Mubane might have her housed. He said he had his folks working on that now. I asked him if he knew where Mubane was right then. He did.

Mubane had several homes and apartments around Thailand. The one where he spent most of his time was the compound where his wife and children lived. The others were for business or sexual liaisons with his many mistresses. Top said that Mubane was a real hound dog and had a varied sexual appetite. I told him that it was my opinion that Angela would need to be at some medical facility, being prepared to lose some of her organs. I told him that we needed to cut the briefing short and get on the road to find Angela. Top nodded and spoke again into the air, asking for an update. A moment later, he nodded and signed off.

Top walked behind his desk, picked up a remote-control device, pointed at the wall on our right, and a monitor lit up with a map of Thailand. He aimed the remote at the monitor screen and a laser dot appeared. He dragged it down to the southwest area of Thailand and held it over what appeared to be a small peninsula. The screen enlarged and the peninsula became an island with a bridge connecting it to the mainland.

I recognized it as the brunt of many R&R jokes back during my Vietnam days. The island of Phuket. Top said Phuket was nearly as busy as Bangkok in traffic and trade. It was also the known center of the human body parts trade in Thailand and the surrounding nations. He said it was rumored that the International Airport there had been enlarged to accommodate the expanded air traffic needed to facilitate the bizarre trade. He shook his head when he said this and added that wealth and power were corrupting this world.

I asked Top if he thought Angela would be held there. He shrugged and said his folks were just now looking at Mubane's flight records to see if any of them coincided with any of his aircraft flights to Phuket I studied the monitor and attempted to form a plan.

I asked Top if Mubane was there now.

"No, he is presently on a small plane that left Bangkok about an hour ago to one of his homes to the north."

He made another quiet call on his earphone and pointed to a screen on the wall. It showed a large car, part of a three-car caravan, driving through a gate. I watched a moment and the picture changed to a different camera that showed the three vehicles driving to a small, prop-driven airplane.

As I was about to ask the Top if he could zoom in on the plane, the picture changed, and we had a close-up view of the plane and the cars just parking and doors opening.

Benz Mubane, his security men hovering around him as if he was a rock star, was a man of medium height with a full head of black hair. He appeared a little overweight. He was wearing blue jeans and a white, baggy dress shirt. He was carrying a small attaché case and holding a satellite phone in his right hand. He had been sitting in the backseat of the large car, and, as we watched, a woman dressed in a traditional nurse's uniform climbed out behind him.

She turned and held her hand out to a third person who was also exiting the car. This person looked like a young girl wearing a white, full-length dress or robe with a hood covering her head. I watched anxiously as the girl came into view. As best as I could tell, she had a light complexion, and I could see a small shock of light-colored hair sticking out of the hood. Guards escorted her up and into the plane. The nurse followed her, and then Mubane. Two of the security men climbed on board and the plane's engines began to turn and the plane began to taxi out to the main runway. The picture on the monitor changed a couple of times to follow the aircraft until it ran down the runway and into the sky.

I looked at Sorensen and asked if he thought we had just seen Angela or if it was Mubane's adopted daughter. He stared a little longer at the now blank monitor and shrugged. I asked Top if he had an opinion and he said that he had seen the daughter a few times on video and in photos, but had never seen her in person.

I asked him if he could return to the video of the girl leaving the car and boarding the aircraft. He pressed a couple of buttons on his remote and it fast reversed to the scene of the girl. I asked him to pause it when it showed her profile and a bit of hair. The picture was clear, but the angle was just too severe to make out any facial features. I studied it a bit more and asked Top to slow-forward it as she walked to and climbed on the plane. I asked Sorensen and Top if she looked like a person who was ill and weak. They both shook their heads. I believed we'd had our first real sighting of Angela since I'd begun this case a few days ago.

I asked Top the destination of the plane and he said that it flew to a small airstrip in a city called Uthai Thani. Mubane had a modest compound there right next to a wildlife reserve. Top explained that Mubane supported the maintenance of this reservation. He said that it appeared to be a favorite place for Mubane to visit. He also added that it was remote and well guarded by a security force of former soldiers. The reserve itself had a large complement of armed Rangers.

Top brought up a map on the monitor that showed Thailand and its surrounding countries, including Vietnam. He then zoomed into the western central area of Thailand, not far from the border of Burma, now known as Myanmar. He walked up to the map, pointed to a little symbol of an elephant and explained that this was the reserve. He then pointed to the west of the reserve and said that all that jungle belonged to Mubane and that his house sat right in the middle of where he was pointing. He then pointed to the reserve, took his remote, and highlighted a symbol of an airplane and said that Mubane had just landed there ten minutes ago. He had no cameras set up there yet, but he was working on it.

I asked Top if he had any map printouts of that area so I could study the terrain more closely. He said he would print some. I then asked him if there was a room Sorensen and I could close our eyes for a couple of hours. I was feeling exhausted and could tell Sorensen was, too. He said that two adjoining rooms had already been prepared. He followed that up by saying he had taken the liberty of setting out some equipment we would need to infiltrate Mubane's compound.

I looked at him closely and, before I could even ask, he said he had followed my exploits for a few years, and when Sorensen called him, he knew there was a good chance we would need some combat gear. He added that this was what he did for several visiting marauders. I laughed a bit, and before I became sick and ruined his impression of me, asked for an escort to our rooms.

Top led us down a side hall to another hidden elevator and we dropped down a couple of floors to the hotel-looking area. He took us to a door with, again, no markings on it. He passed his hand over the wall next to the door and the door clicked. A small blue light came on above the door and a hidden panel popped open on the wall where he had first passed his hand. He instructed me to place my hand in the hole until the light above the door turned green. He had Sorensen do the same thing. He explained that doing so gave us the ability to pass through any door in the building, including his office, if necessary.

He pushed the already open door and it opened into a nicely furnished living room and kitchen area. There was a door on each wall to the right and left of the living room. He asked how long we wanted to rest. I asked him how long it would take to prepare transportation to Uthai Thani. He said he could have it set up and ready in three hours. I told him to let us have four hours.

Normally, I would not allow anyone to have knowledge of my mission plans for so long before I went into action, but I felt confident about Top and his discipline, so I let it go for now.

I didn't bother to shower or do much more than kick off my shoes before I dropped down onto the bed. I was out in a flash but a soft computer-generated voice telling me it was time to get up woke me in what seemed like ten minutes. I startled a bit until I remembered what I was up to. I could hear Sorensen outside my door, speaking quietly with someone. I rolled off the bed and onto my feet as I searched for my shoes. Just then, I saw Top through the crack of the door, standing with Sorensen and holding an AR-15 rifle with some added equipment on its barrel. I recognized a high-intensity flashlight on the side and a small laser sight on the top. I have a number of those in my own arsenal on the island. Dave had built most of them and had added various goodies to keep up with trends.

I went into the small bathroom and washed my face. I have a full beard and mustache, but I normally shave around the outside to keep it presentable. I hadn't looked at a razor in days now, and I was looking shaggy. I visited the john, then walked out into the living room. Sorensen looked clean and refreshed. I figured he had taken advantage of the shower I hadn't. He also wore a full beard and always looked shaggy, so no change there.

I could see some equipment laid out on the floor ranging from two satellite phones with walkie-talkies attached to them for short-range communications to the rifles I had mentioned and six banana-type magazines next to each rifle. I figured the magazines held thirty rounds apiece. There were also two backpacks with stuff hanging on them from larger flashlights to compasses and other things I'd discover a use for later. It all looked heavy, and I decided I would dump mine soon after being out of Top's sight.

Just then, there was a quick one-two-three knock on the door. Top swung the door open to reveal two young Thai-looking men dressed in camouflage jungle utility uniforms. They stood at abrupt attention. Top said, "At ease," and they snapped to another, just as uncomfortable, position. He told them to "rest" and come in. They marched in and again assumed their "ease" position in the living room.

Top introduced them as Lieutenants Smith and Jones. He did not indicate who was who. It didn't matter, as they both looked alike, and I wouldn't have figured it out before it was necessary, anyhow. I said hello and told them they could call me by my first name, Sergeant. They both came to attention again and stared into space. I asked Top if these men were going to be working with us and he said they were. I asked him to tell the men to relax, call me Jake or Storm, and Sorensen by his name. I said we had no time to be this formal.

Top briefed us on his latest intel regarding Mubane, including the fact that he and his entire family were at the Uthai Thani compound at present. Even his grown children and some of his grandchildren. He went on to say that there appeared to be a celebration or big family meeting in the works. There were quite a few service people there, as well as a beefed-up security force—apparently, all on short notice, as some of the security crew were coming into the area from all over Thailand, some driving, some on small planes, and a few on private helicopters.

Top explained that all this movement began only about twelve hours ago. That would have been about the time Frank Gowdy had been at the American Embassy, demanding a meeting with the ambassador. I mentioned that to Top and he said that he had information on Gowdy, too. Gowdy had been looking for protection from the ambassador. He was overheard talking to the ambassador's secretary and saying something about being threatened and followed to the embassy.

My first thought was that he had considered Sorensen and me the threat, but Top went on to say Gowdy said something about the ambassador being able to control Mubane. Gowdy had threatened to reveal what he knew regarding the ambassador, and that the ambassador would know what he was talking about. Something must have occurred shortly after Gowdy left us at the Mandarin Hotel. One thing was for sure: Gowdy was dead because of us. I wondered if he had betrayed us or gotten caught trying to help us. If it was the latter, then our element of surprise had been drastically reduced. I decided to deal with that when it came up.

Top went on to say that he had arranged for an aircraft to take us to a remote airstrip near Uthai Thani. From there, we would take a helicopter to the ranger station at the reserve. He passed us each a small stack of papers. He said they were limited hunting permits for the reserve and would get us clearance into the park. Top explained that Lieutenants Smith and Jones were former rangers and knew the reserve well. I wondered what group they were lieutenants in. I would keep a close watch on them so I could make sure they were following, and not chasing, us. This was going to be an interesting trek.

Top had a set of camouflage, jungle-type utility uniforms for Sorensen and me. The old green-toned ones and not the new, digitally themed ones. We quickly changed and I transferred the ledger from my trousers to the newly purchased, backpack, along with my laptop computer. I was thinking about what to do with the ledger. I didn't want to take it into battle with me, and I didn't want to part with it. I was still thinking about it when Top signaled it was time to leave.

We all climbed into a large, black Chevy Suburban in the parking garage. Top said he would escort us to the small airfield they used just out of town. As we drove toward the outskirts of the city, we came upon our hotel. I asked the driver to pull up to the side door for a moment, grabbed my backpack, and ran into the lobby. I walked over to the mall area and found the FedEx kiosk I had noticed earlier. I had made the decision to send the ledger to Gage under one of his many cover names at a mail drop in Cocoa Beach, Florida. I looked around, saw that very few folks were visible from where I was and placed the ledger into a shipping envelope and then into a drop box. I would worry about that envelope until Gage told me that he had received it and it was safely tucked away, awaiting publication.

When I returned to the car, I tried to act nonchalant about what I had done. Sorensen knew, but he and Top were speaking as we drove off toward the small airport. Very few folks knew that I had that ledger, and many would kill to have it destroyed. Top didn't mention my abrupt stop, so I didn't bring it up.

The airstrip was just that—a strip. Not much more than a narrow road that stretched about a mile. I wasn't sure it was all paved, but the part I could see up close looked fairly well maintained. It was so narrow I was sure a normal plane would have to bounce one wheel on the grass shoulder to use it. There was an old hangar or barn at the end closet to us, and we drove toward it. As we approached, I saw the front end of a single-engine plane that looked far too big for this strip. The side of the building had some Thai writing on it and a couple of cartoon characters riding parachutes toward the ground. I hoped it was an advertisement for skydiving and not flight results!

When I got a clear view of the plane through the hangar door, I saw that it was a long-bodied STOW (Short Takeoff and Landing). A great plane for a skydiving club to use. I'd flown in them from time to time in Canada and Alaska. I had taken the controls a few times. This one looked brand new and was equipped with floats to land on water and wheels below the floats for dry landings. I felt much better about the flight now. Especially the float part!

We were guaranteed a soft landing unless the high wing fell off. Top pointed at it and said it belonged to him. A real nice gentleman had given him the cash to have it built about a year ago. He said the old plane they used to use here would scare you to death. He kept the plane well used as a skydiving training area for his associates. He looked at Lt. Smith and Jones as they were loading our gear into the plane. The only thing missing was a pilot. Sure enough, I heard a truck blasting along the entrance road and slide to a stop, just barely missing our feet.

When the dust cleared, the front driver's door of a huge Dodge Ram 3500, diesel, four-door, pick-up truck, opened. This was not made for Thailand, as they drive on the left, just like England and Hong Kong (at least in theory). Out climbed a little—and I mean little—dark-haired kid who appeared to be about ten years old. He looked Hispanic or Middle Eastern or something. I looked in the front seat of the truck to see if he had been sitting on someone's lap, or at least a built-up seat so he could see over the dashboard. Nothing out of the ordinary there.

Puzzled, I looked at Sorensen. I could see him trying to size the kid up himself.

Top walked over to the young man and shook his hand. He turned to us and introduced the man-boy as Captain Tommy Peoples from Nova Scotia. Top saw our concern and laughed. He said that Captain Tommy was far older then he looked and, five months ago, had flown this plane from Vancouver, Canada, across the Bearing Strait, and down the coast of Russia and China to Thailand all alone to deliver the plane on the agreed upon and promised time. Top said Tommy was his star pilot for all his aircraft, including the five helicopters scattered about the country.

The Captain shook everyone's hand with a surprisingly strong grip that I could see from Sorensen's face came close to matching his. He then shook hands with the lieutenants and greeted them as—you guessed it—Smith and Jones. (Maybe those really were their names!)

Captain Tommy climbed up on one of the pontoon floats of the Beaver and hopped into the pilot's seat like a monkey. He buzzed around the switches and gauges as if he was born for this job and shouted, "All aboard."

I shook Top's hand, thanked him, and climbed on up into the rear of the craft. Captain Tommy pointed to the co-pilot's seat and I jumped over the middle console and into the impressive cockpit with far less grace then Tommy had. I could see then that the rudder pedals had been modified for his short legs and the seat was built up a bit. He threw a few switches and the big, nose-mounted engine began to turn over. It caught quickly and roared to life. We were still in the hangar and I wondered if the prop wash would blow any debris around. Tommy didn't seem to be concerned as he advanced the throttle.

Top and his driver were standing next to their Suburban, watching us roll out. Just then, the big Dodge Ram flashed its lights and swung around toward the main road. I hadn't seen anyone in it but Tommy when he drove up, and because of the blacked-out windows, couldn't see anyone now. I turned and looked at Tommy and he said, "Wife."

I put on a headset and listened in as Captain Tommy announced to the air that he was taking off to the east and would be heading north at five thousand feet. That was standard procedure when there was no flight tower at an airport. Tommy pushed the throttle to the stop, and we took off like a shot down the narrow runway. In a blink of an eye, Tommy pulled the yoke back and we shot off. This was no standard Beaver, and Tommy's grin proved that.

I turned and looked at Sorensen, and he smiled back. Smith and Jones appeared to be sleeping and seemed relaxed. Apparently, Top had not filled them in on my reputation for trouble. That was all right with me, as I wanted them rested and ready to go.

After arriving at five thousand feet, Captain Tommy called the local area air control tower and requested clearance to seven thousand feet and passage to the northwest for some skydiving drops. The tower granted him permission and we climbed quickly. He flew for about ten minutes and then request permission to climb to twelve thousand feet. He was again granted permission. At twelve thousand feet, he banked, did a three-sixty, and then dropped like a rock, leveling out at about a thousand feet. He pointed down at a small airstrip just ahead of us and again announced to the air that he was landing at this field to check on a mechanical problem with the aircraft.

I didn't see any other aircraft in the area, and no one answered his announcement. We lined up on the small strip, dropped out of the sky, and right on the runway. We touched down like a feather and stopped about halfway down the short strip. Captain Tommy was sure proud of his aircraft and again grinned from ear to ear when I looked at him.

He shut down the engine and climbed out onto the grassy area next to the old asphalt runway. He took a small black box from his shirt pocket and pushed a button on its front. A moment later, a helicopter lifted above the trees to our right and headed right toward us. It was an old Hughes helicopter—the same copter Sorensen and I flew around in back in Nam so many years ago. It looked a bit dented up and needed some paint, but it sounded fit as it swooped down next to us.

Lieutenants S & J ran our gear over to the bird and saluted the pilot all in one motion. The pilot, a young Asian female, pointed at Tommy and he pointed back. Must be their form of greeting. I quickly shook Tommy's hand and thanked him for the ride. He winked and said he would be standing by for our pickup back to civilization.

Sorensen and I jogged over to the copter and jumped up onto a skid and into the backseat. I'll bet I did that same move a thousand times before. Sorensen knew exactly what I was thinking and nodded at me.

The pilot yelled hello over her left shoulder and spent a little too much time looking at Sorensen. Sorensen noticed and I half expected them to jump out and run into the woods for a few minutes. They didn't. She went to work flying us up and across the treetops to the northwest.

Jones, or perhaps Smith, undid his seatbelt and kneeled in front of Sorensen and me. He shouted to us that when we landed at the ranger station on the preserve, Mubane's security might be there, but not to be alarmed. He said he would do all the talking and would present our permits to the rangers. There could be many other hunters there, waiting to head out for the day. If we looked the part of two excited hunters, we would be all right.

I nodded that I understood—and, Sorensen was staring at the pilot.

Our rifles and ammo gear were in black carry bags, and Sorensen and I had our pistols secured in our pockets—just in case Smith or Jones was wrong about our greeting.

18

We descended toward a large field. I could see a good-sized airstrip about a mile or so long with a few small buildings lining the field. I also saw Mubane's small aircraft—the one we had seen earlier in videos—parked next to the field. There were two other small, multi-passenger aircraft parked next to it.

Our pilot circled the field, made a few comments on her headset we couldn't hear, and then landed about halfway down the strip. She turned and looked at the Smith and Jones team, and one of them motioned for her to hover to the right, away from the other aircraft and Mubane's security force.

I looked over to the Mubane guys and saw they were paying a little too much attention to us and gripping their rifles as if they thought we would steal them. I hooked one of the black bags with my toe and dragged it toward me so I could get to the rifle if needed.

We all watched the security men watch us as our pilot landed and began the procedure of shutting down. Our lieutenants didn't seem overly concerned about the drama going on across the field and jumped from the bird to the ground. One of them looked across the tarmac and yelled something in Thai to the soldiers, and they appeared to relax their bodies a little. At least they were mostly pointing the muzzles of their rifle upward rather than at us.

I didn't relax much and kept them in my peripheral vision as I grabbed one of the black rifle bags and my backpack.

Sorensen was totally engrossed in a conversation with the pilot—I'm sure exchanging numbers and picking out names for their children. I cleared my throat a couple of times until he looked up, said something pleasant to the pilot, and quickly stepped over to me, grinning that *What?* grin. I just shook my head and asked him if he remembered why we were here. He smiled and said we may need a quick pick-up out there and he was attempting to seal a relationship that would keep her from hesitating if we called. That was a really good one, and I told him so. I glanced over to her and, for the first time, saw her standing upright on the ground. Even in her flight suit, I could see most of the curves. She was all but perfect. Sorensen had a good eye and imagination.

Jones or Smith walked over and said we needed to follow them and check in at the Ranger shack. We picked up our gear and hobbled over to the shack. There we had to sign a couple of forms relinquishing the reservation from any responsibility if we got injured, and another form relating to next of kin and where our remains could be sent if there was anything left of us. I wrote down Benz Mubane, care of Bangkok State Prison. I doubted anyone there read or spoke English. In fact, from the looks of the rangers, I was surprised they could talk.

There were four of them with six teeth between them, total. One of them had only one arm and walked with a bad limp. The other three stood there, smiling like village idiots as Jones or Smith spoke with them and handed them our paperwork. The one with only one arm took the papers and held them upside down as he pretended to read them.

Sorensen looked over at me and gave me the rubbing finger movement that signified money. I took out four one-hundred-dollar bills U.S. and passed them around. There was shock on their faces, and at about the time I was thinking we had insulted them, they surrounded us, smiling and patting us on the back and shoulders. I felt like I had just arrived at my Uncle Elwin's annual Thanksgiving dinner—and then quickly wondered if we were being patted down and measured for a coffin. One of our lieutenants said something and they moved back. Some further Thai conversations were exchanged with a few headshakes that led to a "come on" signal, and then we were on our way into the wilderness.

When we were a distance away from the airstrip, the lieutenants, nearly in unison, asked us to let them do the talking and negotiating, if it came up again, saying that that was what they were paid to do. I apologized, gave Sorensen a dirty look, and tried to look remorseful. I'm not sure Jones and Smith fully grasped what we had accomplished back there, but I knew we had made some new paid-for loyal friends. We were the geese that could lay golden eggs anytime we decided to hunt their reservation. I also knew that they had given Jones and Smith some intelligence, as I'd seen their eyes quickly glance at the security guys during the questioning.

We walked for nearly two hours through paths that were clearly marked. There were even rest areas with roofs and benches about every half-mile or so. It was during the fourth or fifth rest area that we stopped and one of the lieutenants took out a small GPS and stood in the clear for a moment. He then pulled a small map out of his backpack and showed us our destination. I asked him where we were, and he pointed in the complete opposite direction of the airstrip some miles away. I now knew what we had done and why.

He started to explain that we had needed to put on a show and show a lack of any interest in Mubane's compound in order to discourage any tail that they might have placed on us. I signaled that I understood and asked if it was now time to go to work. He smiled and pointed to a small path beside the shed and said that was south. As he held up the GPS, he said that we would follow this trail about a mile and turn west, bypassing the airstrip and main road for about four miles until we reached the edge of the reservation and Mubane's property.

My backpack and the rifle carrier were getting heavy by then, but I nodded and headed out. Sorensen had taken his rifle out, unfolded it into its functional position and strapped it over his shoulder. He had distributed his ammunition clips and the food in his ration boxes across all his spare pockets. He'd thrown whatever else was in the rifle bag into the bushes. I decided to do the same thing but kept the small first aid kit clipped to my waistband.

It had been a while since I had called and briefed the Major, so I took out my satellite phone and speed-dialed his cell phone. The signal was clear enough even in the rather thick overhang of trees. He answered on the second ring and sounded a bit out of breath. I didn't bother to ask him what he was up to as I could well imagine, knowing him. I asked if this was a good time and he said, "Sure."

I gave him the basics in our code speak and he got the general idea of what we hoped to accomplish. He filled me in on his briefs to Thom Cohen and said Gage had been in touch with him earlier regarding what I had just told him. We signed off with the usual, with me asking him to brief the Cohens and try to reassure them that we felt positive at this point.

We trudged along at a good pace. It was a little easier now, not having to carry the rifle bag in front of me. I also took advantage of the food rations and ate a couple of energy bars. Our backpacks were equipped with water pouches. All we had to do was suck on a tube at our shoulders to get a drink. The more I drank, the lighter the load.

We reached the turn to the west and rested for a few minutes. The lieutenants were still fresh and dry. Sorensen and I were soaked with sweat and puffing like spent horses. I took the time to check my gear and the action on my rifle. It injected and ejected fine. The firing pin was intact, and the rounds looked clean and shiny. I would normally not go into combat without testing my weapons, but there had been no time, and I trusted Top had taken care of us. I checked the hand grenade in my pocket by feel. It was secure and only a little damp from my sweat. I'd kept it a secret from our two companions as a little security measure, and, apparently, Sorensen was thinking the same thing. I could see him fiddling in the pocket where he had three or four. He glanced at me as he did it and looked back at the trail ahead of us.

We climbed back to our feet and followed the guys west. It wasn't long before Jones or Smith motioned us to stop and then took off at a swift pace down the trail. He disappeared a moment later, and we got another break. I had gathered my second or third wind and only squatted on the edge of the trail. Sorensen stayed standing and tilted his head slightly like he does to focus on the jungle sounds. I've seen him do this so many times in the Nam, and it normally means trouble is coming.

Sure enough, the lieutenant came jogging back up the trail and pointing to the side, signaling us to get over and down. He didn't have to tell me or Sorensen twice. Silently, we jumped over some brush and into some thick ferns. The lieutenant reached our position, jumped to the opposite side of the trail and disappeared. About three minutes later, four heavily armed Thai security men, most certainly Mubane's, came up the trail at a quick pace.

Sorensen had his silenced .22 caliber pistol at the ready, and I was aiming down my rifle barrel in the general direction of the guards. I looked over at the lieutenant on our side and he shook his head no. I gave the same signal to Sorensen. They walked right on by. Their lucky day, for sure.

Sorensen could have put them all down with four quick silent shots if they had even looked in our direction.

After they had passed and we could no longer hear them, we gathered next to the trail. The lieutenant scout said he had heard them coming up the trail and that there may be more. He explained that with Mubane and his guests at the compound, security was tight, and we should expect more encounters. I asked him to show me his GPS again so I could get a good feel for where we were and where the compound was. Sure enough, we were about a half-mile from it as the crow flies.

I suggested that we cut cross-country until we could get a peek at the perimeter security, seeing how the trail was apt to get very busy the closer we got to the main road. Our equipment was secured, so we were silent as we walked, unlike the guards that we could still hear from time to time clinking and clunking a quarter of a mile away in the jungle.

The lieutenants agreed and we began to slip through the brush toward our objective at a far slower pace than the open trails. Most of the brush was thick and lush and made very little noise as we cut through it. The ground soft and quiet under our feet. Very few sticks to snap and cause us to pause. Toe, heel, toe, heel. The Marines walked that way all over the Pacific, and they managed to sneak up on the enemy even though they were waiting and watching. It works great until that one little stick snaps and sounds to your mind like a bat hitting a baseball. I must admit that the lieutenants had no real walking discipline and made most of the noise. Still, the ground was nearly perfect for silent passage, and I liked that just fine.

Shortly, we came to a smooth trail running east and west. It was covered in fresh footprints. Suddenly, we could smell the compound before we saw the clearing. Food cooking. Also, the sound of voices yelling and laughing. Some kids must have been swinging on a metal swing, making the whining noise they do as they went back and forth. We crawled closer until we could peek from behind the ground cover and see the main house.

It was huge, and there were four or five smaller buildings surrounding the main house. I counted about thirty people on the porch or on the grounds around it. Sorensen pointed to the far eastern end of the compound. There I saw a large, barn-type building that only had a small, regular door on the front. There were several air conditioners on the side, which implied that there were several rooms inside that needed cooling. There were two armed guards standing on both sides of the door. They were paying attention to the crowds at the house. I pointed to the barn and nodded a yes to Sorensen, and then signaled everyone to move back.

It was all but completely dark now, and I could barely see my hand in front of my face. We had moved about a hundred yards east. We were nearly even with the front of the barn. I peeked out at the guards and saw that they were fidgeting around with boredom and fatigue. I don't know how long they had been on duty but they and Mubane must have felt really secure with a company of troops wandering around the woods on the perimeter. We had heard the troops pass a few times as we lay there, waiting for total darkness.

I looked at Sorensen and told the lieutenants to stay where they were to cover us. They looked reluctant, but I knew Sorensen and how he moved, and I was not completely impressed by the lieutenants' footwork. I told them that if we ran into trouble, to fire at the front of the big house first and cause some panic. I emphasized the house, not the people, and then told them to take out any guards they could see and not us. I told them that I had a good fix on our position and, if separated, would meet them at the point in the trail that led us west.

One of the lieutenants took out a small night-vision monocular and looked at the barn. He said he would whistle once if someone came from the west and twice if from the east. We agreed and Sorensen and I went into action. I took the lead and headed right for the south side of the building. There was a lot of noise coming from the house and grounds around it. That and the sounds of the air conditioners gave us great cover. It would also make it difficult to hear a whistle, should they signal us. There was so much light around the houses that if any of the guards were using a night scope, it would be useless.

I crawled back along the side of the barn and avoided the air conditioning units as best I could. There was only a small area from the wall to the brush and cutting through the brush would take too long. We made it to the back of the barn and peeked around. It was the same as the front— one door and two guards.

I needed to see inside that building, and the guards were certainly a deterrent. I weighed my options, but before I came to any conclusion, Sorensen fired two shots and the guards fell straight down on the ground. It was the same conclusion I would have made, but now it was a moot point. I looked at Sorensen and, even in the dark, felt his shrug.

We crawled behind the building and to the door and the very dead guards. I took one and Sorensen the other, and, together, we placed them in the brush and out of sight. I scanned the roofline and wall for any hidden cameras and saw none. Both the guards had walkie-talkies attached to their belts, and we took them. We didn't understand Thai, but we did understand excitement when we heard it. One of the guards was very young, and I felt bad for him for a moment—until I saw what they were guarding.

The door was locked, but before I could go back to the guards to see if there was a key on them, Sorensen grabbed the doorknob with his huge, vice-like hands and twisted the knob right off. The door swung gently open. The inside was brightly lit. There was a small mudroom with a couple of trashcans lined with white plastic bags and a couple of lab coats on hooks hanging behind another door on the opposite wall. I could see some bloody gauze pads in the trashcans, as well as some used latex gloves. I went to the next door and listened but could only hear the air conditioners whirling. The door was unlocked, and I pulled it back a couple of inches while Sorensen stood there with his silenced pistol at the ready.

I saw the back of a female dressed in scrubs. She was sitting at a desk two steps away from the door. I pulled the door open a bit more and saw only a hallway and various doors to the left and right. I showed Sorensen one finger and pointed beyond the door. Just then, she turned, looked at me, and was about to scream when I reached out with my right hand and grabbed her by the throat. I yanked her right up out of her seat and punched her squarely in the left temple. Not hard enough to kill her, but enough to send her into dreamland for a while.

Sorensen grabbed her from me, pulled her into the back room and placed her on the floor. There was a crash cart full of medical supplies next to her desk and I grabbed some rolls of gauze and white tape. I went back to her prone body on the floor and tied her up like a mummy. I shoved about ten of the soiled latex gloves into her mouth and taped it shut.

Sorensen took the left-hand doors and I took the right, opening and searching for more surprises. Sorensen whistled quietly, and when I looked over, he motioned for me to look inside. There were three bodies on gurneys with various openings in their bodies where certain organs ought to be but had been harvested. The first thing I noticed was that they were both young Caucasian-looking girls, maybe twelve to fifteen years old. No one had even bothered to cover them up in reverence. Both had gauze pads over their eyes, and when I lifted one of the pads, I saw that their corneas were missing. Neither of them was Angela.

We continued up the hall, and when I was at the second to last door on my side, I heard a whimper. Sorensen heard it too and lifted his pistol. I squatted down low and pushed the door open. Sorensen pointed the gun into the room and then quickly lifted it up toward the ceiling. I twisted around the doorframe and looked in to see a young girl with dark hair sitting on a small bed. She was tied to the bed with leather restraints around her wrists. She, too, was wearing gauze eye patches. I went to her side and she said hello in English. She wasn't Angela, but she was American, and couldn't be any older than ten. I told her not to be afraid, as I was there to help her. She sat up straighter and I unbuckled her restraints. She reached up to me and felt my face and beard. I took her hands in mine and told her we were going to take her away from here. Asked her if she could walk, and she said she could.

She stood up and asked if we had found her sister. My heart skipped a beat as I pictured the young girls in the room down the hall. I didn't answer her, and she asked me again just as Sorensen came to the door and asked if her name was Janie. She looked toward Sorensen and said she was. He said that her sister, Pattie, was across the hall from her. Janie took a step toward me and I guided her through the door. Sorensen had her sister Pattie and we guided them together. I whispered to them both to be very quiet as there were bad guys very close.

They hugged and held each other for a moment, and then we guided them to the rear door. I quietly asked Sorensen if there were any more girls, and he signaled two and then shook his head to mean they were lost.

As we passed into the rear room, I stopped them and whispered for them to stay for a minute. I ran quietly to the front of the building and took out my hand grenade. I pinched the pin tabs open, grabbed a roll of gauze, tied one end to the grenade pin, and then wrapped the other end around the doorknob of the door to the outside. I carried the grenade and gauze into the closest room and placed the grenade on the floor behind the door. I closed the door and tightened the gauze on the outside door handle before tying it off. Someone—or more than one—would come to make the rounds in a while, especially when the two deceased guards failed to check in. When they opened the front door, it would pull the pin and...you get the picture. I learned that from an old Viet Cong friend of mine. I had used it successfully before. I probably would have used it more often, but hand grenades were hard to come by.

I ran back to Sorensen and he smiled a bit. We directed the girls out the back door, and I saw right away that the white hospital gowns they were wearing stood out brightly in the limited light. I jumped over to the two deadies, quickly removed their camouflage jackets, and brought them to the sisters. I wrapped the jackets around them. I picked up Janie and Sorensen picked up Pattie. We duck-walked up the side of the building to where our lieutenants were hiding and whistled gently to them. We then crossed over into the brush and found the guys kneeling there, waiting for us. Each took a girl from us, and then we moved farther into the brush before the alarm went off.

When we were a distance away from the compound, we stopped and set the sisters on the ground. We helped them put the jungle jackets on properly and explained that we had a long way to walk. I told them to lift their feet high as they walked to avoid tripping on any vines. Pattie whispered that they had stolen their eyes. She went on to say they saw the two men that were to get their eyes. She said they were old, mean men and slapped Janie when she talked back to him.

I asked them the men's last names and they said in unison, "Miller." I asked the sisters where they were from. Janie said Tampa, Florida. I stopped questioning them and told them to be super quiet from here on out.

I looked back over the brush to the glowing lights and thought about Angela. Just then, Jones or Smith told me he had received a message from Top that the girl I was searching for was seen in Phuket Island the day before, and that he had a lead as to where they were keeping her. That took some of the pressure off, as now we could concentrate on getting these young ladies safely out and, hopefully, to an American Consulate office to send them home.

One of the lieutenants was whispering into his satellite phone in English and calling for a pickup. He had an earbud in his ear, so we couldn't hear the response. It must have been positive as he grabbed his GPS, held it up, and pointed through the jungle to the south. He went on to say our pilot was about an hour away and heading in our direction.

I was hoping for a path for the ladies to walk on, but they did very well in keeping their balance in the underbrush we had to cross. They stumbled a few times but quickly recovered with a gentle hand from one of us.

We were about a mile from the rendezvous spot with the helicopter when we heard a very loud explosion. I would have recognized my hand grenade anywhere! I hoped it had greeted many folks going over to the clinic barn for a tour.

Smith or Jones spoke into the phone again and then told us our pilot had heard a lot of chatter coming from other helicopters taking off from a field behind the compound. She said they were doing a search and destroy mission on the area around the compound and the reservation to the east. As he relayed this info to us, we heard a copter heading right toward us. The lieutenants again picked up the girls and began to run far faster than Sorensen and I could toward the south. We did our best to keep up and keep the noise down. The search helicopter was running a sweeping pattern back and forth, which told me they were using an infrared camera.

Just when we thought our goose was cooked and the bird was just about on us, a streak of fire jetted through the air and blew the helicopter to fine bits right before our very eyes. It was such a bright flash that Janie said she saw the light. I had been hoping their eyes could be repaired with new corneas, and that remark gave me some hope.

Just then, we heard the whine of the Huey in front of us. Jones or whoever he was waved us forward and then fell behind. Meanwhile, we guided the girls toward the sound of the hovering helicopter. Just as we arrived at the skids, we heard gunfire behind us. We lifted the girls into the bird and yelled at the pilot to give us only three minutes and then take off and get these kids to an American official. She nodded and Sorensen and I then ran back toward the shooting—not right at it, though. We circled around and out of the line of fire.

I saw the guards' muzzle flashes and heard the familiar sounds of the AKs they were firing. Our guys returned fire from the ground. No one seemed to be hitting anything meaningful, so I looked at Sorensen and he nodded at me. We went to town cutting down everything between us and the bad guys. They were slow to notice the additional firing and, as a result, they, too, went down.

Everything became silent as a grave. I shouted over the silence to the boys to gather their toys and let's go home. They both jumped up and ran toward the copter. Sorensen and I crossed back over and jumped aboard just as she pulled the throttle back and we lifted up. I could see one of our lieutenants holding his leg above his knee, and when I touched it, it felt damp and sticky. I guess the bad guys had gotten a low score, but a score, nonetheless.

I turned on the low wattage light that was on the back of the co-pilot's seat and examined the wound. It was bleeding and needed dressing. I pulled out the little first aid kit on my belt and opened it to find a compress and some gauze. The bandage was a little small for the job and, as I was about to cut off his trouser leg to use as a compress, Ms. Pilot threw a bigger combat first aid kit filled with goodies over the seat. I could have removed his appendix if he wanted! I decided not to say anything like that. Under the circumstances, he wouldn't consider it funny. I taped him up and he drank some water. He lay there quietly as we flew over treetops heading toward what I believed to be the west.

I leaned up into the cockpit and asked her where we were headed, and she said a small city in Burma, now known as Myanmar, about halfway to Rangoon. She said we were headed to a small U.S. Naval Base that operated a rescue post there for boats and aircraft. She yelled back that it was the closest American facility we could fly to. She shouted that the Top suggested she not land in Thailand anywhere near the Mubane compound, for obvious reasons.

I agreed and asked her if we could get the ladies out of there in a hurry. She said there was a small airstrip there that received naval mail and a supply plane every day. The girls would be safe as soon as we put down as it was rumored that some of the rescue team at the base were Seals. I figured the girls couldn't be any safer.

As we flew out of Thai airspace, I grabbed my little satellite phone and called Gage. He answered on the first ring. I had no idea what time it was there, but he was pleasant. I quickly filled him in, gave him the girls' names, and told him they were from Tampa. As we were talking, he must have pulled up their info on his computer because he said they went missing about three months ago from a church group that had floated down some river near Sarasota. I thought of Francis Schultz and figured he was at the root of many missing kids. I felt even better having rid the world of his ugly soul.

I told Gage where we were headed and that we had some info on Angela being down in south Thailand. I didn't mention to Gage that the girls had no corneas for fear their parents would find out before they were properly prepared for it. Some politician might grab up the info and buy some votes by condemning the practice. It never ceased to amaze me at what the politicians would grab hold of and use as their original idea. ("Gun Control." Take guns away from people and no more shootings. Right.)

Very soon, the helicopter began to lose altitude as we approached the U.S. Naval base that no one had ever heard of. I think she called it Point Something, but I didn't catch it. I stuck my head up between the seats and asked her where she got the air-to air-missile that had destroyed the search copter, and she looked back and said it wasn't her. Come to think of it, I hadn't seen a rocket launcher attached to the copter. It seemed guardian angels were watching over this entire case.

I sure was not complaining. I was curious, but not displeased. If someone could arrange all these minor miracles, then why didn't they just do the case themselves? I leaned over to Sorensen and told him his girlfriend hadn't fired the missile. I asked him if there was some invisible force out there that I didn't know about. He said he had never heard of a Navy Rescue Base in Burma. I thought about that, too. I told him that if there just happened to be a small jet waiting to fly us back to Thailand, I was going to freak!

Well, I didn't have to freak, as there was only a small, twin-engine prop plane waiting for us. When we asked the pilot why he was here, he said that several bases had been alerted that there might be an important extraction in the next couple of days, and he thought it might be us. I told him I wasn't buying it and he just put on a poker face and walked toward his aircraft.

Sorensen was disappointed that we weren't spending the night as he had love in his eye for our Ms. Pilot. That was a real shame for poor Sorensen, but good for Angela, as we were closing in on her.

19

Our lieutenants turned invisible as soon as we landed. They didn't even give me a chance to thank them or invite them to the BBQ the Major holds every year to celebrate all his successful endeavors. It's a pretty large affair, and even I have become fond of it, but I still find it embarrassing to be thanked year after year for just doing my job. Did I mention I am not cheap?

Sorensen said he needed to find a head and was gone a little longer than it should have taken. When he returned, his cheeks looked a bit flushed and Ms. Pilot was nowhere to be found. That quick. What a guy!

I noticed a few fifty-five-gallon drums of jet fuel next to the runway and a hand pump sticking out of one of them. I wondered how far offshore the Navy or Marine carrier was that had launched that missile. I figured I should question Top a bit more thoroughly when I saw him next.

I saw that our new ride was looking ready to roll, and the pilot was just standing there, looking at us. I couldn't see any tail numbers on his plane, and as I looked around, I wondered where the Naval Rescue Force was. We appeared to be the only live souls on the base—if it really was a base. Just when I thought it was all smoke and mirrors, a very large helicopter came out of nowhere and landed about a hundred yards up the beach from where we were.

I saw the girls, accompanied by our Ms. Pilot, walk out of a small building and head for the big bird. I started to run over to the girls to wish them well when Sorensen grabbed my arm and said it was better to stay clear for now and not see the folks on the bird. He said the girls would be fine and would love me forever. I looked at him and saw the wisdom of his advice. There was going to be a big stink in this world very soon, and I would rather go bask on my island than have reporters and thrill seekers hounding me. The fewer folks who saw us, the less chance the bad guys get to hound us for retribution.

I whispered, "Be well my lovelies," and let it go. I'm sure I'd get a report from Gage on our next meeting.

I punched Sorensen on the arm and asked if he was ready for some real adventure now as we walked over to the waiting aircraft. The pilot said he had heard some rebel group had attacked a group of rich vacationers, leaving some of them dead and causing a very expensive private helicopter to crash. I told him we certainly didn't want to be associated with that mess and then climbed aboard.

Sorensen sat down, buckled in, and was sound asleep before we even taxied. I waited until we were airborne and fell off soundly. The drone of the plane was soothing, and I didn't move until I heard the engines change pitch as we came in for a landing. I wasn't sure where we were, but I was sure whoever choreographed this adventure had a plan. Sorensen woke when the wheels touched down, but only a small shift in his position indicated that.

As we taxied toward some hangars, I noticed Sorensen change the magazine in his silent .22 and slip it back into one of his side pockets. I had no idea what happened to the rifles on the helicopter—or anything else for that matter. They belonged to Top, but I am sure he did not keep a formal inventory! I missed my hand grenade and hoped it didn't have to live for eternity with the folks it took down. I asked Sorensen for one of his. He flipped one at me and I nearly missed catching it. Wouldn't that be a chapter closer?

The pilot yelled back at us that there were civilian clothes hanging behind the seats and he suggested that we change before we got off. There they were, right size and style. Polo with jeans for me. Brown jungle pants and a yellow, XXXX-sized, Havana-style top for Sorensen, just like he always wore—suggesting that this, too, was all well planned. Had to be Top.

The pilot stopped outside a large hangar and shut down the engines. No one ran out to service the plane or secure it. We just stopped and the pilot pointed to a small car next to the building and said the keys were over the visor. I saluted him and we deplaned.

I told Sorensen he could drive, and I would operate the GPS on my phone. I figured we had about two hours before sunup and needed the cover of darkness to find our way to the address Top had texted us. I knew we were close to Angela. I could feel it in my bones. I really hoped she was still in one piece.

I punched in the address of this Mubane compound and my phone showed where it was in relation to our present position, and then verbally directed us off the airfield and toward the lights of the city.

Sorensen and I were down to two pistols for him and one for me. I had one hand grenade in my pocket and my .9MM tucked into my waistband. This was far too light for possible action. I asked Sorensen to pull over a moment and pop the trunk. Sure enough, there were rifle bags and other goodies tucked inside. I also found a couple of walkie-talkies like the ones we'd taken from the deadies at the jungle clinic and left on the plane when we changed clothes. I hoped Top would find them and their frequencies helpful. I brought the little communicators back with me into the car and handed one to Sorensen. He stuck it in his pocket and asked if we had a supply of hardware back there. I said, "Yup," and he drove off.

We drove for a while and listened to the lady on the phone direct us in and out of side streets. I was sure someone had put a joke application on my phone because I thought I was seeing the same buildings and signs time and time again.

Suddenly, our tour guide announced that our destination was coming up on the right. Sorensen pulled over on his side of the road—meaning the right, as that was where the steering wheel was. He backed into a slot between two cars and shut down the engine. We both jumped out and went to the trunk that he had popped as he was climbing out. We each took a rifle bag and zipped them open. On top of a sweet looking, fully outfitted AR-15, there was a night vision scope and a couple of pistols, both fully silenced. One was a .22 automatic like the one Sorensen had in his pocket, and the other was a higher caliber .380 automatic.

The next item was my newly purchased laptop and my own little backpack. I quickly inventoried it and saw that my numerous passports and credit cards were in place and my collection of driver's licenses still wrapped with a rubber band that has lasted about five years. I put rubber bands around nearly everything I carry to keep them from working their way out of my pockets or being lifted by some sticky-fingered opportunist. This rubber band was the champion of them all. It had outlasted all the others by years. If I could only remember where I'd lifted it, I would buy some!

We left the rifles in the trunk and took the night vision monocles and silenced pistols. Now Sorensen had three and I had two. I felt like I was catching up! We could see a tall wall on the right that our GPS identified as our destination. Even Sorensen couldn't see over it. There were no trees to climb and no telephone poles to shimmy up. I could see a gate in the center of the wall, and a closer look revealed a camera next to the gate to identify anyone ringing the bell.

We walked back to the end of the wall and followed it to the back. There was water back there. In fact, there was a whole ocean. The compound was backed up to the beach, though it wasn't so much a "beach" as a marsh area. The back corner of the wall was washed out a bit, and there was a hole just big enough to crawl through—at least for me. Sorensen was a little larger and wider. I bent down and pulled some more sand out of the opening until it looked wide enough to accommodate my large friend.

The tide was out and the sand dry. I went through first and hid behind a group of bushes. Sorensen came next and set down beside me. There were four buildings and a large house backed up to the rear seawall. There were few lights on, but there were cameras at each corner of the smaller buildings. They were pointed down toward the ground as if watching the building and its occupants. I scanned the big house with the night scope and saw a couple of cameras pointed toward the seawall, but none pointed toward the inside of the compound.

I shone the scope toward the gate and saw three guards standing there, talking quietly to each other. They were very casual and had their rifles in slings over their shoulders. Again, those nasty AKs. One of the buildings had a roll-up garage door with an ambulance front end sticking out. It had all the bells and whistles, including a red-light bar. I figured this was where they delivered the unwilling victims for body stripping.

From where we were, there was no way to sneak over to the buildings for a peek. The bushes we were hiding behind ran the length of the wall as far as we could see, but there were bare spots that would leave us fully exposed when we crossed them. I was also sure that the security lights that were now out would blaze on as soon as they sensed our body heat. We needed a clear view of the area to see whatever human traffic frequented these buildings. The security was light, at least from what we could see. One of the buildings had security monitors for the cameras; that meant there was a guardroom or office of security.

I looked again and saw no egress except a full-out charge using the element of surprise. As I scanned the walls, I noticed a tall building across the street at the front of the compound. It had a flat roof and a low wall with castle-like revetments every two feet or so. These were old decorations, but they might give us some good cover during the day while we surveyed the compound to discover its weak spots.

I was also sure that the blonde, sickly-looking girl we thought might be Angela on the video at Top's office was, in fact, Mubane's adopted daughter. I had a feeling that after the scare at the compound, with so many folks dying and wounded, no one would be in the mood for any organ transplant drama anytime soon. That would buy us some time to regroup.

Sorensen and I crawled out under the fence and went back to the car. We each grabbed a couple of waters and some more rations. I ate an energy bar right away and stuffed some in my pockets. Sorensen grabbed a few other items that we may need. I took one of the black rifle bags and unfolded the AR-15 inside and loaded it. I stuffed it back in and slung the bag over my shoulder.

We both relieved ourselves next to the car, and I thought about how bad I must smell after our trek through the jungle and fantasized about a nice hot shower. Maybe there would be a nice hot tub on the building's roof that we were about to climb. Sorensen moved the car to the other side of the road and into a better parking spot, so it pointed away from the compound in case we needed to make a quick getaway. We walked down a side street and reversed ourselves a few times until we arrived at the old building.

I did a little scouting around the outside and peeked through the dirty windows. It appeared to be vacant, with a few old boxes on the floor inside. I was concerned that Mubane may have some security folks set up on the upper floors, but none of the doors appeared to have been opened in years.

I made my way around the opposite side to Sorensen and found that he had already opened a small window at ground level. This window led to the lower basement area, and a quick flash of my flashlight showed just a mess of old boxes and columns that held up the structure. I slipped in and scooted down to the cement floor. Sorensen followed and I saw he had the small night scope to his eye and was looking for any heat signatures that might greet us. He studied the massive room for a while and then pointed to our right. I looked through the gloom and saw the dark shape of a staircase. I hoped they were cement and not old rotted wood. There was just enough light to see the shapes of the boxes and columns and to keep us from skinning our knees on our shuffle to the stairs.

Sorensen kept peeking through the night scope and guiding us along. When we got to the stairs, I was relieved to see they were, in fact, cement and clear of any debris. Sorensen looked up the stairs with his night scope and then took out a small flashlight with a red lens over the beam. There was a door at the top of the stairs that was partially open and lots of cobwebs crisscrossing from wall to wall. In this case, the spiders were our friends! They can weave webs in a few minutes, but the older webs give you a clue as to how long it has been since the area has been visited.

We climbed the stairs and attempted to duck under the webs so we wouldn't reveal our recent visit. Sorensen really disliked spiders and tried to avoid the webs altogether. I wasn't fond of getting bit by them but ignored them for the most part. Most folks don't realize how many insects house spiders consume in one day. They just get the official family spider killer to remove them as soon as they are spotted. I didn't move any of the little webbers' efforts as we climbed.

The first floor that we came to was much like the basement. Empty boxes and old pieces of furniture were scatted about. Some side rooms must have been office space or storage at one time. I reflected on World War II and imagined that this building surely pre-dated that. The boxes were the old type of non-perforated thicker paper and were mostly drooping from age, and the windows were so dirty that they looked painted over.

Sorensen weaved across the room to a window and rubbed a circle about the size of a small quarter in the grime. He peeked out and pointed up. As we walked past the building entranceway and toward the stairs, I saw that someone had recently pushed the door open from the outside. The debris on the floor was skimmed back in a half circle and there were footprints coming and going. From the sight of them, these prints were made after the last rainstorm, whenever that was.

That dawned on me, too. We had been here nearly two days now and there had been no rain. I seemed to remember that in Nam, a couple of countries over, it rained a lot this time of year. The rain was your friend when you were sneaking about, as it covered the sounds of your footsteps and showed prints you could either follow or avoid as you chose. I said a little prayer to the rain god to help us out a bit when we needed to cross to the compound.

The building was six floors high—seven, counting the basement. We climbed up and scanned each floor as best we could until we got to the fifth floor. Each time we got to a floor, Sorensen would go to the front of the building and look out the windows to check its vantage point to the compound across the way. From the second floor to where we were on the fifth had been all open office space. There were a few old desks and tables scattered about and a lot of paperwork on the desks and floor. I held up some of the papers to the limited light but found they were all in Thai with some English addresses. Mostly shipping forms to San Francisco, Oakland, and Los Angeles. No clue what they were selling until Sorensen found a box of photos showing various groups of people posing in front of the building. They were mostly Thai, with a few westerners posing with them.

The interesting part was there was an American Flag on a post right in the middle of the posers, and it was old. Old enough to have only forty-eight stars. So pre-Fifties, if I didn't miss my guess. I shuffled around further in the box and found another shot that pointed the other way showing the compound across the way. It too had an American flag flying high over the new looking wall and roofs of the buildings. I looked at Sorensen and suggested that this building must have been an American business or office complex back in the day. The flying of the flag normally indicated official American soil. If it had been a normal business owned by an American interest, they would have flown the Thai flag. I wondered who brokered the selling of the compound to Mubane, and when.

As I was looking at the compound across the way, I noticed a windsock on a post on the roof of the main building. There must be a helicopter landing pad in the compound somewhere. That was not a good sign for us, as we had planned to lie on the roof while surveying the area. A helicopter could come out of nowhere and catch us clearly out on the open roof. I told Sorensen that we had better set up shop where we were. It was clearly high enough to observe the compound, and we could shift back and forth from window to window for better views, as needed. It also afforded us the ability to stand up instead of crawling about on the roof.

I could see the first streaks of light coming from the rising sun in the east. I got a better look at the compound and the buildings within the walls. The main house was three stories high and one other building was two stories. The other three small buildings were one story each and looked more like work sheds than offices or clinics. I guessed that the two-story building was the clinic and the most likely place they were housing Angela.

As I looked closer in the better light, I saw that the east wall was also a building or had a couple of rooms built into it. This was where we saw our first signs of life. One of the guards from the front gate walked across the compound, entered through one of the doors in the wide wall, and came out a few moments later with another guard who lit a cigarette just outside the door. The new guy was in the process of tucking in his shirt and adjusting his trousers. I saw that he, too, was a guard. That told us that more than likely, the two doors would lead to the security office and the barracks for the guards.

I had been on the side of that wall earlier and saw no exit door anywhere; that meant the only entrance and exits were inside the compound. The only windows were in the doors, which meant that the people inside had a limited view. That was good.

I also saw that the hole through which we had gained access to the compound was out of sight of the guard office but was clearly in sight of the front gate guards. The guards had a number of slits in the walls they could use as sighting holes and which allowed them to see left and right of the gates as they were set back on the inside of the wall and not at the front. The slits also allowed the guards to see up and down the road in both directions.

We couldn't see the guards unless they were standing in front of the gate openings. Then again, they couldn't see us, either. I cleared the grime a little more so I could observe a wider field of vision, and Sorensen did the same a few windows over. I moved an old desk chair over and sat down. Sorensen remained standing and moved from window to window. He walked around the entire floor area and looked out from every side of the building.

As the sun came up outside and gave us light, I could see where we had walked over the dusty floor. I could also see some other footprints from whoever had come in the front door before us.

I moved about the space while Sorensen observed the compound and found more photos scattered about. They showed a few Thais standing in line at the front entrance of the building. I could also see a plaque on the wall that resembled an American Embassy or Consulate seal. I figured that the compound could have been an embassy retreat and the building we were in could have housed the staff workers. Right now, though, I was more concerned with the activities across the road in the compound.

When the sun had cleared the horizon, we saw a lot more activity around the buildings.

We could smell food cooking and the strong smell of coffee coming from the compound. A woman came out of one of the small buildings pushing a stainless-steel food cart, like the ones you see on passenger planes. There were four chafing dishes and a stainless coffee carafe. The shelf underneath had cereal type boxes and other containers. I hoped she was headed over to us, as I could smell the bacon clearly. Sorensen took out an energy bar and a small bottle of water. I followed suit and we feasted on chocolate and nuts.

The added light in the room gave us a better view of our surroundings. There were many footprints, just as we saw earlier. I walked over and saw where something heavy with sharp feet, much like a machine gun stand, had been sitting on a desk. I looked at Sorensen and we both moved at the same time toward the stairs.

When we arrived on the next floor, I walked to the front of the room and looked out toward the compound. Just in time, I saw two men pass out of my line of vision below the window and heard the front door open. Sorensen took out his pistol and ducked down behind a desk. I walked over to the staircase and ducked under it while we listened to the men walking up from below.

I could see two guards through a crack between the stairs and the wall. One was carrying what looked like an M60 machine gun, and the other had an ammo can and a tripod. They climbed on past us to the upper floor. They had no sound discipline as they were talking loudly and clomping their feet on the floor. I listened to the gun being prepared and loaded. They would be pointing it right out the window and toward the entrance gate to the compound.

It was clear this wasn't an ongoing routine, as there were too few footprints up there. One or two days, tops. That meant Mubane or his advisers were beefing up their security. I guessed we were being noticed around his circle of friends.

Sorensen and I were fairly protected from discovery by the guys above us, but we wouldn't be at all safe once we left the building and ventured into the compound using the hole in the rear wall, which had been our first plan. So far, we had counted five guards on duty at a time. Those were good odds for us; bad for them. I knew Sorensen could walk up to the gate and kill all three in a flash. We could certainly take care of the two guys upstairs from us.

I had been listening for any radio calls that might indicate a pattern that we had to work around. About an hour after they were in place, I heard a screech and a radio voice speaking Thai. One of our neighbors answered in kind and the transmissions ended. I timed it until the next call. One-hour check-ins. We waited another hour and the pattern repeated itself. One hour was plenty of time for us to get in and out before the person on the other end of the calls pushed the panic button. The next question was...when did the gate guards check in, or were they on the other end of these calls from the machine gunners? I was also concerned as to why there weren't any guards stationed in the building at night. A few moments after that thought, I had my answer, for two large vans came bumping down the street and stopped at the gate.

Our friends upstairs began talking excitedly and shuffling their feet. I could hear the tripod holding the gun shift on the table as it was moved. The gates opened wide and the vans pulled through. They stopped in front of the large house and flung the doors open. Eight people climbed out. Four from each van, including the drivers. Three in each van were dressed in hospital scrubs. The drivers were in civilian clothes but carrying automatic pistols in shoulder holsters.

The medical folks stood in front of the building until a man in his late fifties or older came out onto the porch. He stood there a moment and began to speak. We couldn't hear him, but I was sure he was speaking Thai, so it made no difference. He gave orders and the observers nodded in agreement. The porch guy went back into the house and the group turned and walked to the larger of the other buildings.

This was not a good sign. If they were getting ready to operate on Angela, we only had a few minutes to act. I didn't see any sign of Mubane or his daughter. Security was far too lax for him to be there. Whatever was going on was about to start. I looked at Sorensen and he looked up toward the ceiling and back at me. He pointed to himself, took out his silenced pistol, and quietly walked toward the stairs.

I signaled for him to hold up as he started his climb. I wasn't sure killing these two was necessary and whispered that to him. He pointed at his arm where a watch wasn't telling me that we had no time for niceties. I had to agree, but reflected on my future standing in front of Saint Peter at the pearly gates with him shaking his head as he asked me, "No Time?"

Then again, Peter was going to have a full day checking me through with ten scrolls of violations. The only thing I had going for me was that I was a former Marine and I had been assured by my drill instructor, Sgt. Famino, that all Marines went to heaven. Too bad for the guys upstairs.

I nodded toward the upstairs and Sorensen moved like a cat. Sometimes, I had to look at his feet to assure myself he was touching the ground. He never made a sound. I followed him until I saw the two men with their backs to us. As soon as I did, one of them got the itch on the back of his head and turned to see Sorensen standing there, looking at them. Both turned and grabbed for their sidearms. Sorensen let them clear their holsters with their guns before he shot them both between the eyes. Just that quick. He turned to me and asked if that was better. He'd shot them in self-defense.

We quickly dragged the two men into a closet, disabled the M60, and dropped the ammo down a hole in one of the walls. I checked the time and saw we had about fifty minutes before their check-in. Sorensen had taken one of their radios and tucked it into his belt. We'd be able to hear any excitement from the sounds of the voices.

We took off down the stairs and out the rear window. I considered going back to the car and retrieving our rifles but decided not to because two white guys walking down the street would certainly have caused a few cell phones to light up.

The houses and buildings behind the big building appeared vacant. They may have been a part of a group of support homes that had been built before this area was abandoned. We went around the south side of the building and kept low. We had decided to go through the front gate instead of the rear wall hole. There was a camera mounted on the wall next to the gate, but it was pointed toward the north, and it didn't look like it had moved since we saw it at first light. This sure was a low-budget operation, and I was beginning to doubt its importance in the greater scheme of things. The one thing I did know was that the medical team across the street was not up to any good and needed to be stopped in the next few minutes or some human being—maybe not Angela, but someone—was going to cease to exist.

I led the way across the street and up to the wall. I kept my silenced pistol low and close to my leg. Sorensen came after me, looking to the rear in case there was something we'd missed. Just then, we heard a loud scream and a female voice yell, "No!" There was some clattering of metal hitting the floor and I thought of the stainless-steel covers on the food wagon. That was another reason we were moving so fast. Feeding patients before a procedure was a sure sign they weren't supposed to live. Choking on food did not concern these docs.

I arrived at the gate and looked up at the camera. It was still pointed away from us and toward the street. I decided it either did not work or no one was monitoring it. I could see through a small hole in the gate. I couldn't see anyone directly in front of the gate and figured they were to the left in the sheltered area I had seen last night.

Just as I was about to knock on the wooden frame, Sorensen reached over and pushed the gate slightly inward. I recalled there was a wooden or metal slide on the back of the gate that secured it—a primitive method of securing it, but more than effective. I did a three count with nods of my head and pushed hard with my left hand and arm on the left gate, shouldering the right gate at the same time. The gates swung open and struck the three guards standing to the left hard enough to knock them off balance. Two of them were quick to sling their rifles around, and the third went for his sidearm. Neither of them was as fast as Sorensen, who tapped out four shots, putting one in each of the three heads. The fourth round went somewhere else.

I pushed the gates and slid the bar over to secure them. Sorensen was already sprinting toward the building where we could still hear the screaming. This was where the Med Team had gone. It was the largest building of the three, besides the house.

He pointed to the front and ran to the back. I twisted slightly sideways as I ran to make myself a narrower target. Just then, the front door opened and one of the drivers of the van came out holding his pistol in his hand, but slightly down to my left. Big mistake, as I shot him three times in the torso and then in the face for good measure. He never got off a shot and hardly made a sound as he tumbled to the cement walkway in front of the two stairs leading to the stoop. I continued through the door and into a small reception area. I heard two pops I knew were coming from Sorensen's pistol, and then two more sounding a bit closer. I pushed open a swinging door just in time to see one of the medical people dropping to the floor. The other three backed up with their hands in the air. They appeared terrified.

Sorensen pointed to two gurneys with two figures lying on them. They both looked dead. I walked over to the closest and saw it was a young girl

181

with dark hair. She appeared to be about ten years old and had ink lines drawn on her torso like a map. She was still breathing, but only just. I didn't see any cuts on her, though she had a clear tube running down her throat and IVs in her arm. I signaled to one of the docs to come over and pull the tube and IVs out. She did right away and that seemed to revive the girl a bit.

Sorensen moved over to the other gurney and I could see that that girl was in the same shape. I asked if anyone spoke English and the doc, I had spoken to moments ago said, "Yes."

I asked her to revive the two girls, and she said something in Thai to the two men standing there. They both moved to the girls and took the tube and IVs from the second girl. They then took little smelling salt capsules and broke them under the girls' noses. They both coughed and tried to sit up on the gurneys, but they must have been strapped down under the sheets partially covering them. I pointed to the tables and the men unstrapped them. Neither of the girls had the strength to sit up, but they were conscious and looking around.

Just then, I heard a sound from the other room and pushed the door open enough to see a third girl being restrained by a large Caucasian woman in civilian clothes. She was holding the young black girl across the chest and had a scalpel to the girl's neck. The girl was bleeding slightly from the sharpness of the scalpel on her flesh. She must have been the girl who was screaming moments before. The women yelled she would kill her if we didn't let her go.

Sorensen stated he had no time for this nonsense, shot her right between the eyes, and caught the young girl just before she hit the floor. He looked over at me with a "What now?" look.

I looked back at the English-speaking medical woman and asked if there were more victims in the compound. She said no, that there were only these three. I asked her if they were harvesting these girl's body parts. I already knew the answer, and she said yes. I came close to shooting her and her merry men but kept it together. Perhaps they would try something stupid and I'd get to do it then.

I instructed her to wrap the tape around the two men's arms and legs. I told Sorensen to stand by, and I left the building and went through the other two buildings. I found two Thai women cooking in a large kitchen in the small building. They barely glanced at me and I hid my pistol against my leg so as not to alarm them. I cut through the building and came out the rear.

There was a door leading into the big house on the side. I sprinted to it and slipped in. I could hear Thai speaking from a TV or radio in the next room. I peeked around the corner and saw the man who had been on the porch earlier sitting at a table with his back to me, eating and watching the TV. I silently walked up behind him and slammed my pistol into the back of his head. I hoped I had killed him. At least he would be out for a long while. I pulled the electric cord on the TV and listened closely to hear anyone else moving about. I heard nothing but searched quickly through the rest of the house. Seeing no one, I ran back out the way I'd come and cut over to the operating building.

Sorensen had all the medical team, including the English speaker, bound up and stashed on top of one another in the back room. The young black girl was standing with him. I told him there was no one else and he nodded sadly while I picked one of the girls up from the gurney nearest me. Sorensen picked up the other girl and told the black girl to stay close. Out the back door, we ran.

I reached the gate first. Sorensen suggested we take one of the vans and I said we had ample supplies in our car, and it was smaller and more common. The vans were big and memorable. We needed stealth and a plan to get the girls to safety. I could think of no one except Top Friend. He was a couple of hundred miles away but seemed to reach far and quickly. I watched the road ahead as Sorensen looked back. The young black girl held on to my arm as I carried the young, unconscious white girl. She was as light as a feather, and Sorensen carried his girl as if she wasn't there.

We came to our car and quickly placed the two girls on the back seat. The black girl climbed in and gathered them to her. I jumped into the driver's seat, while Sorensen stood outside the car to guard us as I backed out onto the street. I looked at our three little passengers and thought to myself that Sorensen and I were certainly putting a small dent in the female body parts business.

Sorensen jumped in the car and said he'd heard his borrowed radio come to life a moment ago. I then heard it chirp in Thai, sounding quick and desperate. I drove back toward the main part of the small city, paying attention to every car or pedestrian we came upon. No one seemed to pay us any attention.

I looked in the rearview mirror and saw the black girl holding the two younger girls tightly to her, all scrunched down in the seat. I finally asked for her name. She told us she was Emily Tobin. I asked her where she was from and she said San Diego, California as if we didn't know where San Diego was. I asked her when she left San Diego to come here and she said she didn't come here from San Diego but from Hong Kong. I looked at her in the mirror, puzzled, and she continued by saying her stepfather worked at the American Embassy in Hong Kong and that he had given her to those awful people.

I looked at Sorensen and saw it had gotten his attention, too. I asked Emily how long ago that had happened. She said she thought it was about a week ago, but it could have been three or four days. They had kept her in a dark room with the two girls she was holding. She had flown to this place with one other girl in a small, but fancy, plane. She'd heard other kids crying in other rooms and screams when they were taken away.

I looked at the two girls and asked her which one she'd flown with and she said neither. She went on to say the girl she'd flown with disappeared right after they'd landed. She'd been blindfolded when they'd landed and never saw the girl again.

My heart skipped a beat when she said that. I asked her to describe the girl, and she said she could do better and that her name was Angela Cohen. She said that Angela was from Florida. Emily went on to say that she and Angela were able to talk on the flight because no one could hear them in a small room in the rear of the plane. I asked her if it could be as few as two or three days ago, and she said that it was possible and that it could have been last night, for all she knew.

Time had all run together for her, and she felt as if they had given her something funny in her food. She would become very sleepy after eating and fall asleep. She described waking up in a dark room and thinking it was the next day. The two girls were there when she got there. She told us their names were Carol and Sandy, and they were both from Los Angeles, California (again pronouncing California as if we were foreigners.) She said they were friends and went to the same school together.

I drove into the city and asked Sorensen to call the Top. He did and started talking right away. He explained what had happened at the compound, leaving out the shootings, and told him we had three U.S. citizens with us in the car. He told Top we had no idea where we were going but were looking for a place to park. Sorensen was quiet for a few moments, and I could hear Top speaking from the phone. Sorensen said, "Okay," a couple of times, thanked him, and broke the connection.

Sorensen told me to drive due north and look for the airport. I had the area already showing on my cell phone and could see our location as a flashing blue dot with the airfield just ahead of us. I showed it to him, and he told me to pull over into a large apartment complex parking lot. There were a few people coming and going in the lot, but none of them paid us any attention.

I turned in my seat and saw that Carol and Sandy were completely awake now. They looked like they were trying to vanish into Emily's sides. I told them not to be afraid and that we were friends. I asked them their last names, and the one on Emily's right said she was Carol Hopkins. The other girl said she was Sandra Lyons. I asked them how long they thought they had been at that place and both had no idea. Carol said they had been walking to school near their homes when a van pulled up and two men jumped out, grabbed them, threw them onto the floor of the van, then drove off. They both said they were on airplanes and cars and vans, then more plane rides until they were brought to the compound where we'd found them. Sandy thought they had been gone a long time because her hair had grown about an inch since she'd left home. They both said they had been held with other kids in three different places since being taken and the only reason they knew they were not still in Los Angeles was because of the different languages people spoke. They were both twelve years old, and Emily said she was fourteen.

I was dangerously angered by all of this, and that was not a good place for me to be. It was a very bad place for these perpetrators to be with me in this state of mind. We sat in the car for about ten minutes before Sorensen's phone vibrated. When it did, I just about jumped out of my skin.

I had been daydreaming about my pursuit of Mubane. I knew I was going to confront him, and I knew it would be soon. The other reason for my nervous jump was that I had momentarily lost track of my mission focus. That was another reason not to be so overly angered by these thoughts, as it tended to give me a tunnel vision of revenge instead of the clear path of the mission. The problem was that we were again nowhere when it came to Angela. We had accomplished a great deal with the recovery of all these young girls, but I felt we were failing on Angela's behalf. I was sure that Thom and Blanche Cohen weren't especially comforted by our progress.

I re-focused and looked at Sorensen, who had just shut down his phone. He turned it off and asked for the phone I had been using. He opened the car door and threw them under the car beside us, and then told me to find another parking spot down the road. As I drove to the next apartment complex, Sorensen told me there would be a helicopter landing on our side of the airport in about thirty minutes. He said it would land in a field behind some hangars and we were to drive right up to it and board. I asked the girls to be ready to run into the bird as soon as we drove up to it and they nodded in unison.

Sorensen went on to say that we were being sought by the local authorities in conjunction with the shenanigans at the compound and that they had an accurate description of him, at least. I thought again of his nickname "the Tree." In a country where the average height was five-foot-nothing, Sorensen stood out like a giant. Sitting down, he was taller than most folks. I told him to sit lower in the seat and pull his knees up. That did little good.

I asked Emily to tell us about her stepfather as we sat there, waiting for our transport. She called him Father, although he wasn't. He had asked her to. His name was Chris Barton. He was an official at the Embassy and his job had to do with security because he often carried a gun under his coat. He used to work for the Los Angeles Police Department but had had to quit because the other police didn't like him. (I figured he was probably Internal Affairs.)

She explained that her mother, who was back in Los Angeles taking care of her sick grandmother, met him when she applied for a job at some government office in L.A. He came to their house to talk to her mother about her real father, who had died in Iraq when she was a little girl. Her father was not in the Army or anything but had some kind of a job over there that her mother would never tell her about. Emily said she had been listening at the door to the kitchen as they spoke. She heard Chris ask her mother how much her father had told her about his mission in Iraq, and her mother said that she knew very little. Emily knew her mother was lying to Chris, as her father had told her a lot. Her father once told her mother that some of the things he'd told her could get him put in jail. Emily also said that Chris came back many times after that and started having dinner with them and then spent the night until her mother told her they were getting married. She said her mother is white and her father was black and Greek. She said he looked like he was an Arab.

Her mother and Chris had been married about seven years and they had lived in Thailand before moving to Hong Kong this past year. She said

Chris was mean to her and, although he insisted that she call him Father, she felt he was ashamed of her because she was black.

Emily told us that her mother left for Los Angeles about a month ago, but Emily had to stay to finish school. She said that Chris started acting strange and had their live-in housekeeper leave earlier than usual for a few days. A doctor came to their apartment one night with Chris and took some blood from her arm. Chris told her it that they needed to check to see if she had been infected with some sickness that was going around. She'd had numerous shots and blood taken every time they'd moved, so it didn't bother her that much. She asked why they didn't do it at the Embassy Clinic as they usually did, but he didn't answer her. She went on to say that she was not allowed to ask any questions about Chris' work and that he would yell at her when she did. Her mother told her to stay away from Chris, especially when he had been drinking. He had never hit her, but when he yelled at her, he looked crazy.

A few days ago, Chris woke her in the middle of the night and told her to come to the kitchen. Two Chinese men were there, and as soon as she came into the kitchen, they grabbed her and gave her a shot. She woke up in a strange place with another girl in the bed next to her. The room looked like a hospital room but had fancy wallpaper and decorations around the doors like a castle or hotel room. The other girl introduced herself as Angela from Florida.

I asked her if she could remember the last time, she'd seen Angela, and she said that because she was so sleepy and in a dark room most of the time, she could only guess that it was about two days ago.

I remembered that I hadn't checked in with Gage in a while, so I dug out my satellite phone and fired it up. I saw that I had received a couple of calls while it was off. One from Gage and one from Nick in New Zealand.

I called Gage instead of listening to the messages. He answered right away and chided me for the delay in checking in. He said he didn't have enough time to plan my memorial service, much less get me cremated and flushed. I told him that I was dead, and this was a collect call from the Pearly Gates. Saint Peter was asking about him, and if he weren't nice, I would tell him the truth. He laughed and I laughed until I saw the girls looking at me weirdly in the rearview mirror.

Gage led by saying that he'd received the FedEx package and was analyzing it right now. He whistled and said we had grabbed the tiger by the tail on this case. He also told me Nick was home in New Zealand and all was secure.

I briefed him on what we had been up to, gave him Emily's name, and a quick briefing on her stepfather. I held off a moment and asked the two younger girls their last names again. I told him they were both from L.A. and left it up to him to handle the family notification. I advised him to use care while dealing with Emily's family because I believed Barton was CIA. I suggested that Marsh and Mike up in Santa Cruz might be of help housing Emily until we figured out the Stepfather. He agreed and said he would arrange it.

I told him we were waiting on a copter to take us back up to the big city. He said he understood. I asked him to brief the major and call to let Dave know we were still kicking. I would give Nick a quick call. He again emphasized the dynamite contained in the ledger. He said half the world's governments had perpetrators spread across its pages.

I signed off, promising to check in more often, and then called Nick. He answered on the first ring and started out by telling me that he was buying the Island of Tahiti. I told him to go for it but not to change the rules on topless sunbathing. He said that was the main reason he was buying it, followed by a grunt. His wife had punched him in the arm. I laughed and he asked if everything was okay.

I told him that we hadn't found our objective yet but had three small packages ready to ship back to their families. I didn't bother to tell him about Emily's dilemma. I was still trying to work that out. He told me all the stuff was secured and our pilots and aircraft had headed back to some island off East Asia to wait for our signal. I told him that I wasn't aware that they had been permanently assigned to us, but that it was a good thing. In fact, now that I thought about it, it was a great thing.

I hadn't quite finished my daydream about Lieutenant Sally Moore when I heard a helicopter buzz over our heads. It turned and faced west and then turned its landing lights off and on and landed. I cranked up the little car and took off as fast as it would go into the field. The bird never wound down its rotary wing as we pulled right up to its side. Sorensen jumped out with his two pistols held low against his legs and watched our perimeter. I hustled the ladies into the hatch of the copter. I quickly grabbed my backpack and the two rifle bags and threw them onto the floor near the girl's feet. I threw the keys to the car after the gear and jumped aboard. Sorensen followed.

I gave the pilot the thumbs up signal and we lifted off like a shot. The pilot was speaking into his microphone and appeared to be yelling at whoever was on the other end. He stopped talking, reached over to the dashboard, and started throwing switches off as fast as he could reach them. He then dropped the nose of the bird down and headed for what felt like a death dive. I saw the ocean appear as we left the land. He turned right as we all but crashed into the water and headed north, hovering just a few feet above the waves. He was taking evasive action from the radar and anyone else trying to follow us. He was good. Real good.

We sped up the coast about four or five miles and then he popped up and turned right to the east, back over the land. I looked out the windshield and saw another helicopter just in front of us that must be a news chopper, as it had a big camera mounted on its forward belly and large Thai symbols on the fuselage. Our pilot positioned our bird into the rear bottom of the other helicopter for a few minutes, so we were hidden on the radar until we were over a large wooded jungle area. He broke off and again dived for the deck. Soon, we were over water again and he turned left to the north and skimmed the beach at a high rate of speed. He abruptly pulled the nose of the bird up and swung left and landed at a small airport. I saw a small twin-engine plane sitting at the end of the runway with its engines running. The plane appeared to be a Cessna of some model and had Thai markings on its tail. The helicopter pilot landed as close as he could to the plane and shouted for us to get going. I grabbed the bags and little Carol and Sorensen grabbed Sandy and took Emily by the hand. We all took off for the plane, and the helicopter climbed up and off toward the east, doing the same low flight it had done with us.

The door to the plane opened and the stairs flipped out as we came up alongside it. I placed Carol onto the floor of the plane and two strong looking hands grabbed her up. Sorensen led Emily to the stairs and gave Sandy to the strong hands while I slid the gear onto the floor. I climbed in with Sorensen behind me. The girls were all strapped into small comfortable seats and I saw, for the first time in a long time, a man taller and larger then Sorensen. He was so big that he nearly had to double over to stand in the small cabin. He had to be seven feet tall. I squeezed by him to a seat as the plane roared down the runway and took off. Sorensen couldn't get by him until he moved forward to the cockpit and out of the way. Sorensen looked at me and mouthed a *Wow!* as he nodded to the giant. The right seat of the plane must have been custom made for him as he sat back into it.

189

The plane took off and banked hard left to the east. It climbed as it turned and then went straight east. I looked back at the girls all snuggled up in their seats around Sorensen. I could see the sleepy look that Sorensen got when he was about to crash. I was feeling the same.

Just as I closed my eyes for a moment, the engines changed pitch and the plane's nose dropped. I faced forward and saw an airstrip ahead of us getting bigger and bigger as we approached. We touched down and the plane spun around and stopped facing the way we'd come. The pilot did not shut the engines down and Goliath climbed out of his seat and pushed the door open and the stairs down. We unbuckled and walked off the plane. After grabbing our bags and making sure the girls were able to walk on their own, we moved away from the plane. The big guy saluted us and closed the hatch. The plane taxied away and down the runway.

Just then, a black Chevy Suburban pulled up from a narrow road in the brush and stopped right beside us. I saw that Sorensen had his silenced pistol at his side and was watching the blacked-out windows closely for trouble. I wondered if any of these folks dealing with us realized how close they were to death every time they approached Sorensen. He was a real-life fighting machine with a very short fuse. I always think, *Careful* when these occasions arise.

The door to the SUV opened and Top Friend climbed out, looking grim. Of course, he was a Former Marine Master Sergeant and they most always look grim. He perked up when he spotted the girls and became grandfather looking as he approached them. He looked at me and then Sorensen as if to ask what was becoming of this world. I agreed as I wondered what could be worse than kidnapping and killing these precious kids for the almighty dollar. I was feeling that dangerous urge again and tried to brush it off. Top waved us into the car and said something to the driver as we drove off.

20

I introduced the girls to Top and said that he was our good friend and theirs, too. Top smiled and told them they would be safe at home very soon. They would be coming to his house while arrangements were made to get them back home. He had a great big fat kitty named Gunny who just loved little girls. They smiled and sat closer to Sorensen.

We broke through the jungle and onto a major highway. I could see the city in the distance. We were traveling north and, again, I drifted into thoughts of Angela. I wondered how far she was from where I was sitting right at that moment. Top looked at me, and he must have read my mind. He said he would have some good intel for us when we got back to his office.

Top had some thin blankets for the girls to wrap around themselves. They were still in their hospital garments and the air conditioning in the car was chilly. We drove about ten minutes into the city and I recognized Top's building as we turned a corner onto a main road. The driver said something into the microphone attached to his left shoulder and a tinny voice squeaked back. Top told him to keep going and we passed the building. I looked at Top and he said there was some interest from the local authorities, and that was why we were going to an alternate location. I wasn't sure what that meant but kept quiet for the sake of the girls. Sorensen shifted in his seat and scanned the road on both sides. I didn't see anything out of the ordinary but trusted Top's information.

We drove into an industrial area about a mile from the downtown section and slowed down. The driver made four turns in a circle, and then we were headed back in the same direction, just perhaps one road over. The big car turned abruptly to the right on a side street and then into an open garage door at the end of a large three- or four-story factory. As soon as we cleared the door, it slammed down. The driver stopped and jumped out. He quickly walked back to the garage door and looked out of a small window. Top signaled us to wait a moment as he watched his driver at the door. A couple of minutes later, the driver came back and nodded that all was clear. Top opened his door and waved us out onto the cement floor.

This building must be his Plan B, as it was like his big building downtown. There were several vehicles lined up along the wall and two large military-type Hummers facing us from the wall. A door opened on the left wall and our old friends Jones and Smith walked out and headed for the car we had just left. They both nodded. Smith or Jones was limping a bit from his wound, but he looked fit enough. I said quietly to Sorensen that Top must not give time off for gunshot wounds. Top heard me and said the lieutenant had insisted on being placed back on duty. I wasn't surprised at all.

The two lieutenants climbed into the car and spun it around and out the quick-rising door. Top explained that they would drive back and into the main building to see if it flushed out any interest. He led us through the side door and into a hall lined with doors, not unlike his main building. We entered a large lobby area at the end of the hall and a young woman met us with a big smile. It was mostly intended for the girls, but it was not lost on Sorensen, as she looked him up and down a little longer than she did me. She asked the girls to follow her and they all walked down the hallway to the right of the lobby. Emily looked back at me and I smiled and winked. She smiled back and mouthed, *Thank you.* And, just like that, they were gone.

Top led us into a small office, and as soon as we all sat down, a woman pushed a rolling cart in from the hall and the room immediately smelled like a Cracker Barrel restaurant. Breakfast. My mouth watered and I had to stop myself from rushing the poor girl as she distributed plates on the large desk in front of us before serving us. I grabbed a piece of toast and slammed it into my mouth. Great idea of Top's.

After the girl left, I, between chomps, told Emily's story to Top. He said that Barton, her stepfather, had been in Bangkok about a week ago. He was definitely CIA and "a real dickhead." I didn't need any clarification. Top said he was not surprised that he'd given up his stepdaughter. Top had seen a report that the girl had gone missing, and that all the American intelligence officers had been told to be on the lookout for her or to gather any information about her that they could find. I gave him what we knew on Carol and Sandy and he said he would take care of it. He briefed us on Janie and Patty Miller and said they were on a flight back to the States.

Top went on to explain that Washington was abuzz with rumors regarding our escapades and the return of the kidnapped kids. I didn't tell Top about the records or the ledger. I figured I would leave that to the Major and his ring of legal beagles. It would be tough getting that kind of a scandal published, especially with some of the big names involved.

Top turned on a monitor from a remote on the desk. It showed a map of the greater Bangkok area. He zoomed in on an area to the west of the city—a town or area called "Samphran." It was on Highway 4, about ten or fifteen miles from where we were. He showed us a large house inside a tall, walled-in compound. He said that this was Mubane's main residence. He went on to say that after the incident up at the reserve yesterday, Mubane and his family were helicoptered to his house in Samphran.

Early this morning, Mubane's daughter's doctor arrived by car and drove into the compound. He was still there, and there was a small medical clinic in the compound. It had been built after Mubane's daughter was diagnosed with her heart ailment. He said it was staffed with three or four young doctors and four or five nurses. Top's informant had reported that the daughter had had an episode while at the reserve. He believed that she was going to need a heart transplant very soon and that they may well carry out the procedure there at the compound. All the equipment was available there and the doctor who had arrived was the foremost transplant surgeon in all of Asia.

That meant Angela may well be at that compound—or would soon be taken there. The question was where she was now if she was not at the compound. Top said he had every available asset scrambling to learn all they could as soon as possible. I knew this was costing a small fortune and wondered who had authorized the expense. Top, I knew, answered to someone somewhere, but I wasn't going to press him with those kinds of questions at this point. I would find out as soon as this was over—and I hoped it was from the heart and not politically motivated.

I asked Top about the security at the compound and he just shook his head. Not a good sign. He moved the cursor on the monitor and zoomed in closer to show us short towers at each corner of the compound. He again pointed out that Mubane had about twenty full-time former commandos on duty, with dog patrols on top of that. I figured we could get around the troops, but the dogs were another problem altogether. I asked Top if he could print out the picture on the screen so I could study it a bit more. He pushed a button on the clicker, and I heard a printer come to life somewhere in the room.

As it was printing, Top pulled his small cell phone out of his pocket and answered it. He listened for a couple of moments and then signed off. He told us that when the lieutenants drove up to the main building, the local police surrounded them and insisted on searching the car. They were very upset when they didn't find what they were looking for, and one of the supervisors, a high-ranking Bangkok police officer, demanded to know where the girls were and who the American men were who had been in that car. Jones and Smith played dumb and, shortly thereafter, the police released them. Top said that there were two civilians with the cops and that they were surely Mubane's men. That answered our question about whether Top was being watched. At least they were still in the dark as to who Sorensen and I were. We had some cover. I would like to have had Mubane's ledger, which was likely very similar to Schultz's. That way, we could probably bribe our way to the goal line.

Top explained that he was no secret from the Thai government and, in fact, had worked with them on many matters. He said that the U.S. Government had too many restrictions to be able to act quickly and that there were several civilian groups similar to his around the world that only answered to whoever was sitting in the White House at the time. He said that he was probably the longest lasting team leader in existence right now because he had so many good friends and former Marines still working in DC who looked after him. (Sounded familiar.)

I asked him what he thought about Emily's situation, seeing how her stepfather was a company man and it appeared that many of the VIPs were involved in this mess. He said he was working on that as we spoke. Barton was very well connected and seemed tight with a few of the Far East embassy personnel. Instead of being put up at the normally contracted hotels in Bangkok, he stayed at the embassy like a visiting dignitary. Top went on to say he suspected Barton was a little too tight with the politician types who visited the Far East. He was almost always on the security details, even when the politicians brought their own security.

I suggested that perhaps he was more involved in human trafficking than just selling his own kid. Top did a quick take at me and nodded once. "Yes."

That meant we really had no retreat we could trust. I didn't like that, and I could see by Sorensen's stiff attention that he was thinking the same thing. We had Top, whom we could trust, and he had a tremendous spread of assets we could and had used, but as we had just found out from the lieutenants, Top was on the current watch list.

Top sat at his desk, buzzed away on his computer, and made a couple of quiet calls. I used the head and found there were clean clothes laid out. I decided to take a quick shower. I even trimmed my beard a bit and shaved around the outside. I was not at all surprised to find a small bottle of Paco Rabanne aftershave and cologne lying on top of the clothes. Top had really done his homework. I passed on the cologne, as it would give us away at a hundred feet. It was a nice gesture, though. On Sorensen's pile, I saw a small bottle of Irish whiskey. That was funny.

After my shower, I gave Sorensen the heads up and he retreated into the head for a cleanup. Top was still on the computer and phone, so I sat on the long couch up against the wall and closed my eyes for a few minutes. I must have crashed out hard because I heard Sorensen say, "Wake up!" as he kicked my foot. He knew better than to get too close because I often startle when waking and am instantly violent. (I don't get many repeat sleepovers after one of those episodes!)

I opened my eyes and saw Sorensen, looking the same as when he went into the head, but trimmed up a bit, as I was. I was sure he had changed clothes, but he looked the same as usual. I asked him what was up, and he said we had more trouble.

I said, "What else is new?" A rolling cart had been brought in, and I wondered how long I had been out. I also saw some Lipton tea bags and cups, which I jumped on as he told me the latest.

It seemed we were getting popular with the big guys and a full scale "hit" had been placed on our heads—whoever we were. They were also a formable group of thugs. Top came in from the hall and added to the story. He said that two members of the team were American Soldiers of Fortune. He knew them personally, as he had used them a few times for special missions. He stopped using them some time ago because they were a bit over the top. I looked at Sorensen, the champion over-the-top guy in the world, and he looked away.

Top caught that and added, "Far worse than the Tree here."

I smiled a little and couldn't tell if Sorensen was pleased or insulted.

Top explained that there might be as many as twenty local bad guys hired to run us down. The bounty was in the millions and "dead" was the only objective. He said there were a few local law enforcement folks in the group, and that they were well placed in the Bangkok hierarchy. I would not have expected any less. After all, I have a pretty high opinion of myself!

It wasn't going to be easy to take us down. Then again, this certainly wasn't the first time we had been hunted—and, I figured, not the last. I looked at Top, told him we need not bring all this grief down on his little empire here and asked for a few supplies to hold us over. I told him we would slip out onto the streets and be gone. Before he could respond, I told him our main objective was still our Angela. We would deal with the rest of this as we moved along.

Top smiled a moment and said we couldn't get rid of him that easy. When I started to protest, he reminded me that I was still just a Buck Sergeant and he was the *Top*. I shut up.

Just then, he received another phone call, listened a moment, made a quiet reply, and signed off. He picked up his remote and brought up a new scene on the monitor. It was the inside of the Bangkok Airport terminal. Top watched for a moment and then, with his green laser, pointed out a man walking from a jetway hatch.

Top said, "Gentlemen, meet Hong Kong's Chief Agricultural Attache, Chris Barton."

I looked him over closely as he walked purposely through a group of people greeting each other. He just shoved his way through like a bully. He was dressed in tan slacks and a dark brown jungle jacket, like the ones Sorensen and I were wearing. The camera followed him, and then another one picked him up as he approached the Customs lines. He bypassed the long lines and went through a door that I imagined was reserved for those with diplomatic passes. That camera went off and another came on the monitor farther down the concourse area, showing a door he should have come out after passing through the check through. He didn't come out.

Top told us there was an exit in the diplomatic checkpoint to the underground area of the terminal. He said these videos were taken about thirty minutes ago and that someone met Barton down below. He climbed into an official-looking, unmarked van and left toward the city. He said that Mubane's downtown office tower was being watched, but that so many vans of the same color passed in and out of the parking garage, it was tough to determine which one Barton was in. He said he was sure it was a Mubane van and not an embassy vehicle. His people were trying to get a good look in one of the videos at the airport exits to see if they could ID the van, but that would take a while.

I was only interested in the fact that Barton was here in Bangkok but had yet to be greeted by one of his fellow agents. That meant he was here unofficially and may not have the support of the local spooks at our embassy. I also thought about Frank Gowdy running to the embassy, demanding to see the ambassador. Gowdy was then assassinated. He must not have given up our names as I had suspected he had. They seemed to be searching for Americans with our description, according to Top, and not our actual IDs. That gave me some leeway, but not Sorensen, who was easy to spot from across town.

Top made a call and spoke in English to someone about decoy duty. He signed off and asked if we had noticed the two pilots that morning on our flight up from down south. I smiled and said I certainly saw the giant. Top told us that the giant, nicknamed Andre, was going to team up with another American employee of his and walk in front of a few police surveillance cameras. That would confuse the other side for a while so we could make our way to Mubane's compound in Samphran. I piped in and said I wasn't sure Samphran was going to be our first stop. I was still running through it in my head.

I asked Top where these American hit team members would be staying. He said he could only guess but suggested the Suncheon Hotel right next to his headquarters. He brought it up on his monitor and said there were several entrances from his building into the hotel. It was a real fancy building that merged with Mubane's building. I asked Top if the Americans were living in Thailand or were imported. He said they live in Bangkok and worked the eastern Asia area. He brought up their pictures, still shots from a video feed, and they showed two men sitting in the middle seat of a van. It wasn't clear enough to identify them, but I could see that they were the typical Soldier of Fortune types: big, mustached, and working overtime to look mean and tough. I knew the type and did not really care to associate with them.

Top brought up two more pictures of them that appeared to be from

ID cards or driver's licenses. The same mean look. Both looked a little overweight from the lack of exercise often found on "wannabe soldiers." I called them that, as, in my experience, former combat soldiers didn't need to put on that hard look. It came naturally in the eyes. These guys were posers. I wished I could call them up and tell them to go back to the States, as their time was limited on this Earth. I just knew it.

Top went on to describe them as mediocre thugs that came in handy for show and tell. He said he didn't believe they had much, if any, combat experience.

I grinned to myself. "Nailed it!"

The other problem was that they were so much taller than their Thai counterparts that they were easy targets. I looked at Sorensen and he thought the same thing. Still, our biggest problem right now was Chris Barton. He not only presented an immediate concern, but he also stood in the way of our getting Angela back home. His position in the system gave him access to all communications, including names and travel arrangements.

I asked Top if our three girls were on their way out of the country. He told us the two little ones were already down in U-Tapao, a Royal Thai Air Base about fifty miles southeast. Both Sorensen and I knew U-Tapao from our Vietnam days. It was a major U.S. Air Force Base used as a supply center and base for our efforts in the Nam. Top went on to explain that our Air Force still used the base as a training facility and that many U.S. forces were still stationed there.

He said the two girls had been driven there a while ago and were scheduled to fly back to the States on an Air Force MAC flight that was leaving shortly. They were listed as Military Dependents and would land at Travis Air Force Base, north of San Francisco, and then be brought down to Los Angeles by friends of his in a private jet. He realized how important it was to keep all of this as quiet as possible so no one could cover it up before we could spring the news on the American people.

I told him that when all the pedophilic priests were exposed in the Catholic Church, word leaked out and it gave them time to ship numerous priests out of the U.S. and secret them away around the world. He said he was aware of that and had been working to grab a former priest over in Bangladesh for a few years. That priest figured in with many of the pedophile problems there in Thailand. He said that the creep was well protected by the higher-ups who somehow had a relationship with him. I thought of Schultz's ledger.

Top told us that Emily was being housed there in Bangkok with a family he knew and trusted. He said she realized how important it was right now to avoid contacting her mother. Her mother wasn't likely to believe Barton had any part in her daughter's abduction. I had been worried about that. Barton might be notified before her mother. He could then make her disappear for good. Still, I would feel far more comfortable if Emily was back in the States.

So, I began to form a plan independent from Top's that would eliminate Barton first. Barton had to go. There was no other choice. Alive, he would continue to cause us problems.

I asked Top if his people had located Barton yet. He said they were working on it, but he was certain he would surface at Mubane's headquarters shortly. I looked up at the monitor and Top again clicked Mubane's building on the screen. He panned around the outside to show every angle. There were guards at every entrance and some patrolling the perimeter. The only area not covered was the Suncheon Hotel adjacent to the building's left front entrance. Top read my mind and said there were three hundred rooms in the hotel and Barton's name wouldn't be listed as a guest. I wasn't thinking in terms of getting to him in his room but getting into Mubane's building through the hotel.

Top changed the screen on the monitor and brought up a bunch of lines that crisscrossed each other up and down and across. I knew what it was before he told us. A schematic of a sewer system—and I assumed it was Bangkok's. He called it the Bangkok's Underground Highway. He hit another command on the remote and the outlines of square building bases appeared. With his laser, he pointed to a square and said that was where we were now, and then showed us Mubane's building and the hotel a few blocks over. It appeared to be about a half-mile as the crow flies.

I asked him about access points to the tunnels and he said that not only did he have access, but he had a transport system in place that he had been working on for the past five years. He told us to prepare to be impressed.

I asked Top how long before dark and he said it had been dark for a couple of hours. I guessed I had been asleep far longer than I had thought. I asked Top if we could take a ride past the building a couple of times before we started the mission. I wanted a complete picture of its layout before climbing up through a toilet bowl to get inside. He said it would be no problem and led the way out into the hallway and into the parking garage.

I didn't feel comfortable climbing into a van and leaving out through the big door but, as I should have expected, Top cut across the large garage, through another door, into a tunnel, where we walked about a hundred yards. I could see a light at the end that was blinking red and then green. Top spoke into his cell phone and two men appeared next to the door at the end. They both had AR-15 rifles and looked fit. They looked up at the red light, and, when it turned green, they waved us to go through and out onto the street.

Top told us we could slip into the crowds and make our way to our objective or use the tunnel system. He led us back into the hallway and closed the door. Top explained that the lights signified the clear or not clear exit. He said they had cameras watching the roads all around his buildings and that the cameras were connected to a computer that compared vehicles and faces to determine any surveillance just by repeating similarities. I thought that was simple but efficient. He said the computer controlled the lights at every entrance and exit and told them when it was safe to enter or leave. (Oh, yeah, I'm gonna trust a computer with my security!)

He explained that the tunnels had come in handy over the years not just for him, but for generations before. The sewer system had started out as narrow canals used to drain the land after the torrential rains of the annual monsoons. He said that the canals probably dated back two thousand years and became tunnels as the city was built up, but they still served the same purpose. Top said that many were now modern septic systems that brought the household waste and such to treatment plants around the city.

Top walked back through the garage and into his small office, where we saw several weapons laid out on a table, along with ammunition. I spotted my favorite hand grenades in a box on the floor. As he pointed at the charting on the monitor, he explained that the old tunnels used to drain the land were now underground passageways and living areas for a population of Tunnel People. He let Sorensen and I dwell on that for a moment and then went on to tell us there were hundreds, if not thousands, of people who lived in the tunnels and functioned as their own society. He and his staff have developed a relationship with many of these folks, and they serve as some of his best intelligence sources. In return, his group gave them food, water, and clothes to wear.

All of this intrigued me as I had heard over the years of subterranean people living all over the world. I have read some novels that depicted such folks, and it always seemed too real to be complete fiction. Top went on to tell us how important these people were and that we were about to use them as we made our way to Mubane's headquarters.

Again, he reflected on the monitor and told us that he had most of the tunnels charted with small, built-in mini-cell towers, so cell phone signals worked, along with the GPS function on the phones. Top gave us small cell phones like the one he carried and explained that there was an app on them tied into the tunnel's mini cell network. It would guide us around the tunnels like a normal GPS.

I had already decided to take the fight to Barton and his merry men. The "best defense is a good offense" theory has always served me well. I wanted to disable the opposition before they became anymore organized, especially the Americans, so we would have a clear path out once we found and secured Angela. This wasn't going to be easy. A lot of folks were going to get hurt, but they had chosen their own destiny when they became involved in this enterprise.

I could see that Sorensen was anxious to get moving. His left leg was doing its bouncy act as he sat on the long couch.

I nodded at him and asked, "The tunnels?"

He nodded a slow yes.

We picked out our choice of weapons. We both chose about four hand grenades each, and I picked up a silenced .22 caliber magnum automatic similar to Sorensen's little sidekick. He took more ammunition for his piece, and I grabbed five or six magazines for mine. We both took a couple of energy bars and two bottles of water. Top had bulges in his pockets that said he had already loaded up.

Top took us back out into the hallway and turned left this time. A few doors down, he motioned for us to enter. The motel room was like any other I had seen over the years, but when Top pressed a light switch on the wall next to the bed, it rose up and exposed a set of stairs leading down. When he reached in and threw another switch, wall lights came on and showed the stairs went nearly straight down for about fifty feet to a landing or floor. Top led the way and, as we arrived at the bottom, I saw Lieutenant Jones or Smith standing with four or five very short, child-like men dressed in military-type fatigues.

Our Tunnel People, I presumed. They were armed with modified AR-15 rifles and had various pieces of equipment attached to utility belts around their waists. Some of it was Show and Tell, such as the pearl-handled fighting knives and compasses with shiny covers. The kind of things you give to kids to make them feel like they're a part of the game. The look in their eyes told me they were not kids and very serious about the mission. They also seemed disciplined, which was important. I nodded toward them as Top introduced them. I forgot their names right after we were introduced. All I cared about was that they were following us and not chasing us. I did notice none of them had any grenades hanging from their ammo belts, which was a good thing.

I pulled out my little cell phone and found it was already on and reading the passageways. I was surprised to see lights every hundred feet or so and some more green LEDs reflecting in a distance. Top's camera computer system must have been installed down here, too. I wondered why the bad guys weren't aware of these tunnels. I glanced at the five sewer rats and guessed that they would not treat outsiders well.

The ancient system of drain tunnels had evolved from man-dug trenches to storm and cement passageways with a firm dirt floor. I saw little moisture and the humidity was average. From time to time, I felt a slight breeze. There must have been vents to suck out the methane gas that accumulates in underground caves and tunnels. There was little smell, and what was there was musky. All the human waste must go exclusively through the sealed pipes I could see crossing over every thirty or forty feet. I noticed our small guides had large packets on their ammo belts that I was sure contained gas masks. They wouldn't do much against methane but would give them ample protection from the tear gas the militaries use to flush out the enemy. Top didn't issue us any, nor was he wearing one, so perhaps that, too, was decorative.

We moved along at a fast clip. Top spoke into his headset attached to his cell phone and, from time to time, made a hand gesture at crevasses in the walls. I couldn't see any, but I was sure there were cameras installed in them. Top suddenly stopped just ahead of us and his security gathered tightly around him and faced fore and aft. They looked right through the three of us to our rear.

Our lieutenant spoke into his headset in Thai and signed off. Top spoke a bit longer, looked at his cell screen, and pointed to his right down an adjacent tunnel. He spoke to one of the Thais and two of them took off, double-timing it down the tunnel. Top told us that the hotel and Mubane's building were about a quarter of a mile down that tunnel, but a couple of cameras were out of service that were important. He said his soldiers would check it out and get back to us. We all spread out and leaned against the wall to rest a bit. I drank some water and Sorensen pulled a half sandwich wrapped in a napkin out of his pocket. I could see it was bacon and cheese. It looked good. He saw me looking and turned away like a stingy kid. I ate a power bar and made some *umm* noises just to show off. I wished it were a Snickers.

About ten minutes later, the guards returned and briefed Top in Thai. Top listened closely, showed them his cell phone screen, and spoke some more. He walked back to us and said it appeared the cameras had been intentionally disconnected. The guards saw evidence that someone had placed a couple of wi-fi cameras on the ceiling near the Mubane building. The tunnel people were not an unusual sight in the tunnels, so their presence would not necessarily alarm the watchers. He went on to say that we would be doubling back and using an alternate route. Again, Top led the way and, shortly, we took a left into a much narrower tunnel. Not only narrow but lower. I had to tilt my head; Sorensen had to hunch over. Top, the lieutenant, and the guards just walked upright.

There were no lights in the tunnel, but the guards had small flashlights with red lens covers and we could see our way just fine. I knew Sorensen had a small, extremely bright LED flashlight that he always carried in his pocket. We walked single file for about twenty minutes and then stopped again. The two scouts ran ahead and disappeared down the tunnel. As we waited for them to come back, Sorensen and I checked our weapons. I made sure my spare magazines were in their proper place in my pockets, so they were lined up correctly and ready to use when I needed them. The time it takes to look at the individual magazines in order to reload could cost you your time, and your life. The guards had bent, banana-shaped rifle magazines taped together Vietnam-style. All they had to do was pull out the spent clip, swing it around and back into the rifle, and they were good to go. Each one of their clips looked as if it could hold about thirty rounds. They were prepared.

The two guards double-timed it back and reported to Top. He turned to us and waved us along. About a hundred yards in, Top stopped again. He let two of his guards pass him and followed along slowly behind them. The only lights now were the two out ahead of us in the tunnel. The lights kept shining forward and then back at us. It was the signal for us to follow. Sorensen bumped into me slightly from time to time or he was pushing me forward, I wasn't sure which. We had staggered ourselves left and right in the tunnel so one shot with a high-caliber rifle couldn't take us all out at once. The lieutenant was in front of me to the left. I bumped him a couple of times, but he didn't seem to notice or care. At least he didn't turn around and smack me as I was about to do to Sorensen the next time he stepped on my heel.

Up ahead, I saw a red light flash three times and then stay on, waving us forward. When we arrived at the position, the guards stopped, and I could see a ladder on the wall leading up to the underside of a manhole cover. One of the guards had pushed the cover aside about a foot and was standing on a ladder rail with his head sticking up through the space. He ducked back down, said something to Top, and pushed the cover silently farther aside. Top waved us all up the ladder.

After we had cleared the hatch, I looked around. We appeared to be in a huge basement area of a building filled with pipes and large valve wheels. There were some dull lights across the expanse on the wall. I could see some large doors that I recognized as the bases of elevator shafts. They were humming as the cars moved through the shafts. There were staircases on all four corners of the room, but the doors on the wall where the elevators were located were double in size.

A large, garage-type door in the wall to our right probably led to the Mubane building. One of the guards shone his light around the outside of the door and said something to Top just above a whisper. Top turned to us and said it was totally welded shut. One of the guards spoke into his cell phone and, as he did, he moved to the left of the door, shining his flashlight on the wall. He bent down and pushed a bit on the cement doorframe, and it moved inward like a trap door. He shone his light inside the door a while and said something to Top. Top turned to us and just smiled. He told us that he didn't know why these folks didn't own this city. They probably had trap doors in every bank and safe.

Top said something in Thai and two of the guards ducked through the hole, then Top, then three more guards, me, Sorensen, and then the lieutenant. It was another huge basement area with no lights at all. The guards had spread out around the wall where we were standing and then moved slowly to the center and then to the side. I could see a large staircase on the wall to our left as one guard shone his light on it. I noticed that it led to a landing and then turned back toward the center of the building.

The ceiling in this basement was about half as tall as the hotel's ceiling but had the same array of pipes and valves going up the walls and across the ceiling. One of the guards stood at a huge, open electrical junction box on the wall. As I walked closer, I recognized phone lines usually reserved for landlines. Video conduit connected to both cables and wi-fi transceivers. The main power source for the entire system was fed right into the large box. I had never seen such a gross violation of security. The entire building's communication system was all in one place, and someone could shut it down by cutting just one power line. If we disconnected the line, they would lose internal communications, video security feeds, alarms, and early warnings of an approaching threat. I looked at Top and wondered if he had an electronics company on retainer setting up these vulnerable systems all over the city.

Top smiled and winked. He whispered that he needed to get a look in these buildings from time to time and the investment was minimal compared the value.

I nodded and asked if it wouldn't set off an emergency response from security if they lost their system. He told us that they shut it down periodically, so security thinks it's routine and on an irregular schedule. I thought about that for a moment and asked if that included the American Embassy, which I knew was close by. He looked at me and said we would find out in the future if we needed to.

As Top spoke on his phone again, I saw him looking at his cell screen. We walked over behind him and saw he was looking at hallways and office spaces that were mostly vacant since it was after office hours. He scanned camera view after camera view. Suddenly, he stopped and turned to me and showed me a group of men in an office sitting in a semi-circle around a short, round table, with none other than Chris Barton speaking at the head. There was no audio, so we couldn't hear what they were discussing. I was sure it wasn't about the latest winner of *America's Got Talent*. There were five men in the room that we could see, but possibly more out of view of the camera with the fisheye lens. Two American contractors and two Thai. Top said they were Thai Police Intelligence Officers whom he knew to be on Mubane's payroll. I pretty much figured Mubane ran this city, seeing how every time we turned a corner, he had resources. Then again, so did Top.

Top spoke into his headset again and then told us this meeting was taking place on the third floor at the rear of the building. He pointed to the cement stairs behind us and said, "Right next to that stairwell. Four high floors above us."

He spoke to one of his crewmen and the small guard took off across the floor and up the stairs. We waited quietly until the guard returned. He wasn't gone long enough to climb to the third floor, so I figured he had run into a problem. He spoke to Top and stood back, waiting for orders.

Top told us there were two guards at the first-floor landing watching the stairs, and that the Tunnel People knew one of them was a sadistic, former Bangkok police officer. He was so bad that the police had retired him early. Mubane hired him that same day as his Supervisor of Security. Top said he and his people had been looking for a reason to hit him for quite a while. I told Top that Sorensen and I would be more than happy to take care of that little task if he wanted. Top thanked us and said "No." He'd let his troops handle it, so they had the bragging rights.

He spoke some Thai and two of the guards made for the stairs. I thought they were far too exuberant about their task than necessary and figured this guy must really be special. Two minutes later, there was a commotion from the stairs, and we all took up fighting positions. A moment later, two bodies came bouncing down the stairs and landed on the basement floor. The two guards came down after them and pulled them to the side under the staircase. They came out wiping their hands on their trousers. No one said a word as Top pointed to the ceiling and we took off for the stairs.

Sorensen and I pulled out our silenced pistols and climbed up behind the Top and his Merry Men.

The stairway was as I thought—one set up, then a landing, and then another set to the first floor. When we reached the first floor, I could see where the guards had been standing. Cigarette butts on the floor and an ample amount of spit on the floor and walls. One of Top's men pointed to a slip of paper in the crack of the door, which they had set to indicate if someone had pushed the doors open after the guards were taken out. Paper still there and we went on up. Second floor clear and next was the third-floor landing and our objective.

I asked Top to bring the video feed back up on his phone so we could see their positions now. He already had it up, and they were all in the same spots as before.

I saw that each one of the men that I could see facing the camera had at least one hand in their laps at the small table they were sitting around. Barton was now sitting a bit sideways, and he looked as if he was about to jump. I have learned over the years to recognize a sucker punch coming, and we were about to see one any moment. As we watched, Barton sprang up, pulled a silenced, long-barreled pistol out, and shot the police officer directly in front of him twice. His two fellow Americans hesitated a moment, which told me their inexperience in a flash. Barton shot the next Thai cop three times. The two American Soldiers of Fortune then fired their silenced pistols into the two very dead cops and acted as if Barton was the fastest gun in the west.

I had to admit, he was fast and accurate. He could have put all four men down easily. As we watched, Barton and the two men put their weapons on the table and began lifting the dead guys up. I signaled Sorensen and we both moved swiftly out the door, into the hall, and to the left beside the stairwell. I tried the door and the knob turned slightly. Just then, Top and his entourage came up behind us. I waved him back a bit and pulled the door open. Barton and his counterparts were too busy to react fast enough. I put him down first with a bullet to his groin. That really gets a man's attention. Sorensen put the other two down with headshots just as they were reaching for their weapons. I stepped over to Barton and pulled him over and onto the round table. I told him the crotch shot was from Emily and anyone else who wanted to claim a stake in his missing pecker.

He had one chance to live and no time to think about it. I asked him where Mubane was holding the American girl who'd been flown down from Hong Kong a couple of days ago. He looked confused and then asked if she was a young blonde. He was drooling blood from his mouth. Either he had bitten his tongue or the .22 had spun its way up into one of his lungs. I said yes and he said she was dead by now and her heart neatly transplanted into Mubane's daughter. I told him that was the wrong answer and jammed my pistol into his wound as hard as I could. A great deal of blood shot out of his mouth that answered the blood source question. He coughed and said he did not know where the girls were kept but knew Mubane was at his residence on the west side of town.

He looked at me closely and asked, "Storm?" He was looking familiar, too. I shot him right between the eyes before I remembered I owed him some sympathy or twenty bucks or something. Still haven't figured out how he knew me. Perhaps he had seen a photo or two?

Top came in and said it looked like Barton and his boys had a shootout with the local boys and everyone lost. He took my .22 and rubbed the barrel all over the back and palm of a dead cop's hand, wiped the gun and magazine of my prints, and placed it in the hand of the cop as if he had just shot three American citizens. I wasn't that concerned about being accused of murder in these cases since I was sure Top's video would show Barton killing his men and he and his partner's attempt to shoot us first. Then again, this was Thailand and we already knew there was a bit of corruption at the government's upper levels. So, I decided to let them draw their own conclusions when they discovered the dead guys.

I searched Barton and took his wallet and pocket stuff. I searched the shoe on his right foot and found his hidden CIA credential card, just where I knew it would be. Top and Sorensen searched and took all the stuff from the other two Americans. We didn't want to make it too easy for the locals to ID them. I scanned the room and, just as we were about to clear out, saw a briefcase next to a small combination desk and chest of drawers. I grabbed it up and saw a small lug tag that said, "Diplomatic bag belonging to the American Embassy in Hong Kong." I wondered what kind of secrets Barton carried with him on a nefarious mission such as this. Top saw it, raised his eyebrows a couple of times, and led the way out the door.

When we entered the hall, I could see the lieutenant and guards stationed about ten feet to the left of the stairway. They just glanced our way as we walked back to the stairway and then followed once we were clear of the hall.

The second floor was still clear and, as we approached the ground level, we heard voices speaking Thai. Top waved us down and we passed the first-floor door but saw nothing as the voices continued to speak. Perhaps the dead guys in the basement were being missed.

We made it to the basement. One of Top's guards shone his light over the two deadies to show that they hadn't been moved or resurrected. We crawled through to the hotel basement and double-timed it down the narrow tunnel until we arrived at the bigger section. Top stopped and made sure we were all accounted for. He then spoke into his headset, turned to us, and said all was clear back to his building. We proceeded to walk back the way we'd come.

We arrived back at Top's secondary headquarters and settled back into his basement office, thanked our little security force with a hardy Marine Corps salute, and watched them disappear back into the tunnels. The lieutenant followed us back and vanished as soon as we cleared the door. I placed the medium-sized briefcase that I had confiscated on Top's table and checked it over for any booby traps. Top brought over a small meter and scanned it for any signal it may be giving off, and then took a second small instrument and squeezed a small bellows at every side of the case. He looked at me and said there was an AT&T cell phone in there, but no other tracking device, and no sign of explosive residue, but I noticed he stepped back as I began to open it. (So much for his faith in his little toys.)

It wasn't locked, and when I swung it open, the first thing I saw was a pair of men's briefs that were just what that name implied. They looked like the men's European swimsuits that we used to call "grape smugglers" back in Florida. The only difference was that they had a small flap in the front just in case the man wasn't big enough to pull it over the top to pee. On top of that was an I-Phone 5S. Top grabbed it and shut it down. Beneath that was a shaving kit with all the essentials, including prophylactics and a bottle of genuine Viagra. Interesting items to pack when you're on a mission to cover your tail.

I thought about how I hadn't taken my blood pressure or cholesterol meds for days now. Compared to Barton's stash, my meds were anti-sex designed. That made me think of Lieutenant Sally Moore and I realized I had completely zoned out of my current mission. I refocused on the case, avoiding the looks from Sorensen and Top.

First, I saw a clean shirt, and then what I was looking for—four file folders stamped "Top Secret," and two standard college-ruled notebooks. One red and one green. A quick glance inside the red one revealed it was a journal, and the last page revealed Barton's recent conversation with Mubane. It was so recent that he must have written it in the room where he died. He had made a note to tell Mubane that the two Thai police officers were trying to squeeze more money out of him for their efforts. That answered the question of why they'd been executed.

I flipped back a couple of pages and saw that Barton had contacted the U.S. Ambassador to Thailand and warned him that there was an organized effort to "take over our little enterprise in Thailand." I wondered if that referred to the kidnapping and mutilating of children. We didn't have time to peruse the two books as Angela's image crossed my mind. I took them and stuffed them into my backpack, thought better of it, and instead asked Top to make a half dozen copies of them and secure the originals somewhere safe. He grabbed the binders and tucked them under the waistband at the rear of his trousers. (Not exactly what I had in mind as a "safe place," but it would do for now.)

Now that we had removed the latest threats to our endeavors, I asked Top to bring up the image of Mubane's home compound on the monitor. It appeared almost instantly as I stepped closer to study the wall and towers at the outside perimeter. It certainly wasn't the most difficult perimeter I had ever breached, but it was a formidable undertaking at my age and physical condition. A few years ago, I would have sniped the tower guards out of commission, thrown a rappelling hook up, and scaled the wall in minutes. Now, I would need a hydraulic lift.

I had Top zoom in on the front and rear gates and saw that they were designed like a prison: one gate, a stop area, and then a second gate that would not open until the first was shut and secured. There were several possibilities there but all risked being trapped between the gates and receiving numerous volleys of lead poison. I asked Top if there was a schematic or blueprint of the compound filed with the Government Building Department similar to our system in the States. He said there might be, but it would be a long shot, and knowing Mubane's concerns for security, he would have many hidden sections. I asked specifically about the wastewater draining and rainwater run-off. Top spoke into his headset and signed off. He said his folks were checking on that now.

I studied the compound further and saw that it was right next to a park or public area called Rose Garden. Most of the writing was in Thai, but the title of the area was in English. I pointed at it and Top said it was a small government-owned agricultural park often referred to as Thailand's Garden of Eden. It was a favorite tourist destination. I could see that its rear maintenance area was right next to Mubane's northern compound wall. A narrow greenway ran between them, and it looked like our best ticket to gain access to the compound. Top brought up more aerial photos of the park and more of Mubane's compound. Sorensen studied them closely.

Top received a call on his headset and then signed off. He turned and looked at the monitor as a group of small pictures appeared. I could see they were separate pages of blueprints and various permits dating back about twenty years. I studied them closely. As I pointed at one, Top enlarged it. I could see where the hidden sections were. Some of the buildings had whole wings with no interior detail, and one building was nothing more than an outline. When I pointed at it, Top read the Thai wording and said it was for future use. That document was nearly twenty years old. When I had Top bring up the latest aerial photo again, it showed a square building about five or six thousand square feet in size. Closer scrutiny revealed a loading ramp for trucks and cars, and each of the four main doors had ramps leading up from the ground level to the first floor of the building. It looked like a medical clinic of some kind with few windows. I also noticed that tall evergreens hid its ugly facade from the main house. More importantly, it was backed up against the north wall next to the Rose Garden Park. I had the beginnings of a plan in my head.

Top told us he had a meeting to handle and showed us to a room a couple of doors down from his office. He said the meeting was at his main building and might be of help to us regarding Mubane's residence. I told him that we would be ready to move as soon as he returned.

The room had two small bedrooms side by side and a living area with a kitchenette. After the Top left, Sorensen looked at me and told me that he knew what I was thinking, and it made sense to him. I told him we needed to take advantage of the downtime and clean up.

After I had a shower and a quick shave, I called the Major to brief him on the past few hours. As usual, I left out the gore and used our code talk to fill him in. He said he had been speaking with Gage and now had many of the names gleaned from the Schultz ledger. I told him that I had only briefed it but was surprised at the involvement of the many VIPs that I did see. He said that he was not so much surprised as let down by some of the folks he knew and had trusted over the years. I agreed with him and asked him to call Gage and fill him in, although I was sure he knew more about what was going on here in Bangkok than I did. I again emphasized the importance of keeping a lid on our discoveries until we had secured Angela. He agreed and signed off.

Considering the many bad people that I have had to deal with over the years, most folks would think I would have no faith in humanity. On the contrary, I have never lost my faith, and I never will. I don't judge. I take people as I find them. Many souls have departed by my hand, but very few due to revenge or judgment. Mostly, it was due to immediate necessity. If I can't get by them to my objective, I will put them down. Over the years, I have had many hypothetical conversations regarding the extent of force. Kill shots versus wounding. Both Sorensen and I are crack shots and can disable our opponents. However, the logistics of leaving a man alive on the battleground gives you one more concern to your rear as you move through. Then there's the revenge from a wounded adversary who may be rehabilitated enough to be lying in ambush. When I am returning from an objective, I am very aware of the destruction I have left and find it troubling to see that a scene has changed in my absence. Then again, I'm a former Marine. As the saying goes, "Marines don't enjoy killing, they just don't mind it." I let the Lord sort it out.

Sorensen and I sat in the living room and put our feet up. I set my watch to wake me in four hours. From the clock on the table, I could see that it was presently zero ten. (Ten after midnight) Four hours would give us time to prepare and get into the morning confusion at Mubane's estate. I was certainly aware that just because we cut the head of Mubane's effort against us, we were far from clear of any Plan B. I never underestimate my opposition. Unfortunately for them, they do me.

A moment after I closed my eyes, my watch vibrated, and I knew it was go time. I kicked Sorensen's foot and used the head. After rinsing my face and scraping my teeth, I took the offered cup of tea from Sorensen and walked down the hall to Top's office. As I expected, he was sitting at his desk, reading a stack of papers, and making notes on a notepad. He glanced up as we entered and smiled.

We'd had four hours of sleep and he was in a meeting, so he'd had little to none. He looked fresh and spry as he rose and knuckled us cheerfully. He told us that the bodies of the Americans and the Thai police had been found and that the prime minister had summoned the American ambassador to his office. The PM was expecting him to explain the resulting deaths of two of Thailand's most respected law enforcement officers, as well as why a high-ranking member of the Hong Kong Embassy's staff was in Thailand without notifying the Thai authorities.

I was impressed by all the words being used to describe a group of thugs' deaths at a Mubane property, none of which was being mentioned in the press release. Top told us the print media hadn't had a chance to write any articles due to the lack of time, but that the TV stations were in an uproar.

The first thought I had was that Mubane must be very upset. Not only had he lost a high-ranking CIA ally, but two highly placed state cops. That had to hurt in the scheme of things. He knew they hadn't killed each other, and that had to give him the creeps, knowing we were out there and had remained one step behind him for days now. He didn't know who we were, but he certainly knew we were coming after him. I wondered if he had a clue that Angela was our main objective. I hoped not or she would soon become a bargaining chip.

Top turned on the monitor and brought up a new overview of Mubane's home compound. This one was far clearer than the Google Earth-type views we'd seen before. The picture began to move, and I realized a drone must have filmed it. I asked him how old the video was, and he said we were looking at it live. It was nearly completely light out, which made me wonder what the real time was there. My watch was still on Eastern Standard Time.

Top saw me looking at the tiny time indicator on the screen and said it was five o'clock. I looked at the screen again, and he said the camera on the drone was enhanced and giving a brightened view of the grounds while staying hidden in the sky and fairly quiet. I could see a guard standing on the deck outside one of the towers, and he never even looked up at the drone. (I had to get Dave a couple of these! They would save him a trip or two to my island)

The drone drifted over to the Rose Garden Park and I could see the greenbelt area next to the wall. I could also see lights coming on in the clinic-looking building. That reminded me that we needed to move.

22

Top asked us for the little phones he'd lent us so he could download some apps into them that brought up the drone's camera view. It was obvious that the drone was running on a battery, so I asked Top how long it could stay in the air.

He said, "About an hour flying time, and longer when it didn't need to use the light-enhancing feature." He said the batteries could be changed in seconds, and that there were plenty of those with his team near the compound. He also said there were two drone units—the one we were watching and one on standby.

I was impressed. And, ready to go.

I told Top that Sorensen and I would go in alone and that I would appreciate it if he and his group acted as decoys if we ran into too much trouble. He said he already had a plan and his men had been in position for a couple of hours. He glanced back up at the monitor and the camera swung over the top of a building about two blocks away and showed a barely visible man lying prone on the roof with what looked like a rife so big and long I thought it was a bazooka. Top said it was a high-caliber, silenced rifle, and that it hardly made a sound. There were four of his snipers on surrounding roofs and ten men disguised as various workers circling the compound, including the park. All we needed was a catapult and some ladders and we could take the castle.

We left the office and made our way to the garage. Instead of climbing into one of his SUVs, Top led us to the tunnels again. After walking about fifty yards, we climbed a ladder and into the garage of another building. There were three big black SUVs sitting there with four men standing by two of them and our friend Andre next to the third one. Sorensen pointed at him and grinned. He was dressed just like Sorensen and had a full beard now. We walked toward the SUV and Top stopped us and pointed to a small, four-door car that looked like a carnival ride. Lieutenants Jones and Smith were standing next to it and saluted us smartly. Top saluted back and we climbed into the midget car. Sorensen got in the front and Top and I got in the back. We all had the same weapons we had used the night before and all the ammo we would need for a small war.

The lieutenant started the engine as the other three cars exited the building from a large garage door. We went out a small garage door and in the opposite direction. Top said the three-car caravan would lead any watchers on a wild goose chase while we made our way to the compound to the west.

Although Sorensen had the most room, he looked so uncomfortable that I thought he would bust the passenger side door open. The lieutenant was trying to avoid the potholes and sunken manhole covers, but they were too numerous, and every bump made Sorensen's neck redder and redder—a sure sign he was going to blow any minute. I quickly fixed the mood by asking him to view the monitor on his cell phone to see if the greenbelt next to the wall was still clear. He did and I saw him cool down almost immediately.

Top spoke into his headset and, when he signed off, told Sorensen that the scene was about to change as the second drone went online. As I watched Sorensen scan the monitor, he sat up a little straighter in his seat and announced, "We may have a problem."

I pulled out my cell phone and turned it on. The monitor showed the sidewall of the compound and the greenbelt at the edge of the park. I saw right away what Sorensen was talking about—and so did Top. He spoke rapidly into his headset in Thai and gave our lieutenant an order as we turned to the right at the next intersection. What we all saw were two large, dark vans that appeared out of the greenbelt from the direction of the compound wall. Mubane had some cards up his sleeve just like Top—a secret entrance and exit to his compound that most certainly was from an underground level. Two more vans exited while we watched. As soon as these vehicles drove out, the first vans started moving from where they'd been momentarily parked. It was a four-van convoy and they drove right through the park and left through a side gate to the west.

I asked Top how far the drones could follow them. He said not far, and that his team was in a similar van but stuck in traffic. He said we were about two miles away, but there was no chance we could catch up in this morning's traffic. I agreed and asked both Top and Sorensen what the chances were that Mubane was not in one of those vans. No one answered, and that was not the answer I wanted.

As we moved slowly through the traffic and Top spoke into his headset, I realized that we had no chance of intercepting Mubane's little convoy and hoped his destination was close enough for the drone to follow. Top signed off his headset as we watched our individual monitors.

Sorensen saw it first. All four of the vans turned in different directions and moved into the traffic heading to the winds, different directions, to confuse anyone tailing them. The drone circled, the operator waiting for instructions as the vans vanished into the many cars and trucks on the narrow roads.

I asked Top to have his controller bring one of the drones online over the compound again. He spoke into his headset and our monitor view changed as one of the drones turned back towards the compound. There was no doubt Mubane was heading for cover because of the attack on his downtown building last night. I imagined he had his whole family heading for cover.

I asked Top how many possible hideouts Mubane could have, and he said, "Too many."

I understood. I asked Top to drive Sorensen and me to the Mubane compound, as I knew there were some clues there, we could use to pick the trail back up. I thought out loud that there was not much of a chance of Mubane having his daughter or Angela operated on while we were harassing him so much. I also figured his daughter would not be up to the constant moving around we were causing Mubane. Both agreed with me and it seemed to lighten the mood a bit in the cramped little car.

We drove another few minutes and stopped on a side road behind some two- and three-story buildings. Top pointed down the narrow road and said the trees at the end were at the north side of the park. Mubane's compound would be directly south on the other side. I figured the park was about three hundred yards wide at that point so, other than being able to figure out the maze of foliage through the park, it didn't seem that difficult to get to the greenbelt disguised as tourists.

I asked Top if he would exchange some Thai money for the greenbacks I had, and he produced a wad of paper bills. I gave him about ten hundred-dollar bills from my pocket and he said, "Whoa, I only gave you about two hundred bucks there. Take some back."

I told him we were on a nearly unlimited budget thanks to a formerly live benefactor and that he should buy himself a Cadillac with the rest of the money. He laughed and put the greenbacks in his shirt pocket. I gave Sorensen a few bills and told him to buy a red Yugoslavian Yugo convertible. (As I had stated before it's a car that sold in the States for a couple of years back in the Seventies or Eighties. They were so bad that the U.S. stopped importing them.) I then asked Top to drop Sorensen off at the entrance to the park and I got out there in the alley. I told Sorensen I would see him at the greenbelt in a few minutes. Top said he would be in the area and standing by in case we needed extraction. I thanked him and we bumped knuckles before he pulled the door shut.

I walked the length of the narrow road and turned right to the entrance of the park. I could see Sorensen buying a ticket at the entrance kiosk along with several Caucasian tourists up ahead of me. He was fitting right in with the crowd, smiling and pointing to the beautiful flowers surrounding them at the gate. The park must not yet be open, as everyone was standing by the gate and waiting. Again, I had no idea what time it was and no clue when the park opened. I hung back at a little sidewalk cafe and had a cup of tea.

I scanned the fence circling the park and the extremely well manicured plants and bushes. I could smell the faint aroma of night jasmine or the haunting smell of wild roses. I loved the smell of wild roses. It always reminded me of some of the most wonderful times in my life—a soothing feeling I welcomed at a time of pre-mission jitters.

As I sat there, waiting for the park to open and Sorensen to be far enough away from me that we wouldn't be associated, I looked for the exit Mubane's convoys took a few minutes ago. It would be on the west side, according to the drone image, and I was on the north. I could see, at a diagonal, the west side fence line. There were too many bushes in the way, but I could see two brick towers about ten feet high that more than likely indicated the gate. I also noticed a black or dark blue van parked on the opposite side of the road with dark windows. I noticed it because the brake lights kept going on and off every minute or so.

One of the most important things to remember during a vehicle stakeout is to keep your foot off the brake pedal. In fact, don't even place your feet near the brake pedal. Those flashing lights will give you away every time. I could also see smoke come out of the top of the left-hand passenger seat window from time to time. This crew made all the mistakes. I could probably walk right up to them and bum a smoke and they wouldn't spook. That's what happens when you get bored and lose your mission awareness.

Just then, I saw Sorensen and his crowd start moving through the gate. I waited a few more moments, finished off my hot tea, and walked to the ticket booth. The smell of wild roses was even more evident as I stood there at the kiosk. I had to get my head back into the mission. I bought a ticket and donated a paper bill to a bottle for some Thai campaign for something or other. Received my ticket and a nice smile from the pretty clerk and walked to the gate.

As I passed my ticket to the gate attendant, I noticed a small Thai man standing off to the side of the gate, partially hidden in the bushes and looking at me up and down. I also noticed that he had a bulge on his left side under his hanging out shirt. It was definitely a pistol and he was definitely a member of Mubane's entourage. I did my best to look as if I didn't notice him by watching him in my peripheral vision. I passed through the gate and turned toward the guard as if he wasn't there. He did his little act of pretending I wasn't there, too. There was a couple trying to take a selfie in front of a beautiful rose bush, so I asked them if they would like me to take their photos. They smiled and spoke English that I hoped the guard didn't understand when they told me yes. After taking a couple of shots of them, I ended the conversation as the three of us moved along and out of sight of the guard. I could see that he had lost interest in me as soon as I started speaking with the young couple.

After telling them I was supposed to meet a friend on the other side of the park, I shook their hands and moved in and out of the little pathways until I saw the greenbelt and Sorensen's head sticking up above the foliage. As I approached, he walked toward me at a brisk pace and shook my hand as if we hadn't seen each other in years. As he smiled and patted me on the shoulder, he told me there were two cameras pointed right at us and a third pointed at the entrance behind us. As he told me this, we walked away from the greenbelt as Sorensen pointed to nothing in particular to get out of the camera's view. There was a gate leading into the greenbelt that was most certainly the escape route the vans had used that morning. The gate was disguised with vines and flowers woven into it. The giveaway was the crushed foliage and scraps of green debris on the narrow roadway. It was evident this route was not used often.

Sorensen and I walked a bit farther and found a men's room backed up against the greenbelt. I pointed to it and led Sorensen into the entrance. There were four or five couples from Sorensen's original group gathered around in the front, and they all smiled and said hello. We waited a few moments and then entered the smelly, five-holed, three-sink room. I did have to relieve myself and Sorensen looked around at the high windows that gave some vent relief to the stench. After carefully checking for cameras in the room, Sorensen pulled himself up and peered out the window at the rear of the building. The windows folded out and up and were certainly big enough for Sorensen to get through. I took a couple of steps out the door, saw no one in the area, and then waved him to go. He vanished through the window and I followed in a moment.

We landed on some bushes and vines that completely covered us as soon as we made it to the ground level. It was like a wide tunnel area leading nearly unimpeded to the wall.

We returned to the hidden gate and saw that it was indeed a ramp leading up from the lower level beneath the compound. Better yet, down a short, five-step staircase, there was a narrow door next to the ramp's roll-up door leading in and out. We didn't see any cameras around the doors or a window or peephole looking out.

I walked down to the small door and saw that it opened out, toward us. The cement stairs and stoop were covered with debris, clear evidence that they had not been used in quite a while. The ramp had crushed debris from the van's wheels. The door was locked, but loose in the jam. I pulled out my small knife and using it to slide the bolt back and then pulled the door open an inch or two. I could see it was completely dark inside and smelled musty and damp. Sorensen had his pistol at the ready in his right hand. His left hand was holding a hand grenade. I studied it a bit to check that the pin was still in the spoon. I took out my small flashlight and made sure the red lens cover was still attached. I then readied my silenced pistol. Nodding at Sorensen, I pulled the door open about a foot to see inside.

The area was too large for my flashlight lens to penetrate the darkness. I got a sight picture of what was up close on our side of the area. There was nothing. I took the lens cover off my light and peeked across the area again.

219

I could see a couple of vans and some boxes stacked up on the opposite side, near a cement staircase. It was all neat and clean. Too neat and clean. I also smelled the unique smell of Hoppe's gun cleaner. A smell I'd known for many years. A smell that was normally my friend. Today it spelled "Ambush."

Just as soon as I smelled the cleaner, I heard a faint click of what I recognized as the safety being released on an AK-47 rifle. I pushed the steel door shut and saw Sorensen pull the pin on his grenade. He let the spoon pop off, waited two beats, and in one motion, pulled the door open and rolled the grenade in. I pushed the door shut again and quickly moved back to Sorensen's side as the grenade went off. It was a lot quieter than I thought it would be, but it blew the door I had been standing behind back to the wall. If I had remained there, I would be a lot thinner now. Sorensen threw a second grenade farther in this time and we took off toward the east, along the wall.

It was like a tunnel along the wall where the roots of the bushes and vines grew up from the ground. The greenery was high up with little foliage to obstruct our progress. I felt my phone vibrate in my shirt pocket, but there was no time to pull it out to answer it. We were heading along the northern wall and toward the east where the main gate was located. I'm not sure why I decided to run this way except I was familiar with it from the drone shots. That thought reminded me that we had a clear view of what was ahead on the little phone.

We made it to the front wall and turned around the corner. I stopped a moment and took out the phone. It was dark under the bushes and the monitor was easy to view. I could see the overview of the compound with about twenty or more troops dressed in jungle fatigues running from one side of the compound to the other. I don't know how many egress points there were from the lower level up to the ground, but it looked like they were expecting a large raiding party to emerge from the depths any moment now. Most, if not all them, were carrying rifles.

As I looked at the monitor, I felt the phone vibrate that a call was coming in again. I pushed the button and waited until I heard Top say, "Hello?"

I greeted him by saying, "It was nice to be expected." He didn't laugh, nor did I. He asked where we were right then. I told him we were about ten feet from the corner of the north wall, right under the guard tower. Top said there were numerous troops on their way from the Bangkok Garrison and some local police were just arriving at the Rose Park entrance. I gained a whole new respect for Mr. Mubane.

I told Top we were going to make our way back to the fence at the east side of the Rose Park and use the cover of the bushes to get to the north-facing fence near the entrance. As I was talking to Top, I could see the troop activity in the Park area and the confusion it was causing with the visitors. There appeared to be about fifty or sixty civilians running in and out of the paths around the park, and the police moving through the area appeared to be just as confused. They were pointing their rifles and pistols at everything that moved, and from where Sorensen and I were squatting, we could hear the screams clearly.

I moved first, passing Sorensen, and reaching the eight-foot fence. It wasn't as easy to push through the foliage as the compound wall, but we were able to make good progress. The rose thorns were unpleasant but tolerable. I saw a snake in our path and stepped right over it. I didn't mention it to Sorensen, as snakes were not his friends. I didn't need him throwing a grenade at it right now.

We reached the end of the east fence and found that the foliage was a bit thinner and we were about to lose our overhead cover. I looked back toward the northeast guard tower and saw a guard looking our way intensely. He was pointing his rifle at us, too. I quick-called Top and asked if we still had an asset or two on the roofs. He said yes and had already given the order. He no sooner had finished his sentence when we saw the tower guards head come apart into red mist. Just as quickly, the second guard's head followed his buddies into the Promised Land.

Sorensen shoved me forward and we cleared the brush and landed on a small grassy area next to the main road. There were twenty or so people running up the sidewalk and passing us. We joined them, and as we approached the next intersection, saw our little car, driven by our lieutenant, stop on the opposite side of the roadway. I smacked Sorensen on the arm, and we ran across the road to the waiting car.

This time, Sorensen jumped into the empty back seat and pulled out his pistol while watching our rear. I climbed into the front passenger side and the car accelerated to the north. There were still folks swarming out of the park's front entrance and into the street and grassy areas near the gate. As we looked to the west, toward the Park gate, we could see maybe ten police vans and a few police scooters clogging the road. We continued north and then turned east back toward Bangkok.

The lieutenant told us we were going to a safe house close by and Top would meet us there. Sorensen was sitting with his back to the door and his feet on the seat, looking behind us for any tail we may have picked up. Every now and then, a Police vehicle would go charging by in the opposite direction. The cops and Mubane's troops would be chasing their tails for a while yet.

I had a moment to reflect on what had happened, how we'd been set up and led into that trap. When Sorensen asked the lieutenant what went wrong, he shrugged and said, "Top is going over the entire operation from the beginning to try and find the glitch."

I told him the glitch was that it was all too easy from the intel about Mubane's location and our assumption that he would still be there. There was no doubt in my mind that he and his family, probably along with Angela, left out through the park that morning and we were expected to hit the compound as we had all his other properties in the last couple of days. He would be waiting for us now with more surprises up his sleeve. I was also concerned about Top's staff of fifty or more folks that I was sure knew about our general plans.

As we approached the outskirts of downtown Bangkok, I asked the lieutenant to pull over to the side of the road. He did immediately. I looked back at Sorensen, and he didn't need any explanation; he climbed out onto the sidewalk. I told Smith and Jones we would contact Top shortly, closed the door, and stepped over to Sorensen on the sidewalk. The car pulled off into the traffic flow and vanished.

Sorensen was busy checking our perimeter and scanning the road we had come down. I tapped his arm and we walked back toward the west until we reached the next crossroad and went down a southbound road. I told Sorensen that we had depended too long on Top's intelligence and needed to break it off for at least for a few hours and re-group. He agreed with me and added that he felt Top had a mole in his group.

I should have followed my instincts when we entered the Rose Park earlier after seeing the watcher near the gate. I had to settle my nerves and level out my anxiety about finding Angela. I was doing her no good by making these quick decisions without better planning and taking the time to analyze the situation before any action. Even my thinking was blurred. We needed to rest badly, and the further we went without some sleep, the more mistakes we would make. Just to reinforce my thinking, a group of four ambulances buzzed by the road we had just left with sirens screaming, heading for the hospitals downtown.

I was sure there were a couple of pounds of Sorensen's grenade shrapnel riding with them. I took out Top's little cell phone and it still had the last drone view it picked up before being shut down and secreted back in its box. The monitor showed the compound with smoke billowing from several doorways and rooftops. A clear result of the grenades catching some of the vehicles and boxes on fire in the subterranean area. There were numerous folks on the grass areas and parking lots. There were several uniformed men or women near the north wall of the park, facing the compound. That was a sure sign that our cover had been blown and that they were waiting for us to exit the way we had gone in. I had no idea how many minutes ago the picture had been taken. The clock on the photo was of no use, as I had no idea what the time was then. Sometime around 0900, I suspected. The phone should have had the correct time on the screen, but it didn't. Probably programmed that way by Top's techs to function only with an in-house system.

Sorensen was looking at his cell as well and, at the same time, we pulled the backs off them and pulled out the batteries. I didn't want to chuck them into the trash, as I was sure they were extremely sensitive. We could be hacked by the wrong folks. We took the chance that there was no hidden power source running a locator in them and put them in our pockets. I turned on one of my burner phones and called.

As usual, Gage was up to date on the happenings in Bangkok (and everywhere else in the world.) He answered by stating that there were fifteen confirmed dead private security guards and many injured at the home of a prominent Thai citizen. Presently, the news was being blasted all over the airwaves as folks woke to a beautiful, sunshiny day around the world. He asked if we had heard of any of the excitement.

I said, "No, we must have slept through it."

He said that they were blaming it on Muslim terrorists opposed to the government. I told him that must be it and asked for some updates from back in the States. I had to wait a moment or two while two more ambulances screamed by. Gage was silent for a few moments before asking if we were walking away or standing around, looking to get caught. I reminded him I had asked for an update.

Gage first stated that Captain Lee in Rio was sending periodic intelligence reports through Sorensen's network covering Sorensen in Brazil. He said the City of Rio was entertaining the idea of leaving the yacht, *The*

Lady Catherine, on the beach as a tourist attraction at the urging of the hotel and area vendors. I cut in and told Gage that was all very cute, but I wanted to know how our girls were getting on and if any of them had sounded the alarm on the goings on in the Far East. He said it was all still quiet in the news area but expected it to blow open any minute now because lawyers were getting involved and demanding discovery from the State Department. He said that Bangkok was the center of the news right now because a prominent member of the State Department, stationed in Hong Kong, was assassinated along with two of Thailand's Finest by an unknown group of terrorists. I gave him the short version on Barton and Mubane's thugs. He said he had already figured it out.

Gage briefed me on Emily, Carol, and Sandy. He said they were safe. He told me that Marsh Grant and wife took control of the ladies as soon as they were able, so I knew they were alright now. The two L.A. girls were home and Emily was about to be reunited with some of her relatives in Southern California. He said her mother was still being kept in the dark but was told her daughter had been found and was safe.

He went on to say that the Major was forming a group of his closest legal allies so they could standby for the task of the century as soon as it was safe to go public. The Major has a good female U.S. Senator friend we all trust, and Gage said she had been briefed. She was now standing by to expose all those in Congress involved in this mess. Although the Major knew it reached into the White House, he probably hadn't told her that yet. This had the potential to bring down our government and cripple many governments around the globe. We had stepped into some serious crap and it was getting deeper.

As we walked, Gage filled me in on the Cohen and the Davis families in Ocala. Paul Davis's wife and daughter had driven back to Ocala and they were all staying at the Cohen ranch for the time being. Dave was holding the fort on my island. I asked Gage to contact Nick in New Zealand and make sure all was well there and that things were calm and normal. I also asked Gage to check on our female Marine pilots and see if they were still tasked to Sorensen and me. I couldn't think of anything further to say and needed to get my head back into the current situation.

I signed off from Gage and stopped at a sidewalk cafe to grab a coke and a sweet roll. Sorensen did the same, except he is a big coffee drinker and ordered two cups. Sorensen gave me the look and I filled him in on Gage's briefing. He told me that the reports Tom Lee was sending to Miami for him had seemed to have satisfied his boss, who believed he was still in Rio. He said Tom had sent a few photos of the yacht on the beach to show how popular it was to the tourists. He went on to say that several politicians had resigned over the past few days and numerous arrests had been made among Schultz's employees. Sorensen also added that Tom and his small band of trusted counterparts had found ten more kids being illegally held near Schultz's compound. Most of them from Europe and the Middle East. He said that Tom was discovering more and more intelligence regarding illegal activities in and around Brazil and the Caribbean. I told him to put a hold on the rest of his news so I could figure out our next move.

As we sat there and I ran several ideas through my "brain housing group," I noticed that Sorensen was drawing a great deal of attention due to his size and bushy, bearded face. I wondered if our photos or descriptions were being broadcasted on the news. I hoped our friend Andre was still circulating around as a decoy and that that was keeping the local law enforcement busy elsewhere. The sirens had quieted down, and things seemed to be getting back to normal up on the main road. A police van came cruising down the road, but Sorensen was behind a folding sign next to our table on the sidewalk and they never did anything but glance in our direction.

I told Sorensen we needed to split up for a few minutes to break up the Mutt and Jeff routine while I found us a room to re-group and rest in. I could see a small Thai hotel a little farther south and figured it was as good a place as any to start covering our tracks. I told Sorensen that I was going to check in there, then do the usual—slip out the back and grab a room at another.

He and I walked to the little hotel. Did our best to act like tourists. Asked all the right questions about the local sights, restaurants, and the possibilities of bed bugs. I was sure the clerk thought Sorensen and I were lovers. She smiled while she answered our questions in broken, but understandable, English. After paying in cash and giving the clerk a generous tip in greenbacks, we received a key to each for our single rooms with a "very large bed," and then made our way to the staircase leading up from the lobby. As soon as we had reached the third floor, we walked to the rear of the building, then back down, and then slipped out into the alley on the next road over. I told Sorensen to do some shopping while I found another hotel. I told him I would call him shortly.

I lingered a few moments while I covered Sorensen's back, then turned

south and went down the road, looking for a temporary nest. I was
exhausted and my gait showed it as I cut in and out of the foot traffic. The
advantage of having Sorensen walking next to you was that he made a hole,
and I very seldom had to dodge in and out of sidewalk crowds. That
morning', however, I was invisible. I had more folks bump into me and step
in front of me than I'd had in a long while. I spotted another small hotel
and walked in.

There was a young female Thai working the desk. She smiled
beautifully as I walked up to her. (A bright spot in the midst of the gloomy
mood I was in). I asked her for a double and she looked confused. I restated
that I would like a room with two beds. She lit up again and asked for a
credit card. I gave her a hundred-dollar bill for the room and a second one
for her overlooking the credit card request. She was more than happy to
oblige and, in fact, asked if I would like the adjoining room, too. I thought
about it for a moment and said I would. I tried to give her another hundred
and she laughed and said it wasn't necessary.

The rooms were on the second floor and at the end of the hall from the
main stairs leading up from the lobby. The rear stairs were right beside the
door to my second room. I peeked inside and was impressed at how neat
and clean the room was. I checked the second room and it was just as neat
and clean. I unlocked the adjoining door and went back to my room. I
called Sorensen, gave him the location, and said I would prop the door open
leading in from the rear alley. I could hear some music in the background
and figured he had found a honky-tonk that was open early. He said he
would be along in a while. I couldn't believe he wasn't passed out from
exhaustion by now.

As much as I didn't want to crash without knowing Sorensen was in
and secure, I couldn't help but lie down. I was out in a flash. I awoke a few
minutes later when Sorensen tapped on my door to get in. I could tell it was
just a few minutes as the sun shining through the curtains had only moved
its beam about three inches or so on the wall and floor. Sorensen came in
and I pointed to his room, where he disappeared with a glance in my
direction. I heard a flop and knew he was down for the count.

I found the room clock on the little desk behind my backpack and set it
for 1600. It said the time was 1100. That would give us five hours of rest. I
gave Top a quick call to let him know we were all right and nesting. He
thanked me for the call and said he and a select group of his staff were
gathering intelligence and should have something helpful by late afternoon.

That told me two things. He knew he had a mole or two, and that he was not annoyed that we had ditched him. I had an idea that he knew where we were. After all, we had a pile of his stuff and we were even wearing his clothes. I was sure there was a locator planted somewhere on us. I thanked him and signed off.

I looked in on Sorensen and found him flat on his back with a pillow over his face. I also saw he had his pistol gripped in his left hand along his side. It was the closest arm to the door. Sorensen could shoot perfectly with both hands and, in fact, could shoot with both hands at the same time. Many folks can do that, however, few of them are as accurate as he is. Whenever he and I go to a range to practice, it never ceases to amaze me that Sorensen never flinches as he fires—or when anyone else does!

lay back down and thought of Lieutenant Sally, but quickly put her out of my mind and brought up Angela.

In my mind, I concentrated on her face and wondered if her captors were treating her well or tormenting her. All the negative things I could think of rushed through my mind as I batted them away one by one. Thinking positive about her, I believed, would give her energy and some hope. I wondered if she even knew what they wanted her for. I chose to think that they would keep her close to their daughter, perhaps even a companion so their spirits could meld before the operation.

Soon, I was out of it. I dreamt of my island home and sailing my boats. Many quick dreams filled with euphoria. The kind of rest my head needed. All too soon, the clock rattled and attempted to make a pleasant chime to wake me up. It sounded more like a miniature klaxon and, at about the same time, there was a crack of thunder to reinforce the clock's attempts to take me.

It took me a moment to figure out how to turn the alarm turn off. By that time, Sorensen was standing in the doorway, scratching his head and telling me how pleasant a wake-up that was. I told him I had nothing to do with the lightning. He grunted and shook his head.

I went into the small bathroom and washed my face and brushed my teeth. I wondered how long it would be before our next sleep. Thoughts of

Angela cleared my head of such thoughts and brought me back to reality.

I could hear the rain coming down outside and it brought back memories of Vietnam. Even the old familiar smells of the dust and grime being washed down the streets made me drift back to a time when only the present counted, and the future had no meaning at all.

The rain was pounding down outside as I packed my gear back into my backpack and pockets. Sorensen had just fieldstripped his pistols and wiped them down with the oil he kept in a little tube in his pocket. I glanced at my two pistols, blew some lint off one, and stuffed them in my pockets. I peeked out the window, but all I could see was a wall of water running off the roof and some blur of the building next door. I took out my phone and called Top.

He answered on the first ring and I pictured him standing behind his desk, pressing the little button on his headset. Looking at his monitors on the wall and reaching for the ever-present remote control his life seemed to depend on. He greeted me pleasantly enough and asked if I was enjoying the weather. I told him it was great, and I couldn't wait to get outside to play. He grunted a laugh and told me he had a bit of info I may be interested in. I hoped it was good info. The weather outside was quickly dragging down my spirits.

Mubane and his family were seen about an hour ago walking through the rear entrance of a hotel near the airport. Top's informant described two young girls traveling with him, and one description was of his daughter and the other was most certainly Angela. I didn't like the idea that they were at the airport but was encouraged by the fact that we knew where they were at all. There were numerous airports in the Bangkok area where he could fly out with his own aircraft, but he was staging at the big one, which could mean he was leasing a big jet for a long trip.

Top's intelligence was about to get a workout. I asked him to keep us briefed and signed off. I filled Sorensen in on Top's side of the conversation and he shook his head as another building-rattling roar of thunder shook us to the bone. He opened the door to the hall and made for the stairs. I dropped a hundred-dollar bill on my still made-up bed and followed.

I always carried Ziploc bags in my right rear pocket. You could count on them being there the way you could count on my comb. My pockets were a daily ritual with me, and certain pockets held items with no exceptions. A shrink might call it an outward sign of OCD. To me, it was a matter of convenience and time saving to locate and put my fingers on an

229

item immediately when I needed it. The Ziploc bags were one of the habits that I was so well known for that Sorensen just stuck out his hand as we descended the stairs and I placed a large bag in it. In one motion, he placed into it his passport, wallet, and other items I couldn't make out. He held out his hand again and I gave him a smaller one that he placed two phones in and then sealed the bags. I placed the phone that Top had given me into the bag after I reassembled it. I had two more phones in my pockets already sealed in bags. My wallet and passport went into another. I had a few more passports and IDs sealed in my backpack. The backpack had a plastic liner that kept out most of the moisture and, from the sounds of the rain as we approached the door, I figured we should have brought along a couple of wet suits and swim fins!

Just as I was about to push through the door, I heard a faint step in the hall behind us. I quickly turned to see the young girl from the front desk walking toward us, carrying two large, military-type ponchos. The kind with a hood that we used in the Nam. She presented them to us and bowed.

I looked all over the ceiling and walls to see if I had missed a surveillance camera but saw none. I thanked her and started to reach for my cash pocket, but she pressed her hand on mine and shook her head no. She pointed to the door as a big Chevy Suburban appeared under the stoop and she vanished down the hall. "Top."

Sure enough, the driver was none other than our Lieutenants Smith and Jones, smiling as he hopped out of the traditional left side driver's door—in contrast to the right-side driver's positions in standard Thai automobiles. He opened the left rear door for Sorensen and me to jump in. Sorensen slid over to the right side and I sat behind the driver's seat. All he said was "Good evening, sirs," put the transmission in gear, and drove off into the rain.

The traffic was terrible, and the rain made it worse. People dashed across the road without any concern for the moving cars causing drivers to jam on their brakes, which had a domino effect on all the cars behind. Our lieutenant never appeared to get flustered and drove as smooth as he could. There must have been a camera built into the rear of the car, as I could see a small monitor on the dashboard reflecting headlights and some movement. The lens was so wet from the rain that I couldn't make out much, but our driver kept glancing at it as he drove. I looked out the rear window, but all I saw was rain and headlights. Our vehicle was so big compared to the smaller cars and vans surrounding us that we were part of the problem as we squeezed through the narrow lanes. The blaring horns were an added treat.

As he drove, our lieutenant spoke silently into his headset. From time to time, he would turn down a side road, and, after a couple of roads, would turn back east and continue. Obviously, he was being given some traffic advice, and it did seem to help our progress. I asked him how far it was to the airport, as he hadn't mentioned where we were going, and he said normally thirty minutes, but the rain was really backing us up. He said that Top had a helicopter standing by, but the weather was too bad to fly.

I was thankful these cowboys had their limitations. In Vietnam, we relished flying in that kind of weather because it kept the sniper fire down and we had fewer casualties. I looked at Sorensen and could tell by his glance and nod that he was thinking the same things. He and I have spent a lot of time together scrunched up in the rain. The rain gave us a break from the tensions of a mission and some downtime to rest.

My little phone vibrated in my pocket and I saw it was Top calling. I say that, even though you would think it had to be him because the only other people who knew I had that phone were sitting in the car with me. Not so, though. There is Gage. I have had him call me on a pay phone that was ringing as I walked down a street. He had an incredible surveillance system that I never even question anymore. But it was Top, and I answered as soon as I clicked the phone open.

24

Top started out apologizing for the inclement weather and then said it was a good thing, as the airport was shut down due to low visibility. I asked him how close Mubane's hotel was from the airstrip, and he said the rear of the hotel was right on a seldom-used taxiway and the gate to the airstrip wasn't usually manned. He said an airport security van was parked there now, which was an indication that Mubane was standing by to use it. Top said there was no aircraft there yet, but it would only take minutes to get one there once the rain died down a bit.

I looked out of the windshield and saw that the rain hadn't subsided even a little since we'd started driving. I thanked Top and he said he would keep us posted if anything changed.

I briefed Sorensen, and, while I did, Lieutenant Smith or Jones passed his phone back, showing a weather radar application screen. The entire Bangkok area was socked in and there didn't seem to be a break anywhere. I passed him back his phone and shook my head in frustration. The lightning spoke to me, saying, "You're welcome." I thought back, *Not now*. We sputtered on, in and out of roads, making little progress toward the airport.

I took out one of my own phones and called Gage. He asked if we were enjoying the liquid sunshine. I told it as a piece of cake compared to Merritt Island during a tropical storm. Then I told him that wasn't true. The rain was like standing under Niagara Falls during the spring thaw.

Gage was a few years younger than Sorensen and me and was too young for Vietnam. By the time the next war effort came along, he was embedded in the Intelligence Community and far too important to send off to Iraq or Afghanistan, so he hadn't had the pleasure of a real monsoon season. However, he had lived through a few hurricanes, so he could imagine the downpours here. I briefed him on Mubane and our suspicion that he was getting ready to fly out to parts unknown. I told him I was sure he had Angela with him and that I intended to chase him if and when he left. I explained that we were some distance from the airport but that the rain had closed the airstrip down until it cleared some.

I asked Gage for two things: to contact our pilots, if they were still available, and keep an eye on whatever aircraft we determined Mubane might take off in if we were unable to catch up with him at the airport. Gage informed me that our ride was not far off at a base in Rangoon, Myanmar (Burma). He said that our bird was equipped with all the bells and whistles and could land even in the storm we were in. The only thing that could hold them back was Air Traffic Control.

I said that wasn't a problem because Mubane would be under the same restrictions. I told Gage that I suspected Mubane was going to fly out on a large plane because he was at the International Airport, and I expected him to have the plane pick them up behind the hotel he was last seen entering. I still wasn't sure Mubane knew we were chasing him or why. We had messed up a lot of real estate in the past few days, but a man as powerful and wealthy as he was, running the bad businesses he ran, was probably used to being attacked often and from different directions.

Gage said he would pull out all the stops if Mubane got away. He was also sure he could follow him wherever he went. I thanked him and signed off, as the rain appeared to be letting up.

We picked up a little speed, but we were still driving about as fast as I could walk. I looked through my phone list in my little book and found the number for the G5. Captain Cline answered on the first ring. I told her we needed them to get in the air as soon as they could and circle around until they were cleared to land at Bangkok International. She said she had spoken to the spook (Gage) and had already filed a flight plan into Suvarnabhumi International. I was impressed with her pronunciation of the multi-syllable name but knew (I or she?) would forget it as fast as she said it. I asked her to contact me as soon as she was in the area and I would direct her if she needed it. I was tempted to ask for Sally but resisted like a true professional!

The rain slowed even more as we trudged along, now to the southeast. My hopes began to vanish as I heard the roar of a huge jet blast overhead. It had no sooner flown by when the little phone vibrated. I answered it by telling Top I had heard. He said the airport had been opened and that there was a large 767 commercial jet heading toward the hotel from the civilian side of the field. As he was speaking, he asked me to stand by for a moment, came back on, and said Mubane's entourage were climbing into the cars and vans behind the hotel. It was still raining but far less than it was. We were still creeping along at a snail's pace. Top said the plane had reached the gate and a wheeled stair truck had backed up to its side. Then security opened the gates as Mubane's vehicles pulled up.

I thought about asking Top if he could order some sort of deterrent like a couple of gunshots into the air by one of his informants or even call in a bomb threat on the aircraft. None of my ideas would do anything but put Angela and the innocents in more danger than they were in presently. I signed off and called our pilots on their satphone. Sally answered straight away, and I requested they pick us up. I asked if they needed to refuel and she said no, they had nearly full tanks and had filled their spare fuel bladder in anticipation of a long flight back to the States when needed. I thanked her and told her that was wise of them. She said she would call when they'd landed and were requesting to taxi to the FBO called South Ocean Services. I thanked her and signed off. I passed the info to our lieutenant and he said he knew where it was located.

Ten minutes later, we were driving through the gates of the field to the civilian FBOs. I could hear planes taking off beyond and wondered which one was Mubane's. Just as I had processed that thought, both of my active phones rang—Top's and Gage's. I passed Top to Sorensen and answered Gage. He informed me that the 767 charter Mubane was on just filed a flight plan for Hong Kong. I knew that was a ruse because Mubane would already know about the trouble we left there. I asked him to keep a watch on the plane's direction and signed off.

Sorensen jotted down some info on his little pad and then signed off with Top. He looked at his notes a bit longer and sighed once or twice, then said, "Ciudad de Mexico."

I looked at him and said nothing until he repeated it. I couldn't imagine what Mubane was going to do in Mexico City. I knew this was a small world, but Mexico was on the other side of the world. He had to have a good reason to go there. There were a lot of shenanigans going on in

Mexico, so he probably had plenty of dark contacts there. The kind of contacts that included agents who would do anything for a price.

I asked Sorensen if it might be another ruse and he said one of the pilots was on Top's payroll and signaled him as soon as Mubane gave them their destination. I thanked him and signed off. I immediately called our pilots to inform them of our destination. Sally answered again, and I briefed her on Mexico City. She said she would do the math and fill us in when they arrived at the FBO. They may just top-off with fuel when they landed. I thanked her and signed off. I then called Gage back to inform him and ask about what assets we had in Mexico. He answered on the second ring, (I keep score!) and said he would get back to me shortly.

Our lieutenant parked on the side of the building in front of the sign saying "SOS." A cute reference to South Ocean Services. We sat there a moment as Smith or Jones spoke on his headset. He held his hand up for us to stand down as we went to open the doors. He signed off and said there were two unsavory-looking characters in the lobby of the building, and they appeared to be armed. One of Top's sources worked in the office there and had briefed Top a few minutes ago. Mubane, or his security, were covering all the bases.

We had to go through the lobby to reach the tarmac where our plane was going to park. There would be airport security there, too. I could see another FBO a little farther on called "Krong Thep Services." I spotted a very large hangar and some English writing that appeared to say, "Full Service." There were two fuel trucks that had the same logo printed on their sides parked a short distance from the building on the tarmac. I quickly called the pilots and told them about our change in plans. Sally said they had just touched down and would pull over to the FBO without informing the tower. I signed off and told Smith or Jones to head over there.

While we were rolling, I called Top to inform him about the change. He put me on hold and came back shortly. He said he had no assets at that FBO yet, but told us to expect company, just to be safe. I understood what he was implying. I signed off and informed Sorensen. He nodded and re-adjusted his weapons in his pockets. I told our lieutenant to pull over next to some cars in a parking lot before the FBO.

Sorensen pulled out his little monocular and studied the building that was now about a hundred yards away. I saw our ride moving toward us from the main airfield. I called the pilots and told them there may be a little trouble and to be on guard. I asked Sally about the fuel status and she said that they had a normal cruising range of about 6,050 miles and that that was a full load estimate. With the extra bladder, they gained another two thousand miles or so, so they should be able to make the trip without refueling if they topped off there in Bangkok. I told her to do so and to expect us to board just after they finished refueling. I signed off and watched the G5 pull up near one of the fuel trucks.

Sorensen said he could see a uniformed guard or police officer standing next to the gate leading from the building to the tarmac. There was also a large sliding gate next to the building with a keypad stand next to it. I quickly called Top and asked him if any of his sources happened to know the code to the gates. He put me on hold and came back quickly, giving me the current code. I then asked him to call the FBO and inform them that a group of diplomats was arriving for a flight to Manila on a U.S. registered charter. He said that that was not exactly how it was done but he would handle it.

Top signed off and our lieutenant climbed out of his car and went to the rear hatch. He tinkered around a bit back there and then walked to the front of the car. He placed an American flag on a short mast into a holder next to the headlight. I told him that that may buy us some time if we needed it, and he lifted an AR-15 from the seat next to him. I told him that was also a time saver. I also knew we couldn't shoot our way into the sky from a major airport. The Thai Air Force would shoot us down ten minutes after we took off.

I could see the fuel truck pumping fuel into our bird. I could also see Sally walking around, doing her preflight check of the plane. I was still trying to figure out what she may look like in something other than a bulky flight suit. Maybe a bikini, or less.

We sat in the SUV for a few minutes, waiting for the fuel truck to leave so we could drive right up to the ladderway to the plane. As we waited, I glanced at the other FBO and saw two Thai men walking toward the parking lot. One of them had a pistol in his hand and he was looking into each car as they passed. I nodded to Sorensen, who had already seen them. They were coming up on his side of the car, so I slipped out of my side and to the ground. I could see their feet moving under the other cars as they approached. I crawled to the front of our car and then continued until I was just opposite them at the rear of a car.

As they passed behind, I slipped down the length of the car and knelt behind them as they approached our car. Just as the first guy holding the pistol started to take aim at our car, I shot him right behind the right ear. He went down quickly. His partner appeared confused since the airport noise had masked the sound of my silenced pistol. As he bent down to check why his buddy was lying on the ground, I sneaked up and clobbered him on the crown of the head. Sorensen jumped out of the car and Smith or Jones ran around and opened the rear hatch. I grabbed the unconscious guy and Sorensen grabbed the deadie and, together, we heaved them into the rear deck and covered them with a tarp.

Just then, I saw the fuel truck pull away from our plane and we backed out of the space and proceeded to the gate next to the building. Smith or Jones punched in the code on the keypad and the gate slid back just as advertised. We drove right to the plane and climbed out through the door next to the ladderway. I saluted our lieutenant and climbed the stairs without looking back. The pilots were already in their seats and Sorensen lifted the ladderway and closed the hatch. Captain Cline said that the guards in the lobby of the FBO were watching but staying inside.

As she spoke, I could hear the engines coming to life. First one, then the other. I could hear some mumbles from the cockpit, and then we were rolling. Cline must have requested the short runway as we turned and pointed into the wind. She revved up the engines and we were off like a rocket. We were flying west but shortly turned south, then east.

I waited to hear if we were going to be intercepted, but we kept on flying east until I was sure we were in Cambodian airspace. About forty minutes into our flight, Sally came back and said we were out of harm's way and she had filed a flight plan to Manila as I had suggested. She said she would alter that as soon as we crossed the South China Sea.

The smell of jet fuel was strong in the cabin because of the fuel bladder lying down in the center aisle. Sally said we would get used to it. I didn't mention to her that Sorensen and I had had years of fuel–smell-laden flying behind us. Both of us had flown in KC-130 aircraft all over the world from Vietnam to Africa. The only thing slower than a C-130 was a hot air balloon. And, smelly? They smelled as if you were bathing in a diesel tank. So, she need not have apologized for anything.

I was more interested in how far behind Mubane we were. Sally said that his 767 was about two to three hundred miles ahead of us and pretty much could go at the same speed.

Because the fuel bladder was stretched down the center of the cabin, we had to straddle it to get to the rear area for food or coffee. I used the small head behind the cockpit instead of the bigger one in the rear. It made me nervous to walk on the rubber tube for fear a seam could pop open under my weight. Sorensen just walked on it as if it wasn't there.

Sorensen slept most of the trip while I communicated with Gage and the Major. I received one call from Top saying that our lieutenant had made it back from the airfield without incident. I asked if all the contents of the car had been handled, and he feigned ignorance as to what I was talking about. I knew the one guy with the bump on his head was still alive, as he had started moaning before we left the car. I figured he would wake up in some alley somewhere, wondering what train had hit him.

I also took some time to look through my email and answer the ones that were important. Dave always had a running list of chores he had performed or repairs he had made. I checked my bank account to make sure my auto-pay program was keeping me out of debtor's prison. Everything seemed to be working just fine without me. Someday, the computers were going to say, "Get lost," and humans would cease to exist.

Gage kept me briefed on Mubane's flight. The 767 was sending signals to some satellite out in space and gathering mechanical data regarding the engines and navigation systems. Gage was tuned into all that and reported that Mubane and his entourage were on a set course for Mexico City.

Sally came back a couple of times to brief me on our location and the latest ruse of our destination. She had refiled our flight plan several times in case anyone was interested in us. Once, she came back and said we were somewhere over the Bikini Islands. That perked my interest in her flight suit again. I believe she sensed it as she made a point of bending over the fuel bladder and pressing on it like it was a spare tire. An unnecessary move, as you could feel it with your feet as you stepped on its edges. I choose to think she was showing off the outlines of a very well-formed tail section.

As we approached the coast of Mexico, Gage called and said he had a couple of assets standing by at the airport to watch the Mubane folks arrive. He told me an old friend would greet us when we got there, and that he had already arranged for our aircraft to be serviced. I thanked him and woke up Sorensen by kicking him from across the aisle. He woke up slowly, which I knew was faked. Sorensen was always aware of everything around him. Even when he was sleeping.

I briefed him on our location and Gage's info. He told me that our mystery greeter was going to be Tom Lee from Rio. I didn't ask him how he knew that but let him continue by telling me that Tom was still on the case regarding Brazil's interest in the Schultz connection. Made sense, seeing how he and Mubane were informal associates in a worldwide illegal enterprise.

Top said there were several covert investigations going on regarding the human trade market. I was concerned about who was on the teams, as I had seen too many important names on Schultz's ledger—including Sorensen's own leadership. It was going to make for an interesting situation when all these folks were exposed. If we all lived long enough to follow through with it. I was sure we—whoever they thought *we* were—were destined for elimination in their dreams. Then again, I was sure these folks weren't getting a lot of sleep these days.

We landed at Mexico City International, Gage having informed us that Mubane landed about fifty minutes before. We still had fuel to spare, although the fuel bladder was empty and rolled up into the aft galley.

I hoped that our own watchers were on the ball. I looked for a 767 parked at any of the FBOs as we taxied by them. Didn't see any but figured he would have his pilots pull into a shaded hangar. The airport was massive, so they could be anywhere. We pulled into a smaller facility at the far end of the civilian FBOs. There we were instructed to park in between two former U.S. Air 737s being refurbished. They must have had some rain in the past couple of days, as everything was clean. I have landed at this airport many times and there was always dust covering everything. The sky was a deep, bright blue. (Perhaps I'd reset my watch that day.) Meanwhile, I needed intelligence quickly.

Sorensen went from one side of the cabin to the other, looking out of the portholes to check our security. He didn't hesitate at all, so that was the signal that all was well for the moment. Sally came aft and opened the hatch. She looked left and right before running the ladder down. After the stairs were down, she deplaned and began her post-flight check.

I watched as Sorensen tried to figure out the floor compartment's release mechanism. Nothing seemed to work until Captain Cline came aft

240

and, with one finger, popped the hatch open. Great hidey-hole if Sorensen couldn't figure it out.

We both sorted through the stash. I took two more grenades and poured fifty or so rounds of .22 caliber shells into my shirt pocket. I already had some spare .380 caliber rounds for my small automatic. I saw Sorensen place a couple of more grenades in his lower trouser pockets and that was about it for weapons. I noticed a small box with the AT&T symbol on it and found it full of iPhone 5s. I grabbed two and Sorensen grabbed one. Captain Cline said they were clean burners and pointed to a couple of charging cords we would need. I stuffed the phones and a spare charging cord in my backpack and made for the hatch. We would have to clear Customs here, and I had prepared one of my phony passports to present.

It was a clear day with a slight breeze. It was late fall, and, at that elevation, it was cool and dry. Quite a change from Bangkok. Sorensen caught up to me and we walked side by side to the FBO office. As soon as we cleared the door, I saw Tom Lee sitting in a corner, talking on his cell phone. He pointed at Sorensen and nodded at me. I went into the men's head and Sorensen went back on his phone.

When I came out, Sally was just coming in the door from the tarmac. She smiled at me and made for the service counter. I was anxious to get after Mubane as soon as we had some solid intel, but I was also curious if Sally and the captain were staying there to wait for us or heading to parts unknown. I stepped close enough to overhear her talking and was relieved to hear she was asking for a ride to the rental car park. Added up to them staying a while.

Sorensen signed off on his call and walked over to Tom, waving me over as he did. Tom put up one finger and finished making a note on his notepad, then signed off. I was surprised when he stood up and embraced me first and then Sorensen. He acted genuinely happy to see us. I kind of figured he would be upset over my messing up one of his beaches down in Rio. He began by saying he had been following our exploits through Gage and was amazed we were still alive.

Sorensen looked at me and said it appeared that most of the world's perps were offering a price on our heads. Tom said it was strange how Frank Schultz had just vanished. I looked the other way and noticed Sally glancing at me.

I walked over to her and she said she and Captain Cline would be around for a couple of days and then had to fly the bird up to the Marine

Corps Air Station in Yuma for routine maintenance. I had figured the government was missing their plane, and the Marine Corps their two best pilots. I had their cell phone number and told her I would call as soon as we knew our next plan.

She put her hand on my wrist and looked up at me and said, "Don't get dead."

I told her there was no way I would, especially not until I saw her in something besides that flight suit. She blushed a deep crimson and then squeezed my arm harder. We kept eye contact a bit longer until I heard Sorensen clear his throat loudly, and, as I looked over, he gave me a smirk. I knew that look, as it was normally mine aimed at him. I felt like kissing Sally but held back for professional reasons. She looked at my lips and smiled. She was thinking the same thing.

As she walked toward the door, she glanced at Sorensen and said, "Carry on, Sergeant."

He gave her a quick, three-finger salute and winked.

Tom suggested we take a walk out on the tarmac to talk while we waited for the Mexican Customs Agent to arrive. It was interesting how we could have slipped out the back long before any official arrived. Most countries require everyone to stay aboard a private aircraft until Customs arrived to clear you. The captain or first officer was the only one allowed to disembark to start their post-flight check. The drug capital of the Western Hemisphere and their security is crap. Then again, they wouldn't want to upset any drug lords by being too pushy.

We stopped in the shadow of our aircraft, so we had some protection from snooping eyes and binoculars. Tom began to speak when Sorensen cut in and said his source just told him Mubane's group were loading luggage and supplies into a smaller plane as if this wasn't their destination.

I bent down and yelled to Captain Cline that she needed to refuel right away for another chase. She gave me the thumbs up and jogged over to the office. Sally came running out and told us she had already ordered the fueling and, even as she said it, a tanker came pulling up to the plane. I asked Sorensen if Mubane had filed any flight plan for the small plane. He said he was waiting on that info now. Tom was already on his phone, speaking Spanish, looking at his watch, and making hand gestures. I figured he was on it, too.

When Tom got off the phone he said, "Juarez."

I walked over to Sally and whispered the destination to her. She nodded and skipped up the stairs and into the plane. Sorensen was back on his cell, so I called and briefed Gage. Gage said that was both good and bad news. Good, as it was right on the U.S. border. Bad, as it was right in the middle of the Mexican drug lord area. He said that he had many info sources in that area even within the gangs themselves, not to mention the U.S. Government. He went on to say that the missing Mr. Schultz was deeply embedded in the Juarez drug cartels. He would get right on it to see what info he could scare up.

I asked him to call the Major and brief him that we were down and ready to take off again. He said he would and signed off. The three of us gathered again near the stairs of the aircraft and Tom started to fill us in.

He had some sources in Chihuahua, the Mexican state where Juarez was located and said he had his trusted counterparts go through some files they had confiscated and saw that many of the rich drug lords and businessmen in Mexico were beholden to Schultz. There were records of, not only drug deals but of human trafficking. He said there were several financial reports that not only showed the money that had been traded, but also the real names and descriptions of the children who had been kidnapped.

I was beginning to get angry again. Sorensen must have caught it, as he shook me by the arm. I calmed down and began thinking about how many souls we could free during this operation. I thought about how many families had been affected by our actions over the past couple of weeks, and how many would be in the weeks to come. I could feel the metaphysical heat coming down on us from the imaginary cloud over our souls. We needed to get going while we were still alive and able.

I quickly called Gage and asked him to search the ledger for Juarez entries and to see what he could find out about the medical facilities in and around Chihuahua. I remembered some years ago that some movie stars had gone down to Mexico for cancer treatment, and that there were numerous "boob job" factories scattered about the border area. I wondered how many organ transplant facilities were there.

Gage said he would get as much information from his sources as he could and have it ready for me when we landed in Juarez—or wherever we ended up. I thanked him and noticed the fuel truck was pulling away.

I asked Tom if he could ride with us. He said yes but needed to run out to his car to get his bag. Just as he was going through the door to the service counter, a uniformed Mexican Customs Agent walked out. Tom spoke to him briefly and the Agent turned and walked back into the office. Sorensen received another call, signed off, and pointed to the runway to our south.

There was a small commuter jet just winding up on the runway. Sorensen said it was Mubane and his crowd and they had picked up a couple of medical people to ride with them. He said that was Tom on the phone and he'd confirmed that a young girl resembling Angela was aboard. Sorensen said that Mubane's daughter was on a gurney on the plane. That information told me that we had even less time before Angela flew away.

As soon as Tom reappeared, we ran up the stairs and boarded. The pilots were already halfway through their preflight and began winding up one of the engines. Sorensen lifted the stairs and secured the hatch. The fuel bladder was gone and the smell a bit more pleasant. I asked Tom for his boarding pass and he looked at me as if I were serious.

The seating configuration in this plane was for about fifteen people, with small tables next to each seat. The tables had trays that could swing around in front of you for convenience. I told Tom to sit where we all could talk. That was just about anywhere in the cabin. Some of the seats had been removed before we left Rio all those days ago, but it was still able to carry twelve to fifteen folks comfortably. As we spoke, the plane began to taxi out onto the runway. Sally did her safety announcement while Captain Cline had the controls. One of these flights, I was going to ask the captain if I could take the yoke and fly it a bit. I knew the basics of the plane and had watched her fly it for a few days now. All I needed were the numbers, takeoff and landing speeds, and the rest was a matter of figuring out where everything was. (Right. There were about ten thousand switches and buttons.)

We rolled out nicely and took to the sky as a hundred-million-dollar aircraft should. The captain turned to the northwest and continued to climb. I couldn't see Sally from my portside seat, but I was sure she was busy punching buttons and making notes on the pad attached to her leg with Velcro straps.

Everything was running as advertised. I signaled for Sorensen and Tom to swing their seats around so we could debrief. Just as I did, Tom's cell rang. He was surprised it worked at this altitude. I told him the plane was equipped with a repeater system and would reach out to cell towers on the ground when they were available. He answered his phone and looked startled right away. I knew something was up when he spoke quickly and loudly in Spanish. I understood just enough to know someone was warning him.

244

He moved his cell away from his ear and said the airport authorities had just found the body of a fuel tanker operator at the airport—the one who should have been servicing our plane. He said the body had been there for at least an hour. That meant the driver of our tanker had been an impostor. Knowing enough about aircraft and being a quick thinker, I yelled for Cline to maintain her current altitude and for Sally to come back right away. I told her we might have a bomb on board somewhere. I explained the information we had just received, and she thought for a minute. She knew what I was thinking.

She said there was only one inspection cover near the fuel-intake port that the fuel guy would have had access to. The rest of the hatches were locked, and it would have been obvious to her if someone had opened it when she checked her switches at preflight. She said that all the interior safety switches would have had to be reset. She also said that no portside switches had lit up. She explained that the small hatch on the fuselage next to the wing was a pressure bleeder for the port fuel tank and a new feature on this aircraft. They didn't lock it so the fueler had quick access as he fueled.

I told her what we were all thinking. We probably had an altitude-triggered bomb in that little compartment set to go off when we cleared a certain attitude. That was the most common sabotage gizmo used by the drug lords in these parts. Warnings were plastered all over flying magazines and newsletters. Captain Cline's voice came over the intercom asking us to fill her in. Sally went and knelt next to the seat in the cockpit.

I looked at the three most important players in the little war against some of the most hideous perpetrators on Earth. Us. All in one little flying container, passing over some of the least occupied territories in the Americas. We had walked right into it with our eyes wide open. I was hoping that the whole trip from Bangkok to Mexico wasn't a complete setup. I asked Tom how solid his intel was regarding Mubane really being there at the airport. He said there was no doubt.

Sally came back and started to apologize for the mess, saying equipment security was her job. I waved my hand at her and asked her to sit with us. She said that the fuel truck driver never left the port wing area of the plane and that she had had him sign the credit card receipt. So, the only place anyone could have placed anything was in that compartment.

We were still flying and maintaining the same altitude. There were a few different scenarios regarding these types of bombs. If it was a pressure/altitude bomb, it could be set up to detonate at a certain altitude while climbing out. Alternatively, it could be set to explode while passing a certain altitude or while losing altitude to land. The fact that we were still flying and not ground debris told me it was not a command detonator—that is, one that blew when you pressed a button on a little black box like you see in movies. We would direct our attention to the possibility of an altitude bomb and go from there.

I asked Sally if there was any access to that little compartment from the inside of the plane.

She said, "No. It's too far out under the wing."

I asked her what our altitude was at present and she told me we were right at 18,000 feet. "What is our final cruising altitude?" and she said 41,000 feet. I ran every strand of Bomb 101 knowledge I knew through my mind and continued to come up with only one idea. Praying.

Sally and I went forward to include Captain Cline in our conversation. I requested that she notify the folks in her chain of command and asked her to hold off declaring an emergency with the Mexican Air Authorities until we needed to. She said we were about seven hundred miles from the northern U.S. border. The ground beneath us was sparsely populated, so the possibility of collateral damage on the ground was slight.

Cline said the closest U.S. airport was probably Brownsville, Texas.

I brought up the map in my head and realized Brownsville was about a thousand miles from Juarez, and we were losing time as far as Angela's survival was concerned. Less than two hours before, we'd had so much hope for her, and now Mubane was controlling us until we landed or fell out of the sky.

26

I took a moment to look at Sorensen and Lee. I looked at Sally and Captain Cline and decided to put our fate to a vote. I asked Captain Cline where the next serviceable airport was. She looked at her flight computer and said there was a long runway at San Luis Potosi, about fifty miles ahead. She said she was familiar with the airport, as she had flown there during joint training exercises with the Mexican Army. Our approach was over a clear, mountainous area, just in case we came apart on approach. That was as romantic a description of blowing up as I had ever heard. I turned to Sorensen and Tom Lee and said loud enough for all, "I need a show of hands on whether to try to land and drop off our little hidden friend or continue to fly until someone pushes the little red button."

Everyone yelled, "Land!" as they raised their hands.

I was counting on my distant hope that the bomb was an altitude-triggered device and that we could land before we reached that attitude and then defuse it. I tapped Captain Cline on the shoulder and pinched Sally on the cheek. She smiled and jumped into her seat. I went aft and strapped in.

I could see Captain Cline speaking on her headset and figured she was making up some excuse to interrupt her flight for a quick touchdown at Potosi. I swung my seat forward so I could see out the portlight at the wing. I told Sorensen and Lee I would let them know if the wing blew off. I was closest. I didn't get the slightest smile.

I looked out at the rugged landscape and saw very few signs of life. A road on our port side ran north and south. There were a couple of cars heading north. None going south. I considered landing on the road but put that idea aside. If we survived, I didn't want to attract too much attention. In fact, I wanted to take right back off as soon as we were able.

I asked Sally to give us altitude checks as we went down.

She spoke over the intercom and said, "Seven thousand."

That was a good sign. I had ten thousand as the detonating pressure if the bomb was set to go off on our descent. Captain Cline must have requested a straight-in landing instead of the normal circling procedure, as the wheels came down and we dropped quickly to the runway. She turned off at the second taxiway and stopped right away. I told everyone to get off the plane and act as if they were stretching their legs, but to get away from the aircraft and run back toward the runway on our starboard side. I could see the hesitation on the ladies' faces but pointed at the hatch as soon as the engines started to cool down.

Sorensen opened the hatch and ran the ladderway down. I could see a van heading in our direction from the line of buildings in the distance. I asked Captain Cline to intercept them until I could see what we were dealing with. We all climbed off and I ducked under the fuselage on the port side. I saw the little compartment door right away, and, as I reached for it, Sally came up beside me and stopped me from releasing its latch. There was no time to argue, so I let her take the lead.

She pressed the little door up and slowly turned the latch. I heard a click and she let the hatch open about a quarter of an inch. She stood on her tiptoes and tried to look in but was too vertically challenged to see in. I stepped underneath and looked in. I could see it plainly. It was painted flat black and was completely out of place in that compartment. It didn't appear to be attached to anything at all. Just placed in there. I nodded to indicate I could see it and took the hatch lid from Sally. As I did, she pressed herself up against me and I could feel the soft outline of her right breast and the firmness of her thigh. Wow. Talk about a time and place for everything. She was letting me know if I blew up now, I would be missing something special.

I dropped the hatch a bit more and caught the device as it fell out. It was the size of a king-size pack of cigarettes and had a small electrical box attached to it. The van from the airport was about a half-mile away and getting closer. I looked the device over and could see a small blasting cap stuck in what looked and smelled like a small brick of C-4 explosive. I walked to the rear of the aircraft and onto a grassy area and, when I was clear of the plane and Sally, I pulled the little blasting cap out of the putty-like explosive and separated it from the electrical device.

I put the plastic explosive in my right trouser pocket and placed the blasting cap in my left. Sally had secured the little hatch and we both walked over to the rest of the crowd just as the van pulled up. It was a local police officer and an airport employee coming to check on us. Neither of them spoke English, so Sally walked them to the port wing to show them the door and, through sign language, explained to them that the hatch must have come open in transit. A thumbs up signal from her seemed to satisfy them about our unscheduled landing.

Captain Cline showed the police officer her U.S. Passport and military ID card that, even though he didn't appear to read English, either, made him nod as he passed them back to her. I reached into my pocket and pulled out two one-hundred-dollar greenbacks, and they both understood that English perfectly.

They drove back to the small tower area and we all climbed back on the aircraft. Captain Cline requested a takeoff and was granted it right away as she cranked up and returned to the main runway. She never slowed down as we zipped down the runway and into the air, now a couple of hours behind Angela.

We all returned to our cell phones and discovered we had no signal. Sally came back and said they had turned off the assist device and would run it up shortly. She explained that their ground crew in Yuma had instructed them to turn off all transmitting devices except their main radio in case the device had been tuned to a frequency they would have to switch to as we flew toward Juarez. I hadn't thought of that possibility during my prayer session. Tom asked to see the device and I pulled it from my pocket. As he looked it over, he popped a small, round battery out of its side and said he had seen the exact same kind many times over the years. He said it was a gift from the cartels. I told him I would try to return the favor very soon.

We'd flown for about an hour when Sally came back, asking where we wanted to land. Sorensen took my satphone and made a call to one of his sources. I had been so hyped-up from surviving Mubane's sabotage that I hadn't checked in with Gage since Sorensen briefed him on the bomb. Sorensen signed off and said Mubane's aircraft had landed at a small commuter airfield south of Juarez about forty minutes before. The plane was met by three vans and was presently on the outskirts of Juarez, heading to the west of the city. I thought about it for a moment and requested that we land at El Paso International. I knew that the Biggs Army Airfield was a short distance away but felt we would have less explaining to do at a civilian field. Sally agreed and went forward to make landing arrangements. I then called Gage and briefed him on our airport choice. He said he would call his people there to clear us right away.

While Gage and I were talking, Tom must have discovered he had cell service, as he was on the phone and writing notes on a small pad. He stared at me a moment and then went back to jotting notes. Sorensen looked over his shoulder but shook his head at me, which I took to mean it was in Portuguese or Spanish.

I asked Gage to fill in the Major and Dave and then requested that no one tell Thom Cohen where we were for fear he would climb on a plane and try to take matters into his own hands. He agreed, and we signed off.

Tom signed off from his call and briefed us on some info from Brazil. He said they had located and raided another facility belonging to Schultz on the southern side of Rio and found over twenty kids, male and female, who were being held there. Most of them were from European countries, with some from Asia. They were busy identifying them and keeping them safe until they could be returned to their families.

That was great news and, I suspected, would repeat itself many times over the next few weeks. I thought about how many kids were still in the pipeline, kidnapped and waiting for transport to these detention centers. I hoped the process would continue until they were all set free. I also knew there was a possibility that some of them would vanish to cover up the evidence.

I decided to call the Major and tell him to start a media blitz as soon as possible. Mubane was surely aware of us from his actions, and it didn't serve Angela to hold off notifying the world. I told him to coordinate with Gage, and then I asked him to leave out the Mexico connection until we got a handle on Mubane's plans in Juarez. He agreed and said he had prepared a press release already. He was waiting to fill in all the names. I suggested he release the names a few at a time. That way, we had a better shot at finding some more detention centers and, possibly, individual captives being held at some of these big wigs' homes and hideaways.

I also reminded him that Nick had volumes of records in New Zealand just waiting to be scrutinized. I asked him to have Gage arrange for those to be shipped to him by secure service. We decided the only secure transport would be by a private jet. That way, Nick could tag along with a couple of his counterparts for safe measure. I asked him to tell Nick to use some of the money he had for the expenses. The Major agreed and we signed off.

Sally came over the intercom in her best "flight attendant" voice and welcomed us to the United States of America and told us to prepare for landing. She went on with the rest of the spiel, and, as she did, I looked out of the window and saw the very welcomed sight of El Paso, Texas. It seemed like years since I had left my island for this journey. I felt a heavy heart for Angela and looked at Sorensen.

He smiled and then saw the look on my face and tapped my shoulder saying, "Soon." I hoped so.

We landed without any surprises from the explosive device or a surface-to-air missile. I tried to put out of my mind all the possible and negative things that could happen before we rolled to a stop at Atlantic Aviation.

Sally came back into the cabin and told us that she and Captain Cline were going to pick up a few gallons of jet fuel and continue to Yuma for mandatory service. She said they would be on standby for us and could switch planes if we needed them before the service was completed. She turned and opened the hatch. I purposely looked back at Sorensen and Lee to keep from staring at her as she lowered the stairs. I needed to concentrate all my energy on Angela.

It was a bit chilly in El Paso and I welcomed that. Sorensen and Lee followed me down to the tarmac and, as Sorensen did his scan of the surrounding area, Tom pulled out his cell phone and began speaking in Spanish. Sorensen and I had our backpacks over our shoulders and Lee had two small carryon-type bags in his left hand as we walked to the office. I offered to carry one of Lee's bags, but he smiled, shook his head, and said, "No."

Sally stepped over and told me that we did not have to clear Customs. I did remember the two guns tucked in my pockets and, more importantly, the four hand grenades bumping against my legs as I walked. I hoped Sorensen had his handy little diplomatic ID that I knew he carried from time to time, as we were heading right back over the border to Mexico as soon as we could rent a car. Lee would have his Brazilian police credentials, so that left me as the only terrorist in the trio that they might search at the border crossing.

I decided to skip back up into the plane and leave the grenades on the seat but took the pistols. I could get my two, legal law enforcement partners to carry them for me if needed. I climbed back down the stairs and informed Sally that I had left the grenades for her to secure. She thanked me for the heads up and again reminded me not to get dead.

I went into the Service Center and saw that Sorensen was securing a vehicle and Tom was still on his phone, but now sitting down and taking notes. I looked over his shoulder, but it was in Spanish or Portuguese. However, I noted the name Zara. I knew it was short for Zaragoza, as in Papa Zaragoza, one of the top drug cartel leaders in the Western hemisphere. He was known to have a small army of well-trained security made up of former police officers and soldiers from all over the world. (Thanks, Mubane.)

Lee signed off and Sorensen walked up, shaking the keys of our ride. I looked at Lee and asked, "Papa?"

He nodded yes.

Sorensen smiled and said, "Oh, good. I needed to pay him another visit. It's been too long since our last meeting."

Whatever that meant, I was sure it was not good for Papa Zaragoza.

Tom filled us in that one of his people had followed Mubane to one of Papa's extremely large haciendas about five miles west of downtown Juarez. He said the compound was in a rural area but had several large homes surrounding it. His informant said it was one of Papa's least guarded homes and that he mostly used it as a guesthouse for visiting comrades who had their own security. That was a plus, in a dismal sort of way.

We walked outside and Sorensen strolled up to a big black GMC Yukon stretch that matched its sister Suburban. I asked him if it would cause us to stand out a bit across the border and he said it was very common down there. We threw our stuff in the back and climbed in. Sorensen drove, Tom took shotgun and I grabbed the back seat.

Sorensen appeared to be familiar with this area since he didn't call Siri, his phone genie, for directions. I asked him how often he traveled here, and he replied that he had been stationed in Juarez for a few months some years ago. He said it was a great town. His look in the rearview mirror told me that was a bit of sarcasm. I was sure it was a great town, but not for an American Intelligence Agent, especially knowing what was across the Rio Grande River.

I had been there several times. The poverty was criminal. The Native

Central Americans, Hondurans, Guatemalans, Salvadorans, and Native Mexicans were treated even worse than the local poor folks. When you cross over the bridge, there are hundreds of southern refugees lining the road, looking for a handout of any kind. Selling handmade trinkets for pennies, trying to earn money enough to feed the children sitting at their feet. It's very sad, and even though there are aid groups trying to help these folks, it's not enough.

I have always looked at the world as one big family, not separate peoples to deal with differently. I try to help in my strange way of eliminating the Earth of evil as best I can. I also support the efforts of the aid groups by donating and helping sanctuary groups in many ways. Still, it's not enough. Everywhere you go in this world there is tragic poverty. Then I reflected on the Mubane's of the world. My thoughts kept me occupied until I heard Sorensen announce the border crossing coming up. I put my hard brain back into gear and concentrated on the mission. I knew it was going to be tough from here on out.

The big SUV we were driving gave us the appearance of importance as we crossed the bridge. In fact, the uniformed Mexican Border Patrolman averted their eyes out of either respect or fear—it was hard to tell—and totally ignored us. Even the panhandlers looked the other way. They all have seen too much grief and a big black car as we were in spelled grief to them.

Tom had been on his cell a few more times and had been speaking to Sorensen every few minutes. I couldn't hear what he was saying over the sounds of the road and the roar of the diesel engine in our car. Sorensen nodded in understanding, would point from time to time, and say something back. I was content to sit back and wait for a plan to develop. Looking at the poor conditions of the city and thinking about the luxury Mubane was now basking in at the service of Papa Zaragoza, had put me in a dangerous mood and I needed to vent, or I was going to explode.

We traveled west through the city, and as the buildings began to thin out, we stopped on a side road. Sorensen said we were about a half-mile from the compound where Mubane and his entourage had last been seen. Tom said he had "eyes on the ground" and was watching the two entrances and exits from the compound. He had been told there were approximately ten guards in the compound and, along with Mubane's security detail, that meant there were fourteen. Far fewer then I had expected. Sorensen said he had been in the compound a couple of times and had a good idea where everyone would be gathered. To his knowledge, there were no secret passageways in or out like we'd found in Mubane's compound back in Bangkok.

I asked Tom if Papa had ever spent time there. He said that he had been told that Papa was known to keep a mistress or two there and to spend nights in the compound when the urge moved him.

I looked at Sorensen and asked him when the last time was a billionaire outlaw left himself without an escape route. Sorensen looked at me and nodded. He rephrased his statement and said he didn't know if there were any secret passageways out of the compound. One thing was for sure, though—we couldn't drive that big black car past the compound without being made.

I asked Sorensen if there was a little cantina where we could get something to eat and kill some time until dark. He said he felt anything in this area would be under Papa's control and our presence noted. I agreed, but also felt we could turn it to our advantage. Seeing how Papa employed many different folks in his business, we would fit right in. I didn't believe Papa required his employees to wear name tags, and we certainly looked the part. I decided it would work.

As Sorensen drove in little circles away from the compound, looking for a watering hole, we all checked our weapons. I now wished I had taken at least a couple of grenades, seeing we were never stopped and searched on leaving the airport or entering Mexico. Then again, I looked at Sorensen and knew I had a close source for one or two, should the need arise.

We found a small, clean cantina on a side road about a half-mile from the compound, according to Sorensen. We were the only diners. A bartender and a waiter stood at the small bar. With a wave of his hand, the waiter signaled us to sit wherever we wanted. Sorensen made his way to the rear of the small room and pushed two small, square tables together. He and I sat facing the door and Tom sat facing us and the door to the kitchen area.

It was dark outside now and not much lighter in the cantina. The menu was on a chalkboard behind the bar. Tom translated it for us, and we all decided on burritos. The place looked clean, but we all figured we were better off getting something that had been cooked. The idea that we were concerned with our health when we dealt in near-death experiences every day, seemed a bit ironic to me, but I didn't want to die on a toilet seat no matter what I chose to do with my life. Ask Elvis how all that worked out for him!

We ordered and were surprised our waiter, who introduced himself as Paul, spoke English clearly and laughed at our obvious surprise. He said he had lived in the Atlanta area for many years after his parents took him there as a child. He said he'd visited his relatives in Mexico many times, but about five years ago, Border Patrol caught him sneaking back into the States after a visit. He spent some time in a jail camp in Brownsville, Texas, and then, eventually, he was deported back to Mexico. He had a wife and two children who live near Athens, Georgia, who he hadn't seen in three years.

He explained that he was part owner of the cantina with his cousin, whom he pointed as the man standing at the bar. I nodded my head hello and he nodded back. I felt bad for Paul, as I had heard so many of the same stories over the past few years. Paul's wife and children were U.S. citizens by birth, but the new rules on immigration prevented him from staying in the States since he was considered an illegal. I mentioned that we were all illegals unless we were Native Americans. Even Tom was of German and Irish descent.

We gave Paul our orders and he made his way to the kitchen. His cousin served us all a nice cold Mexican beer that I had never heard of. I couldn't make out the name on the label. In any event, I'm not a drinker, but that beer was incredible. Paul came out of the kitchen with some tortilla chips and salsa and asked if we liked the beer. Tom said it was the best he'd ever tasted. Sorensen and I backed him up. Paul said it was his own brand, from his own brewery in the cellar of the building.

Paul returned to the kitchen and, a few minutes later, returned with our meals. The food was just as good as the beer. I was impressed.

As we ate, Paul asked if we minded if he joined us. I had wanted to get into a conversation with Sorensen and Lee but nodded and pointed at the spare chair next to me. Paul sat down and looked at Sorensen, then Tom, and then me. He paused a moment and declared, "You're all Federal Agents."

I stopped eating and was about to spit my food out on the floor when he laughed and told us not to worry or to be offended. He explained that he had run the border so many times and watched so many agents at the detention facility where he'd been caged, that he could pick agents out of a crowd as if we were wearing signs. He laughed again and went on to say he bet we were after his fellow countryman Papa Z.

I was becoming very uncomfortable and I could tell by Sorensen's body language that he was preparing for battle. I half expected a hundred banditos to come charging through the door since receiving a phone message from our brand-new best friend, Paul. Nothing happened, and from our silence, he knew he was dead on. I turned fully to him, stared into his eyes with my best evil stare, and told him that the complete opposite could also be true, and he could be in for a lot of hurt.

He never lost his smile and shook his head, saying, "I'm not wrong." He never skipped a beat and asked what he could do for us.

Again, we were all taken aback by his bluntness and were left speechless for a moment.

Tom said something to him in Spanish that made Paul smile broader. He answered Tom in Spanish and then said, "I stand corrected." He looked at me. "Your friend here is from Portugal or Brazil." He quickly told me he was good with accents.

This guy was amazing, and perhaps foolish for trusting his instincts after talking to us for thirty minutes. I wondered what he meant by "what he could do for us."

After a little more chatter, we finished our meal. The cousin brought us over another round of beers, which I passed on, and asked Paul if we could have a little privacy. He said certainly and went to the bar next to his cousin. They both turned their backs on us, and I leaned into Sorensen and Tom a bit to whisper about my sense of amazement regarding Paul.

Tom said he hoped he was real, as he now had us all but figured out. I agreed. Neither Paul nor his cousin made any cell calls or wandered into the kitchen to give us away. I mentioned that informing Papa or his men about our presence could bring him a few much-needed bucks. I looked over at Paul and they were still looking away. Sorensen piped up and asked what we thought about hiring Mr. Paul to do some scout work for us. I had been thinking the same thing. After all, Paul had asked what he could do for us.

Just then, Paul quickly darted to us, looking very serious. We all went on alert when he told us we needed to leave out the rear door immediately. Sorensen lifted his hand from under the table and showed Paul his silenced .22 pistol, but Paul completely ignored it as he waved us to the kitchen door. I could see the cousin looking out of the small front window of the cantina. He said something in Spanish and looked at Paul.

I decided that it was legitimate and moved toward the kitchen door. Tom and Sorensen followed, walking backward after us. Paul moved back over to the bar area as we passed through the kitchen and to the rear door. Tom had the outside door open and said the cousin mentioned something about "Them nearly here."

I looked out the rear door and saw an alleyway and a fence. Looked too much like an invitation into an ambush rather than an escape plan. Just then, I heard the front door bang open and some shouting. We heard tables being kicked over and then the scream of someone in pain. Tom translated the shouts, saying that the intruders were looking for someone or something. There was another scream and, this time, I could hear a dull thud as if someone had been struck with a club or bat.

That was enough for me. I pulled out my silenced pistol and barged into the dining room area. There were three Mexicans in civilian clothes holding Cousin down on the bar top with his arms pinned. His face was covered in blood and it appeared one of his arms was broken at the elbow. The bigger of the three men was about to slam a club down on his face when I shot him twice in the legs. He screamed and dropped the club.

The other two made the mistake of quickly pulling out their pistols but then fell to the floor with a bullet hole in the very middle of both of their foreheads. I didn't need to look over my shoulder to know Sorensen was standing right there, looking for anything else hostile to shoot. I looked for Paul and found him behind the bar. He was coming to from what must have been a nasty whack on the head. I turned my attention to his cousin, lying on the bar. He was just barely breathing.

Tom helped Paul up and Sorensen and I went to work on Cousin. Here he was dying, and all we knew him as was "Cousin." I turned him on his side so he wouldn't choke on his own blood, but when I did, he stopped breathing altogether. His throat appeared crushed and nearly closed. I let the blood drain from his mouth and laid him back down. Sorensen pushed on his chest to see if he could get him breathing again, but it didn't seem to do any good. I couldn't feel any heartbeat and his one open eye was completely dilated. As Sorensen pressed on his breastbone, I notice the side of his chest bending up unnaturally. His chest had been crushed and his lungs must have been punctured. We could do nothing to save him without an emergency room staff right here, right now.

I stopped Sorensen and looked at Paul. He was regaining his balance with Tom's help and had just now focused on his cousin. He reached over, put his hand on his cousin's cheek, and said something in Spanish. I was sure it was a farewell prayer without needing it to be translated.

I went to the small window and looked out the front. There were a few people gathering on the street a few doors down, but no sign of any more bad guys. The live one on the floor was attempting to get something from his pocket. I nodded at Sorensen and he kicked the guy in the arm. A cell phone fell out and onto the floor. Tom picked it up and saw it was on and transmitting. He put his finger to his lips and listened in. As he did, he covered the mouthpiece and told us someone was calling for these three from somewhere. He said they were sending someone there to check on them.

I looked out front again and saw no threat in the street yet. I turned to Paul and told him we needed to get gone. He agreed with a nod, put his hand out to Sorensen, and asked for his pistol. I started to say, "No, not yet," but Sorensen passed it to him quickly and without hesitation. Paul shot the Mexican three times rapidly in the head. Paul passed the gun back to Sorensen, shook Tom off his arm, and waved at us to follow him out the back.

He reached up toward a shelf on the way out, took an envelope out from between some boxes, and said that that was what they had come for. He called it his weekly insurance payment. I didn't need an explanation.

I did ask him if he needed to call someone to handle his cousin's remains and he said neither of them had any family in Juarez and his cousin's wife had died some years before. As he climbed over the chain link fence in the alley, he said he would call his cousin's family later when we were away from there.

We zigzagged in and out of a few roads and alleys and then stopped to rest. I told him we had a rental car somewhere near his cantina, but he told us to forget it. He said that by now the bandits were aware of us and would find the car right off. A couple of blocks later, he asked us again what we were up to and what he could help us with. It seemed like hours ago that he had asked us the same thing, only it had only been minutes.

We stood in a dark alley and I looked at Sorensen and Tom. They nodded and I briefed Paul with the short version of our mission. Most importantly, I told him about Mubane being at Papa's compound down the road. Paul shook his head and rubbed his eyes a bit. He said he had knowledge of the compound and that the men we just sent to hell were from the same group of bandits. Papa Zaragoza controlled all the illegal trade on that side of Juarez and ran the protection business of the legit shop owners. As with many of the large cities, a "protection business" extorted money to protect folks from themselves. Old story.

I tuned in on the fact Paul had said he was familiar with the compound.

I asked him right off if there was a secret exit anywhere around the buildings. He thought about it for a moment and said there was no secret exit, but there was a third access to the compound from a building to the north of the wall. He said it was where they cooked the food for the guards and delivered it through a narrow passageway from the building. He had worked in that building for Papa for a couple of months when he first moved to Juarez. He carried the food to the door in the wall.

I started to form a plan in the back of my head—one not far removed from the plan we'd had foiled in Bangkok a couple of days ago.

I asked Paul if he knew where we could get another vehicle. I didn't care to rescue Angela and then walk back to the bridge. He said he had several friends with cars that he could borrow. That, I thought, was our priority.

Paul borrowed one of my phones and dialed a number, spoke some Spanish, and then passed the phone back to me. He walked us around a corner in the alley to where we could sit on some boxes stacked up there and said he would be right back. I passed him two one-hundred-dollar bills and he hesitated a moment until I insisted. He had his extortion money envelope in his hand but took the bills and vanished down the alley the way we had come.

I waited a few moments and then waved at Sorensen and Lee to follow me. I went out the same way Paul had gone and crossed the narrow road to another alley just opposite the one we'd been in. From there, we could see the original alley and the road in front. I was just being careful, not really knowing our new friend all that well yet.

We didn't have to wait long before we heard the rumble of a car coming down the bumpy road. We waited a moment after Paul pulled up and went down the alley. No one came after him in either direction, so we crossed over to the little car. Paul walked out from the alley, looking worried and then relieved to see us. I looked both ways again and pointed to the car. Sorensen climbed in the front and Tom and I slipped into the back. It was a small car, but a limo compared to the cars in Bangkok. I had room to stretch my legs a bit—at least until Sorensen pushed his seat back and smashed my legs. I thank him and he said I was welcomed.

Paul drove west on a main road. A few moments later, Paul pointed to a wall and told us that the wall surrounded the main buildings. It was about six feet tall and right next to the public sidewalk. I could see some trees growing up inside the compound and the outline of a couple of high roofs against the sky. I didn't see any security on this side and asked Paul if he knew the guard situation. He said it was obviously light by three men right now but was generally concentrated at the two gates. One in front, he explained as he pointed over his shoulder, and one at the back, which he pointed to and I saw at the same time. There were two civilian-clothed white guys, big and tall. That was the rear entrance. I wondered what the front gate had guarding it.

As we drove beyond the compound wall and pulled over a couple of blocks away, I looked back out the rear window to see if there were any visible cameras on the wall. I asked Tom if he knew what the rear gate consisted of.

He said it was just two metal swinging gates to let vehicles pass through. The front gate was mainly for pedestrian traffic. He said Papa used the front gate. All others come through the rear. I asked him about the *gringos,* and he said that there would be two at the front, too. He said there used to be a former U.S. Government agent who ran Papa's security, but he'd disappeared a couple of years ago. I looked at Sorensen, who turned away as soon as he saw me look. He never did say why he was familiar with the compound.

I asked Paul to take us past the cooking building where he used to work. He pulled out into the light traffic and turned north a couple of blocks later. He then turned east two roads down and stopped at an intersection, a block to the north of the compound. We could see a two-story building in front of the wall that Paul pointed out was the cooking building and sleeping quarters for some of the guards that didn't have homes in Juarez.

I could see a couple of lights on the second floor and the entire lower story was lit up. I looked to the north of where we were parked and saw lights off in the distance. I then realized that I am looking across the Rio Grande River to the west of El Paso. I figured the river was about a half-mile away. I hadn't realized we were so close to the border. I thought about how it might come in handy soon.

We hadn't had a chance to eat any of our food at Paul's cantina and I was famished. I took out four power bars from the plane and passed them around. Paul passed his back and said he was not hungry. Sorensen and Tom gobbled them right down. I ate mine slowly as I studied the building next to the wall.

As I watched, two short Mexicans rounded the corner from the south, walked to the next block, and then turned onto the steps of the cookhouse. They walked right in. No knock or hesitation. I asked Paul about that and he said he didn't recall the door ever being locked but a guard always greeted him when he arrived. He said the same guard opened the rear door when he was carrying the food in. He explained that the guard in the house called the compound and gave them the signal to open the steel gate in the wall. He believed the gate only opened from the inside. He would deliver the food, wait for them to finish, and then take the plates and silverware back to the house. He never had to ask the guards to open the gate, as they watched closely.

I was trying to put together a plan. My first instinct was the element of surprise. Take down the two rear entrance guards. Walk in, shoot everything that moves and then grab Angela for a ride home. Too simple.

I figured there were ten guards, including Mubane's four commandos. Mubane himself was probably carrying a weapon. Possibly his wife, too. Then there was the medical staff they'd brought along. They could be former military and have a good working knowledge of weapons. So, we were looking at fifteen or so on the opposing team.

I looked at the four of us. Possibly three—or three and a half. Paul hadn't been tested yet.

I figured our chances of getting Angela out safely were minuscule, at best. I asked Paul if there were any other guards nearby who might be called to duty once we were discovered. He said he didn't believe so as Papa only spent a few hours at most at that compound. He reminded me that it was a love nest, not a home. He said he was surprised there were any *gringos* there now without Papa.

I raised my eyebrow and he caught on and said if Papa were there, we would know it by the number of guards at the gates and the walking patrols in the neighborhood. I reminded him of the two guards that just went into the cookhouse. He said they were more than likely going on duty.

Just as he said that, two different guard types walked out of the door and headed our way. Paul pulled farther down the road. It was fully dark out and there were few lights on in the surrounding buildings. No streetlights at all. There was a glow from an intersection up ahead and the lights from across the river were brighter here than the Juarez lights. I decided to do a little scouting on my own. I asked everyone to stay in the car and give me an hour to observe the compound.

I opened the car door and slipped up alongside the building we were parked in front of. It was so dark that I could hardly see my feet on the broken sidewalk. I walked back toward where we had come and, as I approached the intersection we had been parked at, I saw the two men who had recently left the cookhouse a distance to the north. It looked as if they were going to walk into the river. I watched them a while longer, and then they turned to the right and disappeared out of sight. The only thing I could see now was the reflection of the lights across the river and a few lights in the buildings around me. I made sure my silenced pistol was loose in my pocket and walked farther west to the next block, toward the road the *gringo* guards were on at the rear gate. I realized if I walked toward them with the lights of El Paso behind me, I would be too visible. I walked back east and turned to the south. Again, I was outlined in light. I walked another block east and then south. I was now a block over and walked three blocks down. I then turned right and, when I got to the next intersection, I was in complete darkness.

I studied the compound and watched the guards at the front gate for a few minutes. They were lax in their attention to duty. They weren't paying any attention to their surroundings. That was a plus for us. I crossed the street to the south and walked the block until I could see the rear gate. There were now two short Mexicans on duty there as equally lax as their front gate buddies. I wondered where the two *gringos* had made off to.

I watched the compound a little longer and then decided I had been gone a little less than an hour. If I stayed gone any longer, Sorensen would be storming the gate. I walked back and located the car. Sure enough, Sorensen was just leaving, and I whistled to him. He stopped and came back to the car. He told me he was just relieving himself, but I knew he was coming after me.

I briefed the three of them on my observations and told them we needed to strike during the next change of the guard. I planned to go through the front gate, disable the guards, and open the side gate to the cookhouse. I suggested Sorensen go into the first floor of the cookhouse and disable the folks there. Paul piped in and said there may be some civilian cooks and maintenance people there. I looked at Sorensen, suggested he disable them nicely, and then leave Paul behind to keep them quiet until we finished our mission. Paul seemed to like that idea better and settled down. I told Paul to brief Sorensen and Lee as to where the help would be working or sleeping when they went in.

I then gave Paul my small notepad and asked he and Sorensen to sketch a diagram of the buildings inside the compound for me. Sorensen, never ceasing to amaze me, drew a large square to represent the walls. Inside it, he drew three smaller squares and a larger one toward the front that represented the main three-story house. He said he was only familiar with the interior of one of the smaller buildings used as an office for the staff and security. It was the building farthest north and the one closest one to the cookhouse entrance.

Paul said he had never been inside any of the buildings but had looked through the window of the main house. The other workers told him it was laid out like a large, normal house. The first floor had a living room, dining room, and large kitchen. He said that the window he had looked through was an office like you see in the movies, with a large desk, bookshelves, and a big fireplace next to the window he was looking through. Paul described the rest of the room as having large chairs and a glass cabinet for liquor bottles.

He went on to say that he had been told the second floor was where Papa had a big bedroom and a number of smaller guest rooms. The third floor was where the help stayed. He said that when Papa was in residence, there were three servants in residence. When the house help arrived, it was the first clue that Papa was coming, as there was no one there when he was gone.

I had seen lights on in the big building on the second floor but none on the third. I wondered what the help's arrangements were when he loaned the house to guests. I asked Paul if he had ever heard of anyone doing any medical procedures in the house, and he said that he had heard that people were often interrogated in the large basement. He then related that there were all kinds of horror stories regarding Zaragoza and that he tortured the people who crossed him. He said that the stories were horrible. Once his supervisor there had threatened him that if he stole anything or ever talked about Mr. Z, he would end up in the "cellar." He couldn't describe the basement, but if there were any medical procedures going on, he would guess the basement would be the most suitable.

I couldn't picture Mubane allowing his daughter to have a heart transplant in a dungeon, but anything was possible. Paul went on to say that Papa supported a large hospital about a mile from there where they treated many *gringos*. He said he thought Papa owned it, and from time to time, part of his protection money was taken for the "hospital fund," and he would have to make up the difference with more cash.

That was more interesting and a real good reason why Mubane would have come all the way to Mexico instead of Hong Kong or the many other cities he had interests in. I believe he also thought this would be the last place on Earth anyone would look for him. He had to know by now that our plane did not go down unless Papa had arranged the bomb and never told Mubane about. It was also possible, now that I thought about it, that Papa might have another motive. Revenge on Sorensen? I decided not to mention it right then.

I told the three of them that we would have to play it by ear until I got inside to survey the situation. I wasn't even sure Angela was inside. It was possible she and Mubane's daughter were at the hospital. I was feeling uncomfortable then and needed answers right away. For all I knew, the transplant operation could be going on in the hospital as we sat there, waiting a couple of more hours for a shift change.

I looked at Sorensen and told him I wasn't waiting any longer. I was hitting the rear gate and storming the house if I had to. Angela was too close to death and I could feel it in my bones. Sorensen was the first to say he agreed. The other two nodded unison. I asked Sorensen to take the front gate and Tom and Paul to hit the cookhouse. The same basic plan, just sooner, and Sorensen and I would hit the compound simultaneously, front and rear. I asked Sorensen to let Tom through the cookhouse gate and for Paul to hang back at the house to keep the folks there alive if they chose to co-operate.

Everyone agreed and we sorted out weapons. I gave Paul my second silenced .22 automatic pistol with three extra magazines. He said he was familiar with the gun. Sorensen was set. Tom only had a small .9MM automatic with no silencer. Sorensen reached into his backpack, pulled out a larger, silenced .22 magnum revolver, and passed it to Tom. He told Tom it was not as quiet as the smaller .22 but would do the trick. I asked him to hold off on using it unless he had to. We would be counting on the element of surprise and even though it was silenced, it would still sound like a firecracker. Tom said he understood and checked the weapon's action.

I called Sorensen's phone and told him I would narrate my movements so he could hit the front and back gates at the exact same time. After making sure we had a clear line, I signed off. In a situation like this, there was no choice on how you took down an adversary. It could only be quick, lethal headshots. I'm not a complete animal and wished there was another way, but with a local police department that was rotten with corruption and hired killers as security, there was no compromise. I'd let God sort it out in the end.

I figured where we were parked was about as good as it got. The car was about the same distance from the rear gate as it was from the front. If we rescued Angela and she could walk or run, we had as good a shot from either of the gates to the car. I asked Paul to put the keys under the front mat and instructed all that whoever had Angela was to get to the car and leave. Not to wait for the rest of us. We would catch up at the border. All of us had credentials showing our American roots. Paul would have to explain in a hurry to Border Patrol who he was if he had Angela. I tore off a piece of paper from the little compound diagram and wrote one of Gage's secret phone numbers on it that he could call.

I took a moment to call Gage, fill him in, and explain what was coming down. He said he understood and would be standing by. He went on to say that there was a small contingent of agents at the border waiting to cross into Mexico if I needed them. I told Gage we might need them at the bridge once we were racing across it. I figured having a positive outlook was the best policy. I signed off from Gage, punched Sorensen in the arm, and slipped out the door and onto the road.

I turned and saw Sorensen and the others going in the other direction at a quick pace. I punched in Sorensen's number and he answered right away. I told him I was just around the corner from the west wall gate and as soon as Tom and Paul had enough time to crash in the door on the cookhouse, I would turn the corner and walk right up to the guards. I told him to be certain there were only two, as things tend to change in a hurry in the Badlands.

He replied, "Yes, Mother."

Sorensen said he could see the two guys and that they had just turned into the side door of the house. I turned the corner, walking right toward the two guards. They were just talking, not paying any attention until I was about twenty feet away. My boot made a scuffing noise on the road and they both looked up. Without issuing an order to halt, they drew their pistols, and I could tell they were going to shoot first and ask questions later.

I had put the cell phone in my top shirt pocket and could hear two quick little pops from Sorensen's phone just as I turned slightly sideways and fired four times in the faces of Mutt and Jeff. They went down without a sound.

I heard Sorensen say, "Beat ya."

I didn't respond as I grabbed both small men and dragged them into the gated entranceway. I lifted a small latch and slowly pushed the gate open. No one was visible inside the gate area. I pulled the two men farther in and shut the gate. Sorensen said he was approaching the cookhouse gate and I spoke, for the first time since taking down the gate guards and said "Roger."

I moved to the first building on the west side of the compound. I saw no movement at the rear or side. I went around the north side of the building and looked in a window. There were no lights on, but I could see that the room was a sitting room with a TV on a stand opposite the window. I crossed over to the rear of the big house and squatted down. I told Sorensen where I was, and he told me he and Lee were beside the office building. He said there were two *gringos* in the front office, watching a football game on a small TV. He believed they were the same guys from the rear gate earlier.

Just then, Sorensen stopped talking, then began again and said there was a small or young girl sitting on the floor. He said she appeared to be nude. I asked him if she had blonde hair and he said she didn't. She was definitely young, perhaps ten or eleven. A dark-haired Latina. He went on to say she was bleeding from her face and had blood on her legs.

This presented a problem. I had planned to sneak into the big house to look for Angela and, if she were there, grab her and make for the border. As I have said before, plans change, and often.

We needed to take out the *gringos* and help the girl, but if we made any noise, we had Mubane's thugs (and whoever was sleeping in the other houses) to contend with. Not a healthy getaway plan.

I made the decision and told Sorensen to get the girl and have Tom take her back to the cookhouse for Paul to sort out. A moment later, I heard a door open over my cell and four quick pops. I could hear the pops from the building even without the cell phone. Sorensen needed to repack his silencer. I then heard the girl start to scream, though it was cut off by what I was sure was Sorensen's large hand. I heard him whisper something, then heard Tom speak in Spanish. There was a little rustling and then silence.

A moment later, Sorensen asked me if he should play Sandman with anyone else in the building, and I said as long as whoever was there remained asleep, leave 'em be. He whispered that once I got a look at the little girl, I might wish I could change my mind. I wondered if they were keeping any other kids there. I decided that a return visit to Juarez might be in order in the future. We could call it a post-operation sweep up.

I told Sorensen to watch for Tom and go to the front of the house. He said Tom was back and they were on their way.

I tried the rear door of the house. It was locked but opened out, making it easier to jimmy open. I peeked in the two windows on the sides of the door and saw it was the kitchen. It was empty, but just as I started for the door, I saw movement through the door to the dining or living room. I did a quick look and studied my memory picture or "sight picture," as you called it in combat or at the rifle range. There was someone sitting on a chair near the doorway. From where he was, I figured he could monitor the rear and front door. I thought about what I had just seen and further pictured white lines on his shirt coming from his head. They were earbuds. He was listening to music or his cell phone. That's why he hadn't heard the pops from Sorensen's pistol.

There was no way I could open the rear door without him noticing me. The air pressure in the room would change immediately and he would look. I couldn't see a weapon in my sight picture, which was fading fast. I whispered to Sorensen and he suggested having Tom tap on the door. He thought the guard was probably one of Mubane's Thai bodyguards. I understood. The Thai would be unsure of the protocols there in Mexico and would, hopefully, not walk to the door, shooting away. I thought about it a bit and decided I didn't like it. At least, not that version. I told Sorensen I was going to slip the bolt on the rear door and, when I had it open a bit, have Tom knock lightly. I mentioned to Sorensen that the guy was wearing earbuds and may not hear the first taps.

I slipped my knife into the jam and the bolt slid back easily. I pulled the door open an inch and checked for any chains or slide blocks. There was none. I whispered for Sorensen to "Go."

I heard the taps coming over the cell. I quickly looked and saw Mr. "On Guard" just sitting there and not moving. I told Sorensen I thought he was asleep and to hold off for a moment as I opened the door. The door was nearly silent—but not quite. It squeaked at the last moment and Sleepy Boy heard it. He turned to the front door, must have seen Tom's shadow, and stood up, holding a small AR or carbine.

I was now standing in the kitchen ten steps or less behind him as he walked to the front. He must have seen Sorensen or Tom, as he quickly lifted the rifle up and I heard the safety click off. I put the little .22 in the back of his head and caught him and his rifle before they hit the floor. I laid him down and quickly scanned the rooms I could see. There was no movement.

I opened the front door, and when Sorensen saw me, he whispered, "Trick or treat?"

I pointed at the guard's prone figure on the floor and then to the stairs. He nodded and Tom scooted around the rest of the first floor to see if all was clear. He nodded that it was and took up a guard position next to the stairs. I pointed to myself and then to the stairs, indicating to Sorensen that I would take point. Not making a sound while climbing stairs was not a job for a three-hundred-pound man. Then again, my two hundred would make little difference. I didn't know Lee well enough to trust his alertness, so I was the logical candidate.

Just before we were about to go up the stairs, Sorensen shone his little LED light on the dead guy's face. He was Asian. A good sign we were on the right track. One down, three to go, by my count. Sorensen stood behind me, aiming up from the bottom of the stairs as I climbed one step at a time and close to the wall molding, where there was less chance of a loose board making a squeak. The stairs turned to the right halfway up and I could see the second-floor landing. No sign of movement or light.

I reached the second floor and stopped to look down the hall. Only the top of my head would be visible to anyone in the hall heading west to my left. There was a closed door to the right. I could hear someone breathing deeply. Almost a snore, but not quite. This would be the front room—more than likely the master. I looked down at Sorensen and waved him up. I pointed to Tom and motioned for him to stay where he was to cover our tail.

I decided to check down the hall first. There were three open doors and one closed. There was an empty chair in the hall with a plastic bottle of water on the floor next to it. I quickly dropped down low and motioned for Sorensen to hold his position. He was just at the first landing, and I saw he could see over the banister and down the hall. He shook his head and nodded to the chair.

I stayed low and duck walked to the chair. I felt the water and it was still cold. I hoped whoever was recently sitting there was off relieving himself and not lying on the floor and sighting down an AK-47. It didn't feel like it and, as I thought that, I heard a toilet flush. It was so loud it covered up the sound of Sorensen creeping up behind me and pointing over my shoulder to a room at the end of the hall. I about jumped out of my skin as his hand passed my head as he pointed, but I kept my cool and pointed after him.

Sorensen moved to the end of the hall where we both could hear the faucet running while our terrorist sentry exercised his good hygiene. The water stopped running and, as he stepped out of the small bathroom, he was met with a clunk on his head from Sorensen's pistol handle. Sorensen caught him before he struck the floor and laid him back in the room. I could hear him rummaging through the man's pockets and the *click* and *clack* of stuff being removed. I looked more closely into the other rooms and saw no signs of life.

28

We moved to the master bedroom and opened the door quietly. The heavy breathing was still going on, so we continued into the room. There was a large bed on the right with two souls lying in it and a hospital-type bed in the middle of the floor. I sneaked up to the hospital bed and saw whom I believed to be Mubane's daughter lying there with an oxygen mask on her face and her eyes wide open. I put my finger to my lips and shook my head.

She blinked and I was sure she understood.

Sorensen was standing next to the big bed, pointing his pistol at the head of the larger prone figure in the bed and then reached down to shake the person awake. Before he could, the person moved and made a peeping sound. He put the tip of the pistol's barrel an inch in front of the eyes of the person in the bed, and we both saw it was a woman. I looked at the other prone figure and saw it was a woman as well, only much smaller.

That person came awake and yawned. It was a young child. These were clearly Mubane's wife and younger daughter. No sign of Mubane or Angela.

I asked the older women where her husband was. She shook her head and said something in Thai that I did not understand. I asked her again and used Angela's name. Again, she shook her head and said something that sounded like gibberish to me. I was about to haul her up by her hair when the girl in the hospital bed took off her mask and asked what we wanted with Angela.

She spoke English. No one ever mentioned that she might be American, too. We'd been told she was adopted as an infant. I walked over to her and told her we were there to take Angela home to her family. She said that she and Angela were told that Angela had no family now. Her father said some very bad people in Florida had killed her family and that Mubane was keeping her safe because the same men were trying to kill Angela.

What a twist.

I didn't see that coming. No wonder Mubane was traveling with Angela so confidently. Angela thought he was her savior. Nice. I asked her where Angela was right now, and she said that Angela had been taken to a nearby hospital after they left the airplane. Angela was feeling sickly and had been drowsy the whole trip from Bangkok. I asked her where her father was. She said he was at the hospital with Angela and that she was going to the hospital in the morning for some special treatment and would be seeing Angela then. Angela was her best friend now and would be happy that some family members were looking for her.

I was trying to keep a clear mind and understand what this girl was saying. I guessed she was drowsy from the meds she was on. I asked her about her family, and she said they were killed in a car accident when she was very young. I asked her about her ability to speak English so well since she'd been very young when she lost her family. She said her father (Mubane, I assumed) had had her tutored in English for years so she could translate for him. I asked her if she had any memory of her original family and she said she didn't.

I heard a clunk and saw Sorensen pick up a little black box that looked like a pager. He whispered that Mama-san there just tried to push its little button. I looked at him and he shook his head, indicating that she hadn't gotten that far.

I saw her holding her arm where he must have whacked her with his pistol barrel. I asked who I believed to be Mary—Mubane's adopted daughter—if either of the two women on the bed spoke or understood any English. She said her little sister spoke some. I asked Mary if she could walk at all and she said she could. I told her I needed to tell her some very important things, but that we needed to get away from that house. The owner was a bad man and very dangerous. I told her to tell her mother and sister to get out of bed and be very quiet.

She told them in Thai and her mother looked defiant. I told Mary that she had no choice. Either her mother came willingly, or we would leave her there for the bad men to get. I had no intention of leaving her behind as she would sound the alarm that we were there. I still needed the element of surprise. As it was, Mubane might believe the attack on the compound was by Papa's opposition.

Her mother looked at Sorensen, his gun, and then at her daughters. She climbed off the bed and went toward the closet. I said no, we had no time. I told her, through her daughter, to put on shoes and come along. All three of the ladies complied. I asked Mary if she needed her oxygen and she said it wasn't oxygen but a breathing machine for her sleep apnea. I wasn't quite sure how important that was right now but asked her again if she needed to take it with us. She shook her head no.

Sorensen walked out in front and climbed down the stairs. I could hear him speaking to Tom at the foot of the stairs. By the time we'd cleared the stairs, Tom had slid the body of the dead guard to the side so the ladies wouldn't see him. We went out the front door and turned toward the cookhouse. I walked up to Mrs. Mubane and told her she would be in great harm if the Mexican bad guys were to catch us. The fate of her daughters depended on her fully cooperating with us. Mary translated and Mama-san nodded.

Sorensen had the gate open and we passed through. Paul was there waiting for us and pointed to the side room where he had tied up the help. I told him to speak to us in Spanish, so they thought we were a rival gang of Papa's. He complied and made some quick, nasty sounding, guttural words that must have been damning to Mr. Z. He used the name Zaragoza a couple of times and spit on the floor. Great act. Then again, he probably meant every syllable.

We slipped out the door from the cookhouse, turned right, and made for the car. When we arrived, I looked at the six of us and figured there was no way we would all fit. I walked Mary a few feet away and looked her in the eyes. I told her to listen to me and not to interrupt until I was finished. I told her a short version of the truth about Angela and her kidnapping. I told her that her father was involved in international kidnapping and worse. I finished by telling her that I believed she had been kidnapped from her own family. I could find them for her and get her home. I then told her that Angela was her heart transplant donor and that was why they were in Mexico. We had been chasing Angela and making it difficult for the operation to take place. I told her I could prove it all by one phone call to

Angela's family. She thought about it and nodded yes.

I dialed the Cohen's phone number in Florida and quickly told Thom, who answered, that we were close to rescuing Angela and that I needed him to speak with Mary, who was right next to me, and convince her I was telling the truth about Angela being kidnapped and her parents still being alive. He was confused but said he would talk to her. I gave her the phone and she said hello, and that her name was Mary. I could hear Cohen speaking to her and saw her eyes fill with tears as she looked at me and shook her head. She asked a few questions and then asked Thom to describe me. He must have done a good job, as she looked me up and down as he was speaking. I made two big boy arm muscles and got a small smile out of her. She passed the phone back to me and started to cry. I quickly asked Thom to brief the Major and signed off.

I let Mary compose herself for a few moments and then realized we had used up too much time. I walked her back to her sister and mother. She said something to her mother, and her mother tried to slap her face. Sorensen caught it early and grabbed her arm. Mary said something else and stood next to me. Her mother looked daggers at her.

I asked Tom if he thought he could get the ladies to the border with Paul's assistance. He said yes. I placed a quick call to Gage, did the short version of the last few minutes, and asked him to inform Border Patrol and Homeland Security that the ladies would be crossing at El Paso and to facilitate their crossing. He said that wouldn't be a problem and there was an outstanding warrant for Mubane and his wife. I asked him when that happened and he said, "In about ten minutes." Good old' Gage.

I asked him to locate Mary's family and he said he would get right on it as soon as she was across the border and he could speak to her. I signed off and helped Mrs. Mubane into the front seat of the car. I took the tie from her bathrobe and tied her hands behind her. I then placed the seat belt around her and fastened her in. Paul got behind the wheel and Tom sat in the back with Mary's little sister. Mary slid in next to Tom and, before closing the door, placed her hand on mine. I told her I would see her soon and tell her the rest. She asked me to please help Angela, as she was still her best friend. I winked at her and closed the door.

Sorensen and I watched the car as it moved on down the road. It turned left and slid out of sight. I looked at Sorensen and asked him if he knew where the hospital was. He didn't but pointed to a blue sign on a post that had to be pointing the way.

We walked about four blocks and saw another blue sign with an arrow pointing to the right. As we turned the corner, I saw a sign in front of a large brick building. It had some Spanish writing and, in English, said "Hospital." The next clue was the name of the Hospital. Zaragoza Medicine Hospital. Tell me we are not the best detectives.

We scouted around the perimeter of the perfectly square building and saw there were entrances and exits on all four sides. The rear had four or five exits and a garage type door for the ambulances to back up into. The main lobby was in the front and was quite small compared to most hospitals I had been in. We could see an information counter and a small flower shop. We could also see a very Asian-looking man standing next to the elevator's doors, along with an armed, uniformed security guard. Not just armed, but well armed. Both men had pistols in their holsters and what looked like either Uzi Machine pistols or Mac-10 sub-machine guns in their hands. I couldn't make it out at this distance, but that didn't matter. They were both capable of ruining your day in a hurry.

The building was six stories high. I figured that Angela was probably being kept slightly medicated to prepare her for surgery. That would account for the fatigue on the flight over from Thailand. I didn't know much about the procedures used in pre-op for a transplant. I knew that in normal heart transplant situations, the donor was a dead person, so pre-op was a matter of the mechanical removal of the heart and transport to the recipient. I found it disturbing that a doctor, or a team of doctors, could be rounded up with another team of operating techs that were all willing to remove a heart from a living person and murder them. Right then, though, it was important for us to locate Angela before any of my morbid thoughts enveloped her.

Sorensen and I circled the building again. It was about an hour before sunup. I could tell by the lighting of the eastern sky. I wanted to be in and out of the hospital by then. Back at the front of the hospital, we could still see the two men at the elevator doors. There was a little more activity in the lobby as staff members were coming to work. We went around to the east side and saw that the workers were using a small door to the left of the rear entrance. As I looked closer, I saw there was a punch-clock on the wall and numerous cards in slots next to it. We couldn't see any sentry or monitoring camera near the door. I could see cameras above the main rear door and one over the ambulance entrance.

As we stood in the shadows across from the rear area, the big garage door at the ambulance entrance began to roll up. A red flashing light began flashing and a beeping noise began. We heard a siren in the distance, and it became louder as the ambulance drew closer. When it rounded the corner, it shut down its siren, swung into the drive, and spun around. It then backed into the garage opening and shut down. The driver ran to the back and vanished into the entrance.

I looked at Sorensen and nodded toward the building. Now was a good time to enter—while some excitement and confusion was coming from the emergency room.

We walked up to the employee entrance and went right in. I had my pistol in my right front pocket just barely sticking up to grab if I needed it. I was sure Sorensen was equally prepared. A hall to the left led to the ambulance bay and a group of folks were moving in and out of view in the bay area. To the right was the rear lobby where I could see two or more folks moving about near another hall leading off the lobby.

I decided to go where there was the most confusion and walked to the ambulance bay. As soon as we had cleared the hall, I saw two attendants leaning over a gurney that they had pulled from the rear of the ambulance. It appeared they were checking the patient for vital signs. As we watched, one of them—most likely a doctor—stood up and shook his head toward a man standing at the side of the gurney with his back to us. I did a second take when I saw the man was carrying a pistol in a side holster and realized it was our Asian elevator guard. I then realized the dead guy was more than likely one of the souls we had provided the Lord with back at the compound.

Sorensen saw it too and pointed to the sliding door into the hospital. I moved quickly and, just as we entered another hall, I saw a red exit sign in English above a wide door. I swung it open and we double-timed it up to the second-floor landing. A window in the landing's door looked out over a long hall. There were many roll stands in the hall and several rolling carts parked along the walls. It looked as much like a post-op ward as I had ever seen one—and I had seen a lot.

A moment later, our gun-wielding Asian guard came around the corner and passed right next to the door we were looking out and then down the hall away from us. About halfway down, he stopped and spoke to someone through a door. Just then, another guard came out of that room and stood next to the door. The new guard walked back toward us and gently knocked on another door about ten or fifteen feet from where we were. The door was on our side of the hall so, again, we couldn't see who it was. The guard bowed deeply and began to speak Thai. After he finished, he turned and walked quickly down a hall he had come from.

Then, in a rush, Mubane came out of the room, walked to the other room, and spoke to the guard standing there. A moment later, a female Asian nurse came out of the room, listened to Mubane a moment, and then dialed a number on her cell phone. She hardly said two or three words when she stopped talking and said something to Mubane, who looked as if he was going to blow apart. I figured he had just learned that his family had been abducted and that numerous members of the compound staff were dead.

I figured one thing out. That guarded room was more than likely where our Angela was. That I was sure about. Just as I was about to ask Sorensen for his ideas, we heard a door below us open and someone began climbing up the staircase.

I pointed toward the stairs going up and we took off silently to the third floor. We waited for the second-floor door to open, but we had no such luck. They were coming on up.

I looked through the window at the third-floor layout and saw a few carts and several doors to rooms. Nothing like the second floor. I didn't want to get too far away from Angela, so I pushed through the door and walked out into the hallway. We didn't see anyone, but we could hear voices and clanging like the staff were serving breakfast. I had spent a lot of time in hospitals around the world—and not just as a visitor—and I knew the sounds of certain events. Also, the smell of food was rich in the air.

We took a couple of steps and the door to the stairs opened. A female nurse stepped out, paid us no attention whatsoever, and walked to the next hall and vanished. We quickly walked back to the stairs and skipped on back down to the second floor.

Same scene as before, only the sentry was in front of Mubane's room and not the room farther down the hall where I thought Angela was. Across the hall, I could see the sun was lighting up the outside, so we had lost the cover of darkness. I figured we had better do something rather than watch our feet go to sleep, so I asked Sorensen to open his phone line to me again. I planned to cross over to the opposite side of the building by going up to the third floor and walking down the opposite stairwell we were presently on.

He asked me the plan and I told him I was still thinking it up. I told him to stand by for my signal, whatever it was, and be ready to move down the hallway to Angela's door. I requested that he not hang around Mubane's door but get into Angela's room and carry her out. I finished by reminding him that whoever got to Angela first had to make for the border. He nodded and I climbed the stairs.

I cleared the door on the third floor and walked down the hall. I didn't look left or right, just straight ahead. The only plan I could come up with was going down to the second floor and acting as if I owned the place until I was close enough to pop the guard. Then, I would grab Angel. I sure hoped she was in there and that we could move her. I also just remembered the nurse that may still be in there. I didn't care to whack her, but she was probably someone involved in the body parts trade with Mubane, so that helped clear my soon-to-come bad conscience. (Yes, I have one of those.)

Just before I reached the end of the hall and the exit door to the stairs, I saw a white lab coat hanging on a chair next to a small desk. It looked bulky enough to fit over my clothes, so I snatched it up as I turned into the stairwell. I thought about it a moment and walked back out into the hall, grabbed a metal clipboard from a wall slot behind the desk, and turned to walk back out into the staircase. Just then, a nurse came out the door from the stairs, hesitated, saw the clipboard and white lab coat over my arm, and smiled as she continued by. I often wondered if people ever sensed how close they were to death at those moments. I did all the time.

As I walked down the stairs, I tried to slip on the lab coat. No way, Jose. I couldn't get my arm in the sleeve. I kept it over my arm and told Sorensen to be ready. I also requested he not shoot the handsome doctor walking up the hall toward him. He snorted and remained silent.

I took a deep breath, opened the door, and walked out into the hallway. I didn't hesitate to analyze the scene. I just walked and acted as if I was reading the non-existent chart on my clipboard. I walked on the right side of the hall so Sorensen could see me clearly. From my peripheral vision, I could see the guard turn slightly to me. I looked at room door numbers and paid him no attention.

Just then, a nurse came out of a side hall near the guard and looked at me in a puzzled way. I gave her a little two-fingered wave and smiled as if we were old friends. She smiled back and said something in Spanish. I had no idea what she was asking and asked her in English what room Mr. Sanchez was in. She smiled and hesitated a moment. She looked both ways as if trying to remember which room Mr. Sanchez was in (it would have blown my mind if she had pointed at a door to indicate where the fictional Mr. Sanchez was residing) but then didn't. She spotted Sorensen coming at her from behind and looked back at me while she sensed the trouble that was brewing.

Hoping she really did understand English, I told her with a smile that we would not hurt her or any patients. She didn't hesitate at all as she smiled back, said she understood, looked at the guard, and then ducked into the closest room.

Just then, the guard who had been distracted by my approach and the nurse's conversation turned and saw Sorensen. Too late, Sorensen reached out with his twenty-foot-long arm and smacked Mr. "See You Later" so hard, I thought a bullet would have been more appropriate. He went down hard and made a little noise. Sorensen grabbed him by the collar and dragged him into a room across the way. It was the same room where the nurse had bailed. I heard him say that the man may need some attention, as he seemed to have fallen ill.

He walked back out and pointed to Mubane's door, showing me his gun at the same time. I shook my head no. He frowned and moved toward me. I was then right next to Angela's door. I was afraid that I would open it and again be disappointed. Perhaps Mubane had foiled us again. I swallowed the negativity and opened the door.

I was not disappointed.

There in the bed right in front of me was Angela. Absolutely beautiful. Even more so then her photos.

There was also a Thai-looking nurse sitting on the opposite side of the bed, holding a magazine on her lap. She looked at me holding the chart, the lab coat over my arm, but she wasn't fooled for a moment. She grabbed a small derringer revolver off the tray next to her and instead of drawing down on me, pointed it at Angela. I couldn't believe I hadn't thought to hold my gun in my hand under the lab coat and was about to throw my hands up in surrender to prevent her from shooting Angela when two small round circles appeared on her forehead. She sat right back down in her chair and, other than the two little blemishes, looked as if she was going back to her magazine.

I turned to Angela, who was halfway in a drug-induced sleep, and put my finger up to my lips in case she was aware of what had just happened. She had an IV in her left hand and some kind of a monitor band above that. Numerous other machines next to the bed were flashing numbers and graphs that meant nothing to me. I walked to her, pulled the devices off her, and then gently removed the IV. She was nude under the sheet, and I could see what appeared to be Sharpie drawings on her chest and side. Like dotted lines and X's. Talk about close; she was all ready for slaughter.

I tried to tell her we were friends, but she was too out of it. There was a hospital gown on the door next to the small bathroom. I grabbed it and wrapped it around her from the front. I lifted her up and carried her to the door. Sorensen opened the door fully and looked out. He waved for me to follow him and we turned right, toward the staircase I had just come from.

There was still no one in the hall—or in any of the rooms we had passed, for that matter. Mubane must have purchased the entire floor for his evil deeds. I so wanted to go back and shoot him, especially after looking in the face of this beautiful child I was carrying. But it wasn't worth the chances of something going south if we took the time to do him right now. What we had been working for all along was in my arms and beginning come to. A little wiggle here and there and then a wide-open stare three inches from my face.

I said, "Hi Angela. I'm your Uncle Jake, and this tall, Chewbacca-looking blob is Uncle Ron."

She looked confused, and so I quickly explained that we were taking her home to her mom and dad. They were alive and missing her very much.

I could see her trying to get her head wrapped around what I had just said, but she was still too drowsy to take it all in.

We continued down the stairs until we were on the ground floor. I hope there was an extension on these stairs to take us down to the basement. There wasn't, and now we were out of options. If we crossed to the employee entrance, the guards would clearly see us from the lobby, and Machine Gun Kelly was probably still on duty—or his relief.

The staircase we were in did not look well used. In fact, there were cobwebs across the door leading out. I looked at Sorensen and asked him if he could requisition a gurney and then check to see if there was a handy ambulance waiting to be borrowed. He looked out of the door window toward the lobby exit and said he had a better idea. He grabbed the lab coat from me and took off down the hall at a quick pace. I watched until he turned right into the lobby. A moment later, he was walking back just behind Kelly, who was looking really pissed off. As they turned into the door, I was holding open, Sorensen smacked him on the head a good one. (I needed to speak to him about his knockout methods the first chance I get.)

Angela was coming around rapidly now and trying to cover up her bare bottom, which I had firmly grasped in my left hand. I set her down and asked her if she thought she could stand. She tested her legs a bit. I looked at Sleeping Kelly on the floor and asked Sorensen to strip him and give his uniform to Angela. She shook out of her hospital gown and put the man's shirt on first. Sorensen and I averted our eyes as she slipped on the man's trousers. Nearly a perfect fit. The shoes were a little large but better than too small. Other than still being a little tipsy, she looked like a blonde member of Papa's brigade.

I explained to her where we were and that we needed to get to the border crossing about a mile away. She asked again about her parents and I told her they were fine and that her dad had spoken to her friend Mary just a couple of hours ago. She was about to ask about Mary when I said we needed to get moving. I helped her stand reasonably straight. Sorensen walked behind her and positioned himself close enough to catch her if she fell backward. She was doing better every second and, by the time we got to the employee entrance, she was on her own.

There were a couple of hospital workers out by the ambulance bay, but they paid us no attention. I took one of the cards from the wall and fed it into the time machine. I wondered what I was being paid. Sorensen opened the door and we were outside. It felt wonderful. I looked both ways and saw only a couple of folks loitering on the next block to the south, but no threats. I pointed to the east and we crossed the road to the other side and walked north a block and then turned east.

I watched Angela as we walked. She was looking a little green in the gills. I asked her if she was okay and she nodded just before she threw up a bellyful of clear liquid. I helped her to a side alley, and we stopped to regroup. She apologized and said she felt dizzy. I told her I felt the same way but hadn't eaten in so long that there was nothing to heave. She smiled a bit and asked if she could sit for a moment. Sorensen walked to the end of the alley and stood guard while I helped her sit on a wooden box by the wall.

We rested a few minutes and just as I was about to suggest we keep moving, Sorensen quick-stepped back to us and said we had company. I helped Angela up and Sorensen picked her up like a pillow and ran down the alleyway. He said there were about ten men with rifles heading down the street from the hospital and they looked angry. We had left Kelly's machine gun in the stairwell, and I wished we hadn't. Might be a good time for Sorensen's hand grenades, but we had no idea who or what was behind these thin alley walls. Not an option right now.

As we moved, Sorensen pushed on doors until one opened. Following his pistol, he ducked in, and I pushed it shut as soon as I'd cleared it. A moment later, we could hear the group of shooters coming down the alley. Someone must have seen us and led them to us. I could also hear them kicking in doors as they progressed. I turned and surveyed the small ground floor flat. There were two very old women sitting in the front, looking at us. One of them stood up. She would hardly make it to Sorensen's waist even if she stood on her tiptoes. She looked at the back door, at Angela, and then me.

Sorensen and I were holding pistols and Angela. The still seated women said something in Spanish and waved her arm toward the wall to our left. The woman who was standing did not hesitate and quickly walked to the wall and slid open a panel. It revealed a little cubbyhole about five feet square that had some boxes stacked in it. The old women pulled the boxes out and motioned for us to get in.

I could hear the doors being kicked in very close now. I pushed Angela into the hole and slipped in next to her. Sorensen turned around and backed into us as the old women slid the panel back in place. I then heard a chair or table pushed up against the wall against the panel.

A moment later, their back door was kicked open and a great deal of yelling and furniture being kicked over ensued. One of the old women screamed and I felt Sorensen stiffen. I grabbed his arm to keep him calm and we waited for the wall to come down. We were both prepared to come out shooting, but the yelling and screaming quieted down and began a moment later in the next flat over. We waited for a few more minutes and then they opened the panel.

I couldn't believe the mess. Everything in the small flat was destroyed. Everything. The boxes that had been hiding in the hidey-hole that they had removed for us were smashed open, and there were dozens of smashed little handmade dolls that the ladies must have made. It was probably there means of income. I didn't know if Mexico had a Social Security system for retired folks, but if they did, it couldn't amount to much. They were wiped out. I thought of ol' Schultz's money in my pocket but decided to wait before handing it out until I was sure the Frito Banditos' weren't coming back.

Sorensen walked to the rear window and ducked out of the way immediately. He pointed to the broken door and raised two fingers. The three of us moved against the back wall and waited.

After a few tense minutes, we heard someone yell something a distance away and the two guards outside our door moved on. I was standing right beside the window and I did a quick memory peek. There was no one there, but we waited a little longer. Sorensen walked to the front of the flat and pushed the curtain aside on the little front window. He looked both ways. Moved to the bedroom and came back a moment later, nodding that all was clear.

The three of us stayed in the little kitchen near the rear door. We could hear people in the alleyway shouting and crying. Kids too terrified to cry were now screaming as their parents tried to calm them down. I didn't need to look outside to picture the grief. The poorest of the poor had been victimized again.

I called Tom as soon as I thought I could whisper a call. He answered and said he was across the border on the U.S. side and all was well. He said they took Mrs. Mubane into custody and that some ladies had taken Mary and her little sister away. He had spoken to Gage and had located Mary's family in Clovis, New Mexico. The local office of the FBI was notifying her folks, and they were being transported to El Paso immediately. Tom said Mrs. Mubane would be cooperating with the authorities when I stopped him and asked where Paul was. He said he dropped them off and headed back into Juarez, but not before giving him one of his cell phones to use.

I asked him for Paul's cell number. It was too long to remember, so I asked him if Sorensen had the number and he said he did. I quickly explained the predicament we were in and said I would call back shortly. He said he would call Gage and head back into Juarez shortly. I thanked him and signed off.

I stepped up beside Sorensen and asked him if his phone was on. He asked me which one. I said, "All of them." He said none of them was on. I thought to myself, *Wiseass. If none of them were on, then the answer was no.* I explained to him that Paul was back in the city with the car. Sorensen asked if Paul could trade it for a tank. I asked him to turn on the phone that Tom's secondary phone would call. He took out his regular phone and switched it on. I asked him if that was his company phone and he said yes. I mentioned that he was very traceable through that phone and he said, "Yup."

As it came on, it vibrated like crazy and then stopped. He looked at it and said, "Mother has been calling."

I knew he meant his bosses and asked if Paul had called in the past few minutes. He looked down, scrolled his phone, and said just a couple of minutes ago. I took out my phone again and asked him to read off the number to me. I then dialed it into my phone and pressed Send. I gave him the "cutthroat" sign and pointed to his phone. He switched it off and said it would do no good because his phone coming back online would light up the boards in Langley. At that point, I didn't care even if one of his supervisors was involved in all this dirty crapola.

Paul answered on the first ring. I told him it was Jake and asked where he was. He said not far from where we were, based on all the armed banditos near the hospital. I told him the short version of our predicament and a general description of where we were. Just then, I noticed Angela speaking Spanish with one of the Mexican ladies, who turned to me and gave me the address of where we were. I looked at Angela and squinted in puzzlement. She then said her family had had numerous Mexican helpers over the course of her life. I gave the information to Paul and he said he knew the area and that it was totally surrounded by Zaragoza's troops. I asked him if he could see my number on his phone, as many of my phones have the caller ID blocked. He said he could. I asked him to park somewhere close and let me know where he was in regard to our location when he was in place. He agreed and we signed off.

I asked Angela if one of the ladies could loan her more suitable clothes than the uniform she was wearing. She asked and one of the women pointed to the floor and shook her head as if ashamed. Angela gave her a little hug and rummaged through some of the things on the floor. She looked up at me as she chose from some of the very few items the ladies owned. I figured this was as good a time as any to pull out a few hundred-dollar bills from my still stuffed trouser pockets. I gave them to Angela to pass on to the ladies.

To say they were shocked at seeing so much money was clearly an understatement. The ladies passed it back and forth between them as if it was a brand-new puppy. Tears ran down their faces and they began hugging us and patting our arms. I accepted their thanks but secretly felt guilty, as we had brought this grief to them in the first place. I looked around and decided to dig into my pockets again and give them even more. The second stack was from Mr. Schultz for his part in starting all this. (Creep.) That brought on more tears and gratitude. I had nearly forgotten we were in a war zone and began to wave my arms and making shushing noises to calm them down. Sorensen was standing at the rear window, looking out from time to time. He didn't tense up at all, so I figured we were still safe for the time being.

Angela walked into the little bedroom and shortly came out wearing a long skirt and beige, puffy shirt. She looked like a native except for the bright blonde hair. One of the ladies noticed too and picked up a long shawl, draping it over Angela's head and wrapping it over her shoulders. With her head hung low and her arms covered, she was ready for the fiesta.

One of the ladies used the word *Bonita* with the other lady, a word I knew meant "beautiful. "I couldn't have agreed more. One of the ladies picked up a framed picture from the rubble on the floor and showed it to Angela. She then passed it to me. The photo was of a young girl wearing nearly the same outfit Angela was wearing. I asked Angela if it was the lady's daughter, and she said no. It was the lady as a young girl. I looked closer and thought that perhaps the skirt and blouse Angela was wearing were the same clothes. Could be. Heck. I still had socks from the Sixties that I still wore.

The shouting had died down to our east and I figured the troops were ransacking the next neighborhood down the way. I pushed the rear door open and looked west and then east. A few folks rummaging through debris in the alley. I knew there was no way we were going to be able to leave that little flat without twenty people seeing us and possibly raising a ruckus, knowing we were the cause of their grief.

I looked at the two old women. They were looking around their little flat, trying to figure out where they could safely stash their money. I decided that the whole neighborhood could use a little cheering up at Schultz's expense. I figured there were about twenty flats in this alley, so I gave Angela about twenty or more hundred-dollar bills. I asked her to see if the ladies would pass them out to their neighbors to help pay for their losses—and, I thought to myself, buy us a little time to slip away without any wild reappraisals.

The ladies agreed and slipped out the rear door. I asked Angela if she was all right and comfortable in her new clothes. She said she was and showed me her large black men's shoes. I smiled and told her she would start a new fashion craze. She smiled and then looked around the room. I knew she was trying to take all this in, but after what she had been through over the past few weeks, she was owed some solace. Such a pretty girl, and with so much strength. I grew angry, thinking about her and the many like her whom these people were hurting every moment of every day. I hoped the Major's opening press conference put the fear of god into all these perps.

I motioned Sorensen over. I told them both we needed to make our move toward the border before Papa was able to bring in even more troops. He agreed and Angela shook her head, as I was sure she was confused about what was coming. I thought about it for a moment and then told Angela I wanted her to go out the door and walk one block beyond where we were and to turn right so she could see the river valley. I told her we would catch up in a few moments. I reminded her to keep her head covered with the scarf and walk a little hunched over. If we did not catch up to her within five minutes, she was to walk to the east, which would be right, until she saw the border crossing at the big bridge. Once she saw the crossing, I told her to walk to the where all the ladies were standing next to the road, selling their trinkets, and sit down as close to the road as she could. If a man named Paul, driving a small dirty blue car, drove up, to get in the car with him and let him take her across the border. Dressed in those clothes, I was certain she would go nearly unnoticed unless the banditos had set up a roadblock. I told her to go, and, after touching me on the arm, she stepped out and was gone.

After Angela was gone, I took out my phone and called Paul in the car. I told him Angela's route and asked him to pick her up as soon as he saw she was clear of the searchers. He said there were many troops still wandering around our area, but I thought the route I'd sent him was the best. I heard his engine rev as we signed off, signaling that he was getting in position. I next called Tom at the border and filled him in. He said he would cross the bridge on foot and watch for her. I hesitated a moment and then told Tom that he had to make sure she got across. Her not making it was not an option. He said he understood.

Sorensen and I took out our spare ammunition magazines and popped a few rounds into them to make sure they were at capacity and ready to go to work. As soon as that was done, I opened the door and quick-stepped after Angela. Sorensen stayed to the left of the alley and I skirted the right. Except to barely turn my head to check my peripheral vision, I didn't look behind us at the east end of the alley. At the first road, we turned right and walked north a block and then turned west at the next crossroad.

I saw Angela first and whistled to Sorensen to stop. He quickly looked around the building on his corner and stepped back a couple of steps. She was approaching two small Mexicans, and both were armed with small machine guns. They were watching her approach and stood blocking her way.

I took off at a fast walk, holding my head down to hide my height. I didn't look at them so they wouldn't sense me coming. When I was about fifty feet away, I saw one of the older ladies from the flat appear out of nowhere and catch up to Angela. She put her arm around Angel and appeared to be speaking to her as they approached the guards.

I moved farther to the right and kept walking. The two guards stopped the two women and one pointed his gun at them and yelled something. He seemed to be asking questions of Angela. She kept her head down as he yelled at her and the older lady pulled her even tighter toward her as she yelled back at the guards. The one guard just standing there with his machine gun reached up and moved Angela's scarf aside. Her blonde hair immediately alerted him.

Just as he swung his gun down into firing position, I fired two rounds into his upper body and then two into his boyfriend once he'd gone down. The second one went down, too. Both guards were still conscious, and one was starting to yell. At that moment, both of their heads snapped back as Sorensen silently placed a round in both of their foreheads.

I wasn't surprised that neither of the two ladies showed any emotion at all. Sorensen grabbed the two bodies, shoved them into some bushes, and took the two little machine guns and a couple of magazines from the men's pockets. He passed one of the guns and a spare magazine to me, and we walked briskly north and turned east toward the border crossing.

I spotted Paul's car up ahead on the side of the road. There was a single guard speaking to him as he stood next to the car. We stayed to the right and in the shadows until the guard noticed us approaching. Paul said something to the guard and waved at us. We kept walking, but now Sorensen had positioned himself in the front, blocking the three of us with his massive body. He had his machine gun held tightly against his left leg and the silenced pistol against his right and at the ready.

Paul looked at Sorensen and quickly stepped back a bit to get out of the line of fire. Just as I thought Sorensen was going to drop the guard, Paul put up his hand and said, "Wait."

Sorensen hesitated a moment and I brought my pistol up and took aim at the guard. The guard kept his gun pointed toward the ground and just looked at us. Paul said the man was his friend and belonged to the local militia. The man was a good *amigo* and he would help us.

I looked at his weapon and his trigger finger. He saw me look and slowly moved the gun to his left hand and away from us. I asked the ladies to hang back a bit and Angela put her arm on the older woman's shoulder. Sorensen approached Paul and his friend first. I lowered my pistol but kept the barrel about halfway between the ground and Paul's friend's midsection. My motion was not lost on the guy. He tried to smile as he looked up at Sorensen but was visibly terrified.

Paul told us his friend worked for Papa but was not one of the thugs we had encountered back at the compound. Sorensen relieved the man of his machine pistol and laid it on the ground next to Paul. Paul went on to say that his friend told him that Papa had placed a price on our head that was very generous. We were described as two giant *gringos* wearing hunting-style shirts and trousers. I stood a bit taller and Sorensen looked at me and then at the distance between my six-two and his six-seven or so. I knew what he was thinking. Anyone under six-four was considered a "little guy" by him. I almost expected him to muss my hair and ask me if I felt like a big boy now. I was much taller than Paul and his friend, so the descriptions were not that far off.

I told Paul to tell his friend that I would reward him generously if he went to lunch and took a siesta right then and told no one that he had seen us. Paul relayed my offer and the guy smiled broadly for the first time. I stood behind Sorensen, pulled out a few hundreds, and gave them to Paul in front of his friend. I told him to hold off paying him until we'd slipped away without a battalion of armed bad guys chasing after us. He relayed that to his friend and tore one of the hundreds in half. He gave one-half to his friend and placed the other half, along with the rest of the bills, in his pocket. His friend said something that sounded an awful lot like, "I go bacation now," and then walked away. I asked Paul to pick up his friend's weapon and put it in his car. He did and we all gathered under a tree on the roadside.

I asked Angela to tell her lady friend to head back home. I told her to tell her we owed her and her roommate our lives and would not forget her. I looked at Sorensen and saw him nod in agreement. The older women took off her shawl and traded it for Angela's. Now, Angela looked different from even her former look. It was very effective. I gave the older women another fist full of hundreds and she shuffled off toward her home.

I asked Angela to get into Paul's car and asked Paul to go and park somewhere where he could make a dash for the border when we signaled him. Angela quickly climbed into the front seat and Paul pointed to the rear. She moved into the back and slouched down some to disguise her height. I smiled and gave her a wink. She smiled back and covered more of her face with the shawl. Paul drove off and turned to the south at the next block. We didn't hear any shooting, which was a good thing.

Sorensen and I followed Paul's lead but saw no sign of his car. As soon as we had a little cover in the form of some bushes next to a building, I stopped and called Tom. He announced he was on the Mexican side of the bridge and was waiting. I told him to wait for Paul to rush the bridge on my command as he got Angela across the mid-point to U.S. soil. Tom said there were several *gringos* in civilian clothes loitering around him. I guaranteed him these were off-duty agents cutting Gage a favor, should we be challenged as we approached the U.S. side. If I didn't miss my guess, there would be some snipers on the cliffside and pointing their weapons toward the Mexican side.

Sorensen walked on the left side of the narrow road and I walked on the right and a little behind. I kept my head turned slightly to the left to watch our rear and left flank. Sorensen's head was turned slightly to the right to cover the rest. It was a little trick we'd picked up in Vietnam, and it pretty much covered us for 360 degrees.

I was getting nervous for Angela and Paul as they were hidden somewhere up ahead of us, waiting for the word to go. I had no idea where or how many of Papa's troops were lying in wait, but I was sure they were waiting for us to break through.

We stopped for a moment and decided to reverse our trek to see what was going on back near the river valley. We had no sooner crossed the first block when we saw a huge motor home parked about two blocks west of the road we were walking. It looked brand new, and it was surrounded by sentries. Most were holding machine pistols and appeared alert.

We tucked ourselves into a bushy area next to a building and watched the activity surrounding the small field where the motor home was parked. It must have just pulled in as there was still dust billowing behind it. The troops standing around it were wiping their faces and stomping their feet as if they had run beside it for a while. Sorensen had his small monocular up to his eye. He made humming noises as he scanned the big, shiny vehicle. Through the front windscreen, I could see a man with his back to us. He turned slightly and, at the same time, Sorensen said, "Hello."

I saw Mubane's face and shiny black hair. He was talking animatedly to someone farther inside the living area of the camper. A small man in the front passenger seat made some hand signals as if he were talking, as well.

The guy must have been translating. Mubane spoke to the shadow and pointed to Papa or one of his top advisers, who sitting in that comfortable coach, probably drinking a nice cold Margarita.

I turned and looked at Sorensen. He said what I was thinking. "There, my friend, sits a major component of all that's evil in this world."

I saw his mind running in overdrive as he looked over the terrain in front of us. I was formulating a plan to cause a diversion so we could get Angela over the border. Sorensen, on the other hand, was thinking way outside the box. He turned to me and asked if I wanted to join him in saving the free world. I thought about it for a moment, looked back at the motor home, and asked him what he had in mind.

He cleared the leaves off a sandy area and drew a square to represent the field where the big vehicle was parked. He drew a rectangle to represent the camper and dots for the fifteen or twenty guards. There was a van parked behind the camper and he drew that, too. Outside of the field, he started to draw little circles and then stopped, brushed away the drawing, and said, "Let's sneak in on both sides and heave four or five of these little round, steel death apples all around the camper."

As he said it, he pulled two of the hand grenades out of one of his pockets, tossed them up as if he were juggling them, and then looked at me.

I thought to myself, *That's as good a diversion as any.*

We laid there a while longer and watched the camper and the guards' actions. They weren't spreading out as much from the camper as they should have been. We saw no one around the field to protect the flanks. All in all, the millions and possibly billions that Papa had couldn't seem to buy him the security he needed.

I nodded to the field. Sorensen pointed right and I pointed left. I took out the four grenades I had, and Sorensen took out a few more he had. We loosened the cotter key-type pins holding the spoons on the grenades and tucked them back into our pockets. I kept one in my left hand and picked up the borrowed machine pistol in my right. Sorensen did the same but held two grenades in his left hand. He elbowed me in the arm and winked. I rolled my eyes. It was one of the signals we used, and it meant if it all went south, we would see each other on the other side.

I told him whoever got within throwing distance first should begin the show. I got one nod from Sorensen. I gave Paul a quick call and told him to get ready. I instructed him to race for the bridge as soon as he heard the first explosion, to look for Tom as he approached the bridge, and to crash through any roadblocks he encountered. He said he was ready. I asked him to call Tom and inform him, too. We signed off and, without looking at Sorensen again, I took off.

I crossed the narrow road and Sorensen vanished into the brush. As I walked as casually as I could toward the field, a couple of sentries looked up at me and then in another direction. I was too far away to recognize and certainly no giant. So, no alarms yet. I turned to the left at the next block and, before clearing the first building, ducked into the bushes and walked west toward the field. I was close to my limited throwing range and expected to hear Sorensen's first grenade go off any moment.

I didn't have to wait long. The concussion nearly knocked me to the ground. I took advantage of the noise and confusion and ran full out until I could see the camper clearly. I also saw numerous men lying on the ground and some getting into shooter positions. Another of Sorensen's grenades went off, and I threw my first and second grenades to my side of the camper. The timers on the old grenades in Nam took about three seconds to blow. These seemed to take less than two. Just time enough to lie on the ground before they blew.

I looked up after my blasts and saw no one still standing. Someone opened the side door on the camper right in front of me and I about emptied the first magazine of .9 mm rounds across the door and the front of the motor home. I could hear screaming from inside and from the men lying on the ground.

Sorensen came charging around the front of the camper, firing into the windshield as he did. I rushed the side door and swung it open. I was about to throw another grenade into the cabin when I saw nothing but prone bodies lying on the floor. I quick looked at the rear sleeping area and saw only a small Mexican leaning against the side of the bed. He saw me and held up his hands.

Sorensen pushed past me and climbed into the camper. Everyone in there was a bloody mess. Mubane was sitting on the floor with blood coming out of his chest and face. I looked closely and saw the guy sitting next to the bed was Papa Z. They both looked close to death. I thought Sorensen was going to do a Sorensen Special and pop them all in the head, but instead grabbed the very dead driver from the seat and jumped in. The motor was still running with a little steam coming from the front, but when he placed the vehicle in gear and stomped the gas pedal, it leaped like a race car out of the field and onto the narrow road.

I knew the rough bumps we felt as we cleared the field were those of the newly departed souls on their way to judgment. I yanked the dead guy out of the passenger seat and sat down. That seat was swiveled to the rear and I had a good view of our passengers. Most were dead guys, but Papa and Mubane were still hanging in there. Papa mouthed, *Hospital,* as he looked at me. Mubane appeared to be in shock but was looking around. I was tempted to put them out of their misery but thought better of it when I thought about the information they carried and the many law enforcement officers and politicians they could bury if they survived. I decided there would be another day to deal with them.

Sorensen turned onto the main road to the bridge and sped up. In our way, there was a zigzagging cement barrier roadblock on the approach to the bridge and the Mexican Border Police standing with their rifles. They jumped out of the way as Sorensen skidded through the maze and out the other side. No one shot at us and we cleared the first part of the bridge. Sorensen was more careful of the folks on foot as he blasted up the bridge. I turned to the front, looked across the bridge, and saw Paul's car parked on the U.S. side of the bridge. I also recognized Tom leading Angela away from the car. As we began to slow down on the U.S. side, I heard a few rifles blast off in the distance, but they didn't seem to hit us.

We stopped behind Paul's car and held our hands up so the U.S. Border Patrol Officers holding rifles on us would not get too nervous. The side door opened and, low and behold, it was Gage climbing in and waving off the sentries trying to rush the door. Before I could jump up and give him a hug or ask what he was doing here, he passed a stocking cap to each of us and told us to put them over our heads and faces and quickly come with him.

I pointed to Papa and Mubane and said, "Happy birthday to you."

He smiled when he realized who they were. He had a small walkie-talkie in his hand and said something quietly into it. We waited a few moments as Gage looked out the side window. He turned and told me again to pull the cap down over my face and opened the door.

Four men dressed in digital desert-colored fatigues carried black body bags. Gage pointed out Mubane and then Papa Zaragoza to the men. A few more guys were lying on the deck, obviously deadies, but the soldiers ignored them. The soldiers quickly picked up Papa, slid a black plastic bag under him, and pulled it up behind his head. One of the men gave Papa a shot with a hypodermic needle when he started to protest. I was sure he was saying something like, "I am not dead yet." He went out like I light.

They zipped him up, left a small opening at the top for air, and moved to Mubane. Mubane had watched what happened to Papa and now he looked like he had a heart attack coming on. They gave him his shot right off. The four men took the two body bags and walked out the door. Gage pulled my stocking cap down farther, put one over his head, and led the way out the door. I saw the men place the body bags into the back of a van and slam the rear doors closed. They drove through the maze and were gone.

As I watched the van leave, I wished I could have had an hour or so with Mubane before his intel was extracted and then buried in some big black filing cabinet for a hundred years before being partially released to some journalist under the Freedom of Information Act. Even then, it would be so redacted it would make little sense. The real bad guys would have bought their way out of it and gone on to do more evil. The bright spots in my thoughts were the ledger and the case of files still in our possession.

I saw the reason for the face covering exercise by Gage. About fifty large video cameras were set up on the bridge and side passageways, and all of them were pointed at us. Gage led us over to a small van and instructed us to sit on the wooden deck. He climbed in behind us and slid the door shut. A driver climbed in and Gage instructed him to head for "the office." Whatever that meant.

There were no windows in the van except up front, and he reached over and pulled off my head cover. He did the same to Sorensen and then took the machine pistol out of Sorensen's hand. After pulling out the partially filled magazine and cocking the round out of the chamber, he slid the gun under the passenger seat. He looked at us and asked, "Well, kids, how was camp?"

He then hugged me and Sorensen at the same time. We all laughed until tears ran down our face. I asked him where Angela was, and he said she was at a sick bay clinic at Biggs Airfield at Fort Bliss. He said Thom and Blanche Cohen were on their way there from Florida even as we spoke.

I looked at Gage and asked how this was all possible on such short notice. I followed it up with: "And what the heck are you doing here?"

He looked at me and said, "There was absolutely no doubt in his mind that we would accomplish our mission and be here right on schedule."

I looked at Sorensen and shook my head. I could tell he was thinking the same thing about our own body bags. Gage went on to say he had twenty bucks on our succeeding.

As we drove along, I leaned back against the wall of the van and for the first time in a long while felt utterly exhausted. I looked down at my legs and boots. I saw the lumps of the last two grenades in my trouser pockets and the bulk of the cash still filling my pockets. The cash seemed to grow every time I fished more out. I also noticed something I hadn't seen or felt before then. Blood on my jungle shirt and a wet red stain down my left leg. I lifted my shirt and saw a large hole in my left side. I was so bruised and banged up, I never even noticed that I had been hit.

Sorensen saw it at the same time I did and went into action. Gage passed him a first aid kit from the back of the van's passenger seat and Sorensen tore open some gauze packets. It really hadn't hurt until then, and Sorensen pouring peroxide and wiping it with the gauze pads changed all that. Gage ordered the driver to step on it, and I noticed there were emergency lights on the top of the windshield that began to flash. Gage busied himself on the walkie-talkie, calling in orders and looking very concerned about me.

I'd had worse wounds over the years and was not at all concerned about this one. Anyway, there was little of importance going on inside the left mid-section of your abdomen to be anything serious. I told Gage to get us to where Angela was. I wanted to be there when her folks arrived, and she was reunited with them. He looked at Sorensen and shook his head.

Sorensen continued to work, and when he pressed hard, putting pressure on my side, I about blacked out. Sorensen knew how important it was to me to be at the reunion and told Gage I would keep for a while. Gage instructed the driver to continue to the airstrip. Sorensen did a fine job of taping me up and then asked me if I wanted a morphine shot.

I said, "No, but I'll take an 'Atta boy' and a pat on the head."

We breezed through the gate at the Biggs Field, swung around a few turns, and then stopped abruptly. Gage opened the door and gave me a hand to the tarmac. I looked around and saw the same thing you see at all military air bases. Tarmac, hangars, and a few grey-painted aircraft all of different designs.

The one thing I didn't expect to see was our very own air taxi and two very pretty female pilots walking toward us. In fact, I noticed one of them walk a bit faster than the other right toward me. This was against military protocol, as junior officers were required to walk slightly to the rear of senior officers. Didn't seem to matter to our First Lieutenant Sally Moore.

She was a woman on a mission.

I was going to be very disappointed and inwardly embarrassed if she threw her arms around Sorensen or one of the other men standing near me. I also noticed the flight suit she was wearing appeared more tailored than the ones she'd worn previously. Nice effect and, boy, was she ever put together well. She must have been sitting in front of her sewing machine all night.

I wasn't disappointed. I was the object of her attention, and other than a perfect salute to Gage, she wrapped herself around me like cellophane.

asked Gage where Angela was, and he pointed to a big Chevy Suburban parked to our rear. There were four Army or Air Force Guards holding M-16 rifles at each corner of the SUV. I could just see several heads bobbing around through the darkened windows, and when the left rear door opened, it was Angela.

She made for me just like Sally did a moment earlier. This time, I turned slightly to my left, lowered my right arm to catch her hug on my less injured side, and held her close. She was still in her Mexican peasant girl outfit, but without the shawl. She was crying and mumbling something about me being the greatest, most handsome, superhero of all times…

Not really.

She thanked me and cried and then dropped me like a dirty pillow as soon as she spotted Sorensen, who was holding me up. He must have been the superhero as she had spent far more time hanging on him than on me. All the while, Sally was clinging to me and attempting to hold me steady on my feet now that Sorensen was preoccupied with Angela.

The Cohen's rolling jet stopped, and the hatch opened, the stairs rolled down, and there was Blanche and Thom Cohen rushing down to the tarmac. Somehow, Angela had broken away from Sorensen and had wrapped herself around her parents faster than I could think. And, thinking was a problem right then. I needed to handle the mission debriefing quickly and get some stitches. I also needed a few glasses of Florida orange juice and some sleep. Through the fog in my head, I was already forming a plan to locate and send some more of the kids that I knew were still out there home—those stolen away from their families and lives.

With Sally's and Sorensen's help, I made it over to the reunion ceremony and stood there a moment until the Cohens noticed me. The three of them turned to me and I saluted them in my finest Marine fashion. I was about to say something clever when my legs gave out again.

The next thing I knew, I was looking up at the ceiling of a hospital room and two IV stands were bubbling clear liquid down clear tubes in the direction of my arms. I turned to the left and saw the pretty face of my lieutenant smiling broadly. Still appeared to be wearing the tailored flight suit, sans blood, and looking fine. My typical male brain reverted to its programmed station and thought of several romantic scenarios, but then I looked around and recalled where I was.

Looking to my right, I saw Sorensen and Gage sitting against the wall, Sorensen in a nice clean civilian shirt, tan jungle trousers, and a smile. Gage spoke first by telling me it was the next day and I was all stapled up and should be ready to go home as soon as the doc came by to release me. He knew very well about my need to get on the road.

I was curious if the Major had done a news conference, but thought better of discussing any business in the environment we were in. He seemed to read my mind and gave me a thumbs up signal. I could picture the panic running rampant throughout the world right now. I needed to get out there and round up as many of these kids as soon as possible before they were all disposed of like condemning evidence.

The doctor came in about mid-morning, according to the shadows on the wall, and checked me over. He said that a bullet had apparently ricocheted off something and slashed my side. I wondered if it was a bullet fragment or one of our own grenades. I looked at Sorensen and he looked up at the ceiling, signaling it couldn't be one of his as he could account for all his shrapnel. Sure.

We left the hospital—Sorensen, Lieutenant Sally, and me. Them walking, me in a wheelchair. Normally, I complained about the ride, but this time, I knew I needed it until I was rested up more. When we slipped out the rear door near the ambulance ramp, I thought to ask where we were. Gage told me we were at the Fort Bliss Army Hospital. It came back to me a bit clearer. As I was about to ask about Angela, I thought about Dave and the Major. All in one sentence, I asked if Dave had been kept up to date about the goings on and if the Major had given his press conference. Gage answered, "Yes and yes."

He went on to say the little ledger was safe and sound elsewhere. I breathed a sigh of relief and he went on to say there were about fifty certified copies of the ledger in fifty different places for safe keeping.

I asked him if the news media were in a feeding frenzy over the press conference and he replied that there was not as much excitement as he had anticipated. I didn't have to ask why. Only a handful of publishers controlled the various news outlets we relied on. Those few folks decided what we read, heard, or saw of the news. I had already figured that those folks would be trying to vet the information we had gathered and were more than likely being bombarded by all the VIPs and politicians involved in this mess.

Gage told me that even I was going to be surprised at the names in the ledger. He went on to say that Nick had delivered the rest of Mubane's documents to the Major, and that they were being analyzed even as we spoke. Gage had called the Major earlier and all the Major could say as he scanned through some of the documents while on the phone was, "Holy crap." about a dozen times a minute. The Major had a meeting later in the day with the Attorney General and a bunch of folks from the Civil Rights Division. As I sat and they stood, a big black SUV pulled up and stopped. Gage said it was our ride. Sorensen pulled me up on my feet and whispered in my ear, "I think we done good, Sergeant." I looked at him, smiled, and quickly told him we were far from finished.

I was able to get a Delta flight to Atlanta and then to Melbourne, Florida, where Dave picked me up in my big Dodge Ram pickup. It had been nearly a month since I had left my island home and, along with my badly aching side filled with stitches and other bruises I hadn't felt until then, Dave gave me a big bear hug and kissed me right on the cheek.

I survived the assault and climbed into the driver's seat of my truck. Dave threw my backpack in the rear crew cab and I drove north to Dave's house next to the Merritt Island Airport. There Dave piloted my pontoon boat to the rear dock of my island paradise.

It looked magnificent. As I looked closer, I saw Dave's Volusia County friends, Tweedledee and Tweedledumb, stretched out on my back patio, drinking from beer cans and saluting us as we pulled in. Dave said he was relieving them of duty and would take them to their truck as soon as I